P9-DUF-532

PRAISE FOR
Highfire

"The anticipated adult novel from Colfer, best known for the Artemis Fowl series, features more of that wild imagination loyal readers have come to love (in this case, a dragon who loves vodka, *Flashdance*, and his Laz-Z-Boy recliner crossing paths with a troublemaking swamp rat)." —*Entertainment Weekly*

"Author of the popular Artemis Fowl books for kids, Colfer has turned his attention to adult fiction to good effect, writing a delightfully funny page-turner with plenty of crossover appeal to teens and sprinkled with genial turns of phrase: alligators' jaws are 'wide like Satan's hedge clippers'; Hooke is 'distributing more mess than a group of finger-painting toddlers on a Skittles sugar high.' Colfer has conjured up voices redolent of the Deep South and delightfully profane. And the characters are simply terrific. But what about those alligators?" —*Booklist* (starred review)

"A fun, unusual contemporary fantasy." —*Kirkus Reviews*

"A twisty, tongue-in-cheek fantasy that's part thriller, part action movie, and wholly irreverent. . . . Colfer's catchy narrative voice suits the characters and their setting perfectly, capturing Vern's world-weary nature, Squib's youthful adaptability, and Hooke's malicious cunning. This no-holds-barred yarn is good fun from start to finish." —*Publishers Weekly*

"Briskly entertaining. . . . With this satisfying and at times hugely joyous novel, Colfer is, like his engaging scaly protagonist, cooking on gas." —*The Guardian*

HIGHFIRE

ALSO BY EOIN COLFER

ADULT FICTION
Plugged
Screwed
And Another Thing . . .

CHILDREN'S FICTION
Artemis Fowl
Artemis Fowl: The Arctic Incident
Artemis Fowl: The Eternity Code
Artemis Fowl: The Opal Deception
Artemis Fowl: The Lost Colony
Artemis Fowl: The Time Paradox
Artemis Fowl: The Atlantis Complex
Artemis Fowl: The Last Guardian
Benny and Omar
Benny and Babe
The Legend of Captain Crow's Teeth
The Legend of Spud Murphy
The Legend of the Worst Boy in the World
Airman
Half Moon Investigations
The Supernaturalist
The Wishlist
Illegal with Andrew Donkin and Giovanni Rigano

COMING SOON
The Fowl Twins

HIGHFIRE

A Novel

EOIN COLFER

HARPER  PERENNIAL

NEW YORK • LONDON • TORONTO • SYDNEY • NEW DELHI • AUCKLAND

HARPER PERENNIAL

This is a work of fiction. Names, characters, places, and incidents are products of the author's imagination or are used fictitiously and are not to be construed as real. Any resemblance to actual events, locales, organizations, or persons, living or dead, is entirely coincidental.

A hardcover edition of this book was published in 2020 by Harper Perennial, an imprint of HarperCollins Publishers.

HIGHFIRE. Copyright © 2020 by Eoin Colfer. All rights reserved. Printed in the United States of America. No part of this book may be used or reproduced in any manner whatsoever without written permission except in the case of brief quotations embodied in critical articles and reviews. For information, address HarperCollins Publishers, 195 Broadway, New York, NY 10007.

HarperCollins books may be purchased for educational, business, or sales promotional use. For information, please email the Special Markets Department at SPsales@harpercollins.com.

FIRST HARPER PERENNIAL EDITION PUBLISHED 2021.

Library of Congress Cataloging-in-Publication Data has been applied for.

ISBN 978-0-06-293857-2 (pbk.)

21 22 23 24 25   LSC   10 9 8 7 6 5 4 3 2 1

For Emily and Jo who gave the dragon wings.

CHAPTER 1

VERN DID NOT TRUST HUMANS WAS THE LONG AND SHORT OF IT. Not a single one. He had known many in his life, even liked a few, but in the end they all sold him out to the angry mob. Which was why he holed up in Honey Island Swamp out of harm's way.

Vern liked the swamp okay. As much as he liked anything after all these years. Goddamn, so many years just stretching out behind him like bricks in that road old King Darius put down back in *who gives a shit* BC. Funny how things came back out of the blue. Like that ancient Persian road. He couldn't remember last week, and now he was flashing back a couple of thousand years, give or take. Vern had baked half those bricks his own self, back when he still did a little blue-collar. Nearly wore out the internal combustion engine. Shed his skin two seasons early because of that bitch of a job. That and his diet. No one had a clue about nutrition in those days. Vern was mostly ketogenic now, high fat, low carbs, apart from his beloved breakfast cereals. Keto made perfect sense for a dragon, especially with his core temperature. Unfortunately, it meant the beer had to go, but he got by on vodka. Absolut was his preferred brand. A little high on alcohol but easiest on the system. And Waxman delivered it by the crate.

So Vern tolerated the swamp. It wasn't exactly glorious, but these weren't exactly the glory days. Once upon a time, he had been Wyvern, Lord Highfire, of the Highfire Eyrie, if you could believe that melodramatic bullshit name. Now he was king of jack shit in Mudsville, Louisiana. But he'd lived in worse places. The water was cool, and the alligators did what they were told, for the most part.

If I tell you fuckers to dance, then you goddamn well better synchronize the hell out of a routine, Vern often told them in not so many words. And it was truly amazing what common gators could achieve with the right motivation.

So he spent his days in the bayou blending in with the locals, staying downwind of the swamp tours, though there were days he longed to cut loose and barbecue a barge full of those happy snappy morons. But putting the heat on tourists would bring the heat on him, and Vern hadn't gotten to the age he was now by drawing attention to himself. Shining a spotlight on your own head was the behavior of an idiot, in Vern's opinion. And his opinion was the only one that mattered, in his opinion. After all, Vern was the last of his kind as far as he knew. And if that was the case, then he owed it to his species to stay alive as long as possible.

He also wasn't feeling suicidal just at the moment. He often did, but mindfulness helped with that. A guy had plenty of time to meditate floating around the swamp's little feeder tribs.

Still, it got lonely being the last dragon. Vern could drink about fifty percent of the blues away, but there were always those nights with the full moon lighting up the catspaws on the Pearl River when Vern thought about making a move on a female alligator. God knows they were lining up for a shot at the king. And once or twice he'd gotten as far as a little nuzzling on the mudflats, which was not a euphemism for anything. But it didn't feel right. Maybe the alligators were close enough to him on the DNA spectrum, but no matter how much vodka he consumed, Vern could not drink himself into believing that he wouldn't be taking advantage of a dumber species. Not to mention the fact that gators had no personalities to speak of and were uglier than the ass end of a coyote.

They were cold-blooded. He had a molten core.

It was never going to work out.

Vern spent his nights in a fishing shack on Boar Island, which had been abandoned sometime in the middle of the last century. The shack sat back from the shore on a little side bayou and was being slowly crushed by the curling fingers of a mangrove fist, but it would do for now, and Vern had it set up pretty nice with a generator and some of the basics. He had himself a little refrigerator to keep his Absolut chilling, and a TV with a bunch of cable. Waxman up the bayou had set up a supply line to the outside world so Vern could keep himself occupied during his nocturnal hours.

It was all about survival, and survival was all about profile, or the total lack of one. Absolute zero. No credit cards or cell phone. No trips to Petit Bateau and no online presence. Vern had set himself up a social media account a while back, cobbled together a fake persona calling himself Draco

Smaug, which he thought was pretty cute, but then Facebook started adding location services and some *Lord of the Rings* fanatics began asking probing questions, so Vern shut it down.

Lesson learned.

From then on, he contented himself with reality shows and surfing the net. All the information Vern needed was out there; he just had to find it.

But no one could find him.

Ever.

Because whenever humans found him, to paraphrase Maximus Decimus Meridius, hell was most definitely unleashed.

And Vern carried hell around inside him, so he could survive it.

But the human who found him would not.

SQUIB USED TO have a daddy.

And back in those days his daddy said things along the lines of:

Don't you go sneaking dollars outta my pocket, Squib, or I'll tan your hide.

And:

You seen my beer, boy? You better not be sipping on my Bud, Squib, or I'll tan your hide.

Or:

How come you ain't minding your business, Squib? You heard about the curious cat, right? That cat got its hide tanned and then some.

It didn't take Squib long to figure out that Daddy's sayings usually ended up with someone's hide getting tanned, and generally that hide was his. Squib reckoned it was probably mostly his own fault, as he did have a little trouble keeping his nose out of other people's business.

It's a free country, he reasoned in his defense, *so everyone's business is my business.*

But then his daddy left on Squib's thirteenth birthday, as apparently buying a gift card for his kid was more responsibility than he cared for, and none of his talk mattered much anymore. And in actual fact that daddy wasn't even Squib's real daddy no matter how much Squib conned himself that he was. Waxman, who lived on a houseboat across the river, said that Squib's real daddy had found this world a bit too much for him, and this guy was just some freeloader who turned up when Squib wasn't much more than a rug rat and his sainted mother was a mess. This replacement poppa was nothing but a goddamn fool who was always shooting his mouth off, as Waxman told it—prison jabber that he most likely picked up in Angola or some other state farm, judging by the ink crawling up outta the neck hole of his T-shirt.

"You and Elodie are better off without that no-account loser," he told Squib when the boy delivered his groceries. "Most he can read is off cigarette cartons. Just taking advantage of your momma's kind nature is what he was doing."

Mostly Waxman was full of bullshit swamp wisdom, but this time he hit the nail on the head, especially where Elodie was concerned.

Squib's momma surely did have a kind nature, nursing folks like she did all hours for two dollars above minimum wage, then coming home to his delinquent ass. Squib was overly familiar with that particular term, "delinquent," being that it was read to him off a report card or charge sheet often enough. Sometimes he thought he should dial it down a notch, the bad-boy act, for his momma's sake, because he loved her so much that it made him furious at all the assholes who had broken her heart: His own original poppa, who had checked himself out when he had folks who relied on him. And then Fake Daddy, who left when he had sucked Elodie's heart dry, like he was some kind of vampire but with a taste for love instead of blood. So Squib tried to rein himself in, but it never took.

Squib could allow that he missed having a daddy, even a fake one, so long as he kept that thought inside his own head.

Even if that daddy did drink beer like it was keeping him alive instead of the opposite. Even if he did raid Momma's coffee tin for change and spend it on lottery scratch tickets.

Even if he did swing for Squib whenever he had a drunk on.

Squib reckoned he'd loved his daddy, a little, anyways. A person can't help loving their kin. But that didn't mean he couldn't hate him, too. And when Fake Daddy left his momma, Elodie, with nothing more than an empty coffee tin and a string of gambling notes running all the way down to New Orleans, which, turned out, the holders had zero problem transferring to his common-law wife, Squib hated his fake daddy with a laser intensity that was pretty focused for a boy without even a scrap of fuzz on his chin.

And now, two years later, Squib hadn't seen much improvement in the fuzz department, but he was half a foot taller and working on a scrappy attitude that had him on the cops' radar even at the age of fifteen. There was a constable by the name of Regence Hooke who got shot down by Squib's momma in the Pearl Bar and Grill one time in front of a packed house, and ever since that night Hooke had himself a hard-on for Squib and made sure to take any complaint against the minor real personal. It seemed to Squib that every time he farted, old Regence would be knocking on the door offering to "forget all about it" for a little consideration from Squib's momma.

Goddamn Hooke, Squib thought. *He ain't gonna back off till someone gets fucked.*

Matter of fact, it had been Regence Hooke who bestowed the nom-de-crime "Squib" upon Squib, whose given name was Everett Moreau. As Hooke had commented, Squib's first time in the station, "'Moreau' like the doctor with the island of freaks, right, kid? 'Cept you're one o' them freaks, not the doctor."

The nickname incident was back when Squib's fake daddy was still bunking in the Moreau shack and young Everett went out on the lake one night fixing to dynamite a few catfish with a boomstick he bought off a kid in school whose poppa had a strongbox. No catfish were harmed in the experiment as Everett had succeeded only in blowing off both the little finger of his left hand and the stern of a canoe he'd borrowed for the job. Regence Hooke had been waiting when the patched-up boy, hampered by overkill manacles, was brought into the station.

"I hear that weren't much of an explosion, boy," he'd said. "More of a damp squib."

And there it was.

Everett Moreau came away from that night with nine fingers and a nickname. So, when the time came for Regence Hooke to really take against Squib on account of his humiliation, they were already acquainted. And Squib wasn't hard to recognize with his hands over his head.

BEHOLD SQUIB MOREAU at fifteen: a swamp-wild, street-smart, dark-eyed Cajun-blood young man with a momma driven to near despair and no future to speak of unless he wanted to work creosote or hump bricks in Slidell. Long on dreams, short on plans most of the time. He was doing his best to stay straight, but it seemed like straight didn't pay the bills, even with his own three jobs and his momma's shifts at the Petit Bateau clinic.

But change was a-coming, for Squib had been presented an opportunity. On this summer evening with the bloodsucking gauze of mosquitoes hovering above the swamp murk and the cypress trees standing sentry on the shores of Honey Island, Squib would be shaking on a deal to buy himself and his mother a little wiggle room from the attentions of Regence Hooke, who was escalating his courtship of Elodie Moreau. Felt like hardly a day went by when he didn't make time to swing by the Moreau landing with some bullshit excuse for being in the ass end of a dirt lane:

Noise complaint.

Truancy office.

Disturbing the peace.

Jaywalking, for Christ's sake—whatever shit he could dredge up. Always with a bottle of sparkling wine packed in blue ice packs in his Chevy's cooler. Blush. Momma's favorite. And it was only going to be a matter of time before Regence got a foot in the door, and then the only thing standing in his way was a fly screen. And you didn't put a halt to a man like Hooke with a fly screen. Squib knew that his momma hadn't warmed to the constable, not nowhere near it, but nights are long in the bayou, and with Regence Hooke pissing all over the boundary, the other dogs were staying the hell away.

"Regence could provide for us, cher," Elodie told Squib one night, eyes heavy after a long shift at the clinic. "And he could straighten you out. Lord knows I can't do it."

Squib knew that his momma must be bone-tired and a long way down in the dumps, having maybe nursed a favorite patient through their final hours on God's earth, even to talk like Hooke was an option for her. He knew that the only reason Elodie Moreau would allow such a world-class asshole across the threshold would be to put a stop to Squib's own criminal gallop, and he felt responsible for that. Sometimes he dreamed of Constable Hooke in some kind of embrace with his momma, with kissing and such, and he woke up in a cold sweat that had nothing to do with bayou heat.

So for maybe the hundredth time Squib swore he would shape up: He vowed it most fervently and, to his credit, believed his words to be gospel at the time. But he was fallible, by virtue of his youth. After barely a week Squib was back to skipping class.

This is me, he realized. *I can't never change.*

And so when school broke up, he had approached Willard Carnahan in the Pearl Bar lot. Carnahan was perhaps the only man in Louisiana who knew the swamp better than Squib himself, and so the boy offered his two hands and strong back to the swamp moonshine runner. A trial run was offered, and tonight was the night that Squib kicked off his apprenticeship.

Just for the summer, Squib told himself. *And just hooch or cigarettes. Maybe machine parts. No drugs, nor people neither. I'll make enough to pay off our debts and maybe get us a place in town. Far away from Hooke and Fake Daddy's reputation.*

AND SO SQUIB crept out into the swamp without bothering to communicate any particulars with Elodie, who was on night shift at the clinic and would have chained him to the water pipe if she knew who he was fraternizing with.

He launched the marine-ply pirogue he had fashioned himself, with some pointers from Waxman, into the water not ten feet from the porch of the Moreau river shack, but decided against starting up the long-tail engine bolted to the stern. *It's all gonna change tonight*, he thought, as he paddled his little flat-bellied pirogue upriver in mud-slick levee wash-off, sticking close to the borders of bulrush.

I got a black T-shirt on and a pack of jerky in case of emergency, thought the nine-fingered boy. *Ain't nuthin' can go wrong.*

———

Regence Hooke was without doubt a colorful individual. There wasn't hardly a crime he hadn't participated in or turned a blind eye to at one point or another. Safe to say that he didn't get to where he was by attending church regular and baking cookies for Africa. Hooke had gotten into law enforcement via the military, and he'd gotten into the military by virtue of the fact that he judged it better than the federal penitentiary. Those had been his options at the time. When eighteen-year-old Regence stood up before a Miami-Dade judge, the clerk had to draw breath before reading the charges, which included, but were not limited to:

Conspiracy, mail fraud, wire fraud, intimidation, bribing a witness, grand theft auto, narcotics possession with intent to sell, assault, and obstruction.

The judge responded to this litany with the expletive "Jesus Christ on a broomstick, kid," which effectively put him in contempt of his own court, and presented young Regence with:

Option A: Army.

Or option B: Baker Correctional Institution.

Regence chose A, got his records sealed, signed up, shipped out, killed a passel of folks, and came home some decades later with a ton of medals, then moved three states west to Petit Bateau, Louisiana, which welcomed the decorated veteran with open arms, having zero clue as to the many and varied sins of his past.

And now, aged two score and more, he was constable of the tiny ward and driving his own vehicle with total impunity. Regence could barely credit how rosy things had turned out. His daddy had always told him, "Good things come to the righteous," so Regence considered every crooked dollar he tucked into his billfold a big *screw you* to his dead daddy, because he sure as hell had never been righteous.

Regence's main source of crooked dollars was running errands for Ivory Conti, who was the New Orleans receiving agent for the Los Zetas cartel. Ivory had dozens of cops on the payroll, but Regence was rising through the ranks real fast due to his unflinching nature and willingness to transport whatever would fit in the trunk of his Chevrolet Tahoe across the Pontchartrain Bridge. Regence did not give a shit what Ivory's boys put in there so long as it didn't leak or seep or otherwise transfer evidence.

On the night our tale begins, Regence parked up his Chevy at Bodi Irwin's boatyard and took his beloved cabin cruiser up the Pearl River for a little talk with a guy who had messed up grievously on Ivory's turf.

It was unfortunate that this talk had to take place at all, because the guy he had to talk with was a useful guy— unique, even. But at the same time, doing this business for Ivory meant he was crossing a line, and crossing a line meant a bump up to a lot more than the usual $2,400 a month.

So fuck you, Daddy, thought Regence and gunned his boat upriver, cutting a swathe through the algae with the *Elodie*'s aluminum prow.

The *Elodie*.

After that runt Squib Moreau's angel of a momma.

Surely to Christ that would bring her around.

Regence knew his own habits well enough to realize that he was on the road to being hung up on that Cajun girl.

"Girl"? Hell, she was a full-grown woman, past her sell-by date and with nothing to show for it 'cept that idiot boy of hers, and Hooke counted him a liability rather than an asset.

Don't get yourself hung up, son, he told himself. *Ain't nothing but pain at the end of that road.*

But Regence couldn't control his yearnings, and it wasn't just a physical thing. Hooke had plenty of slut shacks he dropped in on regular. His interest in Elodie Moreau was more long-term.

She should count her lucky stars a guy like me is so much as letting my gaze linger, Constable Hooke thought several times a day, which didn't make him feel one degree less irritated about how his courtship was progressing. He was smart enough to grasp the psychology of the situation, that psychology being he craved what he couldn't get his mitts on, but knowing the psychology didn't mitigate his needs none.

Maybe if she hadn't shot me down in public that way. Looking down on me like I was some swamp rat come slithering in off the river.

Regence had been rejected by women before, but he often found that decision reversed when he approached it different, for example at four in the morning in a dark alley. Shit, one time he didn't even have to say nothing, just whistled a little off-key and cocked his head to one side.

But Elodie. She had more steel in her than that, the way she stared him down in the Pearl Bar that first time they ran into each other outside the station. Hunched over a mug of coffee, she was still in scrubs after her shift when he came in. Hooke took one look and thought to himself, *Elodie is all tuckered out, so mayhaps her defenses are down.* So he'd sauntered over and dropped the line, "Morning, sugar. Remember me? The name's Constable Hooke, and I would surely like to get my hooks into you."

Cheesy as all hell, but Regence was unaccustomed to making the effort with his sweet talk. Usually just saying any old words did the trick. But not this time. Elodie lifted her head like it weighed a ton with all the troubles in there. She fixed him with those chocolate eyes and responded a bit louder than necessary in front of the breakfast crowd. And what she said was, "Constable, I spent the night scooping old-man crap out of a hypoallergenic bag, and I would one hundred percent rather spend the rest of my life on this earth doing exactly that than let you get a single hook into me."

It was a zinger, no doubt about that. The boys in the Pearl close to split their guts laughing and Regence left with a red neck. Elodie had said nicer things since then, but Regence still felt that burn under his collar.

CHAPTER 2

SQUIB OFTEN FELT HARD DONE BY FORTUNE-WISE. EVERYBODY GOT *some* luck, a bone tossed their way by Mother Nature. Squib's boon was common among Cajun folk in that the maringouins had never taken a shine to him. Maybe it was the French blood from way back, but more likely the Caribbean had more to do with the situation. Squib never could fathom how a person could even tolerate the bayou after sunset with the mosquitoes ripping chunks out of their flesh. You see those tourists in the morning wandering around welted like they got themselves tortured. Some Guantanamo-looking shit. Nothing took the cool out of a college calf tattoo like half a dozen septic lumps. Squib got maybe a handful of bites a season, and even then it was usually some zirondelle on a rampage.

So that was his luck.

Unblemished skin.

Hard to turn a fella's life around on that, less'n he got spotted hanging at the mall by some model scout. And that wasn't overlikely. Squib didn't really *hang* per se. He was a not-enough-hours-in-the-day kind of guy. Always working, making a buck.

His Cajun skin made setting crawfish traps more comfortable, at least. Squib would motor up the bayou toward Honey Island and float half a dozen of those cages near telltale lily pads, then spend a few hours trawling with a scoop net until his traps were bursting at the wire. In all his years night fishing, Squib had only ever been bit the one time, and then it wasn't no mosquito but a moccasin that got itself tangled up in a cage. The snake must have been jizzed out, though, because Squib suffered no more than a nub of swelling around the teeth marks.

Tonight I got bigger fish in my sights, thought Squib, going all melodramatic. *A life of crime.*

Squib knew that he was stepping over some kind of threshold and there wouldn't be no crossing back, but Regence Hooke was a devil in a tasseled cap who had his sights set on Elodie Moreau, so it was up to him to buy them some distance.

Maybe if we're living in the middle of a development with plenty of witnesses, then Hooke might settle down some and back off.

Squib's warped reasoning was based on a child's understanding of evil men. He couldn't know that specimens like Regence Hooke didn't get settled down; they got riled up.

The only time Hooke ever settled down was with a blister pack of Benzedrine, a quart of Old Forester's, and a hooker at the door.

The skinny on Squib's prospective boss was as follows: Willard Carnahan, a purveyor of all things legal and illegal.

Wasn't nothing beneath Carnahan, not so far as Squib knew. There was a story doing the grapevine that Willard had beat a corner-slinger into a coma recently in the French Quarter over a zip of coke that was actually baby powder and turned to rock in his nostrils, so Carnahan wasn't ever crossing the Twin Span again, on account of the retribution that was waiting for him in New Orleans from the hustler's higher-ups. Willard was a swamp sailor: He could navigate the Pearl River without ever once skimming a bank. He worked a tour boat during the day and at nighttime ran his own deals through the tiny feeder tribs—even with his eyes closed, if needs be. Carnahan had his own distillery, which was perfectly legal so long as a fella didn't use it to manufacture white lightning. The official story was that Carnahan was distilling water, but in fact he was engaged in the age-old practice of running 'shine for the alcohol-blind swamp dogs on the bayou. The sheriff's office in Slidell took their payoffs in a jug, and nobody else gave much of a crap. But those jugs were heavy, and Squib reckoned that Carnahan could use a humper who knew the swamp almost as well as he did.

They had arranged a late meet on the old Honey Island dock. Squib reckoned he would be allowed to collect from Carnahan's own dock if he proved himself, but tonight he was being tested.

In case I'm some class of juvenile narc, thought Squib, keeping an eye out for Willard from his pirogue in the cattails on the west bank across the layered slate water from Honey Island itself.

The view was just fine, with the moonlight bouncing off the cypress leaves, and Squib saw Carnahan standing right there at the water's edge in his drainpipe jeans and cut-off T-shirt. But Carnahan wasn't alone. There were two people on the dock: Carnahan, with his Twisted Sister–style ratty hair, and one big refrigerator-sized guy. The big one was Regence Hooke, no doubt about that whatsoever.

What the hell? thought Squib. *Why would Hooke be communing with a criminal like Carnahan?*

He couldn't tell what was going on from this distance—Hooke could be simply interrogating a suspect—but Squib doubted that. Regence Hooke wasn't a man to put himself out, and especially not in the middle of the night.

There was too much bayou between Squib and the suspicious twosome on the far bank to hear what was going on, a fact which would have to be remedied. And if a person had to put his finger on exactly when things went ass-over-balls down the crapper, then that moment was imminent.

I need to get myself closer, thought Squib. *Maybe I can get myself a little intelligence on Hooke in case I ever need a get-out-of-jail-free card.*

And there it was: the moment that would change the course of young Everett Moreau's life. Squib was about to commit the cardinal sin of watchers, spies, and stalkers everywhere, that being: Don't put yourself in the picture. Keep the hell out of whatever's being spied upon, and do not muddy the waters with your own person.

In Squib's exact case, the waters were already plenty muddy, but the boy went right ahead and muddied them further. He cranked his propeller out of the water and paddled to the Honey Island bank, paying no heed to the bullfrogs croaking ominous warnings. His paddle grazed the rough hide of an alligator, but still Squib ignored the omens as he was at that age where every idea he had seemed like the best damn idea in the universe. So the boy forged ahead, keeping his torso bent over low and wishing he had some class of camouflage gunk to smear on his face and arms. Not that he possessed any of that specific stuff, but Momma had every cream under the sun and surely to Jesus one of her pots would have done the job. Still, too late to fret on that now. It wasn't like he could have seen into the future and bargained on this encounter.

It didn't take more than half a dozen strokes to propel the pirogue across the bayou to the overhanging levee of Honey Island. Squib grabbed a fistful of cattails and tugged, sliding his craft into the cover of reeds and roots. The entire maneuver was whisper-quiet, and Squib congratulated himself on his own sneakiness, thinking that in another life he could have been Special Forces, maybe, or one of those ninja characters who favored black slippers and headbands.

Hooke and Carnahan were still jawing away, and now Squib could catch snatches of conversation. He heard Hooke say, "I never saw any sign of it apart from a bend in the middle . . ."

Which could have been pertaining to just about anything from Santa Claus to a police snitch.

And a few seconds later Willard Carnahan remarked, "That wasn't nuthin' compared to this guy I met in Slidell."

Which was even more vague apart from the mention of the parish's main city.

This kind of harmless back-and-forth went on for an age, or so it felt, and Squib was beginning to doubt that anything useful could come of this eavesdropping. With the reeds rustling and the goddamn bugs kicking up their nightly swamp racket, he couldn't track any conversation threads from end to end, and what he could hear sounded like regular bar bullshit.

Willard: "Totally serious, Constable. Motherfucker eyeballed me, 'fore I opened his . . ."

And Regence: "I swear, boy, Momma Hooke had this thing she did where two earthworms . . ."

It was all useless jabber, so all in all, his big plan was proving itself something of a *clusterballs*. And Squib was reckoning he might as well shut up shop and hunker down till Regence took himself off upriver.

I'll shimmy in a little closer, he decided. *Give 'er five minutes, then fuck it, I'm out.*

Squib crawled from the bed of his pirogue to the bank proper and, figuring he couldn't get much lower in life, slithered through the reeds like a serpent, making his way ever so slowly round back of the dubious midnight pair, hoping that he wasn't literally going to get bitten on the ass by some real shithead snake.

He came around the bend of a stump just in time to see a swamp rat the size of a cantaloupe saunter off into the bush. The rat threw him a *you're lucky I ain't hungry* look before its hindquarters disappeared, and Squib was so rattled it took him a moment to pick up on a new tone in the Hooke-Carnahan conversation. Felt like the temperature was dropping a little between those boys.

I should take a photo, thought Squib, and pulled his smartphone from the waterproof pocket of his camouflage-type work jeans. And as is so often the case, things would've turned out a whole lot better if the kid could've kept it in his pants.

HOOKE WAS WONDERING whether there might be some way to avoid dropping the hammer on Willard.

I could just let the idiot walk. Tell him to shave his head and buy a suit. Start calling himself Wilbert instead of Willard. Ivory would never know the difference.

But Carnahan was one of those guys who was just too dumb to grasp the concept of *consequences*. Sooner or later he'd be shooting his mouth off down in the French Quarter about how he dodged Ivory's bullet, and then Hooke himself would be in the crapper alongside Willard.

Shit, he thought. *I ain't got a choice.*

Hooke took the job hoping he might find a little wiggle room somewhere along the line, but now that he was at the end of that line, so to speak, he could see that there was nothing for it but to complete the mission and then figure out some way to fill the Carnahan-sized hole in his own plans.

Because Hooke had big plans that extended a tad further than running out his years as constable in this shithole parish. He had his beady eyes on Ivory's entire operation, which he aimed to consolidate and extend north to Canada, cutting out South America altogether.

He had been drip-feeding factoids about these plans, needing the smuggler to check out his theories, and Willard raised the subject now.

"I talked to my guy at the truck stop," he said. "Ain't

no limit to the number of truckers he can bring over to us. Ivory's guys are bored out of their minds, nothing but gas station hookers for distraction. They'll carry anything, crank or guns. Makes no never mind to those boys so long as they get paid."

"That's good," said Hooke, "real good, Willard. You write those names down?"

"Sure did, just like you told me." Willard handed Hooke a scrunched-up till receipt with names scrawled on the back.

"I gotta say it, Willard," said Hooke, pocketing the list, "you surely are rising to the challenge."

Carnahan accepted the compliment with shining eyes, like a puppy. "Thanks, partner. So, how long 'fore we make our move on Ivory?"

"Soon, son," said Regence. "I got to beef up my own end. I did some surveillance on G-Hop, found myself a few of my brethren. Two definite possibilities."

"And you're set on guns? No drugs? Drugs is awful light and guns is awful heavy."

Hooke had been arguing this point with himself for months, so he was glad for a chance to lay it out for someone who wouldn't be blabbing it in the bar later on.

"Listen close, Willard," he said. "I'm about to set down our entire philosophy. Heroin sales are down, right? Cocaine is cheap and every asshole with legs is trafficking it now. All the gangs. The Mexicans won't need us soon; they got their own people on this side of the border. The Albanians, Russians, Puerto Ricans, Irish—even the Canadians have gangs now. The Bacon Brothers—can you believe that name, Willard? So pretty soon nobody will need Ivory's drugs pipeline. Every thug with a backpack will become a mule. That ship has sailed, even if Ivory don't yet know it."

"The goddamn pipeline is useless?" swore Willard. "What the hell are we taking it over for?"

"The *pipeline* ain't useless," Hooke corrected him. "A pipeline is always useful. Even the product is useful right now. But we gotta diversify."

Willard played his part in the discussion by asking, "Yeah, but diversify into what?"

"Diversify into the famous Second Amendment," said Hooke, saluting. "The right to bear arms."

"We already got that right."

"Some states more than others," said Hooke. "California ain't so lenient. New York makes it near to impossible to secure a permit. New Jersey, Connecticut, even Hawaii. All these red-blooded Americans are crying out for guns. And if there is one thing I know, Willard . . ."

Carnahan completed the thought. "It's guns," he said.

"Exactly. You buy low in Louisiana and sell high in California. That's how the world works. Believe me, the NRA won't hold out forever against the libs. And the best thing is, we keep it all on the mainland. No South American hotheads needed."

"I get it now," said Carnahan. "We're a domestic operation."

Hooke snapped his fingers. "A domestic operation. Go America."

"You got it all figured, Constable," said Willard. "Ain't no way this can miss."

And then Hooke reached one hand into the pocket of his windbreaker, and the temperature dropped.

SQUIB WAS ALL set up now, lying there proud as punch in the swamp gunk with his camera trained on Hooke and Carnahan. Looked like the buddy-buddy part of the evening was over. Wasn't so much laughing and knee-slapping going on now.

"Here's the problem, Willard," Hooke was saying. "That beatdown you handed out in New Orleans."

Carnahan laughed, and Squib saw his teeth glowed black in the camera's night-vision mode. "Fuck that kid, Regence. That shit he sold me weren't no shit. You hear me? Goddamn baby ass-powder. Fucked my sinuses up for a week. Hell, they still fucked up. Every morning I'm waking up, I can't hardly breathe. That ain't no way to do business."

Hooke seemed to grow a little larger, like he was letting the *real* Regence out. "Thing is, son, that kid you whupped? You messed up his brain, so they pulled the plug. His momma had to sign off on that. Can you imagine?"

Carnahan used both hands to tease his hair into vertical spikes. "That's a shame, Regence. A damn shame. But that kid was all about the product, telling me how *gen-u-ine* it was, all that shit. You can't stiff customers and expect no payback."

Hooke draped an arm around Carnahan's shoulders: a bear hugging a deer. Usually the deer has the sense to know it's on the menu, but Willard Carnahan must have been thinking himself indispensable.

"I shouldn't even be paying for blow," said Willard, all unawares, "with all the shit I run upriver for you. But I found myself in a party mood, ya know, so I dipped into my own goddamn pocket for some hard-earned. And what does that asshole do? Sells me fake shit. Me! The fucking coke pilot."

"You got a point," said Hooke, and he did this little upside-down thing with his mouth like he was actually considering Carnahan's argument. "But see, the kid was Ivory's nephew. Trying to prove himself. Wasn't supposed to be on that corner. Young Vincent was supposed to be hitting the books."

This was a lot of information, and specific, too, like Hooke had gotten it from the horse's mouth.

"I . . . Ivory. F-fucking Ivory?" said Carnahan, stumbling over his words. "I didn't have that knowledge, Constable. How could I know that? *Ivory?* He was just some Italian punk on a corner pushing baby powder, far as I was concerned. I got some credit with Ivory, don't I?"

Hooke's fingers clamped onto Carnahan's shoulder. "Shit, boy. You used up the entirety of your credit, and half of mine, too."

Squib was barely more than a kid, but he could see what was coming. This was way more leverage than he wanted. This here was the kind of information a guy volunteered to get lobotomized right out of his own head just to be certain he couldn't testify to it.

"I'm the pilot, Constable," said Willard. "There ain't nobody can navigate the swamp like me. I ain't lost a single package since we opened the pipeline. Not a goddamn gram."

"That is true, son," acknowledged Hooke, actual pain on

his features. "So now you got me discomfited, too, because of how I got to train up a replacement."

Willard had one more argument in his bank. "But we got *plans*, Regence. We're *partners*."

Regence sighed. "We was, right enough," he said. "Until you fucked up Ivory's nephew. I ain't ready for heat yet. My plans ain't been stress-tested."

A fine mist of reality settled on the situation, and the hope drained out of Carnahan. He slumped in Hooke's grasp like a punctured balloon man, and it looked like he might collapse on the spot, but the constable propped him up.

"Now, come on, son," said Regence. "We all got to pay the piper." At which point Hooke whistled a few bars of the reveille. "Get it, son? In your particular case, I'm the piper."

Flat on his belly in the swamp mud, with crawfish and God knows what else nipping at his shoelaces, Squib had himself a Road to Damascus moment. It wasn't God-related—Squib had little time for God or his boys. No, Squib's epiphany was corporeal, vis-à-vis his own mortality. The boy was no fool. He knew in theory that he was gonna die at some distant time in the future. But to Squib, like most kids, that's all it was: a theory. Also, Squib had half a notion that by the time his number was up, the whole death problem would've been solved by scientists.

But right there on the banks of a sluggish bayou, with the silver-dollar moon throwing shine on a dead man walking and the man about to kill him, Squib felt the yawning vacuum of his own mortality open right above him, and he knew with utter certainty that if he gave himself away, Regence Hooke would end him without even breaking a sweat.

"Aw, Constable," said Carnahan, "we's partners, ain't we? Must be something can be worked out."

"Not a damn thing," said Regence Hooke, and he tipped his cap like a good old boy. "Now, listen. I got this single mom back in Petit Bateau waiting for me to crank her open, so I need to finish up here. You understand, right?"

Carnahan sighed, not really on the same page re: his own fate. "Yeah, I guess. Gotta chase that tail, right, Constable?"

"That's right, son," said Hooke, and took his hand out of his windbreaker pocket, two of the knuckles sheathed in the grip of a gut hook. He flicked the blade out with his thumb and sawed it across Carnahan's midsection below the rib cage. The skinning blade opened the flesh in a W flap.

Willard jerked a little. "That's chilly, Constable. Did you just murder me?"

Hooke wiped the blade on Carnahan's shirt. "Yep, son. I did. My sincere regrets."

And he pitched Carnahan into the Pearl like he was ejecting him from a club.

Willard Carnahan toppled onto the bayou, and the scrim of its spongy surface supported his 150 pounds with barely a splash. The wound was so devastating that Carnahan's insides rushed out of him, and almost immediately the bottom-feeders lurking below took hold of this unexpected bounty of tendons and gore, reeling the man in. Willard had barely any strength in him, and all he could accomplish was a sideways leer into the reeds, drawing equal measures of sludge and air through his yawning mouth. For Carnahan, life had slowed to one-third, and nothing he wanted to do was feasible. Watching the world telescope away from him was about all he could manage.

"Hey, son," Regence Hooke called after him, "the swamp is taking you to its bosom. That's fitting, ain't it?"

If Regence had only turned away before casting his final barb, then he might not have cottoned on to the movement in the rushes. Even then, no big deal. Lotta things moving in the rushes this deep in the bayou. However, usually none of those *lotta things* blurted out exclamations along the lines of *Jesus goddamn Christ*, which Hooke was pretty certain he heard coming out of the flora. And even if he hadn't just murdered a person, an inquisitive man such as Constable Regence Hooke would be obliged to ascertain who exactly was playing fast and loose with the second commandment.

What had happened was this: Carnahan had bobbed on past the sagging jetty till he arrived level with young Squib, who'd long since abandoned any notion of blackmail and was wishing he had himself a pair of ruby slippers to click together. Poor Willard had that expression on that was halfway between fucked and dead, and with a pale slickness to the complexion which made it clear he was on the brief trip from one to the other.

Squib found his eyes glued to the dying man, wondering which embodiment of death would win the race to claim Carnahan, blood loss or drowning? Or perhaps a gator? As it turned out, there was another contender. A monster snapping turtle breached like a mottled, domed submarine, coming a full foot out of the water, its predator's beak all hysterical, and tore Carnahan's living face right off his skull, to which Squib exclaimed, "*Jesus goddamn Christ!*"

He had never seen a turtle of this girth: shell the size of a small car, and that long neck corded and erect like the dick his good friend Charles Jr. liked to wave about so much, proud as he was.

Swamp folk often spoke of the bloodthirsty nature of these generally docile creatures, but not many had seen it firsthand.

That was more than likely all she wrote for Willard Carnahan and his modern-day piratical escapades, but the boy did not see him and his flayed skull go under, for Squib's own blasphemous mouth had named him a witness and therefore a target, so he upped off his belly and jinked like a jackrabbit into the island proper.

HOOKE SAW A figure hightail it into the island with the green glow of a phone in his hand and scowled in petulant frustration. "Mary, Mother of Jesus, I cannot believe this day."

In Regence Hooke's mind he had been much put-upon in the past twelve hours.

First the Elodie Moreau thing was souring his mood, then Ivory forced him to gut his pilot, and now some shadowy figure shoots a movie of the proceedings?

Leverage, thought Hooke. That goddamn Ivory was reckoning to tighten the leash. It seemed like he was misinterpreting their relationship, forgetting who had the badge here. Who else could be responsible? Ivory insisted on the hit, then planted some city kid up here to play *Candid Camera*. The drug lord would get even more information than he'd hoped for if he watched that video.

"Not tonight, Ivory," said Regence Hooke, patting the service Glock in his holster. Gunfire traveled crystal clear over flat water, but there was no helping that. Shots in a swamp could always be explained. Video could not.

Regence did not waste bullets firing into the Spanish moss but instead picked his way carefully across the half-rotten jetty to his own swamp cruiser and cast off. He had two reasons for taking the boat: One, the idiot spy had marooned himself on an island, and two, he had a couple of toys in the strongbox.

I'm gonna bleed you with my pump-action, son, thought Regence, *then put you down close quarters with the Glock.*

It occurred to Constable Hooke, as he pushed the flat-bottomed craft back from the jetty, that this would only be the second time in his life he had killed two men in one night.

Oh, no, hold up, Regence. You're selling yourself short. You did that Witness Security guy and his handler last year in Florida.

The WITSEC guy—not an easy hit.

So three times.

Definitely three.

In peacetime.

SQUIB'S FIRST EXPERIENCE of shotgun pellet sting came upon crashing through the mangroves on the western shore of Honey Island. He'd not been intending to crash through anything, but it came upon him all of a sudden, like the cliff in a Road Runner cartoon: One second he was stumbling along what could at a squint be called a trail, and the next his nose was out in the open and there was Hooke out on the water all pumped and ready to unload. Squib saw Regence Hooke's jaw in the red glow of cigar ember, and then the cop's barrel jerked upwards and Squib had himself a gunshot wound on the forearm. It wasn't anything near fatal, not from a distance of sixty yards plus, mostly didn't even break the skin, but he'd be feeling it for weeks to come.

That weren't no shot to kill, thought Squib. *Bastard's herding me.*

The shot's recoil scooted the boat backwards across the bayou, forcing Regence Hooke to tend to his throttle, which gave Squib a second to duck out of sight, shuffle into the interior, and catch his breath.

He lay flat on his back, feeling the buckshot scalding in his arm and the cold swamp mud shrinking his ball sack.

How the hell do I get off this island? he thought. *If Hooke don't get me, the gators sure as hell will.*

The smell of the oil-slick water gave him his answer.

As far as he could figure, Squib's only option was to wait it out. Tours would start motoring through here from Crawford Landing at first light, dozens of out-of-towners eager to catch sight of the legendary swamp bigfoot. Wasn't no way Regence Hooke could take a shot at him then, not with a multitude of cameras pointed his way, because social media sure did love itself a cop-discharging-his-weapon video.

I gotta keep my head down and my mouth shut, Squib realized. *Simple as that.*

But he knew in his heart that this assessment was pure optimism. Regence Hooke was no rookie to the blood-sport game, and he was hardly about to dissolve into a puddle of sniffles because Squib was taking shelter on an island.

This was confirmed seconds later when all hell broke loose.

Squib's first thought was *Volcano*, which might seem like the thinking of an idiot, but in fairness to the boy, although he might have considered himself tough as nails, he had never been within a thousand miles of a war zone and had no frame of reference for the explosive chaos erupting all around. Thousands of man-hours on the PlayStation could not begin to do the experience justice.

The noise was terrific, a thunderous *thooom* rising from the earth and crashing over him in waves of sonic terror. Bayou mud, shellfish, mangrove root, and slate were liquidized and dragged skywards in drapes of swamp slop which fell in a harsh deluge upon the boy, scouring him to his pores. It felt to Squib like he was being summarily interred, buried by the sheer weight of debris tumbling on his slight frame from above.

Momma will never know what happened to me, he realized, and the thought terrified him. He tried to call out, but that turned out to be a mistake as his mouth was filled with falling debris. Squib's eye sockets filled up with mud, and even his T-shirt was shredded by the assault.

I am surely dead, thought Squib. *I can't figure out nothing.*

But gradually the earth's revolutions settled down, and the whine in Squib's ears was intruded upon by laughter from out on the water. Sounded like Regence Hooke was having himself one hell of a time.

"You like that concussion grenade, fella?" he called. "Was that your cup of iced tea? I bet you opened your stupid mouth, didn't you? Took a gutful of swamp shit and shellfish."

Hooke laughed again, and it might have been shell shock, but Squib could have sworn there was an animal tinge to his mirth.

"Every night after a firefight we'd have some fool green-horn running around with his mouth open, getting himself a mouth of shrapnel. We had more busted teeth than limbs."

Squib peeped between the rushes. He reckoned himself camouflaged enough. Regence Hooke was seated on the cabin of his boat, a squat weapon across his lap and his boots kicking against the windshield. His grenade launcher sat in his lap like a favored pet. Squib even knew the model from *Call of Duty*: the MM-1. Funny-looking chunky fucker. The barrel organ of death.

"Lovely night, ain't it, boy? I bet you're wishing you never set foot outside New Orleans, right? I bet you're wishing old Ivory had sent someone else to do his spying."

Ivory, thought Squib. *Hooke don't know who I am.*

This meant that if he could give Constable Hooke the slip, then all he had to do was make it back to his pirogue.

Hooke hiked the grenade launcher to his shoulder. "Son, I bet you're thinking that all you gotta do is crawl snakelike back to your boat and paddle out of here. Well, I got bad news for you on that front. Your boat just floated on past me toward the bay. I guess you didn't secure it none too good."

Squib squinted his eyes mostly shut, thinking that the whites might give him away. Was Hooke shitting him? *Had* he secured his boat?

Probably not.

He hadn't exactly been planning the final step of this mission. So now he was stuck on this goddamn island with the boars and the cougars and maybe a bunch of fire ants forming an orderly line to crawl up his pecker. And if he tried to make a bolt for it, then Hooke would spiral a grenade up his ass like a rocket-powered snow cone.

What a peach of a night this had turned out to be.

Everett fucking Moreau: master planner.

Like that little French guy who used to get with tall ladies to prove a point. Napoleon.

But not like him at all, except for they both ended up fucked on an island, if he didn't misremember his history. Or maybe it was Huck Finn who got fucked on an island.

Either way, he was the idiot getting fucked on a waterlocked landmass this fine evening.

Sorry, Miss Ingram, he broadcast to his social studies teacher, the only teacher he had ever liked in the ten-year history of his education.

"Hey, son," called Regence Hooke, his voice boomy across the sound, "I tell you what. Why don't you toss out that cell phone you got there? It's probably all sorry-looking and waterlogged anyways. Hell, I'll even sign off on your police report for a new one. Because we both know you ain't getting a lick of signal in this stretch of the Pearl."

It ain't sorry-looking, thought Squib. *It's safe and sound in my work pants pocket.*

"You do me that favor," continued Hooke, "and I'll see myself off with my box of munitions and call it a night. What do you say to that? There's a deal you won't see in Target."

Seemed like Hooke was in the mood for chitchat. This was his general mood, in Squib's experience. Waxman once opined that Hooke's brand of chitchat was akin to a prison cake: "All purtied up on the outside with sugar frosting, but you know there's a blade lurking in there somewheres."

It was like how Hooke always referred to Squib as "Monsieur Moreau" when Elodie was around, tousled his hair and such, said he was a fine figure of a *"jeune homme,"* but soon as Momma's back was turned, the constable would lean in close and growl some off-color remark along the lines of *Fine piece of tail, that, Squib. Sooner or later, boy. I'm giving your momma her head for now, then I'll reel her in when she's wore out.* Spittle rimmed his lips as he leered: Regence Hooke, a prince among men.

"Otherwise," said the prince now, "I surely do plan to blanket-bomb the island with half a dozen more of these grenades from this dandy launcher I got here. And just to assure you I mean business, here's another firecracker to set you thinking."

Shit, thought Squib. *Shit and goddamn.*

There was no time to figure the correct course of action. And even if he did have the time, he didn't have the tactical experience. Should he hunker down or make a run for it? Which was best? Both seemed downright fraught with mortal peril.

While Squib was equivocating, Regence Hooke sat back on the roof of his cabin cruiser and, with a squeeze of his trigger, lobbed a metal cylinder high into the night. Up she flew into the drape of mist, trailing a plume of gray smoke, and Squib judged by what he could make out of the trajectory that he had about ten seconds to live.

This entire scheme was a fool's errand.

"Bye, Momma," he whispered, and the regret he would

carry with him to his watery grave was that now there was nothing between Hooke and his mother but a screen door.

"Bless me, Jesus," said Squib, just in case, and "I'm sorry for all the shit I done."

Then he shut his eyes and waited for the end.

VERN WAS ALL set up in his La-Z-Boy watching *Swamp Rangers* on Netflix. Goddamn, but he loved that show. Those Everglades boys tooling around in their golf carts, wrangling tiny gators and such, making a big old deal out of it.

I would fuck those boys up, thought Vern good-naturedly. But in truth he probably wouldn't. They were amusing guys, all confident and shit. It would be fun to see that braggadocio drain down to their boots.

Vern took a slug of vodka soda and laughed. *Imagine their faces. Those stupid goatees would drop off in shock.*

He did his best Jack Nicholson for the only squirrel on the island with enough nuts to sit on his windowsill. "Wait till they get a load of me."

Then he heard the explosion.

"Well, shit," he said resignedly, cranking up his chair. If there was one thing he'd learned from centuries hiding out in various remote spots round the globe, it was that certain things heralded discovery.

Elephants for one.

Elephants were assholes, and no one could tell Vern any different. Those big gray bastards had a nose for dragons, and that nose was called a trunk. There was this one bull who worked for one of the Mamluk sultans way back. Mean fucker with a cloudy eye and a grudge against fire lizards for some reason. Hunted Vern all over the Delhi province for ten years until Vern paid him a visit one balmy night in his paddock and stuck that trunk where the sun historically did not shine. Old Cloudy kept his dragon-seeking skills to himself after that.

Another thing that generally spelled trouble was rows of lit torches coming up a hill. Vern had lost count of the times he'd been dozing in one eyrie or another, only to be woken by the sound of a torch-bearing mob. Humans were stupid fuckers back in those days, attacking a dragon with torches, but they were persistent, and generally a guy would have to move on if he didn't want to spend his days swatting away flaming arrows.

But the number one warning sign that his days in his current hangout were numbered was the sound of an explosion. Goddamn smart-ass Chinese guys with their gunpowder. That shit could get in a guy's scales and itch like balls. And even if the humans weren't searching for him specifically, big explosions tended to shine a light on everything underneath.

"One of these days," said Vern to the squirrel, meaning that one of these days the humans would nail him with some kind of armor-piercing shell that would slice through his scales like butter.

"And then that will be all she wrote for every living thing in a mile radius."

Of course that was an estimate. If Vern's core was pierced, the blast radius could be much more than a mile. When they hit old Blue Ben by total freaking accident with an early-model torpedo, couple of centuries back, he took a large chunk of Cornwall to the bottom of the ocean with him.

"I better check it out," Vern told the squirrel. "Put a stop to whatever this shit is before it can get started."

Vern climbed out of the La-Z-Boy and carefully peeled off his *Flashdance* T-shirt, folding it neatly with the three-precise-creases method he'd picked up from the chirpy Netflix lady. It was one of his favorite shirts, and he didn't want it getting ripped to tatters flying around the swamp.

SQUIB SHUT HIS eyes, cried a bitter tear, and waited for the end.

Except it didn't come.

By some freak of physics Hooke's grenade reappeared from the mist, going right back the way it had come, that is to say retracing its own flight pattern, landing square between Hooke's feet, and clanking off down into the cruiser's gunwales.

Most men would have cursed in disbelief, and many might have fallen to sobbing or collapsed entirely, but Regence Hooke was made of sterner stuff. He grunted a gruff "fuck," then stepped lively off the prow of the boat and into the river. The constable had barely a moment to duck below the water before his grenade ignited and blew a ragged disk from the port side of the cruiser, which frisbeed cinematically into the mangroves and buried itself in the bulbous trunk of a tree with a *whang* like a hillbilly working a saw.

"Lucky," said Squib.

And he wasn't just talking about his own person. Hooke had God only knew what kind of non-standard-issue explosive hardware in his box of tricks. Half the island could have gone up in swamp lumps. They would've smelled the barbecued hog all the way to Slidell.

Squib dared to raise himself to all fours, praying to Jesus, God, Buddha, Aslan, and whoever else might be listening that Hooke was squashed flat between the keel of his sinking boat and the swamp bottom and would die slowly watching air bubbles leak from his nose. But he didn't get to find out if his prayer was answered just at that point because something very strong grabbed him by the waistband of his jeans and yanked him high into the Louisiana night sky.

Two seconds was all it took from earthbound to sky-high.

What in the name of—?

But Squib never completed that thought because:

A: He was too petrified to think rationally.

And B: His balls had been forced halfway up his stomach with the sudden acceleration of what could be fairly described as a supersonic wedgie.

And so as Squib Moreau was lifted high above the bayou, the only coherent thought he could manage to string together before the Gs blacked him out was, *Hey, I can see our cabin from here.*

CHAPTER 3

HOOKE WAS A BENT COP, NO DOUBT ABOUT THAT, BUT THERE WERE degrees of bent. A patrolman taking his coffee on the house every now and then was one thing, but you get a constable systematically subverting his vested power to knock off drug pilots for crime lordlings, and that right there was a whole other level of corrupt.

What set Regence apart were his intentions. Any cop who ever sat down before a congressional hearing or an IA board eventually mumbled shamefaced into the microphone a declaration along the lines of *I became a cop to help people, ma'am. I don't know when that changed exactly.*

Nothing had changed with Regence Hooke. From day one Regence was out to augment his own prosperity—or before day one, truth be told. It was biblical, actually, how Regence's ambitions got forged. His daddy was a self-styled preacher out of Homestead, Florida, who never managed to whip up much of a flock on account of his fanatically strict adherence to the letter of the Bible, mostly the early chapters. Jerrold Hooke might have had more of a pickup in Mississippi, but Florida folk preferred the whitewashed version of Jesus, the one who didn't point the finger at their fur-lined winter coats in church because Leviticus frowned on clothing woven of more than one kind of cloth. And retirees from the Northern states would not countenance a preacher who slapped cheeseburgers out of their hands because Exodus proclaimed that it was forbidden to consume meat and dairy in one meal.

Young Regence had little choice but to toe his daddy's Old Testament line, and it put a serious cramp in his adolescence. Everything concerning beer and balls was off the table, and goddamn if those things weren't the whole world for a teenager. Regence went the traditional route of outright rebellion and got himself spanked for his trouble, actually spanked, in the front yard with his buddies looking on, for flying in the face of Deuteronomy by being a profligate and drunken son. Young Regence, with his face as red as his ass, thought, *Screw this shit, I'll see that Bible-thumper dead and buried.*

It wore Preacher Jerrold Hooke down, how few shits people gave about his churching, and he eventually took to altar wine, and from there it was a short hop to bourbon. And it was only a few hours' sleep from bourbon to self-loathing. And that same self-loathing was passed on down to his wife and kids, as it generally is. Selma Hooke cracked one night following eight hours of preaching spat right into her face by a drunk man o' God and took off with her daughter, Martha Mary, never to be heard from again.

Regence, she neglected to take along.

He was trouble.

It was written all over the boy: a linebacker-looking lump of resentment with violence bubbling under the surface. Selma Hooke knew that there would come a day of reckoning, and she didn't want Martha Mary around to witness it.

This day of reckoning arrived maybe half a year later. Six months of boy and man living on their lonesomes out back of a timber-slat excuse for a storefront church with flaking paint and a spire that wasn't much more than a stack of pallets. Worshippers were limited to the ranks of the homeless, drunk, and addled. And even those poor souls reckoned that old Jerry Hooke was losing the run of himself, drunk as he was most days, whipping that boy around for mostly fabricated infractions of his endless rules.

Seemed like Jerrold was going more Jesus-crazy by the day. He started to invest serious belief in the notion that he'd been chosen by God for something superspecial that would give his life relevance to more than the dozen or so *Walking Dead* extras who inhabited his pews.

When Hurricane Andrew swept in from the Bahamas, Jerrold felt that he had finally found his vehicle.

He told his son, who really could not give a damn, "We shall stand together in the temple though it crumble around us, and then they shall see."

Regence started giving a damn sharpish then because if he understood his poppa's rantings, they were going to stick it out in a church made of rusted nails and plywood while the rest of the city got itself evacuated the hell out of Dodge.

Fuck that, thought Regence.

And so he turned on his father.

Or at least he tried to turn. Regence was big, but Jerrold was bigger. The son got in one good swing before Preacher Dad coldcocked him with his King James.

Regence woke up on the church altar with Armageddon swirling around his head and his crazy-ass father standing naked above him, calling to the Lord to show him a sign.

A sign? thought Regence. *A goddamn sign? Someone is shitting someone.*

And why the hell was his dad buck-ass naked?

None of it made a lick of sense to Regence, and he knew that the hurricane bearing down on them like the world was turning itself inside out was sure to send the both of them to whatever afterworld there actually was. And while the idea of a heaven would have been of some comfort at that moment as Andrew unwrapped the church from around them, flittering it to toothpicks, Regence half hoped the entire heaven thing was bullshit just so his dad's final thought might be something along the lines of *Oh, hell. I was wrong.*

Some tiny squib of Hurricane Andrew landed on father and son, punching the pair straight through into the basement, where they lay gasping and covered with debris while the fury of nature passed above. Miraculously, both Hookes survived.

Momentarily, at least.

Regence was first to gather himself and stood over his father thinking, *Maybe my daddy was actually right. Maybe Jesus delivered us.*

Then Jerrold Hooke opened his eyes and said, "Regence. A pity the Lord did not take you so my survival would have been all the more miraculous. Also, I would have cut a tragic figure for my flock."

And Regence picked up a jagged plank, staked his father through the heart like a vampire, then lay beside him on the mud floor and waited to be rescued.

And right then, lying there with the heavens torn apart above him, young Regence learned that the biggest clouds had the biggest silver linings—if a body was prepared to take advantage of chaos.

I have a gift, Regence had realized. And that gift was that he could keep his shit together while the whole world was freaking the hell out. Years later, a mentor in Iraq would toss out a quote that hit the nail on the head: "If you can keep your head when all about you are losing theirs . . ."

The rest of that Brit poem didn't really suit Regence's purposes, so Hooke took what he wanted and finished it off as follows: *If you can keep your head when all about you are losing theirs, then there is serious money to be made.*

BUT ON THIS night in the Pearl River bayou, with his large frame hunched under six feet of water and his own cruiser coming down on his head, Regence Hooke knew that there was more than cash on the line. His own traumatic upbringing had granted him the gift of presence of mind, which he employed to lunge out of harm's way. That particular harm, at any rate. There were plenty of other options on the harm menu that night, one being the cottonmouth snake which Hooke near to punched in the mouth accidentally while dragging his knuckles to shore, and another being the twelve-foot gator which, shocked awake, was eager to bite something on the ass but too addled to zone in on the constable. And to top it all off, when Regence Hooke dragged himself out of the churned slop, he was met nose-to-nose by a red-eyed boar, which took one look at his murderous expression and decided to break off eye contact and back away.

Hooke bludgeoned a path through the reeds and stalks, his anger intensifying with each swing of his fists. He was pissed about the boat, yes. So much for bringing Elodie around now with his grand gesture. And he was pissed about the ten grand's worth of firepower that had drowned with her. But there were always more bullets and more boats, and this neck of the parish had a surfeit of both. In fact, Willard Carnahan's inflatable was moored around the bend, and Hooke would bet his badge that there were plenty of weapons stashed in the cubbies. And a bottle of Willard's moonshine to drive out the chill would be most welcome.

What had really shaken Hooke's composure was his own confusion. What the hell had just happened? Best he could figure, his grenade had come home like it was on a string. In his long and varied experience of projectiles in general, that class of shit just didn't happen. That grenade didn't operate on any sort of independent guidance system. The direction a person aimed it was the direction it went.

Until today.

He grabbed hold of two stakes of cypress and hauled himself over the ridge of the levee, plopping onto the bank proper.

This ain't dignified, he thought, *lying here on my belly like a washed-up corpse. And what's more, I'm wide-open.*

Though if he was honest, the lack of dignity worried him more.

I get double-tapped now, and this is how they'll find me.

So Regence Hooke rose, sloughing off his jacket and maybe ten pounds of swamp crap along with it.

"Come and get me, asshole," he called into the spectral curtains of Spanish moss. "I got plenty in me yet."

It was true. Hooke was ready to go toe-to-toe. His drill sergeant back in Polk once remarked, "You're like the fuckin' Hulk, ain't you, Private Hooke? The more shit I pile on you, the more you got that glint in your eye. I like that, Private. You're a killing machine, ain't you, boy?"

And Hooke had said, "Yessir, Sergeant. A killing machine is what I am."

But he hadn't said it loud, like he'd been trained to. He said it real quiet, like the words came from his heart.

The drill sergeant near to crapped his camos, and he didn't trouble Hooke too much after that.

Hooke had that glint in his eyes now, and there was nothing he would have liked more than to go rampaging across the length and breadth of this godforsaken island hunting down Ivory's boy.

But . . .

But there had been a couple of explosions which would draw attention.

And his sidearm was no doubt clogged with shit.

And maybe Ivory's boy was already heading toward Petit Bateau, the closest landing, on whatever craft had taken him up here since Regence had been lying about seeing it drift by earlier.

The smart move was to take Willard's boat upriver and maybe get the jump on whoever had been videoing him. That was the smart move.

"Stay smart, Sergeant Hooke," he told himself, imitating his Iraqi mentor, Colonel Faraiji. "Remain calm."

Hooke closed his eyes and counted to ten, breathing in deeply through his nose, which was a relaxation exercise he'd picked up from a whore in the French Quarter. When he opened his eyes again, the killer was tucked away for the moment.

For the moment, thought Hooke. *But something happened here, and I'll be back to find out what.*

CHAPTER 4

VERN OFTEN THOUGHT OF THE OLD DAYS, WHEN DRAGONS HAD ruled decent patches of the earth from high in their eyries. Dragons kept that shit on track for centuries, lording it over the rest of creation, no predators to threaten their supremacy. And Vern was royalty, too: heir to the Highfire Eyrie, including the castle itself and the entire town, not to mention the caverns of assorted riches stashed in the catacombs. It was an excellent package with top-class benefits. But what the dragons in general hadn't realized was that, in the absence of physical predators, time itself becomes a predator. Dragons got accustomed to being top dogs. They started to enjoy the whole shock-and-awe thing. They forgot that humans weren't just dumb sheep with thumbs.

First the dragons grew complacent; then they got lazy. And the universe cannot suffer laziness because it leads to species-killing mistakes. The dragons' mistake was when they started keeping familiars, because before you knew it, the humans had moved on up from carrying logs and shoveling dragon shit to bringing home the bacon.

Next thing, those familiars were doing the books and giving pedicures, making themselves indispensable, making themselves invisible. Dragons allowed those humans to build quarters for themselves inside the walls. Dragons blabbed on about politics and strategy while their familiars were in the room. And goddamn if those familiars weren't taking notes.

It didn't take more than five hundred years and half a dozen failed revolutions before those smart little humans were running the show, and any dragons who had survived the purge were reduced to hiring themselves out as muscle or skulking around in various inhospitable shitholes.

And still humans ran the show, keeping themselves sharp by becoming their own predators, which was twisted as hell. Sure, dragons used to throw down every now and then, but there was no organized slaughter. The era of man was nothing more than a reign of murder and conquest, so far as Vern could see, which was why enjoying human media was about as far as Vern was prepared to go on the whole integration front. Sometimes he fantasized about re-vealing himself to *E! News* and getting his own show, but it was just a pipe dream. Sooner or later all those reality stars went the way of the Hiltons. He would have to make a sex tape to keep his ratings up, and how the hell would that even work? So Vern kept himself to himself and hid out in the Pearl River and tried not to think about the inevitable day when some eagle-eyed CIA motherfucker would spot him on a satellite pass-over and the next thing he knew he'd be up to his ass in drones.

And with all the explosions popping off in the environs, that day could be this day, so Vern needed to know what the hell was going on before he dispatched this kid to kingdom come and slid the body into the bayou, to let the gators make short work of him.

At that precise moment the kid was passed out on the floorboards of Vern's wilderness shack. Poor little bastard had hardly been expecting a night flight. He felt a little guilty for shaking up the kid, but Vern was quietly proud that he'd managed enough vertical acceleration to knock the human out.

You still got it, Vern baby, he thought, pulling on his T-shirt and cargo shorts.

He didn't get to stretch his wings much these days, not since every human over the age of six months got themselves a camera phone. He'd gotten himself all pumped up on Absolut a couple of years ago and taken a quick swoop over New Orleans. Some janitor shot a video of him doing a loop around Plaza Tower and it made the *Tribune*'s website. Fortunately, the video was little more than a shadowy blur which might have been a big flying lizard, but could also have been a kite or a crappy Photoshop job, so the piece never went national. Vern had been lucky, simple as that. But his luck couldn't hold forever.

The kid twitched a little, kicking his leg like a tummy-tickled puppy, and mumbled, "Momma." He was waking up.

Poor little asshole, thought Vern. *He ain't gonna like what he sees.*

Because while Vern fully intended to put the human boy down, he didn't consider himself a cruel dragon. He would have much preferred to dispatch the human in his sleep, but on this occasion questions needed to be asked, and the kid was the only one with answers.

SQUIB CAME OUT of it slow at first, believing himself safe in his own cot, his momma in the next room and maybe a bottle of orange cream soda in the cooler. Then the evidence of hard board under his shoulder blades and the weight of his mud-sopped clothes put paid to that notion, and so the boy opened his eyes and saw what appeared to be on first glance some class of mutie gator up on its hind legs and wearing human clothes.

Squib was at that special age where he was young enough to believe what he was seeing and old enough not to entirely freak the hell out. It was a magical fine line. Six weeks later and he would have gone directly into a shock coma. As it was, he backpedaled into the corner of the shack and took his sweet time looking the creature up and down.

It was some class of a reptile, no doubt about that: swamp-gator-kinda-looking as regards to its hide. Shining black, with lines of ridges, but the snout was shorter and had a couple of tusks curving out of its lower jaw that Squib had never seen on a gator. Also, there was the fact that this fella had wings and was up on its hind legs. And while alligators could rear up, they sure as hell could not maintain the position. The creature had a tail, but it was stumpy, with some kind of arrowhead arrangement at the tip. And there was the small matter of the T-shirt the reptile was wearing, which bore the legend "Flashdance," along with the famous dancer-on-a-chair silhouette.

As Squib studied the creature, the creature studied him, and it occurred to Squib that the creature might be hungry enough to eat him.

"Stay," he said, trying to sound stern.

Waxman had once told him that when dealing with animals, a man's gotta imprint on the beast's mind who the boss is.

"Shit, boy," said the creature, snagging a half-full bottle of Absolut from a cooler in the corner. "I ain't no goddamn dog. I'm what they call an 'apex predator.' You ever hear that term?"

A talking reptile? You'd think a boy would be petrified, but Squib found himself answering, "No, sir, I ain't never heard that one."

The creature took a slug of vodka, then laughed. Real human, it sounded, but alcohol-gruff. "'Sir'? Five seconds ago I was a dog. Now I'm a *sir*. You switch it up fast, don't you, kid?"

"Whatever the situation calls for," said Squib, hoping that the reptile's laughter was of the honest, good-natured type which meant nobody was getting eaten.

"You got a mouth," said the reptile. He reached into the pocket of his army trousers and pulled out a pack of Marlboros. "Smoke?"

Squib shook his head. It was the truth, but he also reckoned that was the smart play: make himself an innocent child. Harder to kill with a clean conscience. If this thing even had a conscience.

"Wise decision," said the reptile. He held up a cigarette and snorted a spark from one nostril to light it, like that was a thing of nothing. "I shouldn't. The way my insides work, it's asking for trouble. Like lighting up in a gas station."

Squib knew he should clam up, but he had to know. "Sir, you don't mind me asking, what are you exactly?"

The seven-foot reptile sank into a scuffed La-Z-Boy and ratcheted up the footrest. "What am I? I guess I'm an illegal immigrant, is what I am. You've heard of us, right? We're taking over the country."

Squib had seen plenty of illegal-immigrant clips on TV. This guy didn't look nothing like those videos. "You messing with me, sir?"

The reptile blew smoke to the tin roof. "Yeah. I guess. I got here way before your folk. By the way you're dispensing with *th*'s, I'd say Cajun, right?"

"That's right. Some Irish Texas in there, too, Momma says."

"Cajun and Irish Texas," said the reptile, grinning an exceptionally toothy grin. "That's a combustible mix right there."

Squib knew the word "combustible." Regence Hooke had said it to him often enough after the dynamite episode.

"Combustible. You some kind of dragon, mister?"

The reptile blew a series of interconnected smoke rings from one nostril. "Yeah, I guess 'dragon' is as good a word as any."

Squib remembered a story Miss Ingram had told them. "You're like that old boy in England? Got himself skewered by Saint George?"

The dragon glanced sharply with his swiveling gator eyes at the shivering human wretch in the corner. "I ain't nothing like *that* dragon. I knew him, though: a full-grown half-wit by the name of Gudmunder who went wandering around the countryside, balls swinging like a bassinet. Shitfaced-drunk most of the time. Got himself shanked by a hunter. Passed out in a village, he was, after a week running around pillaging, fucked up on opium." The dragon shook his head, sparks playing around his chops. "Humans don't play that shit, less they're doing it to themselves. Gudmunder was a dick, kid. He went looking for that shanking."

"But not you, huh?"

The dragon winked. "I'm here, ain't I? The last one, so far as I know. Keeping myself to myself out here in the swamp. Doing you guys a favor. Without me, the boar population would be out of control."

"Thank you, sir," said Squib.

"Call me Vern," said the dragon.

"Yessir, Mister Vern."

Squib hesitated a little before saying what was on his mind, but then thought, *Screw it, it would be a shame to die curious.*

"You don't mind me saying," said the boy. "But 'Vern' don't seem like a good fit for no dragon, name-wise."

"It's short for 'Wyvern.' That's ye olde English, as they say. I abbreviated when I came over here before the war."

"Desert Storm?" asked Squib, who was keeping the conversation going to delay the inevitable reckoning.

Vern laughed again. "No, kid, the war in this country.

The Civil War, and I ain't talking about no Captain America. Desert Storm. Shit."

Squib was a little amazed that once again Miss Ingram's teachings were going to come in useful, God bless that woman. "The Civil War? That's like a hundred and fifty years ago."

"Yep," said Vern. "New Orleans was in the thick of the supply chain. The Confederates even built a couple of submarines to transport their gold. One took to chasing me, so I had to sink the fucker. All hands lost. The gold was lost, too, so far as anybody knows." The dragon winked again, like he was letting Squib in on a secret, and the boy really wished that Vern wouldn't confess things so readily. It was like he didn't care what Squib knew because he wouldn't know it for long.

"I understand, I guess," said Squib. "Loose lips."

"You got it, kid. They sink ships. And by 'ships,' I mean this old carcass. So in the interests of this old carcass, I need to ask you a few questions, and I would advise you to consider the hell outta your answers because I will not tolerate bullshit, which I got a nose for sniffing out, by the by."

"Yessir," said Squib, reckoning that maybe Vern was doing a little bullshitting of his own. "I'll help whatever way I possibly can, trust me on that."

"Good attitude, kid," said Vern. "Now, question one. I urgently need to know what those explosions were about. Was someone looking for old Vern?"

Squib answered smartly, "No, sir. That was some kinda disagreement between Willard Carnahan and the police. A deal that went south."

"Way south," Vern agreed, "and it woulda gone a lot further south for you, kid, if I hadn't batted that grenade back the way it came."

"Thank you for that, mister," said Squib, keeping up the polite act.

"Don't thank me, boy. I just wanted to shut down the ruckus."

"My thanks anyhow. Sincerely. I was a goner for sure."

Vern snorted sparks. "You ain't outta those particular woods yet, kid. And what the hell were you doing in those reeds? A kid like you, up in the swamp this time of night?"

Squib reckoned there was no downside to telling the truth, so he kept on answering the dragon's questions. "The cop—Constable Hooke—he has a hard-on for me and my momma. Different kinds of hard-on, respectively, you understand. I was trying to gather a little dirt, maybe get him to back off."

"Back off?" said Vern and guffawed sharply. "You seriously misjudged that individual, from what I seen. Guys like that don't back off. They ramp it up. A cop with a grenade launcher? I reckon that cannon wasn't no standard issue."

"He's a bad man," said Squib. "Worse than I figured, maybe."

Vern studied the glowing tip of his cigarette, considering this information. "Willard Carnahan. I know him. Runs contraband down the Pearl?"

"Yessir. Best navigator on the river. He was supposed to be my new boss."

"And this guy Hooke had some beef with Carnahan?"

"Some kind," said Squib. "I ain't sure what. It's over now 'cause Willard's fish food."

"And you stuck your pesky nose in the middle?"

"I messed up, I reckon."

Vern thought hard on these details a spell. This was bad news, no doubt, but not catastrophic. Maybe he didn't necessarily have to move on immediately, just keep an eye out for developments. It wasn't likely anybody would be fighting a turf war in the swamp. These kinda deals tended to get sorted out in built-up areas. And maybe with Willard underwater, along with the cop's boat, this whole affair was now sleeping with the fishes.

But the kid had seen him and knew what he was, and that was unfortunate.

Vern tried to think of another way, but he supposed there wasn't one.

Never ever trust a human.

Vern sighed. "I'm sorry about what's coming, kid, but I'm the last of my kind, so you understand why I gotta do what I gotta do, right?"

Squib guessed exactly what was coming. "You don't have to worry about me, mister. I ain't no snitch. Shit, I been keeping my mouth shut since the day I was born."

The dragon rolled the cigarette between his scaled fingers. "Seems like the opposite to me, kid."

"The name's Everett Moreau. Everyone calls me Squib on account of a screwup I had with some dynamite a couple of years back." Squib held up his damaged hand as proof, wiggling his pinky nub.

Vern tossed the cigarette through a gap in the floor

planks. "That was good, Squib. Real good. The amount of information you fit into a couple of sentences there? Making yourself real to me. It's like you read a psychology text. But my game is self-preservation, kid, and I been at that game a long time. A long time. And you know the number one rule?"

Squib didn't know and he didn't want to know, but he had to ask. "What's the number one rule, Vern?"

Vern stood up real fast, unfolding to his full height. The *Flashdance* T-shirt stretched tight across his massive chest, and little pilot lights of blue flame danced behind his molars.

"Number one rule, kid: A human comes in here, he don't come out. It's like Thunderdome, 'cept *no* man leaves."

Vern popped a single claw on his index finger, then sprayed it with nose flame till it glowed white. "I promise you, kid, it'll be real quick."

Nose flame, thought Squib, descending into dreamy shock. *Cool.*

And after that: *Damn, I never even kissed a girl.*

Then the alligators came up through the floor.

Squib would have said that nothing could have surprised him at this point, but seeing that surge of teeth and sinew writhing its way into the room changed his mind real sharp. He felt the balm of shock recede, to be replaced by the fear he'd been repressing: a fear which surged upwards from his boots and took a hold of his guts, wringing them like wet rope.

It was unreal to see the swamp come indoors this way, like the world was on its head. Something about this influx of reptiles felt even more wrong than meeting Vern the dragon.

These gators were *organized*, is what it was. They had *group intent*.

"Fuck me," said Squib. "Oh Lord in heaven."

"Calm down, junior," said the dragon, who'd been on the point of killing him a moment before. "It's just swamp bullshit is all."

The alligators congregated in one corner, snapping and writhing, issuing strange breathy, ratcheting roars. They lashed the shack's planking with their tails and stomped their stumpy legs, splintering entire sections of the floorboards. There was murder in their eyes.

VERN WAS NOT unduly worried. "Come on, fellas," he said. "This is my home. You are messing with a guy's bachelor pad. Invading my space is what it is."

One alligator, a massive bull maybe fifteen feet long and three feet through the shoulders, stepped forward from the herd, waving his head from side to side.

"Really, Buttons?" said Vern. "We gotta do this now?"

Buttons, who Vern had named ironically, for the creature was certainly not cute as a button, hissed, and the pale wattle under his jaw rippled. Whatever this was, it appeared that it did indeed have to be done now.

"Come on, man," said Vern. "I got company here. I'm in the middle of an interrogation."

The gator, who did not understand Vern's words and would not have cared even if he had, lowered his warhead snout and made a lightning sortie, jaws snapping in a scything blur of teeth. Steam rose from his back, and his eyes flashed gold.

"Oh, please," said Vern, not in the least impressed. He'd gone claw-to-claw with a sea serpent in Russia. This guy was no big deal compared to an arctic lizard.

He could have fried the big dumb gator, simple as pie, but the challenger's supporters needed to be taught a lesson in a language they understood, so Vern opted to put on a quick and brutal exhibition. He stomped hard on the gator's neck, driving his challenger half through the rotten boards. Then he shattered the vodka bottle on the ridges of the gator's snout and made a lot of noise.

Vern lit up the alcohol with a snort from one nostril, and suddenly the creature's head was on fire.

"That's right, gators," said Vern. "Your great green hope has got himself a head full of fire." And then, with no apparent effort, he hoisted his challenger aloft and hurled him back out through the window.

Hurt my damn back, he thought, but did not show it.

"Look at me, kid," he called over his shoulder. "The supreme warrior. The goddamn Predator. As a matter of fact, I would kick that Predator's ass back to outer space."

The other gators could not vacate the premises fast enough. They flowed out through gaps in the cypress planking, clambering over each other in their eagerness to be away from the mighty dragon.

Vern might have laughed if he hadn't had enough of fighting for one night. Gators sure looked funny in retreat, though. It was a skill they'd never mastered.

Vern returned his focus to the kid. *Another dumb animal I gotta deal with.*

"You wanna say a prayer, Squib fella? Or should I just go ahead and get her done?"

The kid did not respond, because of course he had gone out the window the second Vern's back was turned.

Smart kid, Vern thought. And then, *This could mean trouble for the Wyvern retirement plan.*

Steps would have to be taken.

CHAPTER 5

S QUIB WENT INTO THE PEARL NOT GIVING A SINGLE DAMN ABOUT whatever might be lurking under the surface. It wouldn't be alligators, not within a swamp mile of this place, not after Vern's display of dragon wrath.

And even if there was one dumbass gator still in the vicinity, Squib would rather take his chances with that lizard than the giant mythological creature who had somehow come to life in Louisiana.

He chugged about half a pint on entry to the bayou, but that was okay; the river water never made it into his windpipe. Squib spat and then struck out for Honey Island with every scrap of panic in his body. It wasn't particularly efficient swimming—in fact, it was downright dangerous with all the thrashing he had going on—but Squib was in flight mode now, and whatever higher reasoning he might've had had gone out the window along with his own self.

Squib was guided back to Honey Island by the beacon of a small blue fire working on the ass end of Hooke's cruiser, which, having yet to sink fully, was poking out of the swamp water. The sky was still some ways from light, but a wash of cobalt was spreading into the black and the moon was calling it quits, so somewhere in the back of Squib's mind he reckoned he must have been unconscious for a couple of hours at least.

A swamp bullfrog the size of a pineapple came hurtling out of the dark and clipped Squib's ear hole a good one, sending the poor boy into a fresh panic as he was momentarily convinced the dragon had some kind of minion deal going with the frogs, but the frog was as startled as Squib himself and breaststroked off downriver, showing Squib his ass and paying the boy no further mind.

Okay, so the frogs ain't out to get me, thought Squib for the first and last time in his life. The toe of his Converse scraped a groove on the mud floor, and Squib near to bawled with relief that he could detach himself from the swamp. He had thought that maybe it might be best to get himself underwater when dealing with dragons on account of fire not mixing with water, though on second thought being wet hadn't seemed to help that gator none.

Vern. That dragon told me his own self that his name was Vern.

What kind of name is that for an apex predator?

Nuts.

This whole entire night was a page of crazy in the book of his life.

Squib found a groove in the ridge and dragged himself onto Honey Island, feeling almost paralyzed by lingering terror and the weight of swamp bilge swelling every fiber of his clothing. *I could stay right here*, he thought, *and just let the algae put down roots. Become a plant.*

Dragons don't eat plants, do they?

Then again Vern, it seemed to him, could eat whatever the hell he wanted.

Also, Momma would freak out if he disappeared. And Squib surely did hate upsetting his momma, after all she'd been through with his actual daddy, his fake daddy, and now Regence Hooke stalking her. Squib knew his momma had two distressed faces: the one she used when he was in the room, which was mostly tight and restrained with sporadic implosive gasps of air, like she was afraid to relax her jaw muscles for too long in case she lost control, and the second distressed face Elodie let out when she thought no one was watching. This face was a heartbreaker every time. Elodie would lay her cheek on the table and weep like there wasn't a sadder situation on earth. She would cry until it looked like there was a spill on the tabletop, and loud, too, like a forlorn cat. Squib surely did hate that sound, and he did not like being the one who brought it on.

On occasion, distressing Elodie Moreau upset him so much that Squib almost chose virtuous behavior patterns over his natural shady instincts.

Almost.

ONCE SQUIB DISCOVERED that his pirogue had not in fact drifted downriver but was actually snarled in the bulrushes, he cursed Hooke with each tug it took him to free the lacquered craft. The engine took a little more work, as every loose piece of crud in the bayou had apparently made a beeline for his mud motor's prop.

The sky was pale slate now and he was a goddamn target squatting out here, tugging at his long-tail propeller. Squib could see his own reflection in the water, and if he could see his reflection, then it stood to reason that his actual self was just as visible to anybody who cared to look.

Anybody or anything.

Spooked was how Squib felt. Every rustle of bamboo sent his head whipping around like a deer at the watering hole.

Time to get gone, he thought.

He pushed off his canoe and hopped in, priming the motor and tugging the cord with weeds still clogging the shaft—bad motor practice, but there was no time to strip the propeller when there was possibly a monster on his tail.

The motor was a trusty Swamp Runner built from a kit, and it justified its reputation for reliability by spiralizing the vegetation and bursting into steady whining life. A sound like that would carry clear to the other side of the river, but Squib couldn't be helping that now. Felt like the lesser of two evils to him.

"The devil's on my heels," said Squib, twisting the throttle wide, not that the cc's he had at his disposal could outrun a determined dragonfly, let alone an actual dragon, but it cheered him some to feel the water sluicing along the marine-ply sides of his pirogue.

The trip north wasn't more than ten minutes, but Squib felt like he was racing against the morning. He reckoned the dragon wouldn't fancy parading his scaly self in front of the various tourists, fishermen, and hunters who relished getting out on the water early. A monster like Vern could hardly have survived by making field trips into populated areas, even to pick up his vodka.

Unless some big-mouth kid eyeballed him.

Yeah, unless that.

The Pearl River ran swollen and sluggish down to the gulf, and Squib's boat skipped along its surface like a palm frond on the front end of a gale even against the flow. Perfect design. The kids now preferred fiberglass—even the locals wouldn't take the time to dig out a pirogue—but Waxman swore by the wooden craft, and Squib was thankful now he'd heeded the ancient asshole's words. All the pirogue needed was a slap on the ass from the smallest engine and it was out of there, slicker than a pike.

Squib kept himself bent over like that would make him invisible from above and ghosted the cypress line until he came upon a little dawn traffic. A couple of old boys saluted him from their crawfish boat, and Squib's heart rate decelerated a few dozen bpms.

Maybe the dragon won't even recognize me, he thought, not actually fooling any level of his consciousness. *Lotta kids with dark hair hanging around the river.*

So get yourself off the damn river, you dumb shit, his little voice told him. *Let this ill wind blow over.*

Sometimes, it had to be said, Squib's little voice made more sense than his big one.

SQUIB GOT HIMSELF off the river, which wasn't exactly a feat of tactical genius. The Moreau house was set in a squirt of switchback back from the main bayou. In truth, the place wasn't much more than a shack on stilts, with a square of deck stained from a thousand catfish gutted by the previous residents. The wooden siding had probably been crimson at some point in the last century, but was now pink and flaking like the skin of a tourist after a day in the Louisiana sun. The only patch of deep red was a rectangle of fresh paint where the landlord had covered up a Confederate flag which somehow defied any attempts to permanently conceal its blue cross and had to be redone once a year.

"Goddamn thing is haunted," Bodi Irwin had commented. "I guess the Rebs will never lay down."

Squib nudged the tiller with the heel of one hand and brought the craft parallel to the dock, giving the engine a quick twist in reverse to put the brakes on. *It ain't much, but it's home*, he thought.

And they wouldn't even have that if it weren't for the graces of Bodi Irwin, the aforementioned flag concealer, who'd been sweet on Elodie since prom or thereabouts, and was prepared to forgo any meaningful rent in exchange for her boy lugging beer crates in his bar a couple of shifts every week.

That was a good deal, far as Squib was concerned. Plus it seemed like Bodi might have left it too long to ever actually ask his momma out, which was how Squib liked it, or at least how he used to like it. Squib was getting to the age where his developing brain was forcing him to consider Elodie as an actual person rather than as simply his momma. Waxman, as part of one of his droning lectures, referred to Squib's insights as the development of his superego, which

Squib thought for a flash meant that he was getting super-powers.

But whatever the reason for his newfound awareness, it had prompted him to take stock of his momma. Elodie was beautiful to him, he knew that. Momma was always telling her nurse friends how her boy Everett used to propose to her on the regular.

When I grow up, I'm gonna marry you, Momma.

And he meant it at the time. Now, a few years after his proposal phase, Squib could see that the rest of town agreed with his assessment vis-à-vis his momma being beautiful. But that was just frosting on the doughnut: His momma was sweet on the inside too; she spent her nights caring for sick folk and her days worrying about Squib. She rarely spent a nickel on herself and would cut both her hair and Squib's her own self. Elodie would turn some fella down gently maybe one time per week and that would be that—except for Hooke; he got turned down flat, which just made the constable come on harder.

I sure wish Bodi would make a move, thought Squib now, especially knowing what he knew about Constable Hooke.

But Waxman had assured him that the bar owner would never ask Elodie out: "That boy's too goddamn ugly. Your mom's a nine, objectively, and Bodi, he couldn't get past a three with reconstructive surgery and a stepladder."

Which seemed a little less philosophical than Waxman's usual lectures so far as Squib was concerned.

Squib tied off on a brass ring which had ended up in one of his crawfish nets a couple of years back. He should sell it, he knew, but the ring had become something of a symbol. People spent their whole lives trying for the brass ring.

And here's Squib big shot Moreau with a big shiny brass ring screwed into his dock.

That must mean something, right? "Auspicious" was the word, according to Miss Ingram.

But "dock"?

Really?

More like a collapsed fence, truth be told.

It had become Squib's custom to rub the ring with his wrist to bookend every day, and he completed the ritual now, his filthy skin smearing the brass.

"Still alive, thank the Lord," he said, and snuck across the deck, avoiding the creaky spots in case by some miracle his momma had decided not to check on him when she was done with her shift sticking clumsy drunks with tetanus shots in the Petit Bateau clinic.

Like most wayward sons, Squib had figured a ninja-type sneaky method of entry into the stilt house. He thought of it as his "window of opportunity," which sometimes cracked him up even as he engaged the maneuver, which kind of ruined the desired effect.

There was no cracking up on this day of days. Today he had been hunted by the two most dangerous creatures he had ever encountered—more than likely the most danger-ous he would ever encounter.

If I die before I wake, most likely one of them two bastards done it.

But the ninja method: Squib's sequence involved one

foothold on a gas tank, a second in the crook of an old anchor hung on the wall by some seafaring previous resident, then, with two hands gripping the upper rim of the windowsill, finishing off with a nice gymnastic-type swing through the skeeter screen, which was only secured on the top end. Done right, this little burglar routine deposited him sweetly on his own cot.

Even in his rattled state, this was the kind of thing Squib could have pulled off in his sleep: one, two, three, and in, reminding himself as he fell to secure the window screen later. But on this occasion as he was already in midair, suspended in hang time with no way to abort the maneuver, Squib heard a voice beyond in what his momma called the parlor, and the voice was not his momma's.

It was Regence Hooke's.

And the voice was saying, "Snake-bit."

Well, ain't that just the sewage icing on the shit cake? thought Squib Moreau before landing on his bed with a thump.

I sure wish I could have left that thump outta my routine, he thought then.

Thumps were like catnip to law enforcement. They couldn't help but investigate. And here was the boy Squib Moreau slathered with just about as much shit as could be heaped on a fifteen-year-old, looking just exactly like a fella who'd just crawled outta the swamp.

The kind of fella Hooke was searching for.

REGENCE HOOKE FELT like shit, was the long and short of it, so he abandoned all notions of strategies and took Carnahan's inflatable upriver just about as fast as he could, which was pretty darn fast, due to the hundred or so horses bolted to the stern. Boat didn't look like much to Hooke, but Carnahan had never stopped singing its praises.

"It's a RIB, Constable," he'd explained. "Rigid-hulled inflatable. Poseidon himself couldn't flip this baby. I can spread a ton of product around the deck and still make top knots. Ordered her special from Canada. They sent a boat on a train. You believe that shit?"

Wasn't much more than a glorified dinghy, far as Hooke was concerned, but he had to admit she handled nice and easy. Turned on a crooked dime and responded eagerly to his touch like she was faking it.

Like that double act in Ivory's club, making out like they never had it so good.

That had been quite a night.

Quite a night.

But nothing like this one. Hooke knew he had to find himself a quiet corner and forensically examine just what in hell had brought this shit storm down upon him.

I gotta take this evening apart like an engine, see if I can't reconstruct it some.

But first things first.

And first thing was to get this boat under a roof.

"I oughta scuttle you," Hooke told the boat. "I oughta cut you to ribbons."

It made sense: Forensics were microscopic these days, plus every character from here to Slidell knew who this boat belonged to.

But Hooke was faced with the practical obstacle that the

sun was clawing its way through the Spanish moss, and pretty soon he would be a big man on a smuggler's bright orange inflatable in the middle of a flat patch of water.

I'd be locked in a sheriff's cell by margarita time.

So it appeared his only option was to pull into the yard and tie off at his shed, then take his time cutting her up.

Except for the engines. Those twins will fetch three grand for the pair.

Hooke's berth was on the blind corner of the Petit Bateau boatyard, which, like most everything else in town, was owned by the town's resident shit-kicker mogul, Bodi Irwin. Hooke had rented one of the outlying boat sheds from Irwin and installed his own security cameras and motion sensors, all of which he could check from his phone.

"Fuck balls!" Hooke swore. Now he had to get a new goddamn phone and set up his shit all over again. He must have twenty goddamn passwords and not a record of a single one.

I shoulda got one of those pouches, he told himself. *Five bucks and my phone would be safe and sound in a plastic envelope.*

Still, spilled milk and so forth. Better to cross the phone bridge when he came to it.

Hooke came up on the boatyard a bit slower than he might usually. Round these parts, a man didn't motor his boat at no snail's pace, no sirree, a man liked to plow a furrow in the swamp coming in to tie off, show he had a little boat craft. Nothing the locals liked more than to sit on the porch of the Pearl Bar laughing their asses off at clueless tourists spinning their rented airboats like goddamn Frisbees on the bayou. Hooke didn't like to be put in that category. He might be a blow-in, but he came from swamp himself and knew how to blow the exhaust out of any craft you cared to drop him in.

Not this morning. Today, Hooke was content to slope into his shed with zero fuss. He didn't want any eyes glancing up from their enamel coffee mugs, wondering about the source of the bass thrum of big outboards, and he didn't want to embarrass himself scraping the gunwales of an unfamiliar craft. So, slow and steady it was.

The shed wasn't much more than a jetty with walls. A few tools and some tackle hung from the siding, and a couple of drums were triangled in the corner. Might have been oil, might have been nuclear waste, who the hell knew? Pretty run-of-the-mill digs for a constable on whatever salary a small municipality could pay him. Hooke was lucky he'd brung his own Chevy Tahoe to the position; otherwise he would have been lumbered with the town's eco-Honda. Who the hell could maintain any kind of authority driving an electric Honda? The mayor owned the dealership, was the problem. He was pretty pissed Hooke wouldn't go around town in his branded golf buggy, but Regence reckoned that there weren't any moonshiners that would give a good goddamn when some out-of-towner pulled up in a car with an electric socket. He'd be a laughingstock. So his angle was that he was saving the city money by bringing his own vehicle to the job. Tough to argue with that.

Hooke tied up and found that he was so depleted that he had to roll onto the jetty.

"What the hell?" he mumbled. Where had his strength disappeared to?

Then he saw his swollen knuckle and realized, *Fuck, I been snake-bit.*

With all his abrasions and the general furor he hadn't noticed till now. He remembered the cottonmouth he had punched.

Looks like I didn't get away with that like I thought.

At least he hadn't done it on purpose. It would be a shame to die a damned fool.

As a parish constable and a St. Tammany Parish road patrol officer before that, Regence had been required to take not one but two first aid courses, and he tried to remember the specifics now regarding the various variables, but his senses were addled and all he knew was: *Get help. Lickety-split.*

There wasn't a jab of antivenom on the premises. He'd been meaning to and meaning to, et cetera, and the clinic was a couple of miles away.

Tarantulas nesting inside every banana leaf and you don't got no antivenom.

Get to the truck, he told himself, *and you'll think of something.*

It was an optimistic plan at best, but Regence was drunk on poison, and before the depression came the optimism.

I'm gonna be all right, thought Constable Hooke, when in fact all evidence was to the contrary.

HOOKE's PICKUP MORE or less steered itself to Elodie Moreau's stilt house. It wasn't more than half a mile down a pine-ridged dirt road: a tin-roofed wooden shack that folk from more northerly aspects could barely credit existed anymore outside sepia images from the Civil War. Alone it stood, lapped by mud water and circled by a cyclone of dragonflies.

The constable must have passed out for a moment at the wheel, but he was roused by a vicious throbbing around his knuckles and was petulantly dismayed to see his right hand puffed up to the dimensions of a catcher's mitt. Hooke poked the swollen mess with a finger and found the skin to be tight as a balloon and filled with electricity.

This is serious, Regence, my boy, the constable told himself. *Elodie will have antivenom. She's a nurse, ain't she?*

Hooke's pigheadedness carried him out of his truck to the Moreau stoop, and he stumbled up the steps using his forehead for leverage, stowing the injured hand close to his belly for protection.

It pained him mightily to appear before Elodie Moreau in this way, brought low, as it were. Elodie Moreau was the only woman with whom he could imagine spending any length of time without it ending in violence. She'd come running into Slidell Memorial after her idiot son blew his finger off, and she near to smothered that kid with love. Hooke had never seen anything approaching that kind of public emotion, and it had repulsed him at the time. But he came around on it and was touched, somehow. The last time Regence Hooke had been touched was never, and so he set his cap at Elodie Moreau and swore a vow that he would try fair means first. For something like six months.

The "fair means" he'd had in mind had not included showing up mud-crusted and snake-bit, but make hay while the sun shines, and so on.

Except the sun ain't shining, and I ain't got no hay, thought Hooke. *Nor no fuckin' lemons neither.*

And then:

Shit. I better knock on this here door.

As it turned out, Hooke had already knocked plenty with his head on the steps, because the door opened and Elodie Moreau's Crocs appeared before his eyes. Sports socks stuck out of the Crocs, and Hooke was flashed back to a high school memory and he said, "Jessica Milton wore tube socks. Used to spy on Jessie through a hole in the shower walls. Skinny ass but huge boobs. Rare combination."

Which was not what he would have led with in normal circumstances, but luckily for him Elodie caught sight of his bloated hand and knew exactly what was going on. She helped the constable inside the stilt house, getting herself covered in mud in the process.

"Dear Lord, Constable," she said, "ain't you right in the head? Walking around bitten like that?"

"Bit," agreed Hooke, tumbling into the room's single armchair. "Snake-bit."

Something thumped in the back room.

"Thump," said Hooke. "Thump?"

Elodie wrestled with Hooke's feet, elevating them onto a coffee table. "That's Everett falling outta bed. He's wrestling a gator or something in his sleep."

Everett? thought Hooke. *Squib?*

And there was something that nagged at him about the boy, but he couldn't be thinking about that right now because right now the nightmares were coming to him through a tunnel which had opened in the ceiling. In the nightmares his father was wielding a fiery crucifix like a hypodermic and saying, *I just gotta administer an antivenom. This will get rid of all the poison inside you.*

And Hooke thought, *You're gonna need a bigger crucifix.*

VERN TOOK TO the skies, which he rarely did these days because of the prying humans and their surveillance. Those earthbound assholes had managed to all but extinctify dragons back in the day with nothing but crossbows and malignant intent, so Vern had no illusions about just how quickly they could finish the job if given a clean shot. In point of fact, with all the technology humans had nowadays, a clean shot wasn't even necessary. All Captain Jarhead needed was one second to tag him with a laser; then a surface-to-air missile would chase him around corners forever and a day.

Well, swim then, Highfire. Keep yourself hidden.

No, you ain't got time for swimming. Times is flying, and so must you.

So Vern did not relish flying as much as he used to, especially at dawn, because a dragon never knew when a warhead was gonna bury itself where the sun don't shine, and Vern had no doubt that he would not survive that detonation.

Hell, I probably wouldn't survive a decent-sized armor-piercing round, he thought gloomily.

Still, on a positive note, the sunrise-tinted water did remind him of the time he'd rammed that Confederate submarine. The water had run red that evening.

Happy days, thought Vern now, and spread his wings wide to catch the thermals.

It was a catch-22-type situation: spread the wings and make a bigger target, or flap more and make a louder one. Vern usually opted to glide. A nice glide had a certain dignity about it, and a fella could pretend he was still Lord Highfire surveying his domain.

He followed the river's lazy meander toward the nearest settlement, Petit Bateau, and soon spotted the foam ribbons of a settling wake. The ribbons led to a hook of switchback, with a little pirogue docked up, still waddling from a fresh disembarkation.

That is quite possibly my boy, thought Vern.

This was about the best result he could have hoped for. Young Squib had the decency to bunk waterside, so the dragon could pluck out this human thorn himself. Any farther inland and he would have had to ask Waxman to make the problem go away, and Waxman had qualms about certain things. Especially kids.

"You're so in love with humans, you should go marry one," Vern had told him once, many years ago.

"I did," was Waxman's response to that. "Twice. First one was an angel, but the second nearly done me in. Brazilian, very fiery, no offense."

But out here on the levee, Waxman's talents would not be called for. That creepy Gladstone bag of his could stay under the floorboards. That bag sure did make an ominous clanking when Waxman hefted it. Even made an old hand like Vern squirm a little.

So, let us see what we can see, Highfire, Vern thought to himself, shifting his haunches forward and wrapping his wings above him in a funnel-type arrangement so he dropped down like he was on a zip line.

If this was indeed the boy's regular crib, then Vern could simply spirit him away and that would be an end to it. He would still need to keep an eye open in the swamp, see if the explosions would draw a torch-wielding mob or the modern equivalent.

Torch-wielding? thought Vern. *I am almost nostalgic for that shit.*

No one had the need for torches anymore. Even your basic hillbilly had a set of night-vision goggles in the trunk to go with their constitutional semiautomatic weapon.

Was a time only a talented and determined bunch of humans could take down a dragon. Now any fool with the right load can do it.

Vern touched down on an iron railing, probably originally V-shaped and salvaged from the prow of a fishing boat but now hammered into a right angle to fit the deck. He gave it maybe half his weight, but kept a thrum going with his wings in case rapid liftoff was needed.

And holy crap, if the window wasn't open: nothing but a bug screen between him and the boy in his bed.

Dragons have the best night vision on earth, and so Vern could easily see that this boy was his boy.

I spy you, Nine Fingers, he thought, *and you ain't sleeping none. Straight into bed and still muck to the eyeballs. Something tells me this slippery character wasn't supposed to be out screwing around in the swamp.*

Vern noticed an orange butane tank on the deck. Looked

like it came off the *Titanic*, old as it was, paint flaked down to the metal and a foot of rubber hose poking out the top.

Like a fuse, thought Vern.

More than likely the tank was empty years since, but if that was where a local fire officer figured the epicenter to be, then that was it, case closed.

Perhaps a fire was cleaner than abduction.

No trace evidence to analyze.

No search party on the river.

Collateral damage, maybe. But Vern's entire species had been collateral damage as far as he was concerned.

Sorry, kid, he thought for the second time that night, and cracked open his jaws. The glands at the back of his throat spurted sulfur oil onto his molars, and he ignited the oil with a gnash which gave him his pilot light.

Vern drew breath to let fly, but it seemed like this kid Squib was blessed by the gods or some such voodoo because at that moment an ambulance surged into view over the verge maybe half a mile down the shoreline, siren shrieking and dome light flashing. Goddamn siren was so loud Vern couldn't even hear the engine.

"Well, ain't this a ding-dong dell?" whispered Vern, which was a twee old saying that he rarely employed in company. Waxman had heard it one time and near to split his corduroy vest with laughing.

"'Ding-dong dell'? Shit, Vern! We ain't graduating from finishing school."

Nevertheless, the saying slotted into this situation neat as pie. "Ding-dong dell," meaning unexpected commotion, which this approaching ambulance certainly was.

"Balls," said Vern. "Balls and double balls."

"Balls and double balls" being a more modern saying.

He hated unfinished business, but that ambulance was bringing more eyeballs than he cared to be looking his way, and the sun was making real strides now against the shadows.

Time to be away, Highfire, he told himself when the ambulance screamed down Squib's lane.

But first he would mark the house for Waxman. It looked like that creepy old bag would be needed after all.

Vern sucked his thumb for a minute, breathing flame on the claw; then he carved a letter into the metal railing with his nail.

V.

Mark of the dragon.

Sorta like the opposite of lamb's blood in the Old Testament.

Everyone in this dwelling dies.

"Later, Squib," he said and launched himself backwards into the river.

Better to swim home.

SQUIB WAS LYING in bed waiting to be killed when a breeze flapped the fly screen and he saw the dragon crouched on the railing, eyes like a cat in the headlights: not angry, exactly. Thoughtful.

Oh, fuck, I'm an ant to him, Squib thought, closing his eyes against the boogeyman, like a kid, like a child. *Oh Jesus Lord, help me.*

Like Jesus would give a shit about a slacker like him.

He opened his eyes when he heard the ambulance and was just in time to see Vern do a backflip with a twist into the water. There was hardly a splash. A very clean entry.

Eight point five, thought Squib, and perhaps more pertinently, *He knows where I live. And Momma, too.*

Squib was marked and he knew it.

I gotta sort this out, he thought. *I gotta get out from under that dragon.*

Which is not a problem most people have to solve in their lifetimes. In general, most folk who get to meet a dragon only get to think about it that one time for about five seconds.

CHAPTER 6

SQUIB WOULD HAVE LIKED TO GET ON THE DRAGON SITUATION ASAFP, but there were things to do. Things like cleaning himself up till he was the squeaky-clean epitome of innocence in five-foot-five Cajun form. Things like destroying all evidence of his involvement in the dragon situation, which was an add-on to the first thing, really. And in this respect Squib caught a break, as the whole Hooke-collapsing-on-the-premises episode had more or less trashed the stilt house's main area. The constable had been all wheeling and splattering, distributing more mess than a group of finger-painting toddlers on a Skittles sugar high.

His momma had ridden with Hooke to the clinic, pausing just long enough for a cursory check on Squib.

"Goddamn that constable," she whispered at Squib, who was probably in shock, which passably approximated just-woken-up wooziness. "That man is a plague on the parish. I'm no sooner out of that damn place than I gotta go back in again. I'm still in my scrubs. You get some breakfast in the Pearl, okay, cher?"

Squib had mumbled, "Okay, Momma," and put his head back down like, *Here I go off to sleep again like I been doing all night.*

But no sooner had the paramedics stretchered Hooke off the Moreau stoop than Squib was up and pacing.

Could be that the dragon wasn't done with him for the day.

Could be he'd come back and torch the whole place with him inside it.

Squib couldn't help thinking that he kinda-sorta woulda deserved that. He'd been sticking his oar into other people's creeks for so long now that he was due some kind of payback. The universe, you know? A person keeps waggling his ass at a shark, then someday that shark's gonna bite. Especially if the shark's a dragon.

But not Momma. Momma's good people. The best. All she does is look out for me. I'm the one waggling my ass.

Miss Ingram would call that a metaphor, he said to himself.

Squib was almost overcome with an adolescent desire to text Charles Jr. over in Riverview Trailers, but he decided that the best thing to do was keep the circle small. The less people who knew, the less people were gonna get hurt.

Should he tell the police?

Oh, sure. Tell 'em that Constable Hooke slit a smuggler's throat, and then his face got torn off by a flying turtle, shortly after which I was abducted by a gator-overlord dragon.

Even if he bypassed the constable's office and went direct to the sheriff in St. Tammany, who were they gonna call?

Ghostbusters?

No, sir.

Regence goddamn Hooke, that's who.

No, Squib, son. Keep this nightmare to your own self. Hooke don't know shit and Vern can be figured out.

Before nightfall, though.

Squib knew that scaly critter was gonna drag his ass back upriver come dusk to finish what he started.

But Problemo A: clean up the swamp mess, which might take his mind off Problemo B: avoid being a dragon's dinner.

Squib switched on the boiler and, while he waited on the hot tank, stripped off his own crusted duds and the bedclothes, too, and balled up the whole lot into a trash bag, along with the woven chair cover Hooke had messed all over and the rug the constable had a shit fit on.

He tossed the sack on the porch, then made a decent try at swabbing the Moreau shack down. After that he patted the boiler to test for heat, then showered his own self in the bath stall.

As he scrubbed the bilge from his crannies, he thought on the whole dragon predicament, pinching his flesh from time to time to remind himself that Vern was real and on the hunt. It would be all too easy in the light of day, and in something of a daze, to believe the monster nothing more than a nightmarish figment, but Squib was determined to figure a solution before sunset brought a fiery reckoning.

Waxman had once advised Squib to keep moving, for that's when answers presented themselves: i.e., when the mind was active.

"Them idlers staring outta windows is just staring outta windows. They ain't solving shit," he'd said.

Keep on keeping on, thought Squib. *Get the cogs turning.*

So he shrugged himself into his second set of clothes,

which was jeans and a cut-off black T-shirt, and, throwing his sack of sodden articles over one shoulder, headed off to the Pearl Bar and Grill.

SQUIB MADE THE short hike to the Pearl in less than ten minutes. The entire township of Petit Bateau boasted barely more than five hundred residences, not counting the various shotgun shacks, trailers, and houseboats dotted around the limits like scattered seed. And fully one-fifth of those residences were boarded up. Currently the mayor was lobbying for a name change, as it had long been a source of embarrassment for the townsfolk that the name "Petit Bateau" had risqué connotations, i.e., *"petit bateau de pêches,"* that being old-timey slang for cooter.

In truth, the town was less of a town and more of a village, and less a village and more of a collection of services sprung up around a landing on the West Pearl River, just off the interstate. Didn't even have its own ramp, just a two-mile-long service road leading right down through the cypress swamp to the riverside.

Bodi Irwin was the town's lifeblood: a benevolent mogul who somehow managed to run Petit Bateau's bar, boatyard, swamp tours, and shooting range. The campsite was presided over by his sister Eleanora, and he employed most of the town, even attracting labor out from the city at the height of tourist season.

Squib could have made the journey in five minutes easy, as he usually walked double time, eager to make a dollar one way or another, but today, post-dragon-encounter, he took himself round back of the trio of Creole cottages that served as town hall, constable's office, and car lot, just in case Hooke had somehow crawled out of his hospital bed and was spying through the slats of his office blinds, watching out for some kid with a bag of swamp laundry.

Also, Squib wanted to make a silent entry via the Pearl's back door so he could load up the bar's industrial washing machine, and maybe grab himself a grilled cheese with hot sauce before Bodi noticed he was present and correct.

He was two bites into the sandwich when Bodi appeared in the kitchen doorway, looking like a refugee from a Grateful Dead tribute act, long graying hair tied up in a Stars and Stripes bandanna.

"How you eat that shit I don't know, son," said Bodi. "That hot sauce will tear the lining right out of your stomach, and that amount of cheese will back up your plumbing big time."

"Thanks, Mister Irwin," said Squib. "Appreciate the culinary advice."

Bodi snorted. "Culinary, my ass. We don't do culinary here, boy. We do whatever the tourists want. Gumbo, crawfish, po'boys. Four different kinds of fries. Chicken wings at a push. Ain't no 'culinary' on the menu."

Squib crammed a triangle of grilled cheese into his mouth. "Whatever you say, Mister Irwin. What you got on the list for me?" Thinking, *Don't send me out on the river, not today.*

And it was like Bodi reached into his mind and plucked out the thought.

"Today," said the bar owner, "I got to send you out on the river. Waxman's vodka came in, and you gotta run a crate down to him."

And what had been fresh bread in Squib's mouth tasted suddenly like swamp sludge.

Well, balls, he thought, but aloud he said, "Yessir, Mister Irwin. Gimme ten minutes to bring my boat around to the yard."

"Take thirty," said Bodi. "First run a rinse cycle on my machine, clean out all that shit you left in the drum."

"That was Constable Hooke made the mess," said Squib. "He showed up this morning snake-bit. Momma rode with him to Slidell."

"I heard," said Bodi. "Your momma done more than I would have. All we can pray for is that no-account asshole don't make it till nightfall."

"Amen," said Squib, with feeling.

VERN SWAM DIRECTLY from Petit Bateau, or specifically the Moreau landing, to Waxman's houseboat on the east side of the West Pearl, maybe a mile diagonally across the river. The houseboat was of the shotgun variety, and sat ten feet wide, set half in the river on cypress stumps. The houseboat must have been something other than swamp-colored at some point in its history, but now looked like it had been camouflaged by experts, when in fact it was simply assimilated. Vern often commented that it looked like "the goddamn Borg gotta hold of this craft," to which Waxman always responded, "The goddamn *who* you say?"

Waxman didn't appreciate modern media as much as Vern. He was more of a reader.

"I just lolls around," he'd say. "Toot some weed, then see

what the fuckin' demon lizard wants this time. Pain-in-the-ass dragon be the bane of my existence."

To which Vern usually responded with something along the lines of, "You just remember where I found you, Waxman. I am your liberator."

Waxman generally chose not to stir from his deck hammock till late afternoon, preferring the hours of dusking sky for business, but Vern considered this Squib situation a full-blown emergency and wanted to engage Waxman's expertise tout de suite.

The swim across wasn't nothing special. Vern dodged a tour boat and scythed through a fishing net, punching a cheeky gator just to burn off some of his irritation, but within minutes was shucking off river water at Waxman's deck.

The houseboat had a fairground candy-striped awning out back that Waxman kept to remind him of the bad times. The awning seemed impervious to even the enswampening of the dwelling itself, shining with a reasonable luminescence while simultaneously throwing the area beneath into deep shadow, which suited Vern on the rare occasion he felt it necessary to show up in person and not send a WhatsApp.

Waxman was surprisingly not laid up in his hammock but sitting in his rocker on the slatted deck, an AK-47 laid across his bony knees.

"Heard me some explosions," he explained. "Figured either a flare or a visit. Praise be: Lord Highfire come to parlay with his subject."

Waxman was a sight to behold.

By all laws of nature, a fellow with that amount of

wrinkles on his visage should be tumbling forth out of a sarcophagus or some such, but Waxman was alive and kicking. Mostly kicking back was how he liked it now. But there was life in the old dog, and so forth. He wore a suit of black-panther velvet and a black bowler hat with a rooster quill in the band. His face might have been any color at some point but had come around to gray mostly, with black in the creases. Sky-blue eyes and a white beard curled down into his scarlet cravat.

Folks who got up close, who were few and far between, said that Waxman's skin looked scorched, like he'd been given the third degree as a little one, which was kinda funny considering the origins of his species.

Which were as follows: Somewhere along the line when dragons were kings of the hill, one would occasionally cross-breed with a human. That didn't usually turn out so happy-ever-after for the progeny. A baby dragon had teeth from the get-go, which didn't augur well for the human mother, and a dragoness's tubes would crush a human baby on the way out. So most of these mutant children never saw the light of day. But life is tenacious, and every so often one of these tough little bastards would pop out looking like he'd spent the night in a cauldron rather than a womb, all burned in appearance. Eventually you got an Adam and an Eve, so to speak, and they took it from there on their own, propagating a new hybrid species neither dragon nor human, and not accepted in either world.

Waxman was one of these guys: full-breed new breed and tough as briar. He wasn't in Vern's league age-wise; he numbered in centuries, rather than millennia. The Chinese called what Waxman was a mogwai, a malevolent-type fairy. But history was written by the victors, and humans had a habit of painting themselves as the nonmalevolent guys in spite of the fact that everyone else was generally swinging from gibbets. And if Waxman was asked, he wouldn't consider himself unnecessarily malevolent. He was a survivor, was all, and a guy did what had to be done.

Mogwai and dragons often buddied up to avoid death by whatever elaborate method the crusading mob favored at the time. Vern ran into Waxman in the early 1960s, when the mogwai was doing some indentured servitude as a freak on a circus train. Vern heard about the Amazing Melting Man and reckoned the circus had a mogwai on its hands and it sure would be nice to have someone to talk to.

So, a little rescue operation, he thought. *Quick in and out. No mess, no fuss.*

Turned out there was *beaucoup* mess and fuss. Vern miscalculated his approach and derailed half a dozen flatcars as they crossed the Pump Slough Bridge, sending them plunging into the Pearl.

"Some goddamn rescue," Waxman often noted. "Broke my goddamned back."

It had been, Vern would admit, a "stoppered cock of a situation," which had been quite the phrase back in the day. Waxman's back had been broken, but luckily Waxman had amazing healing qualities.

"And I almost drowned," was the mogwai's usual gripe.

Which was true.

"'Almost' being the word," Vern always argued. "I fished your sorry ass out of the river, didn't I? I can ship you back to the circus if you prefer? If running the occasional errand for me is too strenuous?"

And Waxman would chuckle and say, "Nah, you ain't the worst, Highfire. You is just the ugliest."

The most useful thing about Waxman, from Vern's perspective, was that he could pass for human—weird as all hell, but still human, which accounted for him living way downriver. And so long as he kept his jacket on, stayed swamp-wild, and paid his bills, then no one bothered him. Of course, every now and then a couple of good old boys would try their luck, but Waxman had more pep in his step than one might assume, and he kept his weapons in good order.

Like the AK-47 which lay across his lap right now. Vern noticed the mogwai's finger was on the trigger, and he knew Waxman was putting those sharp ears of his to work, making sure Vern hadn't picked up a tail.

"Clear, Vern," he said eventually. "So far as I can tell. These days those sharp-eyed motherfuckers could be watching us from off-world."

"Let's mosey inside," said Vern, shaking his wings. "I can't relax none with the sun on my back."

"Ain't that a sorry statement?" said Waxman, and rocked forward in his chair, using the momentum to scooch himself upright. "Too early, you think?"

"Ain't never too early," said Vern, and followed his associate into the houseboat.

WAXMAN'S ORIGINAL NAME was lost in the twists of time. In the days since, he had been known as Winkle, Blackhoof,

Saundersonn, Roachford, Roach, and finally Waxman. The mogwai had never felt the need for a first name or qualifier.

"Ain't but one Waxman," he always said, to which Vern usually replied, "You can sing that, brother."

Waxman used to have family, back in the way back when, and maybe he still did. Weren't no hives left, just spread out and fit in was the plan. Latch onto a dragon if you could, but there weren't so many of those anymore neither, and Waxman had near to gone into early hibernation when Vern dropped out of the sky.

"Shit, your lard-ass descending from the heavens was one of the sweetest sights I ever seen, even if you did shatter my goddamned back."

Vern let the "lard-ass" comment go, and that was the beginning of a beautiful relationship. Half a century and counting.

And the Waxman name worked for the mogwai. Suited his face.

"Makes me seem a character," he said. "'Crazy Waxman' would be better, or maybe 'Scary Waxman' to keep the kids away, but 'Waxman' will do just fine. I'm like Boo fuckin' Radley on crack to these backward-ass folk."

Truth was, Waxman *was* scary, or could be, when the occasion called for it, and sometimes, if he was feeling irritable, when it didn't. Most of the time he was just a swamp character, living out on his houseboat, cut off from civilization; plenty of old guys went off the grid. Kept himself to himself mostly. Something up with his face, but who gave a good goddamn about that so long as he paid his bills? But it had happened, down the years, that some boat people would exercise their human nature and try taking over Waxman's little patch, and then the mogwai would take out his bag.

That creepy-ass bag of sharp things and small corked bottles.

Wasn't no human saw that bag and lived to tell the tale, and Vern often thought that he never wanted anything coming out of that bag with his name on it, because he knew there was something in that purple silk interior that was brewed special for him.

Vern tucked his wings and ducked through the doorway. The inside of the houseboat was a lot more salubrious than the outside. Waxman liked his comforts, even if he didn't draw attention to the fact. The only people who knew how Waxman lived were Vern and Bodi Irwin, who ordered his antiques, and often dropped them off in the tour cruiser, if they were too bulky for the boy who ran for him.

Wall-to-wall rugs, North African mostly, overlapping each other's borders. A forest floor of colors and textures. The walls were pumped full of foam insulation, and there was a nice quiet Honda generator running the electrics when the solar panels on the roof ran out of juice. Where Vern had his cable TV with its treetop combi-dish for entertainment, Waxman had books: three walls of books, which started one shelf off the deck in case of damp or storm, a tactic learned the hard way, the most bitter lesson being a water-damaged first edition of *Ulysses*. The Irish version.

Vern had scoffed, "Irish *Ulysses*? I wouldn't pay ten bucks for that shit. You been had, Wax. Ulysses was a Greek sonuvabitch."

Which had almost put an end to their symbiosis.

But Waxman endured. "You know, Highfire, how come a dragon be so old and so ignorant?"

Which led to huffing on both sides, but they got over it. No choice really. What the hell else were they going to do?

Because of the *Ulysses* incident, there was not one but two dehumidifiers running at all times and a slab of air-conditioning machinery crouched in one corner. Waxman's bed was an ebony four-poster, which had taken some lugging, and he had a rainfall shower plumbed in which Vern envied even as he scoffed at it.

"You gotta watch all this shit when I'm down," said Waxman. "Specially the books. Something happens to my Faulkners and that's the final nail in the coffin as far as this here is concerned."

Vern settled into a velvet armchair with the ass conveniently sawed out of it to accommodate his tail. "You ain't going down anytime soon, though, right?"

Waxman took down a bottle of fine Irish whiskey from the dresser. "Could be soon. I feel this thing in my hide."

Vern accepted a tumbler of whiskey. "Hide? The hell you say. You gone all New Agey on me, Wax?"

"Nah," said Waxman, sniffing his drink, "my skin gets all itchy. Look at me, Highfire. I'm grayer than a badger's asshole. This skin has gotta come off. I can show you if you have a hankering for specifics."

Vern finished his drink in a swallow. "I'll take a pass there, Wax. It's bad enough I got to see your face."

"Feeling's mutual," said Waxman. "Thing is, my entire skin is above regular on the itch scale, which means I gotta go down for the dirt nap soon."

"Shit, Wax," said Vern. "When?"

"As soon as," said Waxman. "Once we sort whatever needs to be sorted. Whatever brings you here in the first place."

Vern was not best pleased with this news. "Come on, Wax, ain't you got some way to bypass that process?"

The mogwai laughed. "Yeah, Highfire. I jest calls up Mother Nature and asks her to speed up evolution. You sure is a dumb shit for an ancient motherfucker."

Vern tossed off his second drink and scowled. "If we got to drink whiskey, you know I favor Scotch."

"Sorry," said the mogwai, betraying his lie with a grin, "all's I got is Irish. Irish like *Ulysses*."

Vern crossed his legs and stared through the golden film at the bottom of his glass down to the marl-tinged shades of the rug under his feet. He twisted his cut-glass tumbler, a makeshift kaleidoscope. "I need the bag, Wax."

Waxman sighed, deep down to his boots. "Come on, Highfire. I ain't needed the bag in years. A guy gets older, you know? You need someone killed, do it your own self. You never had no problem before."

"This is different. I need this fella done quiet. It's a human, if that helps your conscience."

"It does, but not much. Tell the truth, I'm about done with hating the world. It's hard to maintain."

"I know it," said Vern. "Even Ice Cube smiles now and again. But I got seen, Wax. Up close. Flying, conversing, the whole works."

"And this human? You let him escape?"

"Goddamn gator," said Vern. "Came stomping in with a

challenge. I got distracted and the human, the boy, shoots out the window. Plucky little fucker, I give him that."

Waxman sat up. "Plucky little fucker, says you? You got a name to go with that description?"

"I do, indeedy. A stupid-ass name," said Vern.

The dragon didn't need to say it.

"My nerves are twitching up a storm," said Waxman. "Squib Moreau, am I right?"

Now Vern sat up. "Right you are, Wax. These nerves of yours is pretty goddamn specific with names."

"Naw," said Waxman, "I am familiar with Squib is all."

"You're familiar with him? That ain't gonna be a deal-breaker, Wax? You know the arrangement we got."

Waxman finger-combed his beard. "I know it, Vern. Us against them, right?"

"Goddamn right. Like it's always been. The angry mob ain't nothing but one jabbering kid away from our doors."

"Thing is, Highfire," said Waxman slowly, "this kid, Squib, he don't exactly jabber."

Vern snorted. "He jabbered plenty when I showed him the dragon flame. Tried to make himself all familiar. Showed me his fingers and shit."

Waxman smiled, and a person looking closely might spot that there seemed to be a second row of teeth lurking behind the front set. "Yeah, Squib's an operator, sure enough."

Vern was a little surprised by Waxman's attitude. "You gone soft on me?" he asked. "You loving humans now?"

"I ain't loving nobody," said Waxman. "Not even your scaly ass. But Squib. He's a one, you know? Credit where it's due."

"What in blue blazes are you talking about, Wax? 'Credit where it's due'? Have you gone and switched sides on me?"

"Calm down, Highfire," said Waxman; then he actually shushed the dragon.

Vern was not one for being shushed. "'Calm down'? You forget that cage I found you in? Look at you, Wax. You're positively purring over that kid."

"Well, lookee here," said Waxman, clapping his hands. "Highfire is shook up. What the hell happened downriver?"

"Shit," said Vern. "Shit happened. Explosions. Boats sinking. The whole ball of wax. I either gotta tie this off or move on, Wax. Not that I like it here overly, but I don't like it nowhere else neither."

"And this boy, Squib. That's the only way?"

"How I see it. Less'n you got something else up that sleeve?"

Waxman sighed. "I hates to do it, Highfire. That boy does for me like I do for you, if you get my drift. Keeps me in the supply chain. Good kid, too. Resourceful. He ain't the squealing type."

"Sure," huffed Vern, "ain't nobody the squealing type till they get a load of me. Little asshole has probably already done squealed. Only chance we got is that he was messing with Constable Hooke downriver, so could be he won't run to the law."

"How about I do Hooke?" said Waxman, brightly. "I would surely hop to that task. I got just the bottle for that prick."

Vern shook his head. "Hooke didn't see nothing apart from his own ass catching fire. I reckon he'll steer clear."

"You don't know Hooke. That man is trouble. I can smell it offa him a mile away."

"So long as he stays a mile away."

Waxman reached up with both hands and set eight fingers on the brim of his felt bowler hat, removing it delicately and laying it on his lap like a house cat. "You is set on the kid then, Highfire?"

"I can't see another way. I done marked his crib for you. There's this metal rail on the decking. Get it done, is my advice, before he gets to whispering with his buddies after pud-tugging time."

Waxman stroked the hat, which was a downright creepy habit. "No need for the mark o' the dragon, Highfire. Kid should be here in a half hour or so."

Vern found himself both delighted and anxious. "He's coming here? That is downright considerate. I should shake a leg and let you be about your business."

Waxman cackled. "No, sir, Highfire. It is true that Waxman goes where you cannot go, but since you is already present and correct, I'm thinking you can sit a spell and do your own dirty work."

"Come on, Wax. I need to get gone. You the man when it comes to vanishing humans."

Waxman mulled this over. "I been thinking about that. Humans, dragons, mogwai—ain't no bad species nor good species. Ain't you always telling me how your brother was an asshole?"

"He was an asshole," said Vern with vehemence, flashing on his brother, Jubelus, looming over him and mashing pig guts into his face.

"Three thousand years and still you can't let that go," said Waxman. "But my point is that we is all souls. And there is good souls and bad souls. The boy Squib is somewhere in the middle, but I believe he's leaning toward good. So if you want to vanish him against my counsel, then you gotta do the deed your own self."

Vern squinted, considering this. The mogwai didn't offer this level of counsel lightly. Usually shooting the breeze was about as profound as it got at Chez Waxman. Vern had learned to spend a while mulling over anything that resembled the philosophical coming out of his friend's mouth, but on this occasion there was no time for mulling, and no room for soul theories. The boy had got to be got was the boiled-down bones of the truth.

Vern thought that maybe he could pull rank, but really, the mogwai-dragon thing was pretty much an equal-partners class of an arrangement, and he couldn't blame Waxman none for being leery of the job. Wasn't in his nature anymore. Sure, the mogwai had his bag of tricks, but he didn't relish opening it unless completely necessary. And he drew the line at kids of any species. It could be argued that this Moreau boy wasn't exactly a kid, but he wasn't exactly a grown-up neither.

"You ain't for budging on this, I guess?" said Vern.

"Reckon I ain't," confirmed Waxman, threading the feather in his hatband through his fingers like he was stroking a tiny bird.

"Well then, I'll do the kid," said Vern, "and leave you to stroking your hat. Which is creepy as all hell, by the way."

"I'd rather be a hat stroker than a kid killer," said Waxman, which did have a ring of logic to it.

Squib was jumpy as a cat in a doghouse traversing the river. The current tugged at the hull of his pirogue, but the boat rode the catspaws like a leaf and cut across the flow in a series of tiny hops. On another day, Squib might have relished the sunlight on his face and the prospect of passing an hour with old Waxman, who was never averse to beer and cigarettes in the afternoon under that circus awning of his, but today he was hot and bothered by the knowledge that dragons could swim and he was currently on the water.

Dragons can swim? he thought. *Surely to Christ that ain't fair, swimming and flying both? What kind of a chance does a fella have against abilities like that?*

The Pearl River was bustling now—nothing compared to the Port of New Orleans, but by St. Tammany Parish standards they were bang in the middle of rush hour, with tour cruisers heading out for the afternoon shift, loaded to the gunwales with folks itching for a glimpse of the legendary Honey Island monster.

I could tell them, thought Squib. *The monster is real as all hell, but he don't reside on Honey Island.*

These boats could be his salvation, Squib realized. Vern had stayed alive by keeping himself to himself, so could be the dragon would not relish breaching the surface with so many itchy shutter-fingers on the river, so he plotted himself a zigzag course cross-river, bumping up close to the tour cruisers, just a traditional-type Cajun boy willing to flash his poor-ass optimistic smile for the tourists. It took a while longer to make the journey, but Squib reckoned he wasn't in no particular hurry, and the cruisers kept him safe from dragon strike.

Dragon strike. Imagine, that's a real thing. If Charles Jr. knew, he would crap his pants.

This wasn't a word of exaggeration. Charles Jr. had crapped his pants once before, in seventh grade, when some asshole in a clown mask had snuck up on him. His friend would have a pants-crapping reputation still if Waxman hadn't advised him through Squib to climb up on a cafeteria table and drop his jeans, confirming the monster-dick rumors. And as Waxman had predicted, dick trumps drawers any day of the week.

It took a while, but eventually Squib got eyes on Waxman's houseboat, rising up outta the river like part of the cypress forest, all camouflaged apart from a flash of the awning round back. Squib came up on Waxman one time when the old man was down past the label on a bottle of Jameson and learned a couple of things. One, the swamp dweller didn't much care for vodka, and two, he disliked circus folk even more than clear spirits.

Old Waxman never drilled down into either comment much, but it had left Squib wondering why the hell he was delivering crates of Absolut to the houseboat once a fortnight.

For an old boy who don't like vodka, he sure chugs through an amount of it.

As Squib tied off on Waxman's pole, it occurred to him that maybe here was a guy who could offer some advice re:

his dragon situation. It was said in town that Waxman was near to one hundred years old, and surely to Christ a man couldn't live on the water that long and not catch a sniff of a dragon downriver.

Could be old Waxman will have a trick or two up that velvet sleeve of his.

Squib hefted the crate of Absolut from his boat and swung it onto the deck, where it landed with a jangle of clinkings.

"Waxman," he called, announcing his presence loud and clear. It didn't do to sneak up on anybody in the bayou. The human-to-gun ratio in this swamp was about five times the national average, and the shots-fired-to-guns-owned ratio was even higher. "It's your boy, Squib Moreau. I got you a crate of Russian lightning."

"Lug it in, boy," came Waxman's voice from inside the houseboat. It was an out-of-the-ordinary type of voice. Maybe the acid that'd done for his face had soaked through the vocal cords. Waxman sounded like one of those old-time blues singers who spent sixty years in smoky joints and came out the other end with a growl like a junkyard dog. Squib liked the sound; he liked sitting around listening to Waxman talk about long ago, shit that went down when castles had murder holes and battle was waged with honest-to-God axes. Horror stories, but cool to listen to.

"I'm coming, Waxman," said Squib, and rather than humping the blue plastic crate, he just dragged it across the planks, smooth as they were with great age.

Generally Squib would've said "Mister Waxman" or "sir," schooled in manners as he was by his momma, but Waxman didn't hold no truck with formalities: "Just 'Waxman,' boy, less'n you wanna call me 'Handsome Waxman,' and then I know you be lying."

So plain old "Waxman" it was.

Squib pulled aside the screen and nudged the crate through the doorway with the toe of his Converse. He sighed hugely, as though he had completed the labors of Hercules.

"There she is, Waxman. One crate of Absolut, free from additives and colorants. Hell, it's practically a health drink."

Waxman was in his upright armchair, which, according to Bodi Irwin, he had shipped from England, where it might one time have been warmed by the queen's royal behind.

Squib picked up the crate and carried it into the center of the room, lifting his feet over the overlapping edges of the rugs. He plonked it down on a small round table that didn't look balanced right, the stem being off to one side; didn't seem like it could bear the weight, but it always did.

"You should come down to the bar one Saturday," said Squib. "Could be you'd like it."

Waxman stuck out his lower lip and shook his head. "I ain't a fan o' mankind, son. With certain exceptions."

"Me being one of those exceptions, I'm hoping," said Squib.

"You being one, Bodi another. I like you fine, but I ain't about to go buck-sociable, no offense."

"None taken. I'm happy to be liked."

Waxman shifted in his chair. "Sometimes being liked ain't enough, Squib."

"It's enough when you don't experience it none too often. So far in my life, I've gathered three likes and one love. That sure seems enough for me."

"More than I got," admitted Waxman.

"So with that in mind," said Squib, lowering himself into the weird assless chair, slowly, in case Waxman wasn't in the mood for chitchat, "maybe you could advise me on a problem I got."

Waxman frowned. He was obviously on the point of not wanting shit to do with Squib's problem when he threw a quick glance over his shoulder into the shadows and seemed to change his mind. "Well, maybe I could, son. Maybe I could at that. Waxman has seen it all, and what he ain't seen, he can hazard a guess at. So why don't you open on up?"

Squib was hesitant now that he had leave to spit it out. "It's a strange one, Waxman."

"Worse than Charles Jr. and the soiled britches?"

"Yeah, I gotta say. Way worse. I near to soiled my britches my own self."

"Shit, boy. Now I'm intrigued. Lay it on out, and don't spare the color."

Squib took several quick breaths like he was preparing to dive into icy waters and then blurted out the whole thing: Hooke, Carnahan, the face-eating turtle, and, of course, Vern the dragon.

Waxman sagged when the telling was over. "Shit, son. You sketched that real well. Nice and calm, barely a stutter. You've had quite the night, ain't you?"

Squib nodded, allowing that he surely had.

"And your tribulations ain't over yet."

This was a statement not a question.

"If this dragon don't get you, then Hooke probably will."

Squib hadn't even gotten around to fretting on Hooke. "I

guess maybe, but Hooke ain't getting no one from a hospital bed. It's this Vern fella I'm concerned about."

Waxman twisted his beard. "Seems sensible."

Squib realized that he had been neither ejected nor mocked. "Are you saying that you believe me, Waxman?"

Waxman smiled crookedly. "I ain't sure about the face-eating turtle. Sounds far-fetched to me."

"But the dragon?"

"Oh, him? Hell yeah, that old coot's been around for years. The Honey Island monster. 'Cept he don't live on no Honey Island. And he ain't your typical monster."

"Right," said Squib, feeling a little lighter simply from being credited with telling the truth. "He's a dragon."

"I know it," continued Waxman. "That motherfucker is older than the river itself."

This was all well and good, confirmation-wise, but Squib needed a solution. "So what do I do, Waxman? I ain't got no options other than to leave the country."

"You told anybody?"

Squib rolled his eyes. "Told anybody? Who'm I gonna tell? The cops? I'd surely land my own ass in a cell, then I'm a sitting duck for Hooke. Momma? She frets enough already. Thinks I'm scarred by not having no daddy. Also, if she knew the truth, then Vern might do the entire family."

"How about Charles Jr.? The dick man?"

"Charles ain't exactly got his feet on the ground. Last week he swore to me that he was spending his nights in New Orleans man-whoring hisself. I ain't trusting him with no sensitive information. You are the first and only person to hear this story."

"That's good," said Waxman. "Maybe we can bargain with that."

"Bargain? I don't figure this dragon is for turning."

Waxman chewed on that then spoke a bit louder than seemed necessary. "You know, kid, I did hear that dragons were ornery cusses. Butt-ugly, too."

Squib had been far too awestruck by Vern to accept this. "I thought this Vern fella was kinda noble-looking. Big as all hell too. Like a basketballer. You shoulda seen the way he schooled those gators. Shit, I wouldn't have thought it possible."

"Just a pity Mister Noble wants to burn you, huh?"

"Yeah," said Squib, dejected. "If it weren't for that. And I ain't even gonna tell nobody."

"Here's what I hear," said Waxman, conducting the air. "Dragons like their entertainment—cable and such. Got their tastes, too: booze, Pringles, all very particular. Now, a butt-ugly dragon can't exactly waltz hisself into town with a fistful of dollars in his scaly claws, so I'm guessing he needs himself a go-between—like how you go-between for me."

Squib jumped right on that notion, eager as he was for a solution. "Yeah. Like Renfield with Dracula. Vern needs himself a Renfield. I could Renfield the shit out of the bayou for him. Shit, I run deliveries for Bodi Irwin—can't be much different. Whatever a dragon needs."

Waxman grinned wide, and for a second Squib thought something shifted behind his teeth, something like more teeth. "You said 'Renfield' a bunch of times there, kid. The way I remember reading it, Renfield was a pathetic old boy. I reckon Vern's go-between is more of a partner in crime than a bug-eating half-wit."

"Yeah," said Squib, "go in there like an equal. Like I got value."

"Like you got an offer he can't refuse," said Waxman. "Though Vern can be pigheaded."

At the second mention of the dragon's name, something slotted into place inside Squib's brain, and he found himself staring at the bottles of vodka seated on the table and losing himself a little in the fuzzy colors refracted therein while he waited for whatever his subconscious had already figured out to bob to the surface. It was vodka-related, he felt sure. This fraction of the realization was solid as the glass of an Absolut bottle, but the rest was a dark cloud of smoke and terror.

Vodka-related.

Vern can be pigheaded.

Squib felt the blood drain from his face as he consciously joined the dots. Waxman knew the dragon's personality. Waxman was personally acquainted with the dragon.

Waxman is the go-between. Waxman is Renfield.

And:

I done walked right into the dragon's den, more or less.

Squib was so tired all of a sudden that he couldn't so much as lift his head to face his doom.

"Yep," said Waxman, "there it is. I guess you done remembered where you seen the vodka recently. I guess you figured how I know Vern is pigheaded."

"I guess," said Squib. "You is Renfield."

Waxman begged to differ. "I don't see that. We is like partners. We do for each other."

Squib was sinking into shock. His hands dangled loose on their wrists, and all he could do was watch them. "For each other," he said dully. "Right."

"Right," said Waxman. "That's right, ain't it, Vern?"

Squib heard the bathroom door open, and someone stepped into the main room.

Three guesses who that is, thought Squib, and closed his eyes.

VERN STRODE OUT of the bathroom angry. "Why are you talking all that shit?" he asked.

Waxman played it innocent. "What shit? I was just jawing with the kid. Getting him relaxed."

Vern wasn't buying this. "Uh-uh, Wax. You're stirring. Stirring and planting notions is what you're doing."

Angry as he was, the dragon kept his eyes on Squib. The kid seemed to be in a bit of a daze, but he had pulled that dodge before and then skipped out when the chance presented itself.

Fool me once, thought Vern.

"What notions am I planting?"

Vern pointed a taloned finger at him. "'What notions' is it, Wax? 'What *notions*'? Hows about the notion that Squib takes over your position while you're taking the dirt nap? How about that notion?"

Waxman grinned wide, his rows of teeth clearly visible. "Say, Highfire, that ain't a bad idea. You come up with that on your own?"

"Screw you," said Vern, and then clamped Squib's head

in one massive hand, easier than a Globetrotter gripping a Spalding. "Just let me sort this a second."

Vern felt the kid tense in his grip and then slump as the fight went out of him. *Goddamn Waxman*, he thought, irritated. *Stirring and planting*.

He tilted Squib's head back and gave him the double barrels of his sulfur-laden nostrils straight in the face.

Sleep, kid, he thought, *while I sort this mess out*.

"Neat trick," said Waxman as Squib sank immediately into gassed slumber.

"Yeah," said Vern. "Humans can't take the dragon breath. Knocks 'em for six. Apparently they wake up a little dumber, but it's hard to tell."

Vern tumbled Squib out of his chair and slotted his tail through the hole carved into the foam. "Okay, Wax," he said, snagging a bottle of Absolut from the crate. "Make your case, buddy, though I'm warning you, this will be a tough sell."

Waxman composed himself, placing his hat on a low table beside a chintz-shaded lamp. "Tired of that lamp," he commented while he got his ducks in a row.

Vern took a slug of vodka straight from the bottle, which he knew would irritate the house-proud mogwai. "Good start," he said. "Damned if I ain't coming around already."

"Okay, cut the bullshit, Highfire," said Waxman, getting to his feet. "Here's the way I see it. We's both in the unfortunate position of needing a go-between. I got Squib and you got me."

"With you so far," said Vern.

"The problem being that I gotta go under soon, which

leaves you up the creek. Or down the creek, to be more accurate."

"You absolutely gotta go under? You couldn't skip a cycle?"

"Sure I could skip a cycle, and I'd be in a wheelchair by the spring. This old body gotta be nourished, Highfire, and soon. I been putting it off for your sake, and these bones is tired."

"How soon is soon, exactly?"

"Yesterday," said Waxman. "And for three years, maybe."

Vern gaped. "Three goddamn years? You ain't just saying that?"

"No, I ain't just saying it," snapped Waxman. "I got hair falling out in clumps and skin dropping off my ass. You wanna see?"

Vern sighed. "It's been a long day, Wax. No offense to your ass, but I don't wanna see."

"So, we take the kid on," said Waxman. "He sees to me while I'm down and takes up my duties as far as you're concerned."

"Just like that?"

"Yeah."

"A human familiar?"

"I ain't no familiar, Highfire, we done had that talk."

"Yeah, but a human ain't coming in at your pay grade."

Waxman weighed this. "Okay. A human familiar."

"We had human familiars before, at the eyrie. Remember how that ended up."

Vern let that hang over the negotiations. This was crunch point as far as he was concerned. In a thousand years it had never worked out with a human. Let Waxman argue that fact away.

Waxman steepled his fingers, and Vern sensed a speech coming.

"Vern, Lord Highfire as was. The older I gets, the more I realize that we is all just souls. All souls in different bodies. Human bodies, dragon bodies, mogwai bodies. Vessels, as such. Some souls are assholes and some ain't. Maybe it seems like there is an inordinate amount of human assholes, but that's just percentages. And I do believe this specimen of a boy is a good soul. He ain't never tried nothing too shady. He looks after his momma. And he will shovel shit all the livelong day if it's required, which it surely will be. He likes a good story, too, and you do like to deliver a story with flair."

Vern nodded, allowing that he did enjoy spinning a yarn, but it was an absent kind of nod as he was chewing on Waxman's second delivery of his souls theory in one day. Could be his friend had mellowed more than Vern had realized. Maybe the signs had been there and he'd never cottoned on.

To buy himself a breather, Vern asked, "Go back one point. You seriously need all that shit to come out of the hole smiling?"

"If you want me perky as all hell, yessir, I surely do."

"Balls," said Vern. "I ain't no spring chicken neither, you know. The pipes get clogged."

"Eat some fiber," said Waxman. "I know you is all about the protein nowadays, but that stuff will bung up a body if you ain't hydrating."

"Can we swing back to the other shit? The big pile you were trying to sell me?"

Waxman got back on track. "So ultimately what we is

doing here is removing a link from the chain. Making the chain stronger."

"Unless the link is a lying piece of human trash who runs to the newspapers with dragon stories," said Vern.

"So we take steps to ensure that don't happen," said Waxman.

"What steps?" asked Vern.

"We tell him the sad truth," said the mogwai.

"Which sad truth is that, Wax?"

Waxman's black eyes glittered like water-polished stones. "The sad truth that he's already dying."

SQUIB WAS AWAKE a while before he opened his eyes, which was habit rather than master planning, and he overheard a few snippets of Vern and Waxman arguing over his fate. At first he thought the TV was on somewhere and he was listening to a gangster show with a supernatural element, but pretty soon his limbic system whispered to his motor system that he better get the hell out of here, because there was a dragon having it out with some other kind of immortal being about whether or not to kill him or have him shovel shit for all eternity, which he presumed was a metaphor for something.

"Look at the kid," said the dragon. "He ain't nothing but skin and bone. You telling me this specimen can even hump that volume of shit?"

"Sure he can," argued Waxman. "I seen him move a stack of crates higher than his whole self."

Squib thought he better get his speak in. "I can work," he blurted. "Shovel shit for real, or whatever that might mean. Deliveries, collections. Hell, I can do foot massage if you need it, Mister Vern, sir."

The boy opened his eyes to find two very different expressions trained on him. Waxman was grinning as though he was ahead in some competition or other, and Vern was scowling like the food on his plate was irritating him.

"'Mister Vern, sir,'" repeated Waxman. "That's more courtesy than you're accustomed to, Highfire."

"Sure is," said the dragon. "But I ain't interested in courtesy. Humans always start out courteous—then, before a fellow can even retract his balls, it's all torches and spears."

Squib was a mite confused over the retraction-of-balls section of that statement, but he reckoned he could let that go for the moment, though it pained him not to ask a question that was begging to be asked. "No torches and spears from me, sir," he assured the dragon. "I'm a hustler, is what I am, from the day I was born. If you got a paid job for me, then that's the job I'm doing."

Waxman smiled sadly. Squib had seen that class of a smile before in the clinic when he was waiting for his momma's shift to finish. Momma called that class of smile the BLT, for "Bad Luck Teeth." Usually doctors pasted on that smile when they were about to hang a right into the terminal ward.

"It ain't a paid job, exactly," said the mogwai.

"Shit," said Squib. "Am I dying?"

"We is all dying, boy," said Waxman. "Even Lord Highfire here, but you is definitely further along the road."

"Come on, Waxman," objected Squib. "Don't be fooling around. I been a good runner for you these past years."

This was true, and so Waxman reluctantly relented. He had been hoping to spin out the telling a while more.

"Okay, son," he said, "Vern gave you the dragon breath. A full dose. And that is fatal to humans, I kid thee not."

Squib could not believe it. "You killed me for delivering vodka? I can't believe it. My poor momma."

At the mention of Squib's momma, Waxman interjected with the "but."

"But the effects can be ridden out if a fella has access to the antidote."

"Yeah," said Squib miserably, "and I bet the antidote is growing out of a goat's ass on the top of Mount Everest and I gotta go there directly."

"Not exactly," said Waxman, opening one hand to reveal a small shining amber disk. "This here is one of Vern's scales. He molts them all over the place. You need a fresh-dropped scale maybe twice a week for a few months."

Squib took the disk. "And what? I just lay it on my forehead or something."

"Oh, hell no," said Waxman, straight-faced. "That right there is what we call a pessary, which means you gotta stick it where the sun most definitely do not shine."

"Come on, Wax," said Vern, "don't toy with the kid."

"You chew on it," said Waxman. "Like tobacco. Until the color is gone. That should get her done."

"And if I don't chew on it?"

"Cramps initially," said Waxman.

"And then a burning in your innards," said Vern.

"Nausea," added Waxman. "But you won't mind that none, occupied as you'll be with the burning."

"Then you vomit up your lungs."

Waxman disagreed. "Last guy shit out his lungs."

"No, he shit out his shitpipe. Colon, you know. Lungs were up top."

"You is the expert," conceded Waxman. "Either way, everything comes out."

"And then your heart explodes," said Vern.

Squib stuffed the scale in his mouth and sucked it like a baby sucking a pacifier. It tasted bitter, but a fella could endure it, considering the alternative.

"You get the implications?" asked Waxman, while Squib worked on the scale. "You mess with Vern and you don't get your scale. You bring the mob and you don't get your scale. It's a little insurance for Lord Highfire."

Squib nodded. He got it. In his entire life he had never so completely gotten something.

"So, you take up my duties while I recharge. And then in three months I'm back and you're clear."

Vern's brow ridge shot up. "Three *months*, Wax? You total dick. Three years, you told me. I coulda lasted three months without cable. Shit, I can brew my own hooch if I have to."

"Did I say years?" said Waxman, all innocence. "I meant months, Highfire. My sincere apologies."

"You played me, Wax. It's like you don't even want me to kill this kid."

"He's a soul, Vern," said Waxman, earnestly restating his philosophy. "We is all souls. You gotta get with that."

"They're gonna carve that *souls* lecture on your headstone," said Vern, actually kicking the leg of Waxman's bed. "And I don't gotta do nothing because I'm the last dragon."

"So you say," said Waxman, "but it's a big world and you ain't took a squint around for a long time."

"Taking a squint around, as you puts it, Wax, is liable to get a fella killed. Dragons learned that the hard way."

Squib watched them go at it and realized that he could easily have made a dart for the door.

But I got dragon breath in my lungs. So there's nowhere to run.

He figured he'd heard about dragon breath somewhere, read it in a book, maybe. Admittedly, it sounded like horseshit, but only if a guy didn't believe in dragons. When there was a dragon standing in front of a person, it seemed to Squib like that person had no option but to believe in anything and everything.

"Okay," he said, "I accept the job offer, like I even got a choice. What time I got to be here?"

Waxman broke off his arguing with Vern. "What time? I'd say nightfall. That okay with you, Highfire?"

Vern ran some numbers in his head. "At the earliest, Wax. I got to go into production, if you know what I'm saying."

"I hear you, brother. What say we party down some? Have ourselves a send-off. Then you can leave the first deposit on site for the shoveler here."

Squib was starting to get the picture.

Shit, he thought, and then said aloud, "Shit."

CHAPTER 7

HOOKE WOKE UP THE FOLLOWING AFTERNOON FEELING LIKE HE'D come out the other end of the Rumble in the Jungle. Maybe this thought was prompted by the sight of his right hand wrapped up like a fighter's mitt, not to mention the pounding in his skull, which felt like Ali was floating like a butterfly in there, throwing lightning jabs at his eye sockets.

Jesus God, Hooke wanted to say, but he was thwarted in his desire to break the second commandment by a mouth drier than the sand in a fire bucket, and so could barely manage to separate his lips.

What issued forth from those lips was not language so much as an animal growl, but it was enough to attract the attention of a nurse on the other side of the screen which separated him from the rest of the small ward.

The nurse was Elodie Moreau, who looked like she could sleep for a hundred years, given the opportunity.

Girl looks dog-rough, thought Hooke. *Maybe I done picked the wrong woman to yearn for.*

But then Elodie smiled at him and Hooke's doubts were dispelled.

"Constable Hooke," she said. "You all came back to us, thank the Lord."

Hooke wasn't dumb enough to read anything into the Lord being thanked; this was a platitude, pure and simple. But a lot of relationships were sparked off by trauma. Maybe this could be one of those.

Elodie trickled some water down his parched gullet, and when Hooke felt he'd been sufficiently libated, he asked, "How long I been out?"

"All night," she said, "and most of the morning. Snoring like a hog, too. I never heard such a racket."

She's testing my limits, thought Hooke. *People get emboldened, kick a guy when he's down.*

"Careful there, Miss Nurse," he said softly, but with an edge to it. "Even lawmen got feelings."

Elodie stepped back. "Sorry, Constable. Guess my bedside manner could use a little work."

"That depends on the bed," said Hooke, and left it at that. Maybe next week, if this Carnahan storm passed by, he could drive around to Elodie's shack for a proper thank-you.

"Any calls come in for me?" he asked now.

"Nothing came in, but I called Lori," said Elodie.

Hooke grunted. Lori was the secretary he shared with Mayor Shine. Petit Bateau couldn't fund an extra secretary, so the truth was that Hooke did most of his own dispatching and paperwork, but Lori manned the phone most weekday mornings.

"She miss me?" asked Hooke.

"Lori was wondering as to your whereabouts, so I told her you'd been bitten and was resting up here. Nothing much going on in the office. Lori says there was some ruckus downriver last night—some swamp rats dynamite-fishing, probably."

Dynamite-fishing, thought Hooke. *Shit, these people are making up their own narratives.*

"I told Lori that you'd be out for another few days at least. Maybe a week."

"A week? I don't have no week to be laid up here."

This was true. Hooke sensed that time was a commodity he didn't have an abundance of in this case.

How he saw it was like this: Ivory dispatches him into the bayou to deal out some swamp justice to Willard Carnahan. This makes sense for Ivory as Hooke is his man on the water. But then the New Orleans boss decides to copper-fasten his hold on Regence by sending a spy to video Hooke doing the job Ivory dispatched him to do.

A tangled goddamn web, thought Hooke.

So now the whole situation had clusterfucked itself: Ivory's spy was dead or messed up, and the boss knew that Hooke was both onto him and after him.

If it was Ivory, thought Hooke. *'Cause if it wasn't him, I ain't got a clue who to hunt.*

He should have a clue, he knew that, but the venom hangover was clouding his brain. The situation was critical, but Hooke knew he'd better get it smoothed over. Ivory coming after him was interfering with his own plan to go after Ivory, which had always been his endgame.

"You got to lay up, Constable," said Elodie, trying to sound firm. "We just took you off dialysis. The doctor wants to keep you in for observation in case the symptoms reoccur."

Hooke sat up, with some considerable effort. "Just help me out of bed, Elodie. I got a call to make."

"I ain't even told you about the physical therapy," objected Elodie. "You wanna lose the use of that entire arm? Because that's what you're fixing to do by making a call."

"Put a pamphlet under my pillow," said Hooke. "I can look after myself."

Elodie made another attempt to dissuade Hooke. "You shouldn't even be walking, Constable," she said. "Not in your condition."

Hooke swung his legs out of bed. "Honey, I led a patrol across Ramadi with a concussion, so I think I can make my way across the floor."

Elodie flinched some at the endearment but swallowed it down. "You could go blind!"

"Well, in that case," said Hooke, "I'll most certainly go back to bed."

The girl was certainly doing her best to save his life, he had to give her that. Even though she wasn't exactly sweet on him, not as yet.

I'll redouble my efforts. Maybe put her kid in hospital for a few weeks to give me a clear run at her. But right now, there is containment to be attempted with the king of New Orleans.

Thinking of Ivory soured Hooke's mood a few notches, and he forgot his fondness for Elodie Moreau. "Lead me to my phone, woman," he snapped, pulling a drip feed out of his arm. "I got to be about my business."

Elodie had some sass in her and snapped right back,

"Your phone is in the locker, Constable. A man who led a patrol across Ramadi oughta be able to navigate a few feet of linoleum."

Hooke considered punching the nurse with his good hand, then reconsidered. This was a clinic, not a dark alley, and punching a nurse never looked good in print. Plus it might be that he would swing wild and land on his ass. So he smiled as sweetly as was possible for a man like him and said, "My apologies, Miz Moreau. I am a little testy today. Must be the poison in my system."

"No need to apologize, Constable Hooke," said Elodie, her flash of anger disappearing as quickly as it had arrived. "I'm a mite testy myself, so there's a pair of us in it."

Not yet, thought Hooke, *but soon enough*.

HOOKE STUMBLED INTO the dayroom with his phone, glowering at some good old boy with a gashed-up forehead until the man took his copy of *Guns and Ammo* and skedaddled.

Hooke sent a message to an old-fashioned pager number and ten minutes later got a call back from his handler. Regence would have preferred to have a sit-down with Ivory Conti himself in his retro Mafia hotel, but the boss ran his criminal enterprises the same way he'd run his financial-adviser office back in Wall Street, i.e., like a real business. If a street-level operative wanted a meeting with the top dog, it would take six months to find an opening in his calendar, and even then, it would probably end up being five minutes on FaceTime. So Hooke would have to content himself with a call.

That being said, being as Hooke was one of Ivory's pet cops, he would at least merit a grade-A flunky, the Rolls-Royce of bodyguards: the twin.

The single twin.

Tragic story. See, there had been two twins until recently, which was the accepted norm by definition, until one became the first casualty of Ivory's land grab, gunned down outside an inner-city community center by a teenage hit girl.

And then there was one: a big African Creole bruiser by the name of Rossano Roque. Rossano was way into his martial arts. He could chop down a tree with his hands, so they said. Picked up the name Grasshopper in fifth grade after that old show *Kung Fu*, then sawed it off to G-Hop when he grew up some. And G-Hop it was to this day. Only Ivory called the big man Rossano.

"What's the big emergency, cop?" asked G-Hop. "I got business needs attending."

This was reassuring. Rossano was his usual pissed-off self, so nothing out of the ordinary.

"Relax, Roque," said Hooke, trying to sound all casual, like he wasn't laid up with snake bite.

"You wanna tell me what we're doing here, Regence? If the Feds are up on me, then this don't look good for either of us."

"Up on me," thought Hooke, sneering. *Someone's been watching* The Wire.

"If the Federales were up on you, I'd know, and shortly after, you'd know," said Hooke. "You ain't even on their list, small fish like you."

G-Hop snuffled down the phone, and Hooke could

imagine his face, looking all pissed off. It was typical of these slingers: They all wanted liberty *and* notoriety. Difficult to have it both ways.

"Good," he said. "That's the way I like it, Hooke. Anonymity, you understand?"

"Smart move, kid. Stay low-profile. Those old Mafia guys were assholes. All bling and celebrity trim, right? Showboating is why they got their collars felt. I like your way better: low-profile. Nothing special about Rossano Roque."

Roque exhaled noisily. "You know, Hooke, I can't figure the angles on you baiting me. You're crooked, we own you. So why the back-and-forth today all of a sudden?"

Hooke decided to come clean on his condition. "Maybe it's residual venom got me acting all crazy. Nurse said it might happen."

"You got bit?" said Roque.

"Yeah, I got snake-bit. Stupid, right, a man of my experience? But it happens. I just wanted to assure you that in spite of my incapacitation, the job Mister Conti entrusted to me is done. Maybe you already know that?"

"I know now. You got me on the phone for that? You couldn't have sent an emoji? Thumbs-up or some shit?"

"Sometimes communication breaks down," said Hooke. "Then people forget their roles and chaos can't be far behind. Am I right?" Hooke was listening close. Thing was, he was talking complete gibberish unless a person had the code, the code being that Ivory sent a watcher. And if that was the case, then no doubt his head of security had set it up.

But G-Hop sounded mystified. "What the hell, Hooke? I think that venom is all up in your system because you are talking total crap. The only one forgetting their role is you, frankly. I am the boss and you are my dog. A clever dog, granted. An *America's Got Talent* level of dog, but a dog nonetheless. So, I got your message: The job is done. And Mister Conti is grateful, which will be reflected in your envelope. Can we leave it at that? Can we not elaborate around civilians where there could be lasers bouncing off the window? So long as Mister Conti is clear of this shit, he don't wanna hear about it. Are you feeling me, Hooke?"

G-Hop was making a lot of sense. His boss, Ivory, knew more than most how evidence of any sort had a way of making it on to the Internet. Many of his banker friends from back on Wall Street had been sunk by cell phone video or recovered emails.

Maybe I was wrong, Hooke thought. *Maybe Ivory ain't my guy.*

Then again, it was more likely that Roque would make day-to-day decisions like getting some dirt on Hooke to keep him loyal.

"So you didn't send no kid to video me doing the deed?" he asked.

"No, I goddamned didn't," shouted Roque. Then he realized the implication of this question. "Are you telling me that a kid shot video?"

"Could be," admitted Hooke. "There was a camera involved. I'm pretty sure it's blown to pieces, but they make these things rugged nowadays."

"Did you happen to mention Ivory's name while you were conducting business?"

"Now that is a pertinent question," said Hooke. "I might

have relayed a message from Mister Conti—'This is from Ivory' kind of thing."

"Well, that's just fucking great," said G-Hop. "Just fucking dandy. I should just do you, Hooke. Seriously."

Hooke actually laughed at this death threat. "You best not talk trash, son, or you'll go the way of your brother, know what I mean?"

"Goddamn," swore G-Hop. "Look at this for a cluster-fuck. I put you on this, Hooke, because you assured me you were talented and discreet. 'Talented and discreet,' your very words."

"I am discreet," argued Hooke, feeling a tightness in his chest. "I was discreet—but so was the asshole in the bushes."

"And you thought I sent a spotter?" said Rossano Roque. "To keep you on a leash."

"Crossed my mind."

G-Hop took a moment to assess before speaking. "Okay. Here's my take on it, cop. Maybe I did send the spotter, in which case Ivory owns you. But then he already owns you, and a lot more like you. But I'm saying that I didn't send a spotter, in which case you got a problem running around Honey Island Swamp. If I was you, I'd be assuming that I didn't send that spotter and start looking for him on your end, 'cause even if I did send him, there ain't dick you can do about it anyways."

It made sense, Hooke had to admit, if only to himself. If Ivory had the video, then it was now locked in the famous super-safe in his office, which Hooke was not getting into without a specialist. If Ivory didn't have the video, then someone in Regence's own parish did, and he'd better go and sort that shit out before the clip made it back to Ivory.

"The kid who filmed you," said G-Hop. "If not sent by Ivory, then local, yeah?"

"Correct," said Hooke.

More sense from Roque. "Is there a local kid who might like you gone? Some kid who knows the bayou?"

"Shit, Colonel, there's maybe two dozen. But I know who's top of the list."

Squib Moreau, thought Hooke, and immediately felt the rightness of it. *That little prick hates me on account of my future relationship with his momma. If it was him, then it's only a matter of time before the video winds up being played for a jury of my peers, or even worse.*

"And here, Your Honor, is where Constable Hooke guts the drug smuggler with his knife. We can see the intestines clearly."

And the judge would say, "Turn that shit off. I just ate a burrito."

G-Hop was waiting for his take. "Well," said the self-styled ninja, "you got any thoughts on the subject?"

Hooke took his time. "I tell you one thing, G-Hop," he said finally, "I ain't about to talk burritos with no judge."

Which confused the hell out of Rossano Roque.

Just the way I like him, thought Hooke, and hung up without another word.

Squib Moreau, thought Hooke, his heart beating almost hard enough to crack ribs.

Squib fucking Moreau, thought Hooke, and the sight faded from his eyes.

CHAPTER 8

SQUIB TOLD HIS MOMMA THAT WEIRD OLD WAXMAN ACROSS THE river had offered him a little work during the summer, same kind of thing he did for Bodi, and what's more, old Waxman wasn't so weird really, and in fact he wasn't even so old. Elodie asked Bodi's opinion, and they both reckoned it was okay so long as Squib turned in fifty percent of his wages and was in bed by midnight, which Squib promised he would be even as he knew he wouldn't.

Thing is, Momma, I got to run errands for Vern the dragon, else he'll barbecue my Cajun ass.

Wasn't no way he could break that sort of news.

Oh, and I oughta tell you, your boyfriend is a stone-cold killer.

Another fact that would have to be dealt with.

Dragon first, dirty cop later.

But knowing what he knew now, Squib vowed that he could never again allow Regence Hooke into their house.

Waxman WhatsApp'd him to bring meat lovers' pizzas, so Squib stopped by the Pearl Bar and Grill for a couple of extra-large pies before motoring across the river. The Pearl was quiet at this time of the evening, and Squib's own outboard made the biggest fuss, apart from a party cruiser downriver somewhere that was cranking out a bass line that thrummed across the sound.

Squib liked the evening with the molasses of Louisiana sun pouring across the back of his neck and arms. He liked the water, too, on account of how it changed color so quick, like one second it was copper green, and then it became sheet steel with silver curlicues edging the catspaws, and then finally sky blue. A fella could be out here in his own boat, and in between the banks was a sanctuary where there wasn't nothing but river: a few minutes of time-out from the world. Squib spent most of his holiday hours out here when he wasn't hustling or putting in his shifts. He tended his crawfish nets, or he went after old catfish in their holes. And he thought that maybe, when the time came and he was an old man, he would fix himself up a shack in the deep swamp where tourists never poked their noses and just exist out there permanent like. That was if he didn't fall in love, which was a possibility, he supposed. Charles Jr. fell in love once a fortnight, but it never stuck. Squib figured he himself was too far on the wrong side of the tracks for those girls to ever seriously consider him any kind of material.

Squib's father was another subject for thought. Momma couldn't even talk about him. She had tried a couple of times, made a real effort to communicate on the subject, but every time Elodie opened her mouth to say his name, her throat closed up and the tears fell like they might never stop. It got so Squib couldn't broach the subject because if he tried to focus in on any Daddy-centric memories, he felt a lurch in his stomach that was like to make him hurl. Could be his insides remembered something his outside had forgot.

Tonight Squib had no time for aimless ponderings. He had pizzas to deliver to nonhumans.

And beignets.

Waxman had asked for a sack of Bodi's spiced beignets.

I forgot the goddamn beignets.

Way to make a first impression, dumbass.

It was too late to turn back. Waxman was expecting him at nightfall, and that was just about right now. He could always nip back across once the pizzas were divvied up.

Squib had tied off at Waxman's landing maybe a hundred times, but tonight was different. Tonight he was brimful of trepidation. The smell of the pizzas suddenly turned his stomach, and he thought he might experience his very first water heave.

Burned meat, he thought. *It could be me in that box presently.*

But Squib was a sailor at heart, and he swallowed down the bile and stepped neatly to the planking, doing this thing he did where he flicked the bow loop over a decking pole with the toe of one sneaker. Didn't work everywhere, but Waxman's dock was made for it, and it heartened Squib some that he could pull off the little stunt even with the nerves gnawing at him.

I could be a good runner for old Vern, he thought. *The best.*

It looked like old Vern was gone, for it was Waxman alone waiting for him under the striped veranda with the oak copse at his back and a longneck dangling from his fingers.

"You done forgot the beignets, ain't you?" he said from his deck chair. "I can smell pizza, but there ain't no beignets within half a mile."

Squib allowed that he had. "I did forget, but I can zip back over. Ain't a problem."

Waxman grinned. "Considering the alternative, I imagine not. But no, I guess the pizza will do."

Squib relaxed a little, allowing his shoulders to slump. "Where's the boss?"

"Vern lit out. He don't like spending two nights this close to civilization. Anyways, he ain't my boss. Seems like you got yourself four bosses at least. Maybe five, counting Hooke."

"Five, huh," said Squib. "No wonder I don't sleep good."

Waxman finished his beer and placed the empty in a recycling crate. "Maybe I can help straighten out a few things. Give you an induction, so to speak."

Squib delivered one of the pizzas into Waxman's waiting hands. "A training day?"

"Easy, Denzel," said Waxman. "We ain't got ourselves a day. Alls we got is how long it takes you to bury me."

"Bury you?"

Waxman laughed. "Sure, bury me. What the hell you think all that dragon shit is for?"

THE LAY OF the land was as follows. The mogwai went into hibernation once in a while to recharge the batteries. Some ancestor of Waxman's had discovered God knows how that the best dirt for a mogwai to lie in was dragon crap. Apparently it's chock-full of vitamins and nutrients: a superfood, so to speak. The more fresh shit went in, the better a mogwai came out of it.

Waxman directed Squib to excavate a section of his fruit and vegetable patch, which he had already cleared of bananas, squash, and potatoes.

"Hell, boy," said Waxman, as Squib put his back into digging a mogwai-sized pit through the soft loam and coffee grinds, "three months of shut-eye and I'll be good as new. All the aches and pains straightened out. Especially with a good fella like yourself topping me up."

Squib hacked at a root with the blade of his spade. "Are you sure about this, Waxman? It feels an awful lot like I'm digging a grave here. I don't wanna go down for murder in the first 'cause of some eagle-eyed fisherman getting a load of this."

Waxman gestured with a folded slice of pizza. "I got you covered, Squib. There's two letters inside on the table. One is a shopping list for your first delivery to His Dragon Highness, and the other is for my attorney in Slidell. Says I'm gone traveling up to Alaska and you are legal caretaker while I'm gone. Plus the house is yours if'n I don't come back. I am coming back, mind, so don't you go getting no ideas."

Squib severed the root and dragged the tentacle from the suck of wet earth. "I ain't got time for ideas," he said. "Five bosses, remember?"

"I suppose not," said Waxman. "We best get to it then."

"I'd appreciate that, sir," said Squib. "Is there a lot to it? Running for Vern?"

Waxman chewed thoughtfully, thinking back. "Yeah, I guess. He can be a grumpy old lizard—though he ain't a lizard, technically. I call him Lord Highfire, ironic-like, 'cause he ain't no lord no more, but there's times he flashes back to those days and starts shooting off orders, which I ignore, but you gots to take heed, I guess, if you want your scale."

Squib tossed a sloppy swamp divot from the hole. "What kind of orders?"

"Oh, you know, old-lady stuff. Like he has a yearning for breakfast cereal or new clothes at four A.M. and shoots off a message, something like: 'I need a dozen *Flashdance* T-shirts ASAP.' Shit like that."

"He likes *Flashdance*, huh?"

"Oh, hell yeah. That is one *Flashdance*-obsessed dragon."

"No problem. I got an Amazon account. Whatever Vern needs is here in two days."

Waxman devoured another slice of pizza, making no attempt to hide his scything rows of teeth. His mastications made a noise like frogs going through a blender might. Squib had to make a real effort not to wince.

Waxman swallowed. "No. Use my account. Details in the bureau, along with further instructions. The Amazon is set up on a debit card, so just get whatever you need. Bodi has the same card on file, and the general store does, too. I'll be poring over the statements when I get back, though, so no treating yourself to rubber sex dolls or whatever you teenagers waste your money on these days."

"No wasting money," promised Squib. "*Flashdance* T-shirts only."

Waxman squinted at him. "You sassing me, boy?"

"Sorry," said Squib. "Habit. I forgot how our thing has changed, you being not human and all."

"Yeah, I ain't no good old swamp boy, that's for sure. I ate a couple of those guys, though, when they started coming around here poking about, looking for my gold. I ain't even got no gold—Vern's got the gold from that submarine."

Squib kept his eyes in the hole. "You ate 'em?"

"Not all of them," said Waxman. "Just the flesh."

"Come on, Waxman," said Squib, feeling a touch nauseated again. He sincerely hoped it was just the subject and not the dragon's breath eating his insides. "You got to talk like that? It's too much."

Waxman closed the lid on one empty pizza box. "Sorry, kid. It's just nice to be myself around you after all this time."

"I ain't got a problem with that," said Squib, stepping down farther into the pit. "Just the eating-folks stuff. Anything else is much appreciated."

"I can fill you in on the rest in a few months' time, though by then you'll be up to speed or dead your own self."

This opened the door for the question Squib had been leading up to. "You think Vern would torch me now?"

Waxman hung his jacket carefully on the chair. "He could, kid. No doubt about that. Humans butchered Vern's entire family, wore their skin as armor. Hell, humans killed Vern's entire goddamn race save for his own self. And Vern has his own fair share of scalps, so to speak. But you have a window here to make yourself indispensable. Don't be late, don't mouth off, and don't tell a goddamn soul, because everyone you tell is a loose end, and Vern don't suffer loose ends to live." Waxman stripped off his shirt, revealing a torso rippled with waxy folds of skin and fringed slits that might have been gills. "Vern has strayed off the hermit's path these last fifty years. Likes his comforts a little too much. Cable and such. You gotta keep that pipeline running real slick. His wish is your command."

"Got it," said Squib. "He says, 'Jump,' I say, 'How high, boss?'"

"That's it exactly. How are the nights in your schedule?"

"Good," said Squib. "Momma is on the late shift till October, so I'm my own man from eight P.M. onwards."

"That might work out real well. Vern won't need you before sundown any night starting tomorrow."

Squib knew he shouldn't ask, but he was a businessman at the end of the day. "You think Vern might toss a few bucks my way once in a while?"

Waxman threw back his head and laughed, teeth buzzing like an electric razor. "You're a one, Moreau, damned if you ain't. A few bucks, you say. Don't you get it, boy? Vern hates humans, hates them big-time. It's not a casual hatred either, like a guy might hate chicken. This is the real deal. If I come back and you're still breathing, then that will be a win for mankind." Waxman snorted. "A few bucks? Shit, boy. You best get digging and stop asking fool questions."

Squib did as he was told.

SQUIB WENT DOWN about five feet, give or take, and was beyond tuckered by the time Waxman called a halt.

"That should do her, boy," said the mogwai. "Why don't we swap places? Unless you want to go down for the dirt nap?"

Squib reckoned that he didn't fancy no dirt nap and hopped smartly from the pit, though it was up to his shoulders at this point. He was surprised to find Waxman buck-ass naked apart from a slice of pizza, which he used to preserve his modesty.

"You gonna eat that?" asked Squib, trying to lighten his own mood, which was pretty grim on account of being in thrall to a dragon and having to bury old Waxman alive.

"Nah," said Waxman, "I'm gonna absorb it over the weeks. Lay it all over me. Pizza number two. There are a few steaks in the refrigerator. I'll have those, too. And half a dozen bottles of Baby Bio plant food. Pour 'em all in."

Waxman hopped eagerly down into the pit like he was off to Disneyland—and not the crappy Disneyland in Europe either, but the primo one in Orlando. The mogwai's shoulders were a mite broad for the grave, but he wriggled himself flat and said gleefully, "Come on, boy, pile that shit on."

It was a weird and horrific tableau: an elderly fairy-type fella down there with the bugs and snails already squelching toward his pizza jockstrap. Squib had one question. "Waxman, you ain't crazy, are you?"

Waxman grinned. "Crazy? Tired is what I am. Why you asking me that?"

"Well, sir," said Squib, "if you're crazy, then all I'm doing is burying you alive."

"Shit, son," said Waxman, "all the shit you seen in the last day, if anybody's crazy, it's you."

"Yup," said Squib, "makes sense as much as anything makes sense."

"Well, all right, Squib boy. Then you best get to it. Once

that dragon shit dehydrates, you ain't gonna shift it with a lump hammer."

"Yessir, Waxman," said Squib. "Sleep well, I guess."

Waxman closed his eyes. "Hell, kid. I'm already halfway there." The mogwai smiled beatifically, and the expression never left his face even as Squib Moreau filled his grave with maybe a quarter ton of dragon crap.

Squib distracted himself by making observations on the properties of the dragon shit.

Don't smell too bad. Kinda nutty.

And as for texture, I'd say frozen yogurt.

"Hey," called Waxman then, his hand clawing through the dung, "one last thing."

Squib near to crapped himself and dropped the shovel. "Yeah? You change your mind?"

Waxman wiggled his head clear. "Nah, boy, I'm committed. Just take my suit to the cleaners. Dry-clean, mind. Not a drop of water touches my velvet."

"Yeah," said Squib. "Dry-clean only."

"I'll stop jabbering now," said Waxman. "Might make it a deal easier for you to bury me if I stop issuing orders."

It might, thought Squib, but it didn't really.

VERN HAD A feeling in the pit of his gut, like a live thing was coiled in there, gnawing at him.

Dread was the thing's name. Simple as pie. One of those extreme emotions: fear plus anticipation.

I cannot believe it, Highfire, he thought. *You're trusting a goddamn human. When you gonna learn?*

Wax had won him over the previous night with hooch and a couple of lovely boar steaks done just right, burned on the outside and rare in the middle.

"You got your travel bag with you, Vern?" the mogwai had asked him.

"Nope," said Vern. "Left in a hurry on the kid's trail."

"I thought as much," said Waxman. "No matter. I got me a spare waterproof sack here. Got a nice strap and everything."

"What do I need a sack for?"

Waxman had plonked his creepy Gladstone bag on the table. "To get rid of this stuff. I'm done with all the killing, Vern. We're all souls, right? So bury it real deep, far away from my spot. I don't want none of this shit seeping into my garden. Or better still, vaporize the whole package. Use it for target practice, but don't inhale none of the mist; that shit'll rot your insides."

Vern slid the bag close to him. "So that's it, huh? Your murdering days are over?"

Waxman had raised his glass. "Self-defense only, brother. Will you toast to that?"

And Vern, feeling no pain whatsoever after his feed of boar and booze, and well and drunkenly disposed toward the mogwai's *we're all souls* theory, did toast the sentiment, even though he did not subscribe to it his own self.

By morning the dragon had an extra layer of regret laid on top of the self-loathing he usually felt after tying one on, and he got the hell out of Wax's boathouse at first light, scything downriver, letting the tepid river water sluice through his crannies, feeling like he would throw up under-water from pure anxiety.

What the hell was I thinking?

A human familiar.

A goddamn kid at that.

And:

This goddamn river is polluted as shit. I can't taste nothing but diesel and piss.

Which was not helpful when a dragon was already on the queasy side.

Was a time this water was sweeter than lemonade.

This morning it had been most decidedly acidic. No won-der his hide was turning gray, spending all day in cruiser runoff with the gators. When the sun hit the surface the wrong way, the entire river looked like a rainbow slick. Plus he was getting older, no denying that. A dragon only had so many millennia in him before the body began to give out. Was a time he could fly around all day and snort flame fountains for sport, but now Vern doubted he could put in more than a half dozen hours in the air without bringing on palpitations.

That was how the day started for Vern, way down in the dumps. And it only got worse.

My only buddy is gone down for three months.

But it could be years.

It could be forever.

Mogwai often got so comfortable in the earth that they gave up the ghost entirely and allowed themselves to be as-similated. Wax had once told him during that post-interment funk when he was still mud-drunk, "Shit, Vern. A fella stops thinking down there. Everything goes away, you know? And alls you got is peace. An eternity of peace if you want it. That right there is an attractive proposition."

An eternity of peace. That *was* an attractive proposition.

So Vern made it home and slunk back to his shack, ignoring the gators on the bank saluting him with jaws cranked open, feeling his mood darken with every step through the rushes.

Goddamn, he thought. *Here it comes.*

The "it" in question was one of his dark spells. It was only to be expected that any creature with half a brain would get the blues once in a while, especially in his situation. Everyone he loved had been murdered, along with everyone he sort of liked. Even most of the creatures he hated were dead. His mother had been cut up for keepsakes while his father's head had adorned the gates of a local castle portcullis for about ten minutes, till Vern had razed the entire compound. He'd raged, razed, and raged some more. For years his grief exploded from him in extended bursts of dragon fire until he was down to skin and bone, and his mind felt somehow as emaciated as his body, as though it, too, did not have the energy or will to go on. And when the first wave of loneliness had landed like a rock on his chest, Wyvern, Lord Highfire, felt like it would crush him entirely.

The world that had once been his had turned against him. More than that, it had forgotten him.

I just clean the streets I used to own, he thought, paraphrasing winsome crooner Chris Martin.

I am like the rats down in their holes, scrabbling about for scraps.

But he wasn't even like rats, because rats were rats.

Plural.

He was a dragon. The only one.

SQUIB LOADED THE groceries into his boat, day after the burial, ballasting out the mineral water, cooking oil, and other heavier items and whistling like one of the seven dwarves as he worked so he could kid some part of himself that this was a normal evening. He checked the levels on his outboard, then cast off from the bar's dock.

The Pearl River was its usual fake quiet this evening: that is, quiet until a person started paying attention; then the ears picked up the wind sighing through the lace of moss, swamp frogs bouncing their burps across the water, crickets going nuts, and owls hooting exultantly like hillbillies who'd just found a crate of Bud. And under all of that was the constant symphony of water, from the hiss against the levee to the gurgle through the root bridges of water cypress. Usually Squib didn't notice all this so much as become a part of it. Usually the swamp folded around him like a blanket, but tonight he felt as glaringly visible as a big-ass bug on a small windscreen.

Goddamn dragon, he thought.

But still.

But still there was a part of him, the kid part maybe, that was a little excited about working for a mythical creature.

A goddamn dragon.

If he kept his mind right and made himself indispensable, as Waxman had suggested.

Before you buried Waxman, said his little voice.

Yes, before he asked me to bury him.

If he made himself indispensable, then maybe the dragon might help him out with the Hooke problem. After all, Hooke was up to shady shit in the swamp, and if Vern wasn't king of that swamp, then Squib was a gator's granddad.

And I ain't no gator's granddad.

Squib felt a ray of light puncture his funk.

Maybe Vern could help.

Long shot, said his little voice. *Vern hates the entire human race.*

Squib could allow to himself that this was true, but hadn't his momma often told him that he could charm the birds from the trees? He certainly could charm dollar bills from tourists. In fact, the only person who had proved immune to his charms had been Regence goddamn Hooke.

Maybe old Vern might find himself warming up to the Squib-man.

It might not be much of a plan, but it was something like hope, and Squib determined to hold on to that feeling just to see him through the night.

SQUIB WAS A little overexcited and took a couple of forays up the wrong tributaries before arriving at Vern's digs. When he did finally get there, he found the shack deserted. On the table was a single scale acting as a paperweight for the note pinned beneath it.

"Shit's out back," said the note, and followed this with a short shopping list that included vodka, the latest *TV Guide*, and a vegetable spiralizer, which Vern must have seen on QVC.

Not a dragon in sight.

Squib popped the scale into his mouth, thinking, *This job ain't as exciting as I'd hoped.*

And, *Looks like Vern ain't of a mind to help me after all.*

CHAPTER 9

OOKE HAD OVERDONE IT WITH HIS CALL TO G-HOP, AND AS
Elodie Moreau had predicted, his snake-bite symptoms
recurred and his eyes quit on him for almost a week.
The doc also said there was some permanent damage to his
kidneys, which Regence could give a shit about. The constable got himself hooked up to dialysis, morphine, and
industrial-grade antibiotics. He wasn't so contrary about bed
rest now, as he found that he did some of his best thinking
while under the influence of narcotics. Also, there comes a
point when a man realizes that being pigheaded just leads a
fella to slaughter.

So medical attention it was, and on day six Hooke's sight
returned and the mask of civility that he wore for the general public slipped on account of his dozy state.

He opened his eyes, took one look at the nurse, and said,
"Shit, Elodie, you done let yourself go."

To which the nurse said, "I ain't no Elodie, asshole. She's
on the night shift."

Regence reckoned that this lady mustn't be aware of his

nature or she wouldn't've been mouthing off. This was a good thing, as it meant his cover was intact. He preferred the reputation that preceded him to be one of civic responsibility, and so the constable did not admonish the nurse as he would surely have liked to do but instead apologized for his own rudeness, blaming his insensitive comment on the drugs coursing through his system.

The nurse did not look in the least mollified and treated Hooke to a withering glare, the likes of which was usually reserved for unemployed cheaters on cable TV shows.

Hooke gave the nurse time to finish her rounds of the small ward, then packed up his gear, dragged on his trousers, one leg at a time, and got the hell out of there.

Ten minutes and one signed waiver later he was in his Chevy and back on the job.

Because Regence Hooke did have an actual job he was supposed to be doing while he was clandestinely pursuing his dreams of constructing a metal pipeline up the Pearl and from there to California and NYC. He was the one and only constable for Petit Bateau and was two years into a six-year term. What had drawn Hooke to this ward was the vague nature of the qualifications required: An applicant needed only to be of good moral character and be able to read and write the English language. Hooke could read and write just fine, and he considered his own moral character to be in line with his ambitions. Luckily, the constable's office was part-time, and so long as Hooke submitted reasonable expenses and kept up with his justice of the peace subpoenas, he was left pretty much alone. It was an open secret in Louisiana that the office of constable was a dinosaur from the previous century which was outrageously exploited all across the state by entrepreneurial part-timers who bumped up their expenses to hundreds of thousands of dollars per annum. There was a time when a smart operator could grease the right wheels and hold onto a constable's badge for two or three decades, but with the advent of published expenses, the public was wising up to some extent and unlikely to re-elect someone riding the city gravy train. So a constable's options were to do the job right, or grab as much as possible over the six-year term.

Hooke did the job right. He served whatever needed serving, no matter how deep into the swamp it took him, and he claimed his delivery fees and mileage back through his salary. He worked whichever three days a week suited him and did a little enforcement work on the side for the mayor and his buddies in the next ward. And in return, Mayor Shine gave Hooke the use of an office and secretary. Hooke wasn't technically supposed to take on any city police duties, but constables generally did, and the Petit Bateau residents were glad to have an army man around to break up bar fights or transport the occasional burglar to the Slidell lockup.

The previous constable had been the local bus driver, and it was said in the local bars that old Derrick didn't know how to spell "good moral character," never mind possess a bunch of it. So the public were satisfied enough with Hooke, who was, admittedly, a little intimidating, but there had been a vertical drop-off in larceny since he took it upon himself to walk a beat around the town in the evenings. And Hooke wasn't a letter-of-the-law kind of guy either, in that he employed a live-and-let-live code. Drunks were generally dropped off at their own front doors rather than locked up, and kids smoking weed were given a swift kick in the seat of the pants rather than getting themselves a record.

The townspeople felt safer in their beds, and Regence Hooke's cover was complete.

When he cashed out of the army, Hooke had put considerable research into where he would pitch his stall. The Colonel Faraiji model had appealed to him: i.e., get into law enforcement and open trade links to other regions. He had picked Petit Bateau because it was a gateway to the North through the swamp. Also, he had heard of this guy Conti through the dark web: a wannabe gangster who was buying up any soldiers on the force. Any force. Paying good money, too.

The first thing Hooke did when the city hired him was spend his days off surveilling Ivory's family, so when his hothead nephew Vincent got himself thrown into the beatdown room of a strip joint for pawing the dancers, Hooke was able to step in and defuse the situation, which got him on a bar stool adjacent to Rossano Roque, which led to an offer from Ivory. So now Hooke had two salaries, plus the sizeable nest egg from the military-fuel racket he'd had going in Iraq. That had been a sweet scam which had fallen apart months after Hooke's discharge, resulting in a hundred-plus enlisted personnel and military officers being convicted of theft, bribery, and contract rigging valued at tens of millions of dollars during their deployment. Hooke had laughed his ass off when that news trickled back to him stateside.

Tens of millions of dollars? Hundreds would be closer to the truth.

He wasn't worried it would ever come back to him. The army had barely scratched the surface, and his involvement was way subterranean. Subterranean *and* labyrinthine.

In the negative column, his long-term plans vis-à-vis Ivory Conti's infrastructure had hit a bump. He would need an act of God to dislodge Ivory from his perch at this rate, and where the hell was he supposed to come across one of those? Surviving that hurricane back in Florida was probably about as much as any god was prepared to do for him.

Maybe if I hadn't staked out Daddy like a vampire.

Still, no use crying over spilled blood. Better to clear out his in-tray and turn his focus to Squib Moreau.

Once his sight returned, Hooke was reluctantly cut loose by the hospital. He'd had to sign a waiver and was told by the doctor that he was lucky to be out so quick, that his heart had been put under considerable strain and he should take it easy for a couple of months, all advice Hooke intended to roundly ignore because, as fate would have it, Squib Moreau had fallen neatly into Hooke's in-tray that very morning. He'd called Lori from the Chevy to see what was urgent, and the answer was "Nuthin' much, Constable." The half a dozen papers needing serving Lori had already foisted onto the college linebacker Hooke had sworn in as his deputy for twenty bucks a pop. It was money well spent in Hooke's opinion, and easily earned, in the opinion of the college kid Duke McKlusker, who was known by all and sundry as Kluskerfuck, on account of how he would fuck a person up if'n they resisted his subpoena service.

The only other matter of any note was a weeks-old noise complaint from one of the Beaujean brothers who lived downriver in a converted train carriage on the bayou. Maybe, Lori suggested, Hooke remembered that someone had been dynamiting catfish down there? It would mean a lot to the brothers if Constable Hooke would have a stern word with the usual suspects.

Usual suspects, thought Hooke. *I know exactly who's king of that hill.*

He swung the Chevy around in the general store lot and set its grille toward the river.

HOOKE DROVE SLOW down the Moreau lane. A couple of things were different from his last visit. There were no spinning wheels this time around, and his right hand was pretty close to normal, apart from a compression bandage which reminded him of the support tights his mother used to wear—he made a mental note to check if those bandages came in any other color besides nude.

He shuddered, then wrenched his mind away from his mother's varicose veins and to the problem of Squib Moreau.

There were two ways he could proceed with this investigation, and it was best to settle on one before making his approach.

There was a saying Colonel Faraiji used to throw about, "Softly softly catchy monkey," to which Hooke often replied, "Shooty, killy motherfucking monkey."

A response which never failed to pain the colonel, who saw Hooke as his padawan.

"But Regence, my boy, what if you wish to interrogate the monkey?"

"Then I shoot him in the leg." Which Hooke still believed was a valid argument.

But for today, he thought that perhaps the *softly softly* approach was the right one to take. Regence was fine with this approach and could pull it off easy enough, apart from one thing. Or two things, to be precise.

His eyes.

Another quote from Faraiji: "The eyes are the windows to the soul. But not in your case, Sergeant. I see no soul."

Hooke had to agree. He sincerely believed that his soul had been excised, or at least forfeited, so his gray eyes were windows to bedlam. To look into Regence Hooke's eyes was to understand that this man's religion was a blend of avarice and chaos.

Hooke knew that people found it difficult to hold his gaze. They felt it in him, the deep well of aggression, the boundless need for conquest.

Hooke could twist his mouth into a grin and relax the tension in his shoulders, but he couldn't do shit about the eyes.

So he bought himself some Wayfarers to disguise the animal bloodlust.

Hey, it worked for Tom Cruise.

HOOKE RAPPED ON Elodie's front-window glass through the bug screen. He could have just as easily knocked on the door, but he'd found rapping on windows freaked people the hell out because they assumed that whoever had been knocking on the window had probably just been peeking through it. And most folks' default emotion when they discovered a peeper was to feel guilty their own selves. Hooke liked interviewees to feel guilty, even the innocent ones.

The curtains were closed, but they were threadbare, and Hooke could clearly see Elodie asleep on the sofa bed, face deep in the cushions, the curve of her thigh rising like the swell of surf, and he thought to himself, *Someday, Regence, son.*

But not today.

Even so, he resolved to take it easy on the girl. No need to burn bridges entirely.

He rapped again, and Elodie jerked like she'd been prodded, rolling backwards off the sofa onto all fours, an unconscious but practiced move.

There ain't one goddamn thing I'm seeing here that I don't like, thought Hooke. *I know there are finer women who don't need persuading, but Miss Elodie is a peach, no doubt.*

Inside the house, Elodie climbed up along the table leg, then stood in place, swaying slightly.

That goddamn woman is asleep, Hooke realized, and gave one more knock at the window.

Barely a minute later Elodie appeared at the screen door. She hadn't needed a minute to shrug on a dressing gown, being as she was still in her night-shift duds.

Hooke was disappointed.

A little slovenly, he thought, *a person sleeping in her clothes. That's something I'll have to fix.*

Still he kept his professional face on, hiding his eyes behind the Wayfarers, hoping the Polaroids reflected the light both ways so she wouldn't see the lasers coming out of him. Not yet, leastways.

Elodie opened the door, eyes down, in the manner of sleepy people. Hooke's navy uniform trousers with their gold piping were enough to shake half the sleep from her system.

"Constable Hooke," she said, taking a barefoot step back, surprised to see him at her door, especially so soon after his snake bite. It was true that he had called on her before, but never out of the blue. "Constable."

Hooke approximated a friendly smile. It came out something like a guy sucking on a slice of lemon.

"That's two 'Constables.' Hell, that near to makes me a captain—Captain Hooke. Get it?"

Elodie shook her wedge of dark hair.

Hairdo looks like someone hacked it off the back of her head with an axe, thought Hooke. *I believe she does it herself. Squib's, too. Guess she only knows that one style.*

"Oh, I see," mumbled Elodie, rubbing one eye. "*Captain* Hooke. Like in the book."

Stupid Cajun, thought Hooke. *I like that.* "I think you might find it was a movie," he said kindly. "If you went and looked into it."

Elodie blinked maybe half a dozen times, thinking that maybe she was still dreaming.

"I'll do that. You know, there's no need to come around, Constable. You done thanked me already, at the clinic. Maybe you don't remember. You was all drugged up at the time."

Hooke held up a hand to stop the flow. "No, Elodie. Miss Moreau. It ain't that. It ain't that at all. I'm here about something else."

"About that something else," said Elodie, placing half her head behind the flimsy protection of the screen door. "I don't think there is anything else, Constable."

Hooke knew what Elodie was saying. She had seen him stripped down to the bones personality-wise and thought now that there was no future for them romantic-wise. This surely was a pity, but Hooke had encountered resistance before and he felt confident he could charm his way over that molehill. But not today. Today was for more pressing issues.

Hooke casually nudged the toe of his boot into the frame, in case he had to apply pressure to find out what he needed to know.

Could be I'll end up here for the day. Six hours shenanigans, two hours cleanup. Then burn the place to the ground.

Hooke always kept that card in his back pocket, which was probably why that telltale glint never left his eyes. Every time he met someone, Hooke was figuring how to murder them and get away with it, in case the need arose.

But this time, it was better to turn that burner down real low. There was an endgame here beyond the usual gratifications.

"I ain't here about personal stuff," he said, "though I surely wish that was the case. No, I done had a complaint about your young 'un. Ain't the first time neither."

Elodie came completely awake like a switch had been flicked. "Everett? He ain't done nothing. The boy promised me."

Hooke sighed like it pained him to be delivering bad tidings. "They promise, don't they? Sun, moon, and stars.

But words don't mean shit to boys in the long term, pardon my language. They is just convenient at the time."

Elodie had a bit of fight in her as far as Squib was concerned, her hackles rising even in the face of Hooke. "What's Everett *supposed* to have done?"

"This time," said Hooke keeping up the gentle tone. "What's Everett *supposed* to have done *this time*. Because this surely ain't the first time."

Elodie squared her shoulders some and her chin cranked over to one side, which the hunter in Hooke knew as a sign that this lioness was prepared to protect her cub. "Well then," she said, the steel in her voice challenging Hooke, "what's he supposed to have done this time?"

"Nothing too serious. Just a spot of dynamiting on the bayou. Stun those catfish to the surface." Hooke wiggled his pinky finger. "He sure has got previous experience in that particular area, if not expertise."

Elodie gripped the screen-door slat tight with one hand and her entire frame stiffened, and Hooke realized that with that one little gesture he'd forever blown his chances. It always amazed him how much some mothers actually loved their offspring. Not his, obviously, which was why he found it hard to relate.

"It's been a while since that incident, Constable," said Elodie. "Everett's done straightened up. Boy's working three jobs trying to get us out of the hole his daddy done dug."

Hooke was interested. "Three jobs? You don't say? Mind running those down for me?"

Elodie counted down on two fingers. "One, the boy has

his own graft on the water. Crawfish, catfish. Sells to Bodi direct. Which is his second port, working the bar and grill, being as Bodi cuts us a deal on this place."

"Yup," said Hooke, thinking, *Cuts a deal, does he? I wonder, is old Bodi taking his rent in kind?*

"Three," continued Elodie, on her thumb, "Mister Waxman has taken him on as his assistant. He's doing all sorts of chores over there. It appears Mister Waxman likes to loaf about mostly, and he has Everett keep up his house. My boy is spending every hour the Lord sends on the water. Won't even take the Sundays for himself. He's a good son, Constable. Lord knows he sneaks a beer on occasion, but that's all he does these days. He swore to me, and I believe him. I ain't breaking my back to throw it all away on bail money and medical fees."

Hooke tipped his cap back on the crown of his head. "That's a pretty speech, Miss Elodie. You surely do have a way with the words."

"Truth makes its own way," said Elodie, shifting one foot back like she was primed to end this conversation.

"That's all as may be," said Hooke. "Unfortunately, I have this here complaint and I got to check it out. So, if you could present the young fella, we can get this cleared up in a jiffy."

"I can't present him," said Elodie, sounding hard like she wouldn't present him if she could. "He's at the Pearl, filling Waxman's shopping list. I don't know when the boy sleeps. Can't be getting more than two hours in the bunk every evening."

Hooke allowed his mirrored gaze to wander all over

Elodie's person, taking his sweet time, moving his head as well as his eyes so that she knew he was looking, because at this point he was pretty sure his chances of getting his hands on that person legitimately were pretty much zero, but he gave it one more try.

"Maybe I could come by later and catch up with the boy? Maybe bring a bottle of that sparkling wine you like?"

Elodie rubbed her neck. "I can't, Constable. I'm on the late shift all summer. We need the money, Lord knows we do."

Well now, thought Hooke, *there's the clincher.*

He considered snatching the Wayfarers off his own face then, letting this no-account Cajun see exactly what she was turning down. How her life was hanging by a thread every time they spoke.

Take off the glasses, then one hand around her throat, and walk her backwards into the house.

Wasn't no one around to see. The kid was on the clock.

But that didn't solve his problem. There was someone out there, maybe with a video of him slitting Carnahan's belly, but at the very least an eyewitness.

And even after that problem was solved, he had Ivory Conti's empire to deal with.

It had to be done clever.

He flashed back on a night in Iraq, sitting on a breeze block beside an oil-drum fire, and Colonel Faraiji showing him a stump of cracked wood before he tossed it into the flames.

"Do you see this piece of wood, Regence, my friend?"

"I see it, Colonel," Hooke had said. "And I bet there's

more to it than wood. I bet nature's teaching me a lesson I ain't understood yet."

Faraiji's smile was pained but indulgent. He'd never had a son who would listen to the lessons passed down through the generations, so Hooke would have to do.

"This wood is split and weakened. Good for nothing but the fire. How did this happen?"

"Fuck knows," said Hooke.

"How would you destroy this piece of wood?"

Hooke's patience was wearing thin. Faraiji never just came out and said stuff. There was always the big buildup.

"I guess I would take an axe to it."

"And how would the wood feel as the axe came down?"

Sometimes Hooke felt like he was being trained by Yoda. "I guess the wood would shit its wooden trunks."

"Exactly," said Faraiji. "So we must take our cue from the desert moisture. Seep into the wood, as a friend, then freeze in the night and split the wood."

"Fight from the inside is what you're saying?"

"Exactly, my friend," said Faraiji. "And even as the wood lay dying, it would not blame the water."

Fight from the inside, thought Hooke now. *Be a friend to all, until the time comes to stop being a friend.*

He flashed Elodie a smile that was broader than it was deep. "Hey, you can't blame a fella for asking, right?" He slid a card from his breast pocket and proffered it to Elodie like he'd pulled it from behind her ear, magician-style. "Ask Squib to give me a call when you see him. It ain't nothing serious, but I do want to hear from him, okay?"

Elodie took the card, careful not to make fingertip contact. "I surely will tell him, Constable."

Hooke adopted a jokey Southern drawl. "Don't make me come back here, hear?"

"I hear ya," said Elodie, an unconvincing good sport.

Hooke tapped his brim. "Ma'am," he said, and returned to the Chevy, leaving Elodie Moreau shivering in the thump of ninety-degree Louisiana heat.

The Hooke-Moreau hookup was never going to happen now, and they both knew it.

But, thought Hooke as he climbed into his vehicle, *there is surely more than one way to skin a Cajun.*

CHAPTER 10

VERN SNUCK INTO HIS CABIN THAT SAME AFTERNOON KNOWING full well that he shouldn't even be in there during the daytime, in case one of those swamp boys plucked up the courage to set foot on the island. Lord knew he had disappeared a few of them over the years just to send a message to the rest, but there was always some bane-eyed simpleton looking to make a name for himself by tracking down the Honey Island monster.

"This ain't even Honey Island, you dumbass," Vern had shouted at the one guy before he sank him in the bayou.

But he didn't do that anymore.

What he usually did was slink into the water and hide out till the latest baccy-chewing would-be monster-killer went on his way, praying he wouldn't stumble across Vern's shack with TV, beer cooler, and satellite line snaking down from the cypress canopy.

Not today, thought Vern, cracking the seal on his first bottle of vodka of the day. *Today I torch any motherfucker who sticks his nose into my hallowed ground. Screw it, I am done hiding.*

Vern was no fool. He knew what was going on.

The black dog has got me in his jaws.

These spells were unpredictable and often accompanied by a migraine so severe that Vern felt like the top of his head was gonna peel right off. His core temperature went sky-high, and he could melt his way through a tub of ice in twenty minutes, if he had a tub, or if he had any ice to spare.

Problem was that the blues used to creep over him slow: a gradual trough, then a slow climb up the other side. But now his mind knew what to expect and ramped things up straightaway, from zero to critical in a matter of minutes. The slightest trigger could set him off. A fish bone in his teeth. A bad bowl of gumbo. Or, in this case, the slightly more serious matter of his only friend going into the earth. The depression had taken hold of him when old Wax had gone down, and had only gotten worse since.

When these moods came over him, Vern felt like he was trapped in a dark tunnel with nothing ahead but more darkness. Endless night with only momentary flashes of light to distract him.

Light? he thought now. *What fucking light? I can't even go out in the daytime no more.*

And that was when the thoughts came, like:

Why bother? Why the hell bother? Ain't you lived enough?

The temptation that lurked closest to the surface was to go out in a blaze of glory. Just load up on fats and make a beeline for Belle Chasse. Swoop in there and go full scorched earth. See how much damage he could do before the navy got the tarps off their big guns.

Shit, I could probably burn that base off the face of the earth.

It tickled Vern some to imagine the worldwide shit storm that would follow an event like that. The humans would straight-up crap themselves. Washington would be terrified of an impending dragon takeover. No stone would be left unturned, that was for sure.

And this was where Vern's gung-ho fantasy ran out of steam. If Vern cut himself a fiery swath through some armed forces, then you could bet your last quarter that the government would scour every remote corner of the earth looking for more possible threats. And if he wasn't the last, if there were a few of his brothers and sisters hiding out somewhere, then Vern's actions would condemn them along with himself. Or even worse, they would be taken alive and subjected to a whole raft of intrusive testing.

Also, Wax's new pacifist ethos must be rubbing off on him because Vern didn't enjoy killing humans like he used to. The red mist was lifting a little. He hadn't gone on an unprovoked rampage for more than a century, though the way Vern figured it, every rampage had been provoked if you followed the river back to its source, so to speak. Vern had only killed in order to survive for quite some time, and even then, he'd kept a clean slate for close to eight years, ever since an asshole monster-hunter had actually found what he'd been looking for.

I outta get one of those flip signs, Vern thought. *"No homicides in: 2923 days."*

So, no flying into naval bases.

But Vern still yearned to just *not be* on occasion. And he would probably have to weather many such occasions before he made it through this spell of gloominess.

And he'd made several attempts to get that done. Back in the day he realized that his neck was simply too stubborn to be snapped by any kind of rope-drop combination. Deadly nightshade just gave him a knee-trembling case of the shits. A bullet to the brain never made it through his skull, though he did manage to damage his sinuses when he stuffed a flintlock up his nasal passage. Vern took a high jump a time or two, but chickened out before impact. Once he chickened out a hundred feet too late and inflicted a bum shoulder on himself for a couple of decades. It still twinged from time to time.

Frankly, it was too much pain for too little gain.

Or it had been. Until now.

Because Wax had given him his bag to destroy, in case some dumbass found it and mistook the vials for aphrodisiac. The Gladstone bag of murderous playthings, chock-full of death-dealers that had been passed down through the centuries. Usually Waxman didn't have to dig too deep into his bag for the appropriate murder weapon, but there were a few hidden pouches just in case. Sure, the mogwai could slice and dice a person better than most, but he could also drop a parasite into an ear or smear toxic bacteria on the back of a neck, all kinds of subtle but fatal shenanigans. When it came to creative ways to kill a person, the mogwai made humans look like koala bears. And it seemed to Vern that mogwai in general had a real taste for that macabre element of the job, but lately Waxman had lost his gusto in the homicide department. He'd held on to the bag, though, because you never knew, and now Vern had the bag, stashed inside his wet sack for the swim back here. And he knew there was something in there that could do him in because Waxman had told him so, maybe fifty years ago, when he started putting the bag together.

Vern remembered the first day Waxman had plonked the Gladstone bag onto the orange crate which had served him as a table before he went all antique-collectory.

"You see this, Highfire?" he'd asked, like it wasn't sitting right there. *"This here is my murder kit. 'Cause you know people are going to need killing if we plan to avoid dying."*

"Amen, brother," Vern had said, because truer words had never been uttered.

The bag was in its infancy at that point, but still Waxman laid out a fair collection on the crate. Blades, bottles, pills wrapped in tissue.

"That's a lotta shit," Vern had commented. *"That bag is like a goddamn clown car."*

This had been back when Vern did a lot of circus references just to piss Waxman off, considering how he'd been rescued.

"Screw you, Highfire," Waxman had said. *"You see, it's comments like that is why I have this beauty here."*

The "beauty" in question was a small patty of herbs and mud wrapped up in a boiled nettle leaf. Covered in wax paper, the leaf looked like a hipster vegan snack. Except it wasn't.

"Dragon's Bane," explained Waxman. *"Because some dragons are assholes who get to thinking that maybe they can*

beat up on their mogwai whenever they feel like it. I'm here to tell you, Highfire, I don't hold with that kind of abuse, and I won't stand for it."

Which kind of put them on an even footing.

And now, seventy years later, dragon and mogwai had grown tight, and there was a ball of Dragon's Bane sitting on the table in front of Vern.

So easy, thought Vern. *I pop this little fella down my gullet, lie down in the swamp, and let Wax's pill work its magic.*

Lie down in the swamp so his body wouldn't ever be found.

And once the notion had him, it wouldn't let go. Where a fortnight ago he had been a dragon who was prepared to kill whoever it took in order to survive, today there he sat in his recliner, slugging vodka from the bottle, a creature who could not think of a single goddamn reason to live.

"Dragon's Bane," Vern had said back in the day. *"Sounds painful. Even rhymes with 'pain.'"*

Wax had grinned, his rows of pointed teeth twinkling. *"No, sir, no pain. You just get a little buzz, talk some shit maybe, then take a nap and don't wake up. I don't want no cramping dragon using his last remaining minutes to fry my old ass."*

No pain, thought Vern now. *Just take a nap.*

An appealing notion.

A nap.

What else was he going to do? Live in a goddamn swamp until some tourist got a photograph of him?

No. Better to go out on his own terms.

My own terms? Rotting away to nothing in the swamp mud, when we used to rule the skies?

Not anymore.

Not for a long time. Humans saw to that. Time to finally face facts. The dragon era was over, and it had been over for a long time. He was like the last guy in the world listening to an eight-track. That shit wasn't ever coming back.

The Dragon's Bane sat on the arm of his chair now. Seemed like the wax paper was crinkling of its own accord, daring him to grow a pair and get this shit over with already.

It's been a while since I had the blues this bad, Vern realized. *Guess I was due.*

And so Vern made a decision.

I am gonna drink for the next day or so, and if this funk hasn't lifted by then, I'm gonna eat that there Dragon's Bane and take myself a final swim, somewhere nice and deep.

And that is exactly what he proceeded to do. Apart from the final swim. That bit didn't pan out as planned.

SQUIB MOREAU, ALL unawares that Constable Hooke was on his tail, went about his unique business. Every day the same thing: Up at midmorning and shake off the sleep funk. Grab some breakfast at the Pearl, followed by his bottle-boy work behind the bar. Help Bodi set up for the lunch crowd, flirt a little with Shandra Boyce, who waited on the booths. Sometimes Shandra would split a cream soda with him in the lull, but usually not, because Shandra was after an upright boy and Squib hadn't been in that bracket long enough to prove himself. He was like a junkie a couple of weeks off the gear: He needed a few more clean months under his belt.

After lunch Squib was out on the water tending his nets and traps. Whatever haul he managed went back to the Pearl kitchen and was added to his weekly tote. There were usually a couple of items to be picked up for Vern in the general store. The staples were vodka, palm oil, and fresh meat, and there would always be a few extras. These would all have to be packed carefully in a cooler, and then Squib would take himself on a quick spin downriver, making damn sure to avoid any sort of human interaction lest he get himself followed and be forced to forgo his precious scale.

After the drop-off, Squib would collect that day's shopping list and suck on the dragon scale that weighed the list down. Then it was out back to collect the shit bucket and take himself over to old Waxman's place for a spot of fertilization. Sometimes he talked to Waxman, told him how much of a pain in the ass Vern was being, how he had barely set eyes on the dragon these past ten days. And how he sure could use a little remuneration for all these hours he was putting in. Even gas money would be something.

Squib felt like he'd been on tenterhooks forever, even though it had only been a couple of weeks. He felt like he couldn't remember the sensation of being relaxed, though he could surely picture times when he must have been: smoking reefer out on the levee with Charles Jr., for example, or joining his momma for a viewing of *Highlander*, which was her favorite movie. Those were easy times, when he had surely felt his troubles lift off his shoulders for a couple of hours. But he couldn't put his finger on that sensation right now. Seemed like those things had happened to another person in another life because this particular version of Squib Moreau was in thrall to a dragon.

It was nightfall on the bayou, and a weekend to boot, so things were heating up in Petit Bateau. The Pearl had managed to somehow secure the services of Aaron Neville, who had history with Bodi Irwin. It was a secret gig, but as soon as the word got out that the king of New Orleans was burning up the Pearl's little stage, half of Slidell piled into the diner and the other half filled up the dock and patio tables.

On another night Squib would hate to miss such a buzzy evening, but he was on the clock now and Waxman had been very clear that he shouldn't *ever* be late. His duties for the evening were twofold: swap over shit buckets and deliver Vern's groceries, which included Cocoa Puffs, Lucky Charms, Cheerios, and a gallon of soy milk. Apparently the dragon was a breakfast-for-dinner kind of guy.

So far as I know. Could be he's feeding Cheerios to the catfish. It ain't like I ever lay eyes on him.

So Squib was no less than dumbfounded to find the dragon actually present when he wheeled the cooler into the shack that evening. Vern was lolling in his easy chair, plates and scales glowing in the TV light, a bottle of vodka drooping from two clawed fingers of one hand and what looked like half a protein cookie in the other.

The boy was further surprised when Vern said, "Looks like you ain't the one dying after all, kid. Looks like it's me."

The dragon was inebriated as all hell, judging by the slump of him, but Squib had heard a boatload of drunken declarations working Bodi's bar, and he felt this one had a ring of truth to it.

"Just one more bite of this here shit biscuit and off to sleep I go. Bye-bye, cruel world. Then you can blab to whoever you like, but no one will believe you."

This was confounding to Squib, as he didn't know what action to take. Should he let the dragon go his merry way, if he even had a choice in the matter? Or should he do something to save him?

"But I brung you cereal," exclaimed the boy, which seemed a lame thing to mention given the situation. "And mineral water, too. From France."

The dragon cocked his head like this might change his mind. "Nope," he said then, tossing the rest of the biscuit down his gullet. "Ain't enough."

Vern washed the snack down with a slug of vodka; his teeth clunked against the bottle neck. "Off home now, boy. I don't know exactly what side effects this Dragon Bane is gonna have. Could be I'll go full *Exorcist*."

Squib had seen that movie mostly because his momma had absolutely forbidden him to watch it, and a dragon unleashing a fire-hose puke was not something he wanted to be in the path of.

But still.

A good puke might save him.

Squib's little voice had a problem with that.

Save him? Why'n hell would you want to save him? Just let the big lizard go, and that's fifty percent of your problems off the board.

Yeah, but. Dragon, you know?

Screw it. Fuck him. And to hell with extinction. Get your ass back in the boat, and keep the groceries while you're at it.

Even Waxman couldn't blame him for Vern checking out like this.

The dragon's eyes were hazy. "I seen things, kid," he said softly. "I watched C-beams glitter in the dark near the Tannhäuser Gate."

That snapped Squib to a little. "That it, boss? All you gotta tell me is ripped off from *Blade Runner*? Tell me something real before you go."

Vern squinted and wagged a finger at Squib. "You got me there, kid. *Blade Runner.* I thought you probably wouldn't have seen that one, young as you are."

"I seen it," said Squib. "I seen all the old movies with Momma. She loves the *Highlander.*"

"Shit!" said Vern. "There can be only one, right?"

"There can be only one," agreed Squib. "And you're it. The one dragon. You wanna go out like this?"

Vern blinked slowly like it was an effort. "I don't wanna go out and I don't wanna stay in. Know what I mean?"

Actually, Squib kinda did know. He had some experience with people who didn't care none for living.

"I do get what you mean, Mister Vern. Times are tough. But we all got shit to take care of."

Vern burped. "Not me. I got nothing. You all saw to that. Not one of your kind ever did squat for me nor mine."

The dragon leaned forward, elbows on knees, drooling a little. "What's the point?" he asked. "Maybe the sun will come out tomorrow, you know, but I'm sick of watching the sunrise alone."

Squib remembered something his momma had said one time when she came home real tired and found him in bed with the whooping cough and her new boyfriend was smoking reefer on the back porch and could not give a shit about her kid sick in bed. And as she was mopping his brow, Momma talked a little about his original daddy, which she rarely did.

"If only I could have seen him through to sunrise," she had said, a tear dripping from her nose. "But we weren't enough, me and you."

So when Vern made that crack about sunrise, Squib felt himself getting angry. "Screw you, Vern," he said. "You ain't dying on me."

Vern drooled some more. "That is correct, son. I ain't dying on you. I'm dying on myself."

"The hell you are," said Squib, and sprang into action. Or, more accurately, ran around in a tight circle while he considered what action to spring into. He remembered when his friend Charles Jr. had accidentally taken a swig out of a bleach bottle, with the reasoning that the container was similar in dimensions to his daddy's rye whiskey bottle. Miss Ingram had taken Charles by the neck like he was a turkey and jammed three fingers down his throat till he puked all down her forearm. Took the color right out of her blouse.

Miss Ingram had admitted later that this technique was homegrown and frowned upon by the medical profession, but hell Charles was alive, wasn't he?

And even if he did try the Ingram method, it could be that dragons didn't puke in the same manner as humans, but Vern had referenced *The Exorcist*, so Squib reckoned he might as well give it a try.

Still, he thought, *those teeth look mighty sharp.*

Squib widened the radius of his run and snagged one of a dozen T-shirts hanging from a peg. He wrapped it around his forearm, then said a quick prayer. "Jesus God, help me now."

"I met Jesus," mumbled Vern, his head coming up. "He weren't even a good carpenter."

No more revelations were forthcoming as Squib stuffed as much of his fist as he could down the dragon's windpipe. He really put his weight behind it, grunting with effort, and flashed on a time, years before, when he and Charles Jr. had punched into a bucket of drying concrete to see how far in they could go, except this was tighter and ridged with muscles and teeth. Squib met Vern's eyes, and it seemed like the dragon was outraged, for he stood suddenly upright and took Squib bodily with him—and still not a sign of a puke, so Squib wiggled his fingers in there good, like he was running a finger race, and then planted his feet on Vern's barrel chest and yanked himself free.

Maybe a pint of gel-like substance came with him, and Vern hawked and said, "The goddamn nerve!"

Then he puked up whatever he'd been keeping down in a multicolored, multitextured heave which washed across the planking like so much bilge.

"Ah," said Vern. "I see what you done."

Squib wasn't concerned so much about saving the dragon's life no more as he had moved on to the next stage of his evening, that being panic, for the gel-like substance which preceded the vomit had already eaten through the T-shirt, leaving nothing but strands of crisped cotton.

"Oh Godawmighty," said Squib as the gel marched on, going to work on his arm hairs, crisping them like a thousand tiny fuses, and then sinking into the pores, raising tiny funnels of smoke from each one. He yelped in pain and slapped at his arm like he could smother dragon flame.

"Urgh," said Vern, then, "Fugg."

The dragon hawked and spat a lump of gel which burned a neat circle in the floor.

"Okay," he said, "you ain't gonna like this, kid, but it's better than losing an arm."

Then Vern dropped his cargo pants, magicked his dragon tackle out of somewhere, and pissed all over Squib's arm.

Mostly his arm.

A HALF HOUR later, dragon and boy were seated on the deck watching the gator eyes pop up and down on the river's surface.

"Like Whac-A-Mole, every goddamn night," said Vern. "Like I'm gonna do something unusual after a hundred years."

"You pissed on a kid," said Squib, "so that's unusual, I guess."

His arm was smooth and a little raw-looking but no worse than the time he'd tried one of Momma's wax strips out of boredom. Sometimes when a guy's momma works nights, he gets into things.

Vern shrugged. "Technically, I marked you. You's lucky I did, kid. Dragon piss got all sorts of properties, including some kind of healing chemical in there. They reckon mogwai are made mostly from that chemical, which accounts for their healing abilities."

Squib wasn't in the mood for a science lesson. From his teenage perspective, getting pissed on was worse than being burned. Having said that, he did mentally add dragon piss to the list of things which might grant him superpowers.

Dragon-Boy. Not bad.

"The way to think of it," continued Vern, "is like it's aloe vera times a million."

Aloe vera did not sound like something an X-Man might have a use for, so Squib went back to being annoyed.

"Aloe vera? Why'ncha write me a book about that and I'll read it when I'm old and can't do nuthin' fun no more."

Which was quite a turnaround in attitude for the Cajun boy so far as Vern was concerned.

"Hey," said the dragon, "watch your mouth, kid. I'm still an apex predator, hear?"

Squib rubbed his arm. "I ain't minding my mouth. You's gonna murder me anyhow."

"How d'you figure?" asked Vern, who was actually considering the opposite, if not murdering was the opposite of murdering.

"I gotta chew on a fresh-dropped scale, don't I? You were set on dumping yourself in the swamp. So I reckon my life don't even figure on your list of priorities."

"That's true," admitted Vern, "but I ain't so set on killing you no more, not since you punched my windpipe from the inside. Even if you only did it for your scale."

"I only thought of that scale this second," muttered Squib, snapping off a dozen crisped hairs from his forearm.

It sounded so like the truth that Vern was visibly taken aback. A dragon being visibly taken aback took the form of his twin eyelids flickering some and his snout wrinkling so the nubs knocked up against each other.

"Bullshit," he said. "That ain't the human way."

Squib screwed his courage to the sticking place, glared at Vern, and said with no little accusation, "You ever think that maybe Waxman was right? Maybe we're all souls?"

"Wax don't know humanity like I do," Vern countered. "That boy is only a few hundred years old. Anyway, the whole scale thing was a crock. Dragon's breath might dumb you down a little, but it won't kill you."

Instead of relief, all Squib felt was more anger. "Goddamn you, Mister Vern! Messing with me left, right, and center! Ever since I bumped into you, I been living on my nerves. Ain't you seen the movies? Meeting a dragon is supposed to be cool."

Squib ran out of steam somewhat at this juncture and reckoned that maybe shouting "Goddamn you" at a dragon was the new number one on his dumb-moves chart.

For his part, Vern took a moment to let the developments of the past few minutes sink in. After all, these were minutes he hadn't been counting on living to see.

"Cool, huh?"

Squib was staring at his forearm like it used to be invisible but now he could see it. "You know the problem with you people?" he asked.

Vern was surprised. "'People'? I got people now?"

"Dragons. Humans. Anyone who's planning on taking their own life."

"No," said Vern, a touch irritated. "Why don't you tell me, kid? After all, you been around for all of ten seconds."

"The problem is, you don't give a shit for the folks that get left behind."

"I don't got nobody left behind," Vern pointed out. "Wax is gone down. And anyways, maybe I've been here long enough. Most people don't believe in me, and those that do want to make me into a nice pair of boots. You ain't got no idea what it's like to not be believed in."

"That's maybe true, Mister Vern," said Squib, "but I do know what it's like to be left behind. I know how it feels to carry it around in your gut like a lump of gristle that won't pass. I seen what it does to a fella's momma. All my momma does is cure folks, but she couldn't cure my daddy 'cause what he had was invisible. Weren't no reason for it but chemicals."

"Your daddy, huh?" said Vern, seeing the light regarding why Squib chose to save his life. A fella didn't have to be a genius.

"Yeah," said Squib. "He bought himself a version of your shit biscuit."

Vern didn't have it in him to sympathize with a human just yet, so he kept his own counsel and listened to the worms popping out of the swamp mud.

Finally, the dragon grinned a little. "So I ain't cool enough for you, boy?"

"I don't know," said Squib. "I can't tell. Too busy crapping my pants, burying my friend in shit, and running vodka downriver."

Vern was surprised to realize that his own black dog

was loping off. The kid's funk was pulling him out of his, and damned if he didn't wanna cheer up the little swamp rat a little. "You brung vodka?"

Squib scowled. "Yeah, I brung an extra quart, just in case. Lucky I did, huh? Now you can get your drunk on and chew on another shit biscuit."

"You brung the mineral water, too?"

"I told you that already, boss, but you was all Tannhäuser Gate and stuff."

Vern dipped his scaled feet in the water and flexed his webbed toes, thinking. "Okay, Squib Moreau. New deal, if you're up for it."

"I'm all the way up for shitcanning the old deal, if that's about the same thing?" said Squib, keeping up the belligerence 'cause it seemed to be working for him.

Vern grunted, which signaled the end of his tether might be approaching regarding Squib's attitude. "Seeing as you saved me, I'm gonna upgrade your contract. One-time offer, mind, and no negotiations. You keep running for me while Wax is under, and I'll pay you one fifty a week plus a performance bonus if I don't have to pull you up over tardiness or the like. Wax looks after the cash, seeing as I got nothing but gold, so we settle up when he claws his way through the patch. You keep tally."

"And you won't kill me?" asked Squib.

"Not unless completely necessary is about as far as I can go with that."

Squib chewed on this. "And if it is completely necessary, then just me," said the boy. "You'll leave Momma out of it."

Vern reckoned he could do that, so they shook: dragon and boy.

Well, holy shit, thought Squib, feeling the dragon's tough, scaly fingers wrap around his so he couldn't even see his own fist no more. *Now here's something I wasn't expecting the summer to bring.*

Which was more or less what Vern was thinking.

After a long contemplative moment, the dragon asked, "Say, boy, you surely know how to make a martini, you working in a bar and all?"

CHAPTER 11

SQUIB HOPPED TO HIS DUTIES A LITTLE SMARTER THE REST OF JULY now that there were wages at stake, and Vern, for his part, showed up most evenings for a chinwag, though on some occasions he still kept himself to himself. Squib relished these little talks with the dragon, as he reckoned he was the only human on God's earth engaging in such conversations and looked forward to the day when he could share his secret with Charles Jr., or maybe even get himself on James Corden, who was one funny *Downton Abbey* cheeky servant-type guy.

Squib pitched up at the shack one evening with an old calendar he'd picked up on eBay the previous week but had never found the right moment to pass over. He wasn't even sure if this was the moment, but Vern spotted the curled edges poking out of the grocery crate. He plucked the calendar out, had a quick peruse, and was appalled.

"What in the name of God's balls is this, son?" he said, flicking through the summer months.

"That? That is a genuine dragon-fetish calendar," said

Squib, squaring six bottles of Absolut away in the refrigerator. "You would not credit the amount of ladies perving on dragons. It's like a fetish or some such. They call themselves Scalies, can you believe it? Goddamn Scalies. Look at them, getting all hot and bothered over some guy dressed up as a dragon."

Vern laughed. "You remember that time recently when I was gonna kill you, boy? I feel that time coming around again."

"Come on, Mister Vern. These are pretty ladies."

Vern settled into his easy chair. "Not to me, kid."

This raised a question for Squib. "How come if human ladies are so ugly you wear those *Flashdance* T-shirts with the picture on 'em?"

Vern winked. "That there is a martini question, boy."

"Everything is a martini question with you, Mister Vern."

But Squib wanted the answer, so he mixed the dragon his cocktail in a peanut butter jar, olives and all, and waited while Vern took his first sip.

"Not bad, kid."

"So, what is it about *Flashdance*? That movie was nothing special."

Vern growled, embers wafting from his nostrils. "You hush your mouth, boy. That was an inspirational movie. The woman goes after her dreams. She gets there in spite of everything." His eyes lit up. "And her main job is welding. She works with fire, get it?" He purred and closed his eyes. "What a feeling."

Squib was skeptical. "That's it? She works with fire? That's your big connection?"

"Well, not entirely," the dragon admitted. "There is that moment when she's on the chair. And the water comes down."

Squib knew that moment. It was still teenage boy top ten, even after all these years. "Yeah, but she's a human—we're ugly, right?"

"That's true, Squib, my boy, but when the sheets of water hit Jennifer Beals in silhouette, if a guy hits pause at the right moment and maybe squints a little, then it almost looks like she's got wings, and maybe a tail. And goddamn if she don't remind me of a Chinese lady dragon I spent some time with up on Mount Sagarmatha. We melted some snow on that peak. Cold as hell, but worth it on that occasion. I could tell you about it, but I better not on account of you being a minor."

Squib helped himself to a Pepsi from the cooler. "I reckon a guy would have to practice a lot with the pause button to get that effect."

"Years," said Vern. "Decades."

HOOKE WAS NOT twiddling his thumbs while all this dragon-boy heart-melting stuff was going down. That was not the Regence Hooke way, especially with a potential murder charge hanging over his noggin like the sword of Damocles. Hooke knew all about the sword of Damocles because his pops liked to reference it whenever the pressure of running a failed storefront ministry was too much for even the bourbon to alleviate.

One time he'd charged into Regence's bedroom in the

early hours, raving like a jonesing tweaker. "You ain't got no idea," he shouted at the bleary teen. "You ain't got no idea the strain doing God's work puts on a body. Even the Lord Jesus Hisself tried to wriggle out from under it. But there ain't no escaping the sword of Damocles, boy. It hangs over me every second of every day. And the instant I weaken, down she comes."

Hooke checked out this famous sword and found that it wasn't even mentioned in the Bible. Some Greek guy invented the whole thing to make a point.

Spider-Man's Uncle Ben said it better: With great power comes great responsibility.

And more serious consequences too, I guess, the young Regence thought.

Still it gave him a notion, and one night while his poppa had his drunk on, Regence suspended his hunting knife from the ceiling fan over the passed-out pastor's bed, using a string of Plasti-Tak rolled real fine.

The knife hung there glittering with each revolution, but it didn't fall until Reverend Jerrold rose to take himself a piss. His pops never noticed a thing. He never heard the thunk. Never saw the boy sitting cross-legged in the rocking chair.

Balls, thought teen Hooke, retrieving his knife. *I guess Poppa lives to preach another day.*

Now Hooke felt that metaphorical sword over his own head. Maybe "sword" was too strong an image. Maybe "mosquito" was better. Squib was an irritant, nothing more. Something to be dealt with. Hooke was confident that if he stayed on his path, solutions would keep presenting themselves as they always had, until they didn't. That was how life worked and there wasn't no point fretting on it. A fella fixed his eyes on the prize and kept going until some greater power decided enough was enough and called a halt.

So do you believe in God or not, Regence? Hooke often asked himself.

And the answer to that question varied, depending on his mood. Often it boiled down to something along the lines of: *I believe in God enough to hate Him.*

A conclusion which made Hooke smile.

BUT SQUIB. SQUIB Moreau was behaving just like that one mosquito that proved impossible to catch. Most skeeters hovered around, legs dangling, just waiting for the rolled-up magazine that would flatten them. But there was the occasional insect that seemed possessed of more smarts than the rest of his species.

What was the word for those guys?

"Pesky."

Squib was proving pesky.

Of course, Hooke could simply wait on the dock and lift Squib straight out of his precious pirogue any day he felt like it, but there was more in play now. Squib was working for Waxman. Maybe that deformed old coot knew more than he should. Maybe Squib Moreau had confided in him, or in his other boss, Bodi. Maybe Squib had whispered tales of crooked constables to his mother, or his pal Charles Jr.

Goddamn ripple effect, thought Hooke, and laid his plans.

Which were as follows: take a few days' personal time, just as his doctor had suggested, and dedicate himself to tailing Squib Moreau, military-style.

Hooke was pissed off that he was being forced to exert himself to tie off a loose end, but better safe than sorry.

Also, he was pissed that he was taking sick leave when he had planned to fake an illness later in the year to attend a dark web sniper camp in the Ozarks.

Squib's gonna lose a lot more than a finger this time around.

THERE WASN'T NO need to go full military, not really, but truth be told, Hooke enjoyed tinkering with the tools of his trade, and he didn't get too much opportunity in Petit Bateau. Occasionally he would stake out a moonshine operation or a pot farm, but that was state police business, and Hooke didn't want to draw any attention by playing hero local cop, so he generally just kept watch to see if there was anything in it for him. The previous year he had been so bored that he started blowing up meth labs. The plague was creeping into Petit Bateau and drawing in the sheriff's office, which was hampering his own operations, and so Hooke decided the best thing would be to help those crystal chefs carbonize themselves. Simplest thing in the world to put an incendiary round into a gas tank and let the phosphorus do the rest. Hooke retired three industrious swamp factories in half a year, and then called it a day before some eagle-eyed deputy smelled something off. Turned out he'd done enough and the crystal meth addiction flowed back downriver to New Orleans like a saltwater tide.

When Hooke thought about that campaign, it was so unlikely that he sometimes wondered if he'd dreamed it.

Fun dream.

So truth be told, Hooke was content enough to take his kit from behind a panel in the boat shed and let loose his soldier sense. And if the opportunity arose to feed Squib to the gators, so be it, just so long as nothing could be traced back to him. It would be a cosmic joke to get out from under one murder rap just to land right under another one.

Softly softly catchy monkey.

You said it, Colonel.

The first night was strictly remote recon, but what he observed was enough to convince Constable Hooke that he was definitely on the right track. He set himself up nice and comfy on the flat roof of his boat shed and trained his night-vision monocular on the Moreau dock.

Let's go, Squib, he thought. *Ain't you got a job to go to?*

And Squib did.

Soon as his momma set out for the bus stop, Squib was pottering around on the decking, loading cargo into his boat. Looked like regular groceries. Hooke could see the little bastard clear as day through his scope.

Look at that eager beaver, he thought, *all happy in his labors.*

Hooke felt a millisecond of jealousy. What must it be like to be happy for a few minutes every day?

Nah, he thought, *fuck that. Happiness ain't no kind of motivator.*

But Squib did look happy, dancing around to some tune

in his head. And Hooke was offended by this and contemplated shooting the kid there and then, but the revenant of Faraiji stayed his hand.

Patience, Sergeant. We must gather intelligence, not destroy it.

And so Hooke left his rifle in its bag and kept watching, chewing a Cuban and looking forward to sparking her up. But not yet.

Down on the Pearl, Squib cast off and started his engine right there in the cut-back. Nice watercraft, Hooke had to admit, and it occurred to him that should Squib prove sufficiently bent, he would be an ideal replacement for Willard Carnahan, being a swamp guy through and through. But Hooke quickly dismissed the notion. He was done with swamp guys. They were unpredictable and slaves to their appetites, not to be trusted. Hooke was aware enough to realize that he himself was inherently untrustworthy, but he preferred his own subordinates to be loyal.

If that ain't irony, it'll do until something better comes along.

Hooke bit a chunk from the end of his cigar and sucked on it like chewing tobacco. He was warm, and that didn't feel right to him.

Seems like if a soldier is on night surveillance, then the desert chill oughta be keeping that soldier frosty.

Except this wasn't Iraq and he wasn't a soldier no more.

Below him on the water, Squib did not navigate cross-river, as expected; instead he stuck close to the Pearl's fringe of reeds and set his course downriver.

Downriver, thought Hooke. *Toward Honey Island. Where*

that grenade somehow reversed its own trajectory. Where someone bore witness to me gutting Carnahan.

This was an interesting development, and a positive one. Could it be coincidence, or could it be that Hooke had struck gold on the first try?

Is Squib my guy?

It sure would be good to plug that leak.

And there might be a most welcome side effect. In Hooke's experience, grieving parents dropped their defenses way on down. A heartbroken mother might do just about anything for some strong arms to comfort her.

Hell, I could even pin Squib's murder on some fall guy and present myself as a white knight.

Regence had enough self-awareness to realize that offing a kid and dating that kid's mother was about as coldhearted as a guy could get, but it didn't bother him none. In point of fact, he was kinda proud that he hadn't yet arrived at the limit of his callousness.

I guess the colonel was right and I'm one of them sociopaths, thought Hooke. *Like Spock.*

He had taken an online magazine test once, to find out just how sociopathic he was, and was delighted to score in the top five percent, right up there with the big-business boys.

Hooke had lost points because unlike most sociopaths, he did actually have a very focused life plan and he learned from experience.

I'm a sociopath who thinks ahead, thought Hooke, smugly. *King of the crazies.*

When Squib's canoe meandered around a bend in the

river, Hooke lit his cigar and enjoyed a quiet smoke, thinking how pleasant it was being up here, watching the world, visualizing his focused life plan rolling out.

Squib. Ivory. Metal pipeline.

It occurred to Hooke that the most valuable blocks in Conti's infrastructure were the pet law enforcement officers.

Shit, we don't need nobody but ourselves. All those gangster types are more trouble than they're worth.

What he needed to do was lay waste to Ivory's hub of operations and then reach out to the police on his payroll.

Those cops will already be hooked on blood money. Shouldn't be none too hard to tempt them over to Team Regence.

HOOKE WAS ON his third cigar and was feeling the raspy effects in his throat when the monocular picked up Squib, maybe ninety minutes later, tacking cross-river toward Waxman's place.

I love this night vision shit, thought the constable. *There ain't no place to hide.*

Even at a distance of maybe a thousand yards, Hooke was able to count the fingers on Squib's left hand, which was wrapped around the tiller.

Four digits. All present and correct.

And the constable smiled to himself remembering the night of Squib's misfortune.

Dynamiting catfish. That boy sure has his dumb spells.

The pirogue was riding a little higher in the water, so Hooke reckoned whatever cargo he'd ferried downriver had been delivered. There was a small sealed drum in the prow which hadn't been there before, so the boy had obviously picked it up wherever he'd stopped over.

What's in there? Radioactive waste?

Probably nothing much. Bait or salt. Probably Squib was just checking his traps and dropping off a few groceries for some swamp bachelor. Probably.

Still, probably wasn't definitely, so best to keep a lookout.

Could Squib be running some kind of operation? Was Waxman dealing in contraband, if anybody even used that word anymore? These were all questions that needed to be answered.

This is my water, Hooke thought. *I am Regence, king of the Pearl River, and no one runs shit through here without my say-so.*

Even thinking like this made Hooke grin. He had options now. He could take out Carnahan's inflatable and motor across to Waxman's boathouse, have a little word with them both.

Or.

Or he could follow some more, increase his stock of information. After all, it was a lot easier to surveil a subject if a person had an educated idea as to where that subject was going.

Hooke set up farther downriver for the second stakeout. This time he went full bush and spent the day weaving some cover into his old sniper veil.

Shit, he thought, all nostalgic. *How long has it been?*

Truth be told, the veil probably wasn't necessary, but

Hooke enjoyed the feel of the netting in his hands, and if he was honest with himself, the camo cloak made him feel powerful, gave him a little edge. It had always pleased him to deliver death remotely because he imagined his targets' last thought to be, *What the fuck?*

If all the guff his pops had spouted was true, then the victim's soul would be levitating toward the heavens still looking around for who the hell had shot him, and Hooke would be there all invisible in the brush. Sometimes, if the op zone was completely clear, then Hooke would flip the bird skywards just to add insult to mortal injury.

Hooke wasn't actually a scout sniper by trade or rank, but he'd taken it up for some freelance work in-country, mostly for Faraiji. He wasn't the worst from five hundred feet, but after that his vision let him down some. Slight presbyopia, the eye doctor told him. Apparently he had trouble bringing things into focus.

Like the future, thought Hooke. *But I'm working on it.*

Hooke took one of Bodi Irwin's rental skiffs out on the river. The craft was built with a draft so shallow it could float in a bathtub, and an aluminum hull so light any idiot tourist could drag it off a sandbar. He left the boatyard late afternoon, looking for all the world like a recuperating cop taking advantage of a mild day to dip a line in the Pearl.

I got all the trappings, don't I? thought Hooke, one hand on his tackle box, which was filled not with lures and spinners but with batteries, bullets, and grenades from Carnahan's stash.

Hooke could not be completely sure where Squib had been for that hour and a half the previous night, but his best guess put the boy somewhere near Honey Island, where all the shit he was concerned with had gone down.

Where I lost the Elodie *and all my gear,* Hooke thought, taking a minute to mourn his cruiser and all the wonderful ordnance that had gone down with her.

Hooke took his sweet time motoring downriver, waving at passing pleasure craft and shrimp boats, the brim of his fishing cap pulled low over his eyes, trying to make himself look ordinary.

I ain't here, he broadcast to the universe, and the universe seemed okay with that, because once he cleared the Petit Bateau southern meander, traffic thinned out, and soon Hooke found himself alone on the river so far as humans were concerned.

It was tough for a guy not to enjoy himself out there on the Pearl. Fish were swimming so thick they butted the keel on occasion, and the weather was that rarest of Louisiana sorts where the sun was penned behind a stubborn haze and the humidity was having a little mercy on the folks below and easing up for once. Hooke found that he could mouth-breathe deep as he liked without the usual lung constriction.

So it was tough for a guy not to enjoy himself, but Hooke persevered.

Again it occurred to him that maybe a man could be happy, but the notion didn't hold much weight.

Happy? What's the damned point in that?

His poppa had never been happy, no matter how high he'd clambered on Jacob's ladder.

In his youth, Hooke believed that he himself experienced happiness as an emotion per se whenever he put an enemy down, but now he reckoned that was more of a triumphant rage, an *I'm still here, motherfucker* kind of thing.

Close enough, thought Hooke. *And I'll still be here long after that bug Squib Moreau is crushed.*

So he lit a cigar to chase the mosquitoes away and settled back into his usual grim funk.

SQUIB MOTORED ALONG the same stretch of river some hours later, his pirogue evenly weighed down with the day's groceries, which included:

A new card for Vern's satellite box so the dragon could watch the pay-per-view fights.

One carton of Krispy Kremes, which were definitely not ketogenic.

And:

A gallon of fungus ointment, which Vern did not want to discuss.

Squib WhatsApp'd Vern to let him know he was on the way and then relaxed on the wooden slat seat he had built into his craft, having a little fun with the throttle, weaving in and out of a cypress and tupelo wetland slalom course.

Ain't life awful curious? he thought. *One minute there's a dragon on my ass with murder on his mind, and the next thing I know I'm on the payroll.*

Squib was squarely in the sweet zone age-wise when it

came to accepting such a frankly astonishing turn of events, information which would surely have driven most adult types to distraction. Not only had dragons ruled the world, but there was one left and he, Everett "Squib" Moreau the Third, worked for him.

Actually, there weren't no Everett Moreaus the First or Second, but it sounded cool, so Squib sometimes tacked it on in his mind. He'd made the mistake of mentioning it to Charles Jr. one time, and for maybe a month his friend had referred to him as Everett Squib Moreau the Turd, which wore thin real quick.

Squib popped in his earbuds while he steered. No doubt Vern would make him listen to that ancient jazz stuff he liked, which sounded almost as old as the dragon himself, so he stuck on some Green Day, who were favored by his number one boss, Bodi Irwin, and Squib did have to admit that those boys knew how to shred a guitar.

Ten minutes later Squib skirted Honey Island and nudged up into Vern's switchback just as the sun tucked itself into the treetops. If a guy didn't know the old dock was there, then he would never find it behind its curtain of moss and bamboo and a slop of lily pads on the water looking like they hadn't been disturbed in a thousand years. But Squib had memorized a bunch of markers for himself, and he knew by the five fingers of cypress root poking through the scum and the brown horizontal slashes on a water oak trunk that he was where he needed to be, and so gave his engine one last rev before cutting the power altogether and drifting the last ten feet, steering with the dead prop.

Squib considered today's questions for Vern as he unloaded the pirogue:

Have you ever fought a bigfoot?

Did you ever meet Dracula?

And the big one:

What's that trick you do with your dragon junk, making it disappear like that?

On further reflection, Squib figured he might lead off with the dragon-junk question, as Vern often ran out of tolerance for interrogations real quick. Or maybe he'd soften Vern up with the bigfoot softball and put the junk question second.

Once settled on this course of action, he decided that he should maybe take a sniff of the fungal ointment, see if he couldn't get a handle on where Vern might be intending to slather it, seeing as the dragon probably didn't suffer from no human-type ailments.

Lotta crevices, though, thought the boy. *And he does live in a swamp.*

Squib had the top half screwed off the ointment container when he heard a snuffling, which cut through the fading final chord of "Basket Case" in his earbuds. He looked up guiltily, reckoning that maybe Vern had caught him red-handed interfering with his medicine.

But it wasn't Vern. It was a red-eyed boar the size of a small cow. The bristles quivered on its back.

"Easy, boy," said Squib like he was talking to a dog. "Easy now."

Unfortunately, the boar didn't speak canine and charged like it'd been shot out of a cannon.

Fuck, thought Squib. *Spared by a dragon and done in by a boar. This is some bullshit.*

VERN WAS IN his favorite subaqua cradle while all these boar-centric shenanigans were about to unfold on his dock. The cradle was a natural hammock of tangleweed and soft shale which had bedded itself into a mud bank. Not only was it slowing down the erosion process, but the little niche provided a nice heat trap for a fella who might like to eke the last red rays outta the Louisiana sun, and there was a tiny icicle of salt water that somehow snaked up this far, which kept a dragon cool, and so Vern was reluctant to climb out even though the kid was already on the dock. He could see this because he had elevated the top end of his cradle with a turtle-shell pillow which fit neatly into the crook of his neck, so he could open his nostrils when he needed a breath and see pretty clear through the few inches of water.

There be Squib, he thought, sucking out a heelsplitter mussel. *I wonder did he get that ointment?*

Vern cleaned out the mussel, then crunched on the shell, which had the double advantage of scraping his teeth and toughening the gums: his version of a visit to the dental hygienist.

Ten more minutes, thought Vern. *Then I'll go over there and educate the boy about jazz.*

Ten more minutes, just enough time for one more breath.

Vern opened his nostrils and breathed in. A scent crept in with the air: a familiar scent, if a mite stronger than usual.

Boar, thought Vern.

But not just any boar. This particular guy was the pig master on Boar Island, and he would have been top dog entirely had it not been for Vern. The boar had made a couple of snuffling forays over Vern's border, and Vern had sent him scurrying off with a shot of flame to his hindquarters the last time he came around, burning his hide good.

It was stupid toying with the boar, really, because wild animals as a rule didn't tend to learn their lessons. Hell, not even the gators had learned to stay clear of his patch, and he'd been throwing them around for years/decades.

I should have barbecued that fella because now he's making a move on my boy Squib.

When he raised his head, he spotted the animal, and even from this distance Vern could read the boar's body language. The big pig was quivering like he was plugged into an outlet.

If that boar's head goes down, thought Vern, *then the fat lady has sung.*

The boar's head went down.

Goddamn, thought Vern, and made his move.

Vern managed to flap his wings underwater just once, which is a bastard of a maneuver to accomplish considering the resistance, but it was enough to lift him clear of the surface, sending water sluicing through the grooves in his plates, which had evolved for exactly that purpose. Once airborne, he threw his hindquarters backwards, which jerked his head upright, and from that position, maybe six feet out of the water and from a range of fifty yards, he squinted for clarity, hawked, and spat a single blob of dragon flame, which was reflected in the Pearl as it covered the distance between dragon and boar in less than a second, catching the boar in midleap and pinning him to the trunk of a water oak, where the poor animal crapped himself and squealed like the hog he was until the dragon flame burned through to his heart and shut him up for good.

By the balls of Blue Ben, thought Vern, which had been quite the saying back in the day. *It's a pity Squib had his back turned to that move.*

Because, goddamn, it must have looked awesome.

HOOKE WOULD CERTAINLY not dispute that the display was awesome in the true sense of the word—not awesome like good pizza or doing some sort of flip with a skateboard on YouTube. But awesome as in *very close to incredible.*

He'd scouted the area and decided to set himself up in a horseshoe wetland that would most probably be an oxbow in five years and an island in twenty. There was the usual huddle of ancient trees on the central hump clustered together, fighting for root space, and every spare inch of mud was populated by bamboo. Hooke was able to wade ashore and wedge his skiff between two trunks under a quilt of moss until it was invisible to the untrained eye and damn near invisible to the trained eye.

Hooke admired his work and was satisfied. "Hey, Pop," said Hooke to the heavens, "I am gazing upon my work, and damn, it is good."

Which made him smile.

He went a little craft-crazy then, hacking out a nice hide for himself maybe eight feet up where two cypress trunks were twisted like lovers. He enjoyed that kind of work; it cleared out his head for a while. When a fella was swinging through hardwood with a short-handled field axe, there weren't space for nothing but the blade and the timber, unless that fella didn't mind sacrificing a finger or two.

The job took longer than it should have because Hooke was forced to suspend his labors whenever a boat came around the bend.

Shrimp boats. Pleasure cruisers. Swamp skiffs. Pirogues. Hooke had never realized there was so much traffic on the river. But at least the breaks meant he kept himself hydrated, which was important at his age.

Hell, Regence, he thought, *you're sneaking up on fifty, boy. Who'd've thought you'd last this long?*

Nobody, most especially not Regence himself.

Shit, the grim reaper must have had me in his sights a dozen times or more.

Eventually, once Hooke had the hide set up to his satisfaction, he climbed on in there and wiggled himself comfortable, with the camouflage veil draped over his head and shoulders.

Okay, Regence, he thought, *nothing for it now but to wait.*

And wait he did, for several hours, staring through the sights mounted on his old Browning rifle, watching with some satisfaction as Squib came downriver in his dinky canoe, doing some dipshit maneuvers in the tree line. It was light enough that Hooke didn't bother changing over to Starlight.

He watched the kid tie up at a concealed dock and begin unloading his cargo. Then a boar showed up and Hooke thought, *Shit, maybe nature's gonna solve my problem.*

But nature never got the chance because the boar's ticket got punched in a most unlikely way.

HOOKE HAD BEEN on stakeout for hours at this point and had transitioned into that sniper fugue that made the world seem somehow illusory. Veteran shooters often spoke of how pulling the trigger on a target didn't seem real after hours spent looking through a scope.

Which was why, when a large creature erupted from the water maybe fifty feet downriver, Hooke didn't fall out of the tree with shock. His first thought was, *You murdered your daddy in a church during a hurricane. It was only a matter of time before you started seeing demons.*

But he quickly realized this wasn't no hallucination. That thing was real as the water it came out of and the sky it flew into.

Goddamn Honey Island monster, thought Hooke. *It exists.*

He kept stock-still, as he had no idea as to the potential of this creature, but he guessed that a winged bear-sized animal with tusks like a walrus could probably inflict a lot of damage.

He ain't pointed my way, he thought. *Let's just see how this goes.*

He imagined that it would go something along the lines of:

Boar craps itself.

Boar runs away.

Monster eats boy.

But he was wrong on two out of three of those points.

The boar did indeed crap itself—but only after the monster nailed it with a ball of flame which it shot out of its mouth, looked like.

A ball of honest-to-God, I-shit-thee-not *flame.* Dragon-style.

Nice, thought Hooke; then, *Is that what I'm dealing with here? A dragon?*

A part of him was pleased that he was continuing his keeping-it-together-while-shit-went-crazy streak going.

I am not bothered by extremes.

Not extreme religious fanatics of any kind.

Nor, now, by extreme animals.

Though Hooke did notice his hand was shaking slightly.

Hell, most guys would have vibrated right out of this tree, thought Hooke. *A shaking hand just means I ain't stupid.*

The surreal sequence of events went right on unfolding, oblivious to Hooke's bearing witness. The dragon, if that's what it was, glided across to the hidden landing, and not only did it not attack Squib, but it seemed to know him.

It looked like they were . . .

Could those two assholes be . . . ?

Actually *conversing?* In actual *language?*

The light was fading now, so Hooke hurriedly reached

into his pack for his monocular and switched on the night vision.

And there they were, plain as green day: kid and dragon, chewing the fat.

This is unexpected, thought Hooke, sharpening his focus and thinking absently that he must trade this monocular in for a newer model with autofocus.

But old gadget or not, it was working well enough for Hooke to see the dragon dismember the boar with a few casual slashes of its claws and then chew on a charred leg right out there in the open.

That motherfucker is dangerous, thought Hooke, and then: *More than dangerous, he's like the wrath of God.*

The wrath of God: exactly what Hooke had been searching for.

"Thank you, universe," said Hooke under his breath, and made a mental list of what he needed to do:

Take more time off.

Step up the surveillance to include audio and video.

Get hold of some heavy-caliber weapons.

CHAPTER 12

SQUIB WAS PRETTY SHAKEN UP AFTER THE BOAR EPISODE. HE reckoned that Vern should quit riling up the wildlife.

"Maybe you shouldn't oughta go around antagonizing vicious predators?" Squib had argued. "First the gators, now the boars."

Vern had an answer for that, too. "Yeah, says the goddamn human. Don't talk to me about vicious predators. How many species have you humans wiped out? Including my own, almost."

Which was a fair point, so Squib calmed himself down and had himself a slice of charred boar haunch, which he had to admit was delicious, especially as Vern allowed him a beer to go with it.

"Don't tell your momma," Vern warned him. "We don't want Elodie taking against your employer."

"Don't worry, boss," said Squib in between mouthfuls. "I reckon keeping secrets is second nature."

"Good to know," Vern said, rooting out some freezer

bags and starting in on butchering the hog with his claws. "It certainly is a requirement of the job."

After maybe ten minutes he said, "Shit, this old boy is cooked through. I can't save none of this meat. You wanna take some home to your momma?"

"I sure do," said Squib. "We don't get this quality of free-range stuff too often. I'll tell her Mister Waxman sent it as a gift."

If Squib had to name his favorite thing in the world, if he was straight about it and let his heart show, he would have to say his favorite thing was the look on his momma's face when he did something good, right out of the blue. The way her face lit up like a lamp. The way her smile seemed like she'd had clean forgotten about the rest of the world and all the troubles it held. Squib knew pulling into the jetty with this meat would earn him one of those smiles.

Vern heated up one talon and expertly carved a dozen steaks. "These'll be good for a couple of days. Have someone over."

"I know who'd like to come over," said Squib, his mood souring. "That murdering asshole Constable Hooke."

And then the enormity of what had almost happened hit Squib like a punch in the gut and he puked all over his own shoes.

Vern patted his back. "Yup," he said, "there it is. Sometimes the shock gets too much. I was wondering when you'd reach your limit."

CHAPTER 13

SQUIB HAD ANOTHER SHOCK WAITING FOR HIM WHEN HE LUGGED the cooler of meat in the back door at three A.M. Hooke was waiting in the Moreau shack, relaxing in the armchair like he owned the place. This turn of events set Squib's heart beating so hard that it felt like his entire body must be blushing.

"What you got there, Squib?" asked the constable, sitting forward like he actually gave a crap.

"Boar steaks," said Squib, happy to have an easy question to answer because he certainly wasn't up to a complex debate. "Mister Waxman's been hunting."

"Uh-huh," said Hooke. "I hope that old coot's got a license. Otherwise I might have to pay a house call."

Squib humped the bag to the refrigerator and began loading up.

Just talk like you talk, he told himself. *Keep on keeping on, same old same old.*

"He sure does, Constable Hooke, sir. I seen it. He's

forever flashing it. Like 'Waxman, FBI,' 'ceptin' it's a hunting license. A joke, see?"

Hooke laughed. "FBI? Shit. That Waxman is a funny fella. He was probably around when they established the FBI, old as he is."

Squib hid behind the refrigerator door for a second, wondering what the hell was going on and how the hell he could get out of it.

Hooke whistled. "Say, boy, come on out of there. I need a word."

Squib swallowed hard a few times, then poked his head out. "Just saying, Constable. But I'm a minor, you know. And my parent ain't here."

Hooke wasn't in the least put out by Squib's legal points. "Hell, son, we can wait for your momma if you prefer. Shoot, the only reason I dropped in at this god-awful hour is to spare Elodie a little drama. She's got enough going on with her minimum-wage job and that man of hers digging a debt hole all those years. Not to mention all the family tragedy you all have got going on."

These facts hit Squib like a *one-two* combination. It sickened him to know that a man like Hooke had so much information on the Moreau family.

"But you can't just come in here."

Hooke stood as though about to leave. "That is true, son, but the door was wide-open, and in the spirit of small-town friendship I strolled on in. All I want to do is rule you out of my investigations because your momma assures me, *assures me* no less, that you have seen the light, so to speak.

And maybe she didn't mention, but you was supposed to call me."

Squib nodded slowly while his mind raced. His momma had mentioned the whole dynamiting thing, but of course Hooke knew full well that the swamp explosions had come from his own grenades.

He's fishing, thought the boy. *He's trying to find out if maybe I was the kid in the reeds.*

"Momma did say," said Squib. "About the dynamiting, right? I done learned my lesson there, Constable. A fella's only got so many fingers." And he did his nub-wiggling trick to make the point.

Hooke pulled some kind of grimace that maybe was intended to be a smile. "I believe you, boy. I do. You ain't top of my list anyways. But I got to eliminate you nonetheless. So I'm gonna need your phone."

Squib was puzzled. "My phone? How come you need my phone?"

"I got to take a swab," said Hooke. "Like they do in the airport. Check for explosives. See, guys often wash their hands to get rid of trace evidence, but people don't wash their phones. So usually there's transfer."

"Do I got to give you my phone?"

"Absolutely not," said Hooke. "It's like a voluntary thing. Otherwise, though, I need to make it formal and take you in. This way we're one and done in half a minute."

Squib considered this. It should be safe enough. After all, he hadn't been near explosives in years, far as he knew. Except the ones Hooke had lobbed at him.

"I guess it's all right," he said, and handed over his smartphone.

"Password?" asked Hooke.

"You need that, too?"

"Affirmative. I wanna check your recent videos. You'd be amazed how many dumb kids video themselves doing illegal shit."

Again, Squib had to think, and it was like his thoughts were edged with fever. His phone was clean: Vern had warned him against pictures and videos. All message threads were instantly deleted. It was a deal-breaker if he couldn't manage his phone, the dragon had said.

"'FOOTLONG,'" said Squib. "All caps."

Hooke laughed. "In honor of Charles Jr.'s snake, right?"

"Yeah," said Squib. "Seems kinda stupid now."

"Not at all," said Hooke, dropping a wink. "Big reptiles need to be celebrated."

Squib did not like this wink one little bit. A wink like that had all kinds of connotations. Maybe Hooke had some inkling about the secret swamp dwellers, or maybe he was just tossing out some bait.

Either way, Squib knew he couldn't afford to overreact, so he just smiled a bit, like Hooke's remark was somewhere about a five out of ten on the funny scale and said, "I guess they do. Someday Charles Jr.'s reptile is gonna be famous."

"Yep," said Hooke. "Famous, or shot to pieces."

"Shot to pieces?" blurted Squib, before he could button his lip.

Hooke gave him the wink again, and it was downright

creepy. "You know, by a jealous husband or the like. People hear about a lizard like that and they go looking."

And the constable turned and walked out the front door.

HOOKE SAT INTO the Chevy and made a big show of swabbing the phone screen in case Squib was peeking, but the swab was just an ordinary wipe, and there wasn't no spectrometer in his car in any case, as if the parish would spring for something that expensive.

What he'd said about checking Squib's videos had been true, though, which was indeed why he'd needed the password, but a cursory check revealed nothing but the usual bullshit teenage videos and a quick swipe through the recently deleted file revealed even more teenage bullshit, with date stamps all around the night of Carnahan's murder but nothing from that night. Which didn't prove or disprove anything other than Squib was smart enough to move any evidence against Hooke off his phone. Either way, the boy would probably have gone to the authorities by now if he had anything.

So either Squib was not the guy, or he was too scared to talk.

A week earlier, Hooke would have arranged an accident for Squib, just to be on the safe side, but that was PDS— pre-dragon-sighting. It was a different ball game now.

A ball of fire.

Step two in Hooke's phone plan was a little more technical. He popped the boy's SIM card into a mini USB cloner and quickly copied it over onto his own phone. Now any text the boy sent would show up on his screen, and he could force-activate Squib's microphone whenever the phone was powered up.

Operation Dragon Watch is a go, thought Hooke and went back inside.

SQUIB WATCHED THE constable dick around in the cab of his truck.

No way that asshole has an explosives-swab machine in there, he thought, although he couldn't be entirely sure, not when Hooke appeared to have access to a lot more equipment than your regular constable. It wouldn't have surprised him if Regence Hooke could call in a SEAL team to blow up the entire shack.

But judging by the constable's face when he came back inside, all was well. Though a fella could never be sure with Hooke's face, seeing as it didn't arrange itself like normal faces.

"Looks like you're off the hook," he said. "No trace of explosives."

"I'm keeping my nose clean, Constable, sir," said Squib, accepting the phone. "Ain't no future for me in being bent. Momma is set on me earning an honest living."

"So I hear," said Hooke. "You listen to your momma, son." Hooke did a fake jab. "And put in a word for me."

"Sure thing, Constable," said Squib, thinking, *In your dreams, shiibird*.

But Squib was relieved to be in the clear for now. Hooke had no evidence that he was the boy in the bayou.

I can get on with earning an honest buck. Ain't nothing illegal about fetching groceries for a dragon.

"I guess I'll be heading out," said Hooke, tipping his cap. "You play your cards right and you won't see me again, professionally at least."

"Don't worry, Constable," said Squib. "Straight as an arrow, that's Squib Moreau."

SQUIB WAS PRETTY certain that Hooke was full of shit in regards to him being in the clear, but as July rolled itself through to August and the temperature nudged up a couple of degrees, the boy had plenty on his plate to occupy him other than worrying about Constable Regence Hooke. And glory be, the constable appeared to have given up his pursuit of his momma—in fact, Squib barely caught sight of the man other than occasionally spotting his silhouette fussing over paperwork in his office beside the car dealership.

Elodie even mentioned this development to Squib one morning when they were passing each other at the screen door. Squib's momma was tuckered out and disheveled as per usual following her shift, but she always had energy for a smile and a hug. Squib thought that maybe her smile was a little brighter this morning.

"You feeling good, Momma?" he asked her.

"Matter of fact, I am," Elodie said. "No one died at the clinic. We didn't have a single fool drunk showing up with blood on his shirt. I got paid, so lunch is on me if you can slow down long enough. And . . ."

Squib felt that maybe the "And" might be the real reason for his momma's smile.

"And what, Momma?" he asked.

Elodie waited a moment, like she was weighing up how much Squib needed to know.

"What the hell," she said. "You're a working man, right?"

"That's right," said Squib, and then, since he was a working man, he said, "Damn right."

Elodie tousled his hair so it looked more like her own. "*Damn* right? Okay, big man. I guess you can hear this then."

"I guess I can," said Squib, mirroring his mother's smile.

"It's Constable Hooke," she said, and for one horrible gut-punched moment Squib thought his mother was about to announce her engagement, even though that made not one lick of sense.

Elodie put him out of his misery. "I think maybe Regence ain't as sweet on me as he was," she said. "I've seen him when he was weak as a kitten. A lot of men can't abide that."

Squib was beyond delighted. "You think he's really cooled off? All it took was you nursing him some?"

Elodie crossed her fingers. "Sure looks like it. He drove right past me yesterday without so much as a tip of his hat." Elodie hugged him tight again and felt his ribs. "You're so skinny, son. You want some grits? I think we have bacon."

But Squib was already gone. "Ain't got time, Momma. I got business to take care of."

Elodie called after him, "You take care of business, my big man. Then get back here for dinner. We're celebrating."

Squib threw his hands in the air. "Woohoo!" he crowed. "No more Hooke—goddamn!"

SQUIB TOOK TO thinking in those seconds between his diverse employments. *Maybe things are looking up.*

Mind, those thinking moments were few and far between. The outlying wisps of a tornado lifted a section of roof off the Pearl Bar and Grill, so Bodi Irwin defied the parish's health and safety guidelines and had every able-bodied teen up on the roof nailing down tiles, which gave Squib a chance to catch up with Charles Jr., which was nice for the boys, and his friend solemnly swore to him that he had given up on the man-whoring and was keeping his pecker behind bars from now on.

I work for a dragon, Squib wanted to say, but he kept this information to himself.

Keep the circle small.

Without a doubt the favorite hours in Squib's jam-packed schedule were those he spent in Vern's company. He never tired of staring at the dragon's person, trying to memorize every scale and armored plate, seeing as photographs were absolutely forbidden. This scrutinizing pissed the dragon off a little, but he tolerated it so long as Squib kept the vodka martinis coming.

Squib learned pretty quick to avoid the subject of Waxman after he'd motored into Boar Island one evening with a mouthful of questions along the lines of:

So what is Mister Waxman anyway?

Is Wax actually a male guy? I didn't notice no dick, what with the pizza.

Which made Vern like to choke with surprise. And Squib had more questions in the pipe:

This whole dragon-shit thing ain't just another joke? Only I'd hate to be humping barrels of dung upriver every night only for you two to be laughing your asses off next fall.

Vern eventually made a new rule. "We ain't talking about Wax, okay? I miss the guy enough already without your fool mouth yammering on about him. Let's just say he's on vacation and leave it at that. We clear, kid?"

Squib saluted. "Clear, boss."

"Good," said Vern. "I ain't much for prolonged conversation. Maybe half a dozen sentences per evening is fine by me."

"Don't worry, boss. You leave the talking to me."

"That ain't what I was driving at," said Vern, treating himself to a rare beer. "Didn't your poppa ever tell you that young 'uns should be seen but not heard?"

Squib packed away the evening's groceries quietly for a shelf or two, but pretty soon the boy found himself talking. "My daddies never taught me much. Neither one. The first guy, my real daddy that is, he was mostly in the back room, far as I remember. Had himself a headache every damn day. He showed me some ABC's one time. The second guy was an asshole and all he taught me was how to dodge a punch, and that's all I want to say about him. I imagine he's dead or doing time—either is fine by me."

"Shit, son," said Vern. "You had it worse than me."

Squib snickered at the idea that he had it worse than

the last dragon and finished off squaring away the groceries, which included a charcoal exfoliator Vern favored and a drum of palm oil to fuel Vern's own fire. As he folded the bags for recycling, Squib flashed on a little Internet research he'd been doing. "So, I looked up 'Wyvern' on Google and—"

Vern growled, and sparks danced behind his teeth. "Kid, don't bring that up. You done earned a few sympathy points. Don't squander 'em."

But Squib was a teenager, and therefore curiosity trumped caution. "And the Internet said wyverns were like this runty version of a dragon. I wrote it down." Squib swiped his phone till he found a note. "According to Wikipedia, 'Wyverns tend to be smaller, weaker, not as intelligent and ultimately inferior to the much more ferocious and powerful dragon.'" Squib closed the screen. "'Ultimately inferior.' Fucking ouch, right, boss?"

Vern lost his shit at warp speed. He let loose a roar that sounded like there was a lion tussling with a gorilla inside his belly, and stamped a webbed foot right through the shack's floorboards, and it was only when they'd splintered and he'd punched clear down to the swamp below that Vern stopped stomping. But he wasn't done fuming; he was simply on to the next stage, which turned out to be berating someone who wasn't there.

"'Ultimately inferior'? Who's 'inferior' now, Jubelus? Who's still standing?"

Squib didn't know who this Jubelus character was, but Vern clearly wasn't a fan, that much was clear.

"Who has man hands now, Jube? Not Lord Highfire, that's for damn sure."

And then, as an exclamation mark, Vern turned a funnel of fire on his own La-Z-Boy and melted it to slop.

Squib decided to state the obvious. "That's your own chair, boss," he said, then scooted outside to escape the acrid fumes billowing in toxic clouds from the dissolving leisure chair.

He sat on the decking counting gators until Vern stomped out and sat beside him.

"You shouldn't oughta have brought up that wyvern thing," he said. "Now you got to get me a new goddamn chair."

Squib bit his tongue, holding back the question, on account of the dragon was quick to aggravate and there wasn't no other furniture handy.

So instead, he said, "Sorry, boss. I guess we all got our touchy areas. Mine is egg-and-spoon races. I can't stand even hearing the phrase. This cheating motherfucker by the name of Moon Lipton tripped me in second grade sports day. Otherwise I woulda taken that medal for sure."

"Whatever," said Vern, but he was mollified a little. "I suppose you wasn't to know."

Squib took advantage of the softening in Vern's tone. "So who's this fella Jubelus, boss? Some knight guy?"

Vern lit a cigar with a snort. "I wish. Then I coulda smoked the asshole. Nah, Jubelus was my baby brother. The prick."

Squib had heard all about the downside of having kid brothers from his classmates. "Yeah. Little brothers never get in trouble for nothing."

"You can sing that, boy," said Vern. "Jube was the apple of his mother's eye. Always the damn favorite."

"So you kicked his ass, right?"

"I wish. Fucker was ten feet tall. We was even-stevens for a year or two, but after that he shot past me. Truth be told, I was the runt of the family."

"Yeah," said Squib, "but there musta been a time there when this Jube fella looked up to you. Before the growth spurt."

Vern did a comical double take. He hadn't thought about little Jubelus in a long time. And no human had ever prompted him to talk about his own family. It was all: *Can you grant wishes?* Or: *For the love of God don't kill me.*

"I guess," said the dragon. "We did shit together before it got all competitive. Sat on mountaintops with Granddaddy. Flame-grilled cows. I remember Jube made me a thing once, I guess you'd call it a pendant. Ugly as all hell. Some kind of rodent skull on a string. Rat maybe. Still, I wore that thing day and night until Jube got big enough to kick my ass. Didn't take too long for that day to dawn. I wasn't exactly no prize specimen."

"You are now," said Squib loyally, adding, "Also, you got the whole firepower thing going on. And the superhuman strength, too."

Vern tapped his forehead. "What I got is the smarts. I keep my head down and don't make no friends. Well, not too many, leastways."

Squib took this as an olive branch. It filled him with something like pride, to have a dragon for a friend. Maybe.

He took advantage of the moment. "So what happened with Jubelus?"

"It irked him that I was Lord Highfire. Irked my daddy,

too; in fact, he was real irked, so he gave Jubelus plenty of latitude when it came to throwing insults my way. I think they were both hoping we'd get to fighting and Jube would win out."

"Sounds real human," said Squib.

"'Man-hands' was the favorite insult," said Vern. "'Hey, man-hands, don't break a talon lifting up that rock.' Shit like that, and on a daily basis: Every time he saw something weak or puny, he'd call it a wyvern. Like: 'That ain't no real tree, that's a wyvern tree.' Or, 'A dragon is like a wyvern, only better.' Got to be like a thing."

"I can't imagine you swallowing that long-term, you being Lord Highfire and all."

"No, you're right there. I was all set to challenge, had my mind made up, so I went up into the Highlands to toughen up a little."

"So what happened?"

Vern's posture slumped. "You happened. Humans. Elephants, too. Chinese powder and cannon. Blasted us right out of that eyrie. Our familiars drugged our wine and let the mob in. They tore the place apart. It was unbelievable—like being attacked by monkeys."

"But you survived."

"Yep, on account of I was in the Highlands, beating up rocks. Eighteen dragons died that night. We didn't know at the time, but all over the world, humans were dominating. That was the end of the Dragon Age. From then on, we kept to ourselves."

"Shit," said Squib. "That's awful."

"My granddaddy had been alive for eight thousand years,

kid. Old Gnarly Head—had eight rows of horn nubs. *Eight.* Humans drowned him."

"*Drowned* him?"

"Yeah," said Vern, "put out that heart flame but good. Jubelus fought as best he could, but he couldn't spark up, drugged as he was. He took a stake from a war machine right in the gut. Bled out slow."

"What did you do?"

"It was over by the time I got back. There was nothing left of my family but corpses. I lost my head for a few months, razed a couple dozen villages, then they set those damned elephants on me, so I hightailed it outta there. Haven't been back since."

"Razed a couple dozen villages?"

"More, probably. It didn't mean nothing. I was up high so it was like destroying anthills. Burning that chair meant more. But I tell you something, a fella can't burn away the pain."

Squib shivered, and it was nothing to do with the skein of mist floating over the swamp. It hadn't before occurred to him that he was getting all pally with a hulking mass-murderer with some class of a complex. Inferiority maybe, or Napoleon. Maybe Miss Ingram would know.

Screw it, he thought. *I got a dragon friend and he ain't Pete's dragon, all furry and dumb. He's the real deal.*

So he said, "Hey, boss. What d'you say I mix you a pitcher of martinis right now?"

Vern was still a bit moody. "I dunno. I started on beer already."

"Come on. Wax told me you wasn't supposed to be

drinking beer. Ketogenic, right? I got some low-carb vegetable chips."

Vern was interested. "Low-carb?"

"Martinis and chips, boss. And maybe you could use some of your dozen sentences to tell me about history?"

"It's possible. If you patch the floorboards."

"Deal," said Squib.

"Goddamn right, deal," said Vern. "Like it's a democracy."

HOOKE, KING OF the sneaks, was recording everything from his hide across the water. He thanked God for the first time in his life: He thanked God for Everett "Squib" Moreau, a teenager who asked more questions than Congress on a witch hunt. Hooke took to wearing a Bluetooth earpiece during work hours so he wouldn't miss a minute of dragon-boy exchange. He even bought a smart watch so he could read their communiqués as they came in without having to root about for his phone.

So far as intelligence gathering went, Hooke had never had it so good. These two fools, having no idea that they were being surveilled, spoke freely about all manner of shit. Including but not limited to:

Squib: "Hooke was in the house the other morning, Mister Vern. Couldn't believe it. Walked in and there he was on the chair."

Vern: "That prick. I heard shit about him."

Conclusions: *Vern was the dragon's name, and he spoke English.*

And:

Squib: "Hooke thought I might be the guy hiding in the reeds watching him do his murder on Willard."

Vern: (chuckles) "He thought right."

Conclusion: *Squib, you little asshole. Everything coming to you, you got coming.*

And another time:

Squib: "Shit, boss. You need all this cooking oil? Shit's heavy."

Vern: "Quit your bitching, employee. I need every drop of that oil. No oil, no flame. Get it? That shit's like rocket fuel to a dragon."

Conclusion: *So Vern is definitely a dragon. And a dragon needs oil to keep him lit. Interesting.*

Vern and Squib talked a lot about history, which seemed to interest the boy, who credited a Miss Ingram for this educational bent. Hooke wondered, would the boy confide in her? For if he did, then it was permanent retirement for the high school teacher, too. Hooke gleaned that Vern was three thousand years old, at least, and that he had lived all over the world. He was a little runty, so far as dragons went, and he still bore a grudge against his brother Jubelus, who sounded like a hoot to Regence.

Still more revelations:

Squib: "What's your opinion of *Game of Thrones*, boss?"

Angry clattering of furniture.

Vern: "*Game of Thrones*? Are you trying to push my buttons, kid? *Game of fucking Thrones*! Those dragons are like servants—you see me doing any fucking mother of dragon's bidding? I'd never serve humans!"

Squib: "I didn't mean nothing—"

Vern: "Goddamn lapdog CGI motherfucking fire lizards. Heap of shit."

Conclusion: *Vern really did not like* Game of Thrones.

And the intelligence kept coming:

Squib: "You was playing 'Blue Bayou' the other night, and I thought I heard crying. So I stayed out on the bayou till the song finished."

Extended coughing.

Vern: "Yeah, I smelled you out there. I can smell you all the way from Petit Bateau, good as I know you. That song was part of something on TV. An old movie. Good song, though. Great tune."

Conclusion: *Vern had himself a dose of sentimentality and an excellent sense of smell.*

The info piled on up, and it got so Hooke was obsessed with the files he was amassing.

I got my act of God out in the swamp, he realized, *but he ain't no use to me there 'less I can get Ivory upriver to check out the new run I am about to be proposing for his product.*

Hooke had long believed that the Pearl River was an ideal way to traffic upstate. Ivory had never agreed to commit more than Carnahan could personally carry, but if a few of his regular deliveries were hit, then maybe he could be persuaded to come take a gander. But that plan seemed unnecessarily complicated.

Colonel Faraiji would laugh his ass off at that plan.

Keep it simple, stupid.

Faraiji once said, "Do you know the difference between a sundial and a wristwatch?"

Hooke had allowed that he knew many differences, but

perhaps not the specific one Faraiji needed to get his message across.

"The difference, Sergeant, is that a sundial has no moving parts. Sundials do not malfunction."

Hooke could have pointed out that sundials weren't portable, or that sundials were no use in a sandstorm, but he knew that these observations would just drag out the lesson, so he nodded like he got it.

"A plan should be like a sundial, understood? The fewer moving parts, the better."

So it made no sense to move Ivory's crew to the swamp. It made more sense to lure Vern to New Orleans.

But what did you use to lure a person/dragon to where you wanted them?

You used that thing the person/dragon loved.

Vern might not love Squib, but he sure was fond of the boy.

And Squib is a pain in my ass anyways, thought Hooke.

Two birds, one stone: win-win.

Except for Vern.

And Squib.

Also Ivory.

CHAPTER 14

HOOKE COULDN'T FIGURE IT OUT. THAT DRAGON FELLA MUST surely have a yearning for vegetables, the amount of effort he was putting into their cultivation, sending his boy down here with a barge-load of manure most nights for a start. Though Hooke did get a perverse pleasure from watching the boy shoveling shit.

I must keep this chore going when I'm shacking up with his momma, he thought. *Just for the hell of it.*

But back to the dragon and his veggies.

A guy wouldn't think it, he mused from his position in the oaks behind Waxman's houseboat, *a dragon loving him this many vegetables.*

But then everything he knew about dragons was gleaned from TV and other such unreliable sources.

Never figured dragons actually existed, he admitted now, but he wasn't all agog over Vern's actuality anymore; he'd gotten over that. In fact, the shit-shoveling surprised him more than the dragon.

It seemed to Regence Hooke that old Vern walking the earth was the answer to his prayer.

Vern shall smite mine enemies and lay waste to them who would oppress me.

Hooke smiled in the darkness, thinking how happy he was, nestled in here among the bamboo stalks with fireflies alighting on his camo veil.

Whaddya think of that, Pop? "Smite mine enemies." Sure sounds biblical, don't it?

Imagine, a heathen like Regence Hooke having his prayers answered. Just went to show that blessings could land on any shoulders. It was what a person did with them that counted.

Hooke knew exactly what he would do now: He would lure Vern to the Marcello and use the dragon to excoriate the mob hotel.

And then Regence Hooke here will take advantage of the chaos. Just like always.

At the very least, he would be rid of Squib Moreau, and at most, he would be right there in position to step into the vacuum created by Ivory.

It's all good, thought Hooke. *For me.*

He allowed Squib time to tie off and fill the barrow with the night's steaming pile. It pleased him to watch a teenager engaged in physical labor since they generally took so hard against it. But when the boy was maybe a dozen shovel-loads in, Hooke had a mind to get on with his evening and threw his camo sniper veil back over his shoulders. The veil looked a bit like a Snuggie, he'd always thought, but you couldn't argue against its convenience. Folded up neater than a handkerchief.

My very own cloak of invisibility.

Hooke came out of the copse slow and quiet, picking his steps so's not to spook the kid, but he needn't have bothered because Squib had a headful of his own tunes, piped direct into his skull by tiny white headphones.

Hooke wondered what the boy might be listening to. Rap, most likely. Or hip-hop, whatever the difference between those two might be. Hooke didn't care too much for music in any case, though occasionally, in times of stress, he would catch himself humming a snatch of "When I Survey the Wondrous Cross," which was the only hymn his father considered not to be sacrilegious—which only went to prove that the dead never really did die.

This notion pleased Hooke almost as much as watching Squib dig dragon shit.

I sure do hope there's a scrap of you floating around, Poppa, bearing witness to all the devil's work these hands of mine are doing.

Hooke flexed his right hand, testing for residual snake-bite damage, but there was nothing much. Maybe the ghost of a twinge? If anything, Hooke was feeling less with this hand since it shrank back down to its original size. Nerve damage, probably. His aim might be off a tad, but he could punch shit harder.

Hooke stepped silently over to Squib all the same. The boy had proved himself a slippery customer in the past, so no point in giving young Moreau points in this spread. Best to keep the game one-sided from the get-go. He was tempted to tap Squib on the shoulder before punching him, just for a little theater, but the kid could swing a shovel, and shovels had blades.

Nope, keep this streamlined, Regence, he told himself. *If everything goes right, there'll be theater aplenty later in the evening.*

SQUIB NEVER SAW it coming. One second he was trying to be a good Renfield, giving "What a Feeling" a listen and the next it felt like the back of his head had been stoved right in and he was facedown in the shit he'd been shoveling so assiduously.

Holy Christ, I musta been struck by lightning. Surely to God I am dead, was more or less what he was thinking, but there wasn't any concrete shape to his thoughts, just a spew of pain with sharp edges.

Squib somehow managed to roll his face out of the shit and hoist himself upright, only to realize that the rolling and hoisting had been assisted by someone.

Squib heard a ringing of feedback in his ears like he'd come off a plane, and then a voice hacked through the membrane and the voice said, "Time for a reckoning, Squib. You gotta pay the piper, son."

Squib did not immediately recognize the voice, but he knew who it was just as sure as the Lord recognized the devil when he spoke to Him in the desert.

Hooke, he thought. *He found me.*

"You hearing me, son?" said the voice. "Anybody in there?"

Squib felt his jaw go slack, and he might have drooled like a baby. Also, he could still hear music in the background, so it was like his misfortunes had a soundtrack.

"Huh?" he said. "What?"

Hooke laughed. "'Huh? What?' I reckon I scrambled your brains, son. Or maybe the stink of that dragon shit did that."

And that statement smartened Squib right up, scything right through the brain fog.

Dragon shit? Hooke knows about Vern?

Hooke tossed Squib back down in the dirt. "What are you doing here, boy? Every day shoveling shit? Old Vern loves his vegetables that much? I can't believe it."

Squib coughed, and his head felt like it might fall to pieces like a busted egg. "I just put the crap on the patch," he muttered almost to himself. "Orders from the boss."

"Vern's orders, huh," said Hooke. "Fair enough, I suppose. Each to his own."

Squib made a stab at loyalty. "No. *Waxman's* orders. I see to his patch while he's down. Down South."

"Yup," said Hooke. "Sure, okay, whatever. You are misunderstanding the situation, son. I already know what I need to know. That information is banked, you get me? For your part in this unfolding scenario, all you gotta do is keep breathing till you die. Simple, ain't it? Shouldn't be no problem for you, even with a busted head."

Squib couldn't rightly figure what was going on. The soggy earth was seeping through his clothes, and his head throbbed like pain incarnate was living inside there. It seemed like Hooke had the situation all figured, so far as Vern was concerned. He had enough sparks left in his brain to ask one vital question.

"You ain't gonna kill me now, Constable?"

"Kill you?" said Hooke. "Don't you know a thing about hunting? The best kind of bait is the live kind."

Squib watched his hands sink into the mud and felt the worms on his skin. *I'm the bait.*

"What are we hunting, Constable?" he asked. He didn't have the strength to lift his head so he could look Hooke in the eye.

Hooke turned him over with the toe of his boot so they could face each other. "I think you know what we're hunting," he said, looming above the battered teen. "We're hunting chaos incarnate."

Squib wasn't sure what the word "incarnate" meant, but he reckoned the word "chaos" referred to Vern.

"Chaos," he mumbled. "You can't track chaos."

Hooke screwed a cigar into the corner of his mouth and lit it, grinning all the while. "Ain't you the clever dick, son? You saying chaos can't be tracked on account of there's no pattern? But what I can do is *lure* chaos: get it where I want it and see what happens. I wonder how well Vern does in enclosed spaces."

It was clear that Hooke was all up to speed as regards the whole dragon thing, so Squib decided to abandon all pretense of ignorance on that front.

"Vern will tear your enclosed space to pieces, dipshit," he said. "You ain't got no idea."

"Hey, boy," said Hooke. "Your sentences are coming back. How about that. Guess I didn't bust your fool head hard enough. Never mind, that's an easy fix."

Hooke reached under his camouflage poncho, pulled out a shotgun, and showed Squib the butt end. "Nighty night, Squibster," he said. "See you in the Big Easy."

Squib closed his eyes and allowed his jaw to hang loose, which was counterintuitive, but Charles Jr. had once told him it would save his teeth in the event of a head trauma, and Charles Jr. should know as he'd rammed his quad into more walls than he had limbs.

This is sure gonna hurt, thought Squib, while Hooke was swinging his Mossberg. *If I can even feel a higher level of pain with my head in smithereens.*

"Smithereens," he thought. *One of Waxman's words.*

And you know what they say: *Think of the devil and he shall appear.*

HOOKE WAS HAVING the time of his life, busting up Squib's noggin and setting up crime lords. A guy had to wonder if life could get any sweeter than this.

Sure it can. Soon I'll be tangling with a dragon.

Across the river, he could see a bonfire throwing light against the night sky and thought, *I better check that shit out. Prob'ly Bodi burning his trash again.*

And in a case of mind-bending irony, Hooke gave himself a mental pat on the back for his professionalism, tending to the law even on his day off. *I ain't even full-time, and here I am looking out for the environment.*

Because Regence Hooke took his job seriously, in spite of the way he gleefully shattered the state and human laws on a regular basis.

Two separate things, he told himself. *We all got duality in us. Dark sides and so forth.*

Which was why cracking Squib's skull didn't bother him none; in fact he reveled in it.

Don't kill the boy, though, Regence, he reminded himself. *A dead hostage ain't nothing but a sack of meat, and no dragon is going to come out of hiding for a sack of meat.*

And so Hooke held back a few pounds of force when he brought the wooden stock down on Squib's head, but nonetheless he enjoyed the dull thunk it made, like an axe going into a tree trunk.

That boy is gonna have a nasty welt, he thought. *Still, that's gonna be the least of his problems considering the mutilations I got planned.* He wondered if there was ever a version of himself who would have had some qualms about taking his blade to a kid?

Probably not, he admitted. *Even before Daddy lost his mind to God, I wasn't big on conscience and the like.*

"Yep," he said to the unconscious boy, "first I'll take the gut hook to you, then old Vern is gonna do my bidding, and when I'm good and satisfied, I'll put that monster down."

What happened next surprised Hooke, and truth be told, he didn't really understand what was happening until it was over. And even then, he would spend long hours mulling it over, wondering if it could have gone any other way—like, could he have wrung some advantage from the situation.

Squib was facedown in the vegetable patch with the stink of manure cut with the sharp odor of coffee grinds rising up out of the earth, which was all well and good, but then the earth took to humping and rippling like something was coming up out of there, which couldn't be right unless a cypress root was shifting, which Hooke had seen happen before, or maybe like a bubble of swamp brook was winding to the surface.

Hooke was more interested than alarmed, as there wasn't much to fear from roots or swamp water. But the shifting increased in amplitude, and goddamn if a pale arm didn't come shooting out of the clay, followed by more limbs and the approximation of a head.

"Shit," said Hooke. "Lotta teeth."

Which was his first impression. And the constable was not wrong: Whatever that thing was, it did have a whole lot of teeth, which were buzzing in a very disconcerting fashion, and it did not take a whole lot of imagination to realize what those teeth might do to a body.

Hooke decided to negotiate. "Hey!" he said, "Hold your horses there, fella."

But when the creature, whatever it was, obstinately persisted in emerging from the swamp mud, Hooke decided enough with the diplomacy and brought his shotgun to bear.

"Vern!" said the swamp thing, but that was all it managed as Hooke's first shot took its face off below the jaw and set it seesawing on its breastbone.

"Shit," said Hooke. "Is that you, Waxman? You ain't human, son—all this time?"

And right there in front of his eyes, Waxman's jaw swung upwards, strands of flesh reaching for the upper jaw, questing to be realigned.

"Vern," said Waxman again, and he was most of the way out of the mud now, and his hand was reaching for Hooke, and not in a friendly fist bump kind of a way.

Everything was happening too fast for Hooke to be spooked, or even to consider his options, one of which might be to leverage Waxman to get to Vern somehow. But now Waxman—or whatever it was—was out of the hole, the dirt falling off its torso in clumps, leaving the creature naked apart from a triangular jockstrap of some kind.

"Shit, son," said Hooke. "Is that pizza?"

Waxman, still trying to shake off his grave funk, didn't respond.

I guess getting shot in the face didn't help none, thought Hooke. It was a pity he had had to plug the old guy, because this was fascinating stuff and most days life on the bayou was so goddamn dull.

My eyes have been opened, Poppa, he told the ghost of his father. *This swamp is surely a land of wonders.*

Waxman's face kept right on repairing itself. The old geezer shambled from side to side.

Like a zombie, thought Hooke, but then corrected himself. *No. Not like no zombie. Zombies were human at some point. Old Waxman sure ain't human.*

"On your knees, son," he ordered whatever it was that had emerged from the earth. "Hands behind your head."

But that was just reflexive talking; there wasn't no police work going on here tonight.

We're all of us in the swamp now, Hooke realized.

Waxman either did not hear or chose to ignore Hooke's commands regarding his knees and hands and kept right on coming, spilling some kind of black bile from his shredded throat.

Hooke pumped another shell into the barrel and took a breath to issue a warning, but instead changed his mind and used the drawn breath to say, "Fuck it."

And he shot Waxman's left leg from under him, sending the creature down in the dirt beside Squib.

Waxman oughta been driven near to insane with agony, but the pain seemed to sharpen his wits somewhat. "You asshole, Hooke," he said, wriggling onto his back. "You done shot the wrong mogwai this time."

"A mogwai," said Hooke. "Is that what I'm talking to?"

Waxman pawed the earth till he found his leg, then held it close to the stump, which immediately began to spin a web of new sinew, stitching the leg back on.

"Well, balls," said Hooke. "It seems like I'm wasting my cartridges here. You don't die like normal people, huh?"

Waxman concentrated on his leg, like he was healing it with mind power. "You ain't got the stuff to kill me, Hooke," he said.

Regence drew out his gut hook knife. "Oh, I got the stuff all right, Waxman."

Waxman glared at Hooke with golden eyes. "You ain't killing anybody, Constable. Soon as my leg grabs hold, I'm gonna eat you like a goddamn crawfish, suck the brains right outta your head. You'll never see a nugget of that Reb gold."

Reb gold? thought Hooke. *This gets better and better.*

The constable squatted down. "Shit, Waxman. You're awful perky for a gunshot victim."

Waxman nodded at his leg. "This ain't nothing. You ain't got the first clue how to end me. Better men than you have tried."

"Maybe a *better* man ain't what's needed in this situation," noted Hooke. "Maybe what you need is a worse man, and I surely am one of those."

And Hooke couldn't be sure, but it seemed that old Waxman blanched a little at that. But just a little.

"I been in worse situations, Hooke," declared the mogwai. "I dealt with worse people than you. You think you're bad, son? I seen bad and you ain't it. I ate bad and shit it out all over this bayou."

"Yep," said Hooke, "you surely do talk tough, lying there hanging onto your magic leg, but all you're doing is trying to buy time, hoping for a miracle. It ain't coming, old man. Ain't nothing coming for you but the void."

This hit home. It was evocative rhetoric: *Nothing coming for you but the void.* Hooke could see Waxman's confidence meter was falling.

Let me just hurry that process along, thought Hooke, grabbing Waxman's leg and twisting it clear of the mogwai's body, tearing the fresh-grown tendrils. Waxman flinched some but refused to cry out.

"Interesting trick," observed Hooke as fresh tendrils reached out for Waxman's person. "I wonder what your range is." The constable tossed Waxman's leg to the riverbank, then watched the new tendrils wriggle and die. "I guess less than six feet," he said dispassionately. "I should make a note or something."

"I'm gonna make a note on your forehead with my finger-nail. 'DOA,'" said Waxman, but it was clear he didn't believe it himself.

"Of course you are, son," said Hooke. "Now here's what's actually going to happen. I'm gonna finish you off, Waxman. Sure as day follows night, you're going to meet your maker. And after I do you, your pal Vern is next. And after him, the boy. And that's just God's honest truth. None of us think it's coming, and maybe you got more of a right to believe that than most, but time's up for you, old man. Time's up, and that's the way it is. Now, you look in my eyes and tell me it ain't so."

Hooke watched as Waxman did as he was told. The creature looked into his eyes, and Regence knew he saw nothing in there but sense of purpose.

Yep, he thought. *It's sinking in.*

Waxman changed his tack and tried to appeal to Hooke's better nature. "You know what you're doing here, Hooke? This is more than murder. Ain't you got no heart?"

Hooke ran his thumb along the curved blade of his gut hook. "Reckon I don't, but I aim to find out exactly where yours is at."

IT TOOK HOOKE a good half hour, but he finally located Wax-man's heart, in his left ass cheek, of all places, and the mogwai talked all the way through, spouting threats and bile like there was still a chance he was coming out the other end of this encounter.

"God sure does have himself a sense of humor," muttered Hooke as he severed Waxman's arteries and lifted the dripping heart out of its cradle of bone. And just to be sure of the job, he hacked the mogwai's head from his shoulders with the blade of Squib's shovel and laid the lot out in a gruesome tableau around the boy.

"Say cheese, fellas," he said, snapping off a bunch of photos with Squib's cell phone. He would send the best shot to Vern with a nicely phrased provocative message, see if he couldn't entice the dragon out of his shack.

It occurred to Hooke as he dumped Waxman's remains into the swamp that he was likely unleashing all manner of hullaballoo on the parish.

And I'm gonna be the guy holding his nerve while all around are losing their shit.

Which was another version of the old poem.

Hooke remembered that old Waxman had a nice shower in his back room. He was covered in mogwai slime, among other things, and he had a lot to achieve.

You ain't looking your sharpest, Regence, son. Best you smarten up for a trip into the city.

So, first a good long shower, then let loose the dragon.

Sounded like a plan.

CHAPTER 15

HOOKE WAS NOT EXPECTING TO BE WELCOMED WITH OPEN ARMS when he presented himself at the Marcello elevator, and he was right to have low expectations. In fact, the only open arms were the constable's own, as Rossano Roque frisked him with a thoroughness that would not have been out of place in Gitmo.

Of course Hooke had not simply strolled in the revolving door with the kid slung over his shoulder in a duffel bag. He considered it, but there was blood blossoming through the canvas, and that would have been too brazen, even for him. So instead, the constable parked out back and lugged Squib in through the deliveries entrance, stashing him in the meat freezer behind the kitchen. One of Conti's lower-tier goons with spirals shaved into the side of his head was dumb enough to challenge him, so Hooke had cuffed him hard enough to knock the grille right out of his mouth and set him guarding the freezer until he could persuade Ivory to station someone there who was a little lower on the dumbass scale.

Ivory Conti was waiting for him when Rossano Roque pushed open the heavy double doors. The capo was standing behind one of those adjustable desks which rose up on a motor so he wouldn't develop curvature of the spine from too much chair-time writing figures into a leather-bound ledger. That was the world he came out of: Wall Street and hedge funds, one of maybe a dozen of the real high rollers who cashed out in 2007, which was optimum cash-out time. You can believe he laughed his waxed balls off when the crash came the following year. If cash was king, then Ivory Conti had graduated to emperor.

Ivory had decided that the only guaranteed market for his money was contraband, or, more specifically, drugs, and so he invested a large part of his fortune in resuscitating the mobbed-up gang model of the 1950s, when his grandpa had been consigliere for Carlos Marcello, the Tunisian godfather of the Italian Mafia in the French Quarter: a truly international enterprise.

Ivory had heard all the tales from dear old Grandpa—about how the movie stars flocked to New Orleans and Vegas to fawn over the made men, how there was no finer job for a real man than running his own numbers syndicate—and little Ivory had bought it hook, line, and sinker, even though Poppa had worked himself to death to keep Ivory out of the life. And yet here he was, balls-deep in wise guys looking to be like him, a force in the New Orleans drug scene. And he was a force: medium-sized as yet, but getting bigger, all thanks to the army of crooked but excellent lawyers who'd kept him out of prison on Wall Street, and the legion of police from various institutions across the

US, Mexico, and Canada who were very well compensated for having his back.

Soon those guys will have my back, Hooke thought now.

Ivory had been known to say, "Don't expect to make money in the first five years. That's when you sow the seeds."

This was a revolutionary business model for drug dealers, who usually expected to see hefty returns right from the off, but Ivory had money and what he wanted was the Life, which was not to say he was one for giving cash away. Ivory applied the same acumen to his drug deals as he had to his funding of hedges, or vice versa.

"I'm building bridges now," he had told Hooke as part of his recruitment patter. "But in five years' time this town will be mine. It's all about infrastructure, cop."

Hooke had been impressed at the time, that time being a long time ago.

Ivory Conti looked the part, it had to be admitted—if the part in question was a classic-era mafioso with a pin-striped gray suit, slicked-back hair the color of copper wire, and an almost luminous blue tie fatter than a cottonmouth.

"Ivory" was Conti's mob handle. He'd arrived from New York with the pseudonym in place. "Anthony" was the actual name on his birth certificate, but that was too on the nose for a guy who was actually mobbed-up: "Tony the Mafioso." No, "Ivory" sounded good, and it suited him too. Ivory Conti: the little white count, on account of his super-pale skin. He had de-fanged any ribbing that might come his way over the complexion by sticking it into his name. Clever.

Hooke thought that this self-applied nickname told a person a lot about Ivory Conti, about how he could control a situation. *But shit*, he thought with some contempt, *a god-damn hurricane couldn't control Regence Hooke.*

Now he ignored Ivory Conti, deciding to take himself a look at a large painting in an ornate gold frame. Some guy buck naked, more or less, tied to a tree and porcupined with droopy arrows. Guy still looked all holy and shit, like the arrows didn't bother him none 'cause he was off down the yellow brick road or whatever to see his Lord.

Hooke knew that look from his own father: the holier-than-thou look. He sniggered. *This guy is certainly holier than me*, he thought. *In every sense.*

"Saint Sebastian," said Ivory behind him. "By Botticelli. A fine example of chiaroscuro. You familiar with chiaroscuro, cop?"

"Something to do with how light falls on the subject," said Hooke, dragging up that nugget from somewhere. "That's it, right?"

"That is it, Constable Hooke," said Ivory. "Look at this, Rossano: The cop knows his art."

Hooke turned from the print. "I know enough to know that's a fake, boss man. Ain't no Botticelli in the French Quarter."

Ivory winced, pained. "It's a *print*, Hooke. Not a fake. And someday I might get the real one up there. Maybe I already have it." He jerked a thumb over his shoulder at the titanium walk-in wall safe, which, rumor had it, doubled as a safe room.

I surely would love to get me a peek in there, thought Hooke. *An Aladdin's cave of wonders, I bet.*

"It's important to have goals," he said.

Ivory went back to what he'd been doing, which was counting money right out on his standing desk.

"Constable Hooke," said the self-styled kingpin. "A cop in my den."

Cold shoulder, thought Hooke, so he thought he might push the boundaries a little, shake this little mafioso out of his Capone fantasy. "Gauche," he said, nodding at the towers of cash.

This term was unusual enough for Ivory to spare him a glance. "What's that, Constable? You trying to educate me?"

"What you're doing there, son. Gauche. Unpolished."

Well, that was enough impudence to stop Ivory in mid-stack. "You know I'm Italian, right? Sicilian, as a matter of fact. And you're coming in here calling me unpolished in front of my boy?"

Now Hooke had his full attention, which was the point. "No, Mister Ivory, I'm just trying to help you along the road to the big time. The boss don't count money. The soldiers count money. You didn't know, son—how could you know, being as you're starting out? Grunt work like that gets delegated."

Ivory stopped counting the money. "What are we talking about here, Constable?" he asked, and Hooke thought that maybe he was smarter than he looked in his Armani suit.

Hooke eyeballed Roque until the big bodyguard shifted himself out of the way, and then the constable sat uninvited on the chaise longue. "What we're talking about is how far up the ladder you're aiming to climb, Ivory."

Roque piped up, "I'd say Mister Ivory's on the top of the ladder, cop. Look around you."

Thank you, dumbass, thought Hooke, but he did indeed look around him, taking his sweet time. "Yup," he said, "this is a fine building you got. Pillars and the whole works. I guess you're pretty much in control of all the corners you can see from up here. Every single one."

Ivory was no fool. He knew blatant sarcasm when he heard it. "I know what I got, cop. I know who I am."

Hooke lit a cigar. "Maybe—but do you know where you're going?"

Ivory came around the desk. "I'm trying to figure your agenda here, Hooke. A fucking constable on my payroll who runs minor shit occasionally through a swamp coming in here with all this talk about where I'm going? You gotta know this don't end well for you. Maybe you're just insane. Is that your deal, Hooke?"

Hooke took a deep drag. "Psychotic I would say. Yeah, that's fair. Insane? That's a little too much for me to take from you."

At this point, Ivory had no choice but to stop wondering about Hooke's agenda and take action. "Okay, that's it. I got no more time for you, Hooke. This one single building I have is a busy place. I gotta oversee all these corners. Gets real busy here in the city."

Hooke interrupted before Ivory could get to the part about making Sicily great again. "Okay, Mister Ivory, maybe I approached this all wrong. No disrespect intended and so forth. I just need to know what kinda balls you got in your silk shorts. I've worked with big players in Iraq, on both sides. On all sides, actually. I'm talking mountains of co-caine, shipping crates full of weapons. I'm talking billions in profits. You got that same look in your eyes those guys had. Ambition. But I need to move you on a few squares because there ain't time to develop naturally."

Ivory found himself strangely flattered by the constable's comments, but also intrigued. "Thanks a fucking bunch, Hooke. I don't need any cop to tell me I got ambition. A fucking constable? You ain't even a sheriff."

Go on, thought Hooke. *Ask me.*

Ivory fought the urge, but he had to know. "So, go on, motherfucker. Why ain't I got time?"

I should make this melodramatic, thought Hooke. *These boss types love them a slice of melodrama. Or even better, something from the Bible.* And just like that, the appropriate reference leaped out at him.

"You don't have time, Ivory," said Hooke, "because like Jesus in the desert, you are about to be sorely tested."

"Tested?" said Ivory, and then, for appearance's sake, "Who's gonna test me? I own the police, I'm tight with the cartel, and this building is a fortress. I got a dozen men on every floor and enough firepower in this room alone to win a medium-sized war."

Hooke pretended to be impressed by all this exposition. "You know, I do believe I brought this situation to the right place."

"What situation might that be, Constable?"

Hooke fidgeted with his cigar. It wasn't a simple thing, to present this case. Blurting out the facts would get him laughed out of the building or, more likely, carried out.

"Okay, son. Here's the deal. There are a couple of strands, so pay attention."

Ivory pawed his face like he would pull it off. "Constable, you're the one testing me. The chances of you surviving this encounter are slim to none unless I like what you say next."

The twin, knowing a setup when he heard one, drew a 9mm and stashed it behind his back.

"Okay, G-Hop, settle down," said Hooke. "What we have here is a once-in-a-lifetime opportunity. The brass ring. A chance for us all to elevate our positions."

"This I gotta hear," said Rossano Roque.

"Well then, maybe you might consider shutting the hell up, son." He ground the cigar under his boot heel. "So, the first strand. I got the boy who witnessed that little job on Honey Island tucked away in your freezer. No longer a threat."

Ivory was surprised. "I hope the second strand is better than the first because I sure as shit never told you to bring a witness here. You sure you're an officer of the law, Constable? Because you don't appear to know a whole lot about it."

"Relax, Ivory," said Hooke. "You own the law around here, myself included. And the Feds ain't sniffing around you yet. All's you got is a hotel and a half a dozen corners. That there's penny-ante shit to the Feebs."

"Fucking Hooke," said Ivory, and Hooke could see those words made his so-called boss feel better, so much better that he repeated them. "Fucking Hooke," and added, "I rue the day. I surely do."

Hooke grinned. "Well, that's all about to change, son, because strand two, this kid, he's got himself an employer. More of a friend, really."

"A friend?" said Ivory. "I hate friends. Friends do illogical things for friends."

"Ah, but this friend is special," said Hooke. "You need to open your ears now because this is important. This friend could move the earth for us. I don't wanna say too much about him, but you've seen *Game of Thrones*, right?"

"I've seen a few episodes," said Ivory.

"*Game of Thrones* is genius, man," said Roque. "The amount of ass on that show is insane."

Hooke dropped Ivory a wink, like they both knew his soldier was an idiot.

"The point is," he continued, "the little blonde lady, she's nothing without her friends, right? What if we had a friend like that?"

Ivory's eyebrows shot so high it looked like they might take off and fly away. "Like a *dragon*? Is that what you're saying, Constable? What if we had a dragon on the payroll?"

Hooke grinned. "A dragon? Come on, Ivory, I ain't no crazy guy coming in here with dragon stories. But this friend, he's something to see. So I think that's the best way for this to play out: just let you eyeball him. And I reckon he'll be here any damn second, busting down your door."

"He's gonna come in here looking for beef?" said Ivory. "Who is he, your fucking brother?"

Hooke laughed. "Good one, boss. You zinged me there. He's a character, ain't he, Rossano? But no, this guy ain't my brother. You've never seen nothing like this guy. And if we can capture him and get him hooked on product, go a little *French Connection*, get him on our leash, then we can bust this city open like a clam."

This was Hooke's fallback, if Ivory's men actually managed to subdue Vern.

"He's that good?"

Hooke considered his answer. "There's a term—kids use it all the time. 'Awesome.' That's what this guy is, in the true sense of the word. This guy is awesome. He's Godzilla and Thor and goddamn Batman all rolled into one, and he's gonna pop in here any second and wipe out half your men without breaking a sweat. You gotta sound red alert and get loaded with armor-piercing rounds—gas, if you have it; whatever the fuck is in your box of tricks. Because Vern don't play around."

Ivory snorted. "Vern? Some guy called Vern is gonna off half my people?"

"At least half. More if he sticks around."

"A guy this powerful, why would I want to kill him?"

Hooke guffawed. "You ain't killing him. All that shit might just slow him down long enough to get a spike of crank into him."

Rossano laughed. "Crank? Fucking old-ass bitch be talking about dog food and dragons."

Hooke was not a man for swallowing insults unless there was an upside, and in this case, he couldn't see one. In fact, Ivory could use a lesson right about now.

He moved fast, while seeming to move slow, which is about as difficult as it sounds and involves every muscle from the neck down. He had seen a French merc in Iraq operate in this underwater fashion: Old Serge could slice a fella's neck like he was opening a greeting card, and people never saw him coming. Hooke had studied that technique and practiced it until he felt confident enough to go public with Serge himself, which he figured was the ultimate test.

Hooke passed; Serge passed on.

He leaned forward easily and grasped Rossano's knee, which was at his eye level. "Sorry," he said, making it look like an accidental graze; then he tightened his grip and pistoned his arm, pushing the knee in a direction knees don't like to go.

"Oops, hey," he said, still playing the bumbler, "watch out there, buddy."

Roque went down, his face the color of swamp scum, and as he fell, Hooke drove an uppercut into the bodyguard's jutting chin, which carried Hooke to his feet and almost took Rossano's head clean off. It certainly drove the life from his body.

"One punch," said Hooke. "I always wondered."

To give Ivory his due, he didn't quake or gibber but stood up tall for the fight to come. The boy had probably had to show some moxie along the road, dealing with all those senior-type mafiosi hooked up to breathing machines over in Saint Margaret's.

"You wanna go for a gun?" Hooke asked him. "I know you got one in your fancy desk. Smart move, I'd say, because it would be real stupid going toe-to-toe with me."

"I don't need a gun," said Ivory, balling his fists. "I ain't scared of you."

Hooke balled his own fists a touch mockingly. "It ain't Marquess of Queensbury, boy. Getting to the top might be about brawling, but staying there sure ain't. Rossano had to go because he was distracting you from the Fourth Horseman of the Apocalypse who's about to drop in. We can finish this right now, or you can get on the intercom to your floors and get them set up for a breach and maybe make something of yourself. Get out from under the family's shadow. Be the next big man."

"I am the big man, Hooke. All I gotta do is holler and a roomful of hurt is gonna come running in here."

"That's your call," said Hooke, though it wasn't really. "But I wouldn't waste resources just now." He gave Ivory a few seconds to think about it, then said, "Come on, son. Clock's ticking."

"Okay," snapped Ivory, "we do it your way for now. But soon as this super-fucking-assassin is strapped to the table, me and you are going to have a long talk."

"Of course, boss," said Hooke.

Boss. Like Ivory was still in charge of anything.

CHAPTER 16

VERN DIDN'T GET THE PHOTOGRAPH ON HIS PHONE UNTIL HE CAME out of the water at sunset. At first the dragon didn't know what he was looking at, figuring the boy was pranking him, which seemed to be a popular pastime on the Internet, but then he took a closer look and realized that someone had sliced Waxman up like so much gator bait and placed the pieces around a knocked-out Squib. Vern was no stranger to savagery. He'd seen enough of it in his life, mostly concentrated around the time of the purge, when humans had inflicted just about every atrocity on dragon-kind that they could come up with. Vern had seen the looks on the faces of those humans in the aftermath and figured that they had surprised even themselves with the innovative forms of murder they'd freestyled with maybe half a dozen swords, a couple of elephants, and a vat of oil.

Vern had seen it all and his heart had broken and his mind had snapped.

But hearts and minds can heal.

And now Vern was plunged into hell all over again.

Waxman was dead. The human Hooke had done the deed and Vern felt the deep blues creeping over him like a storm cloud and his thoughts slowed and it felt like blinking and breathing was just too much trouble.

Then a text buzzed through. Squib had set the text alert to light saber.

The text read: Hey, dragon. Didn't you get my picture? I got your little buddy here.

The text was signed with a hook emoji, which made it clear who was sending it.

Five seconds later the light saber buzzed again.

He don't look so good. You better get down here.

This was followed by a Google map pin on the Marcello Hotel in New Orleans.

A third buzz.

Ivory Conti says kill him now, but I'm gonna give you an hour before he ends up like Waxman.

This one came with an attachment: another picture of Waxman. This time just the mogwai's head sitting on a post.

Hooke made a mistake, thought Vern. *He shoulda killed Squib, too. Now I got something to live for.*

For sixty minutes.

TEN MINUTES LATER Vern was in the air and in a state of disbelief about current events in general.

For one: He was entering New Orleans airspace for the first time after all the shit with the janitor's video a couple of years back.

For another: He was risking his scaly ass for some kid he'd known barely a wet week because—because what? Squib ferried vodka and dragon porn to the shack: hardly worth killing or dying for.

And for the third strike: He was allowing some asshole cop to get him so riled up that he was flying into a den of gangsters, in no small part to win a pissing contest.

Whatever happens on this night, Regence Hooke ain't walking away from it, nor crawling neither.

"You have plumb lost your mind, Lord Highfire," he told himself strictly. "Turn yourself around right this minute."

But he didn't turn around because Squib was a good kid. Good and loyal.

I'm rewarding loyalty in humans. Next thing I'll be swearing allegiance to a goddamn sheep.

And still Vern did not turn around. Hooke's actions could not be allowed to stand, even if it was an obvious trap.

Vern flew low across the Gulf, enjoying the warm updraft in his membranes.

Enjoying the updraft, are you?

Well then, Almighty Wyvern, if you ain't turning around, then at least get your goddamn head in the game.

Which was a fair comment.

He might be a powerful dragon, and they might be nothing but a clatter of dumb humans all conveniently clustered together for easy slaughter, but sometimes dumb gets lucky and powerful gets dead.

Focus, Vern baby. Remember the time Grendel took out that longhouse of Vikings? Let's do it just like that. Except for the Vikings, read Italians. The longhouse is a downtown hotel. And the swords are semiautomatic weapons.

Vern was beginning to realize that metaphors were not his strong suit.

NEW ORLEANS WAS lit up like the whole town was a carnival. Monolithic slabs of skyscrapers, garish tombstones against the night, were not half as pretty as their painted-on reflections. Especially the Superdome, a purple boob of a building which reminded Vern of a lady dragon he'd met one time in Brazil, as it was now called.

South American drago-ladies. Shit.

Vern drifted over the Delacroix marshes barely ten feet above the Mississippi port. He kept his wings as tucked as possible, and his mouth shut tight. A single hint of flame and he'd be lighting himself up for whatever cameras were pointed his way. And if there was one thing Vern knew, once you hit civilization in this century, there was always some dick with a camera. And nowadays the dick could even be a robot. Roll on a dystopian technology-free future, then things might get a little easier for a dragon just trying to survive.

Vern sent a message to his pigment cells, which blended him in pretty well with the Mississippi to the casual observer, gave himself a little lift to avoid the party cruises, but stuck to the river, following it northwest to the French Quarter. From there his sense of smell went insane with the sheer variety of scents drifting up from the streets, a cornu-copia of spices and perfumes which were making it difficult to think about anything except gumbo.

I need a little cover, Vern realized. *Some space to spy on the hotel in the photos; then I grab that motherfucker Hooke and rip his pumpkin head clean off and maybe pickle his balls in vodka.*

And then a moment later, a little shamefaced, *And also rescue Squib. Do that first.*

VERN HOOKED A talon around St. Louis Cathedral's middle spire and squared himself away in the shadows way up there with a bird's-eye view on the modern-day Gomorrah laid out below him.

I must look amazing, he thought. *Big badass dragon hang-ing off a steeple. Christopher Nolan would shit himself if he saw this.*

No one would see him, though. That was the whole point. Resisting the urge to show off for the crowd was how he'd stayed alive so long. But it was so difficult for a guy who was totally magnificent in action to rein that in. Vern thought he would give a decade of his life to cut loose just once.

I don't even know how much damage I could do, he real-ized. *That's how long it's been.*

The Quarter below had that downtown vibe where gloss was painted over vice, so the tourists could stuff po'boys down their gullets or flash their college breasts without ac-tually feeling threatened. Or, if they got really loaded, maybe buy some fake voodoo charm to get into someone's pants.

That used to be a carnival thing. Now it's all the damn time, thought Vern. *The dicks are coming out, too. I'm surprised it took menfolk so long to get into the game.*

But the French Quarter's paint job was patchy, and the underworld poked through at the corners and down the alleys. Vern smelled the scouring sweetness of cheap spirits, the oily plastic stink of burned crack, the rank musk of all-day drinkers. He saw the boisterous out-of-towners all whooping and hollering like they were invincible, like there wasn't a 9mm or switchblade within five feet on every side. Like they couldn't be snuffed out without much thought or effort. He saw the workers, industrious as ants, moving through the crowds, selling baggies, picking pockets, wheedling marks into their establishments. It was all going on as it had for centuries, apart from a week of reduced service due to multiple FEMA fuckups after Katrina flooded eighty percent of the city.

On another evening, Vern might have enjoyed the exotic change of scenery, but tonight he was on a mission to avenge Waxman's savage murder, rescue his boy, and bury Constable Hooke so deep they'd need an archaeologist to find him.

Vern's heart couldn't believe that Wax was actually gone, but his gut was churning with that old familiar *friend/family member killed by a human* feeling that he remembered so well.

Vern knew from way too much experience that revenge wouldn't magically make that feeling go away but it sure would dull it some.

Vern spotted the Marcello Hotel right away. This guy Ivory sure liked his columns. Must've been half a dozen of them out front of his establishment, couple of blocks behind Rampart, knocking up against Treme, all painted gold in the grooves, festooned with concrete vines and grapes. And, of course, the sign was gold, too: "The Marcello Tower. Classic Elegance."

Where did this guy think he was? New York in the '20s?

It occurred to Vern that once upon a brighter day, he would have torched the entire building simply because the sign irritated him.

Glory days, he thought. *You said it, Bruce.*

He fancied a closer look, so he risked a five-second glide to the building opposite the Marcello, which was a redbrick apartment building with honest-to-God gargoyle heads peeking over the rooftop.

How convenient, thought Vern.

There was one guy on the roof, all set up for the evening with a lounger and reefer. Vern dropped down behind him like he was on a wire and breathed a lungful of fumes all over the guy's head, knocking the stoner out cold.

"Cheaper than weed," said Vern, "but a bitch of a sulfur hangover."

The dragon dropped to all fours and crawled to the lip of the roof, where the gargoyle heads sat up on the cornerstones. From there he had a decent view of the Marcello. Even better, he wasn't overlooked on any side.

There was no real need for him to do what he was about to do, he realized, as his pigment cells were still okay at this distance, crude as his coloring was.

But what the hell. Live a little.

He wriggled one taloned finger into the seam of desiccated concrete connecting one gargoyle to the wall and in less than a minute had the bust separated from its groove.

"Let's go, little fella," said Vern, and wiggled it slowly backwards off its perch.

Not a bad likeness, he thought, inspecting the gargoyle. *Needs a little more forehead.*

Dragons didn't look much like gargoyles up close, but from below at night, it would definitely fool ninety-nine percent of humans, eighty-three percent of whom were dumber than pig shit in a slop bucket.

And then he slid his own head in the gargoyle's space and gazed down on New Orleans with impunity.

THE MARCELLO WAS four floors of solid steel and stone, with heavy granite columns and a beveled double doorway. Built in this century to withstand a hypothetical Katrina II, the hotel wasn't in the least flimsy. Plus she was a hive of activity. Plenty of soldiers out front keeping things moving, and a bustling Italian restaurant that took up half of the ground floor. Most of the windows had decorative iron grilles bolted across their frames, and there were Hollywood spotlights lighting up the facade. This Ivory guy was probably going for an updated version of classic Italian, architecture-wise, when he had the front done, but plonked down in the middle of a row of colorful stucco Creole town houses, the Marcello looked like the Vulcan embassy: i.e., humorless and bland.

Even with spotlights on it, the place is boring.

Vern yawned just looking at it.

This groove is actually pretty darned comfortable, he thought. *Power nap?*

Ten minutes would set him up nicely after the flight in.

But what about Squib?

Probably better to lift the kid out of there and then have a nap.

Vern focused his awareness in both nostrils. *Where are you, Squib boy? Where you hiding out?*

Dragons had a better sense of smell than the average bloodhound once they had a scent to follow, although this sense tended to deteriorate over the years, due to sulfur deposits along the nasal passages. Vern had been almost completely bunged up for a couple of centuries at his previous digs in the Everglades, until this nice Thai lady who lived on a river shack talked herself out of a barbecuing by offering to candle his nostrils. It was a dangerous travail, working with flame right next to a dragon's person, but Lily got clumps of crap out of Vern's nose and goddamn if he couldn't smell into the future afterwards. He slept better too with clear airways.

And so Vern let Lily go unharmed, and she in return set the mob on him. And that was all she wrote for Florida. Since that time he'd hung out in Honey Island.

But it was worth it. You ain't got nuthin' if you ain't got your health.

Vern thought that once he snatched his troublesome familiar, he would have Squib do a little Internet research on candling and see if the boy couldn't do a session on his nostrils. Though the buildup was nowhere as severe as it used to be, on account of he rarely got to *flame on* these days.

Which might be about to change.

Vern had brought an old shirt of Squib's from the shack. He tugged it from his cargo pants pocket, held it to his snout, and sniffed.

Come on, twitchers. Seek and find.

Of all the places Squib could have gotten himself stashed, New Orleans in general was the worst, and the French Quarter in particular was the worst of the worst. All the usual odors hung around: carbon monoxide, human fluids, swamp musk, restaurant vents, street smokers, food trucks, with that added Katrina shake-up after-smell which still hadn't dissipated. So you took all of that, made it super-spicy, added a cloying mist of the lemony bleachy street wash-down, and the occasional waft from Cancer Alley's leaking drums over in the River Parishes, and it made for one hell of a bouquet.

Not for the faint of nose.

Most humans can't smell shit anyhow, thought Vern, but his fourth sense was working just fine, and he almost immediately picked up Squib's scent on the third floor of the Marcello. The kid wasn't hard to find, scrubbing as he did with that cheap-ass soap that came in pillow-mint-sized packets. More industrial detergent than anything else. Poor ignorant Squib didn't know it, but he was slowly bleaching his own skin.

That scent, along with Squib's own signature blend of sweat, adolescence, and attitude, was so clear to Vern that he could read it as clear as tendrils of neon smoke reaching out to him from across the street.

Third-floor rear, he thought. *In and out. Anybody who gets in my way—well, not my problem. I'll try and keep the body count low in respect for Squib's feelings about homicide and Waxman's souls theory, but in my defense before the fact, these are all bad guys.*

Vern shifted backwards, inching his head from the

gargoyle's niche. He was pretty sure no one had spotted him. Camouflage cells plus nighttime plus drunk-ass humans equaled virtual invisibility, or so he sincerely hoped.

Vern did a few push-ups, then popped half a dozen burpees just to get his blood pumping. He considered some split squats, but he hated that exercise with a passion.

Those bastards are harder for me, he reasoned. *My center of gravity is lower.*

Push-ups and burpees would have to do, and of course a cursory check to make damn sure his dragon tackle was tucked up about as far as it could go.

His little voice piped up, *Are you nervous, Wyvern? Holy shit, are you scared?*

Vern answered back under his breath, "I ain't scared, asshole. I'm prudent, is all. It's been a while, and I'm the last dragon, so far as I know. The world can't stand to lose me."

But Vern was nervous, and possibly a smidge scared, which wasn't necessarily a bad thing, though he wouldn't admit it to his little voice.

Even Adele gets stage fright, he told himself. *Be like Adele and use the energy.*

And before he could change his mind, Vern took a running jump off the roof and aimed his armor-plated head at the third-floor window's grille.

And missed by a country yard.

VERN WENT IN through the wall, which is a tough breach, even for a dragon. Luckily, though the blocks were stone, they were cavity blocks, with nothing more than plasterboard on the interior. The wall barely qualified as a wall by the standards of some of the medieval castles he'd busted into. Three feet of solid rock, those bastards were, with some fucking Norman pouring boiling pitch onto your back, which really gunked up a guy's scales. So he broke through, but his wings got torn up some and there was dust everywhere.

"Fuck," swore Vern. "Fucking dust and shit."

Which was his way of blaming the environment for his aim being off.

He shook the stars out of his eyes and lifted his haunches from the floor before the fat pooled in his ass and the mafiosi came upon him lolling there like a steer ready for the bolt. Vern found himself jammed in a corridor, which wasn't good: In here, he was restricted. A dragon generally preferred a little room to maneuver: get a little scything going with the talons, do some damage with the tail. In an ideal world a dragon wouldn't even touch down during battle, but no one had ever accused the French Quarter of being perfect, unless in the tone of *Oh, perfect. That's just fucking perfect.*

Two guys came around the corner, and one seriously misinterpreted the threat level.

"Hey, man," he said to Vern, kinda smiling, kinda not, "you like some cosplaying motherfucker?"

The second man was slightly more on point. "Holy shit, Alfonse, that's the real deal right there. It's a fucking gargoyle."

Which was a low blow, in Vern's opinion.

At any rate they both skipped over negotiating and went straight for shooters.

I got no choice, thought Vern. *I gotta go operational.*

Yep, said his little voice. *Like that was never the plan.*

Then the first bullet from a semiautomatic hit him square on the chest plate. Fortunately, Vern had been in crisis so often that the plate's valves had seized up and stayed permanently rigid, which was a bitch when he was trying to sleep some days, but paid off when there was a wiseguy taking shots at close range. Still, the impact smarted a little, so Vern the amiable swamp dragon went away for a spell, and in his place emerged Lord Highfire, battle dragon.

Battle dragons do not listen to their little voices.

They go directly to war.

Which is what Vern did.

His fight-or-flight instinct pumped extra blood into his armor plating to further toughen his shell. His pigment cells picked up the navy blue in the corridor's wallpaper, and the glands at the back of his throat spurted sulfur oil onto his molars.

Here we go, thought Battle Vern, chomping his back teeth together, causing a spark, which ignited the oil, providing him with a pilot light.

Feed the fire, thought Vern, and converted ten pounds of body fat into plasma, which he breathed onto the pilot light. This ignited the plasma, transforming it into that particular stream of flame which has been written about for centuries, which the victims rarely survived.

The stream of flame had already charred the two armed heavies down to their bones before Vern got a grip on it and tightened his lips to a tight whistle, narrowing the stream to a perfect tube which he used to carve a hole in the wall at the end of the corridor. Then he swallowed his flame and barged through the embers ringing the hole, expecting to find Squib on the other side.

But there was no Squib—not an entire Squib, at any rate, just one of the kid's toes on a napkin. Scribbled on the napkin was:

"Fuck you, lizard."

Vern sighed.

Goddamn, Hooke. He ain't got no idea. Poor fool figures he can trap me like I'm a wild animal.

And then it occurred to him: *Hooke mutilated my boy.*

Vern heard the particular rowdy clatter of a mob barreling down the corridor.

Now ain't that a blast from the past?

He turned to see a dozen or so assorted hoodlums hustling toward him, all stoked for gunplay.

I can smell the coke from here, Vern thought. *A little Colombian courage.*

These guys sure were dumb. Hadn't they ever watched 300? Never overload a narrow avenue with bodies. It don't matter how many people you have: Two at a time was all that had to be dealt with.

But Vern thought, *I ain't got the time, patience, nor inclination to be dealing with no two at a time.*

And so he sparked up and opened his jaws wide, sending a five-second burst of viscous flame down the corridor, which reduced his would-be assailants to piles of bones and set their ordnance popping off every which way, knocking chunks from the masonry. The unfortunate wiseguys never even had time to get a good look at what they were charging.

Does anybody even use that term anymore? "Wiseguys"? Seems a little dated.

Vern raised his nostrils, reaching out for a fresh trail, and found two, fainter than the toe he was standing over but unmistakably Squib Moreau.

More digits, the dragon guessed. *That goddamn sadist*, he thought. *This is torture.*

Yeah, said his little voice, *says the guy who just torched an entire battalion.*

At least they went quick, argued Vern. *My fire don't burn slow. No one ever got mildly scalded from dragon flame.*

"Fulminated" was the word, or used to be.

Two *separate* scents: which meant that Hooke was leading him on a wild-goose chase which was supposed to end in his goose being cooked. While that was unlikely to happen, who was to say that this Ivory wannabe didn't have a rocket launcher waiting for him beside one of the toes?

Vern took a moment to consider. A rocket launcher would definitely leave a mark.

If I had a restaurant and a hotel at my disposal, where would I stash a boy I didn't want smelled?

The answer came to him pretty quick.

Even a dragon found it difficult to smell through aluminum.

But in his long experience, the meat locker was always at the back of the kitchen, and if there was one thing Vern could smell, it was a kitchen.

He went back out the way he came in, this time digging his talons into the stone and crawling snout-first down the wall.

Down the wall and into the kitchen was the plan, but being a little out of practice with facades and with his meter tipping over into reckless because of the adrenaline blast, Vern dug in a little deep with one set of claws and pulverized a block.

Shitballs, he thought as he lost his grip and went plunging headfirst toward the pavement.

No time to spread the wings—and even if he had managed to get a little span going, it wouldn't have slowed him down much—so Vern instinctively tucked his chin in and prepared to take the brunt on his armored crown.

Luckily his two-story plummet was broken by a couple of wrong-place, wrong-time doormen, who were also broken by the two-story plummet. Vern didn't feel bad about it because they were armed and he was in the moment.

However, crashing into a French Quarter sidewalk outside a restaurant was a little higher-viz than Vern would have liked. There must have been a couple of hundred tourists meandering along this section of the street, with dozens more looking out through the restaurant windows. The humans shrank back from the impact like ripples from a stone in water, and Vern found himself bathed in streetlamp glow, in full view of the public he had shunned for so long.

Nice job, Lord Highfire, he told himself. *Still think this rescue operation was a shit-hot idea?*

Once upon a not-so-distant time, folks' first reaction to a dragon dropping unexpectedly into their environs would have been to fall over themselves running the hell away. You could generally expect a couple of the more lily-livered youngsters to crap themselves or pass out. All of these things happened now, but a large percentage of the witnesses also reached for their cell phones. It was all about the documenting of the moment in modern America. As recently as ten years ago, the documenters would have had to reach all the way into their handbags or pockets for their devices, and even if they did get their phones out in time, the video would've been virtually useless in this light. Now, however, every individual on the continent over the age of two was in possession of at least one fully loaded HD movie studio clutched in their sweaty hands at all times. After all, people couldn't be expected to eat, sleep, work out, or jack off without a smartphone.

So when Vern came down, the humans made two noises. The first was a collective gasp, and the second was a variation on the word "Record."

Also, two possibly drunk girls flashed him.

Goddamn it, thought Vern. *Now I either gotta leave Louisiana or get myself killed. Humans don't understand what kinda hoops a dragon has to jump through just to get Wi-Fi.*

He was tempted to flex a little, spread the wings, to give the folks their money's worth, but he hadn't survived this long just to blow it on a moment's grandstanding.

So the dragon leaped from the pulped doormen straight through the restaurant window, showering a bar mitzvah party with glass and tangling a red velvet drape around his shoulders like a superhero dragon.

"Mazel tov," Vern said to the stunned kid in the hat, then scooted along the tabletop and through the swing doors.

He moved fast, quicker than he had for decades, and he could feel his heart ramping up.

I gotta do more cardio, he told himself. *This is ridiculous.*

Time was, I could fly the length of this continent without breaking a sweat. Now I can't even run through a restaurant without panting.

Nevertheless, Vern was still the fastest living thing any of these humans had ever seen—which is why they didn't see him, not clearly. He was a bear-sized blur that left a general impression rather than a detailed image.

The bar mitzvah kid, Tony Cohen, said later to Fox 8, "I thought it was two alligators fucking."

Which went viral, getting more hits than any footage of Vern himself. Clearly little Tony had been sneaking vodka shots, which is what his parents get for throwing a bar mitzvah in the French Quarter.

Vern hit the double doors with his noggin and took them clean off the hinges. There was one of Ivory's soldiers in the corridor, hitting on an obviously uncomfortable waitress by showing her his gun, so Vern palmed the guy into the Sheetrock on the way past. A chef in toque blanche was holding a Baked Alaska on a silver tray, which Vern set alight with a squib of flame, just for giggles.

I mean, how is a guy supposed to resist that? he thought as the dessert's *whoomph* of blue fire set off the sprinklers.

As he had surmised, the meat locker, a walk-in aluminum job, was buttressing the back wall. There were two goons on the door.

Guarding the beef? I don't think so.

All credit to Ivory's boys, they did manage to get their guns out before Vern reached them, but this was probably because of the minute or so of chaos which had heralded the arrival of some form of threat.

That, and the fact that the cop Hooke had told them, "Guard the door with your balls."

One of the guys had queried the instruction. "Hey, cop, ain't that supposed to be 'guard the door with your life'?"

And Hooke had answered, "No, son. Balls. 'Cause that's what I'm gonna hack off if you let anybody or anything in there."

Constable Hooke backed up his threat with a mean old stare, and this, coupled with the evocative nature of the verb "hack," ensured that the guardians of the refrigerator stayed frosty.

That being said, they had assumed that whatever threat they were to face would have a human face.

The threat streaking toward them was surely not human.

Vern was alternately amused or irked by humans' reaction to his appearance. On this occasion, he experienced both emotions within a second of each other.

The first guy blurted, *"Hail, Satan."*

Which was presumably a last-ditch attempt to change saviors to appease the devil heading for him.

This made Vern smile, until the second guy said, "Fat fucking super-hog."

Which wiped the smile off Vern's face. *"Super-hog"? What the hell?*

If Vern had slowed down a little, the kitchen staff might have gone batshit crazy at the sight of him, but as it was, reactions were trailing a couple of seconds in his wake and the hysteria wouldn't make it into the kitchen until Vern was long gone.

He hit the fridge guardians hard, flattening their rib

cages like concertinas, which pulverized their hearts. One guy did manage to squeeze off a shot, which pinged across Vern's upper thigh and would surely have clipped his dick had he not had the foresight to withdraw it earlier. Dragon junk does not have protective plating, and a dick nick could easily have had him bleeding out on the kitchen tiles.

Not exactly a noble way to go.

Vern's blood was up now, and he yanked the freezer door right out of its frame when he could easily have turned the handle, which caused his back to twinge. Hard to believe, but when he picked up that back injury all those years ago, he had been doing nothing more strenuous than eating a horse.

The freezer was a big walk-in job with frosted sides of beef hanging in rows like dry-cleaning. Squib was squatted down at the back between towers of ice cream buckets with his T-shirt pulled over his knees and a candy-red pool of blood frozen around one bare foot.

"Hey, Vern," said the boy. "Am I dreaming you?"

"No, son," said Vern, "you ain't dreaming. There's an honest-to-God dragon come to save you."

Squib smiled weakly. "Not all of me. Hooke done took his gut hook to my foot."

Vern squatted down and breathed sulfur over Squib's head.

"Are you putting me to sleep, Vern? Why you wanna do that?"

Vern popped out a claw and blew flame on it till it glowed white.

"'Cause you don't wanna be conscious when I seal those wounds, kid."

"I guess," said Squib, one eye already closing. "We gonna fuck Hooke up, boss?"

"That guy is already fucked," said Vern, "all the trouble he's brought to Ivory's door. Hooke is super-fucked, no doubt."

"Super-fucked," said Squib. "I sure do like the sound of that."

And then he was asleep, so Vern elevated his boy's leg and got to work.

Funny for a dragon, but the smell of burning friendly flesh always made Vern gag a little. He could give a shit about hostiles, but there was something about cauterizing a familiar that turned his stomach.

Squib had lost three toes, which made his foot look like it had a Mohawk, which caused Vern to giggle and took his mind off his stomach. He quickly finished up the field surgery, then took a fist of frost from the freezer wall and ground it onto the melted flesh, rising up a fierce hiss and cloud of steam. Squib did not even moan throughout the process, though he'd feel it plenty tomorrow.

Poor little bastard will be hopping around like a pirate for a few weeks, he thought. *But he'll live, providing I make good on my rescue boast and get us out of here.*

The human world was beginning to cotton on to the fact that something out of the ordinary was in their midst, and Vern didn't have to test his senses to the limits to find evidence of this. Chatter from the kitchen was maybe three octaves higher and fifty decibels louder than it ought to be. A couple of heads poked around the crumpled doorframe, only to hurriedly withdraw.

From on the street, Vern heard sirens indicating the police were approaching, drawn by a commotion which was above and beyond the usual, even for the French Quarter.

I sure wish I could stick around to watch Hooke explain what he's doing here, thought Vern, but his own desire to send the constable to meet his Maker would have to take a back seat. There wasn't time for a full-scale rampage at the moment, not now that cruisers had shotguns and SWAT rode around in tanks.

The best thing for it is a quick-style exit and back to the bayou. Still, he added to himself, *guess there's always time to fuck up a Mafia hotel.*

Vern picked up Squib with a sight more tenderness than he usually employed when laying hands on a human, wrapping his wings around him like he was a little baby dragon. He stepped out of the refrigerator and then used a technique which, once upon a time, was known as "calling the cavalry." He blew a dense column of roiling flame which burned the living hell out of anything it touched, and scoured a series of holes straight through to the night sky. That was the thing about dragon fire: It was closer to the fourth-century-BC Greek fire than your common or garden fire: an incendiary liquid flame which ate through anything unfortunate enough to be in its path and did not give a shit about someone dumping water on it.

Even Vern didn't fully understand his own physiology, because that level of understanding came with a price tag, and that price tag would include anesthetic, restraints, a gurney, and a team of medical types in scrubs. Which, as prices go, was a little Wolverine, in Vern's opinion. He had let this Italian polymath guy poke around a little in the fifteenth century, but all Vern had learned from that was that his flame was a "nonadhesive petroleum distillate"; plus the guy had done a sketch of Vern having a fight with this lion, *balls out*—when Vern had *specifically* told him his balls were *in*.

Goddamn polymaths.

So Vern sent up a blast of petroleum distillate which blew a six-foot-wide shaft right through the heart of the hotel, letting a silver dollar of Louisiana moon peep through up top.

Voilà, thought Vern. *Exit stage right. Thank you, and good night.*

And then: *Please, God, no helicopters.*

HOOKE HAD TO admit that he was surprised by the actual volume of ruination Vern was visiting on the Marcello. He'd been expecting maybe SEAL-team-level destruction, but this dragon was more like a natural disaster: some kind of whirlwind–forest fire hybrid. All this and barely seven feet tall.

Impressive.

Looks like maybe old Vern will do me the courtesy of taking care of my pain-in-the-ass boss. So no need for plan B.

Now all Hooke needed was to get into the vault.

Once the elephant-sized shit hit the windmill-sized fan, cracks started running like black lightning along the penthouse walls and San Pellegrino went spraying everywhere.

"What the fuck was that?" said Ivory, falling back against his fitness desk.

"Well, it's like this, boss," said Hooke easily. "It looks like a dragon showed up after all." He reckoned the truth was an easier sell now that the building was wobbling like a tower of boxes in the bed of a speeding pickup truck.

"Fuck you, Hooke," said Ivory, but a part of him believed it. Humans have race memory, after all, so consequently everyone believes in dragons in a pinch.

Hooke thought that maybe Ivory Conti was entitled to a little self-pity, firstly on account of how he looked corresponding so perfectly with his name—viz., White Count—which no doubt accounted for his variation on a Napoleon complex. And secondly, because of the fact that ten minutes ago he was king of this little castle with a pretty solid business model, and now his best guys were dead, his authority was under threat, and there was a giant death-breathing fire lizard he might not even believe in coming to barbecue him in his very own fortress.

Poor little fucker, thought Hooke.

At least Ivory was finally taking the situation seriously now, even if it had taken a dead bodyguard and a shaky building to motivate the man. He unlocked the walk-in safe at the back of his office and, appropriately enough, walked in.

"Oho," said Hooke, actually rubbing his hands. "So Ivory Conti's been hiding his toys. What you got in there, son?"

He followed Ivory into the safe—and into an Aladdin's cave of goodies. Regence Hooke was impressed, and he'd seized a fuck-load of treasure in Iraq.

"What is this place, boss?" he asked like he didn't know. "This ain't no regular lockup."

"It's a safe room," said Ivory. "Take a good look 'cause you won't ever be seeing it again, *capisce*?"

"*Capisce*"? thought Hooke. *Really*?

Ivory took a spanking-new modular combat rifle from its brackets. "Your dragon ain't the only one with *fire*-power," said Ivory. "Let's see how he likes a gutful of this."

"I admire your attitude, boss," said Hooke. "You got spunk. We come outta this and the city's ours."

The safe room really was impressive, guns displayed like that, all regular-spaced and lined up. People underestimated the care and attention to detail that kind of arrangement required. It was a goddamn exhibition, is what it was. Hooke had heard that Ivory hired an art installer from a gallery over in the Warehouse District to come in here and lay out the weaponry. Took the guy a week and cost eight grand, or so he'd been told, but it was worth the inconvenience and price tag, because he'd be willing to bet it made Ivory want to jerk off every time he came in here; plus he'd let his competitors get a glimpse from time to time just so they knew what caliber of a man they might be thinking about fucking over. Because guys in Ivory's business thought about fucking each other over 24/7, 365.

Hooke eeny-meenied his way along the various weapons hung on the wall, passing by the more pissanty models, until his eyes lit upon a Barrett Light Fifty.

"And the winner is," he said, reaching for the .50-cal and taking its weight like it was a barbell.

It will be interesting, he thought, *to see if this portable cannon can punch a hole in an actual dragon*. It would also be interesting to see what Vern did when Ivory irritated him with his peashooter.

Dragon's gonna be pissed, and that's when I take my shot.

Ivory took a sniper's stance, elbows on his fitness desk, barrel aimed toward the door.

Maybe he expects Vern to knock.

Meanwhile, Hooke stood back, keeping one foot inside the safe room, which he figured was called "safe" for good reason.

They didn't have to hold their positions long, it not being exactly the hunt for bin Laden. Within seconds a roar like someone had brought thunder indoors ripped through the building, and a good quarter of the floor was consumed by a bolt of solid flame which punched straight through the penthouse to the sky above.

"Fuck!" said Ivory, his eyebrows crisping. "Fuck balls momma—"

Which pretty much spoke for the room.

As terrible as the column of flame surely was, there were a couple of positives, in Hooke's view. One, it completely destroyed any evidence of his recent homicide, and two, it was short-lived. Nothing caught alight, as such, just glowed around the edges.

The fire winked out like it had never been, and it was immediately obvious to Hooke what the point had been.

Old Vern is carving himself an escape route, he thought. *Which leads directly through this sorry-ass penthouse.*

He nudged Ivory's ass with the toe of his boot. "Lock and load, boss," he said. "Here we go. Enter the dragon."

Hooke snickered. *Enter the dragon.*

VERN'S CLIMB THROUGH the hotel was pretty uneventful so far as journeys through the circles of hell went. Climbing was no biggie for a dragon, as historically they favored altitude. True, they usually flew down to their eyries rather than climbed up, but a fire lizard was equipped with crampon talons and could scale a sheer cliff if he had to, so a four-story New Orleans hotel shouldn't pose a problem so long as nobody was foolhardy enough to get in the way.

The second floor was absolute chaos, dust everywhere and embers flittering in the afterburn. The sprinklers were sputtering in a half-assed manner, and a couple of Ivory's soldiers were stumbling around, dazed by the vapor. They were pretty shaken up and did not really compute Vern's appearance, well, not until he burned most of them down to their bones.

"Was that a gargoyle come to life?" the only survivor mumbled to himself.

"Gargoyle"?

That was twice now.

Up Vern went, cursing Squib, even though the boy with three steaming toe stumps was in deep REM sleep.

"Goddamn familiars," griped the dragon. "You open your heart for five goddamn minutes, and next thing you know you're burning escape shafts in Mafia hotels."

Yeah, like you're not loving this, said his little voice.

He went up quick, digging in the talons, pretty happy with his progress considering he hadn't done a whole lot of climbing for a few decades.

I'm gonna feel this tomorrow. He knew this from experience: You neglect the glutes and they will bite you in the ass.

The climb stopped being uneventful at a definite point, and that point was when he caught a glimpse of Regence Hooke on the top floor.

"Bonus points," said Vern, thinking that he was going to enjoy the hell out of what he planned to do next.

Chop toes offa my boy, will you? Dismember my drinking buddy? You are about to learn what happens when you poke a dragon, Regence.

Vern's arrival at the penthouse level had been met with a hail of automatic weapons fire. The bullets pinged off his forehead, but damn if it wasn't irritating as hell, like someone was spitting ball bearings at him.

Vern frowned, and not just because he was annoyed, but because the frown brought a thick plate of brow down over his eyes, shielding him from the assault.

Is there no end to my talents? he thought, peeking out from under the shelf of bone to see who besides Hooke was wasting their ammunition. Little fucker in a Tony Montana outfit was screaming something about his momma and balls, which was inappropriate from any species. Guy looked hysterical in his black shirt with Bee Gee–wingspan lapels and a white waistcoat.

Vern thought about saying it, the thing Pacino said in the movie, and he was on the verge when he caught sight of Hooke, hanging back a little.

"There you are, motherfucker," he growled, but instead of growling, Vern should have been sparking up because Hooke had raised up some kind of mini cannon and blasted off a shot. Two things stopped Vern from dodging the bullet: One, he wasn't overly concerned, and two, fast as he was, Vern could never go supersonic without a run-up, so the .50-cal was always going to outpace him.

The big bullet clipped his brow, lifting a flap of flesh and chipping the bone, inflicting a level of pain on Vern like he hadn't felt in many a long year.

Once the blood started flowing, Vern went all heat-of-the-moment, red-mist crazy. He dragged a roar out of prehistoric times and sent a wide-bore *kill 'em all* blast of flame into Hooke's corner, somehow managing to incorporate the words "'uck you, 'ooke" into the assault, which was the best diction he could manage with an open mouth.

When the mist cleared, Vern surveyed the devastation he had wrought and he saw that it was good.

No way Hooke is walking out of there, he thought. *Fucker is probably a tiny little diamond, considering all the heat I blasted at him.*

This was a pleasing notion, and it calmed Vern's heart rate down somewhat. "All this inconvenience for a kid," he said to the moon.

Jubelus would laugh his ass off.

The notion that a dragon would take a missile to the face for a human really would've had his brother cracking his scales with laughter. Vern would have laughed, too—after all, how desperate would a guy have to be before he gave a solitary sulfur fart about the fate of a specific human?

Exactly this desperate, thought Vern, giving the torched penthouse one last squint, just in case Hooke, slippery customer that he was, had somehow managed to wriggle his way through death's door. Then he felt the entire building exhale and sag. He clawed his way to roof level. The night air felt cool on his back, which was nice, and he stretched out his shoulders for a second before he spotted a chopper in the night sky. The spotlight slung under its chassis was scything through the darkness toward him.

I never torched a chopper, Vern thought. *Could be fun.*

Then Squib stirred in his makeshift cocoon, and the dragon thought perhaps he'd better hightail it back to the bayou.

Vern patted his stomach. All this sparking off was costing him his reserves of fat.

I'll stop off at the Pearl Bar and Grill, he decided, *siphon off a few gallons of cooking oil from their stores, just in case there's any fallout from this bullshit and I need to light up an angry mob.*

You didn't hear so much about angry mobs anymore, but they were still out there, just waiting for a burning cross to congregate around, putting in time between causes screaming at pregnant teens on TV. The losers usually went after their own kind, which was hilarious to Vern, humans hunting down humans because of skin tone, or which port they used in a storm, so to speak. That was the problem with humans: They couldn't be reasoned with. Vern had had himself a pal, back in medieval England. Nice guy. Lived in a region called Fatfield. Smoked a lot of hashish. Anyways, he always maintained that a mob could be reasoned with. *You give them a demonstration of power, then they'll think better of it and go back to their farms.*

The Fatfield dragon held on to this point of view right up to the day when a bunch of Norman Crusaders used cross-bows to stake him down in a marsh and let the elements take care of him.

"Reasoned with"?

If there was one thing Vern had learned, there was no reasoning with humans.

So why are you here, dickhead? asked his little voice.

Vern didn't have a good answer to that. *I am here because it feels right* didn't really stand up to argument, but it was as close to true as he could get.

Squib was a good kid doing his best in a shitty situation, so if Vern had to pick a side, he would pick the one that Waxman had been on, that being Squib Moreau's.

And I just burned old Regence's team to ashes.

"A good night's work," said Vern, then shook out his wings, thinking for the umpteenth time that he should Google how wings worked and learn something about himself.

"It's something to do with lift and drag," he told the unconscious Squib, then grabbed the boy's waistband and soared into the New Orleans night sky.

"Good-bye, Constable," he said, mentally ticking off *Kill Hooke* on his to-do list. "Burn in hell."

CHAPTER 17

OOKE WAS NOT BURNING IN HELL. IN POINT OF FACT, THE CON-
stable had significantly more life left in him than might
be expected. There was barely a scratch on Momma
Hooke's boy apart from a few blisters on his fingertips where
he had been a mite slow letting go of the safe room door.

Things that had saved him:

1. Steel fire doors.

2. Oxygen tank with handy face mask.

3. Dimwit mob boss who turned his back on what he
thought was the lesser of two evils.

Sayonara, Ivory, thought Hooke, sucking down the sweet
oxygen. *You served your purpose*, paisano. *You kept me alive.*

And in return, when Vern had sent the lightning, Hooke
had shut the boss out of the safe room.

Ivory Conti must have been one paranoid little Italian
mobster because that room was a mini fortress built to withstand the very worst that nature or the New Orleans underworld could throw its way. Turned out, the room itself
was a modified bank vault that could shrug off a hit from

a hurricane or an RPG with barely a buckle in its plates. Hooke had seen similar setups in Iraq, but nothing with air-conditioning and deep-pile carpets.

Ten million, this place cost, he estimated. *Easy.* And that wasn't even counting the private elevator.

Little Ivory must have been expecting a siege-type situation.

Besides the impressive wall of guns, Ivory had kept his stockpiles of cash in the safe room, along with his records, all burned onto labeled CDs, which was a little archaic but very handy. The surveillance feeds from all over the building were either completely dead or glitching, but the item which interested Hooke the most was a simple Moleskine notebook with the words "Pet Pigs" written on the cover in correction fluid.

"Hello, future," said Hooke, pocketing the book. He also stuffed two duffels with cash, a selection of car keys, a couple of gold ingots, and a lot of automatic weapons, because a dirty cop can never have too much of the pimp life. The final item to be requisitioned was a man-portable air-defense missile system, which Hooke almost missed because it was semi-disguised among a pile of cardboard poster tubes.

"Ah, my Russian friend," said Hooke, stroking it, "together we shall wreak such beautiful destruction." The logic being that if a .50-cal could put a hole in Vern, then a Russian MANPAD would shut the lizard down but good. He slung it over his shoulder, summoned the elevator, and three minutes later was nudging his brand-new Humvee out through the underground parking garage's security gates.

The Marcello was beginning its slow collapse to the

ground, shrieking and groaning like a dying behemoth, and Hooke knew he had underestimated Vern.

Barely seven feet tall and with a paunch—I thought maybe a little flamethrower-type action, nothing like this. Goddamn, that boy can party.

But so could Regence Hooke.

We are as the great adversaries of history, thought Hooke, feeling a little grandiose. *Ahab and the white whale.*

Vern was probably Moby-Dick in that scenario.

Hooke patted the duffel of ordnance strapped into the passenger seat. "Well, boys," he said to the guns, "I guess we'll have to write ourselves a new ending to that story."

And since Hooke was Captain Ahab in this scenario, he would need to find himself a crew.

VERN OFTEN THOUGHT that somewhere along the line one of his ancestors must've been a pigeon, because he had one hell of an internal compass and could generally find wherever he was looking for with his eyes closed, though this was more a figure of speech than a boast since his inner eyelids were transparent.

Tonight, though, his compass was all over the place, and Vern found himself out over the Gulf with his mind a thousand miles away instead of concentrating on getting Squib home ASAP. This kind of disorientation often clouded his senses after a battle. One time he'd had a run-in with these Spanish Inquisition assholes outside Seville. There were harsh words on both sides, but it might have blown over had not this one martyr-looking motherfucker in a sackcloth cassock called Vern an "abomination." Next thing Vern knew, he had six bloody crucifixes strung around his neck and he was touching down in Iceland. Frickin' Iceland! That was no climate for a dragon. Still, he'd hung out in the Blue Lagoon for a spell until his presence started interfering with the local ecosystem and actually increased the water temperature and mineral composition.

Tonight, he'd felt it again: the battle rage. Combine that with fat loss, and it was no wonder he was a bit out of his head.

I need to get some fat into me, Vern realized, *before I drop right out of the sky.*

And so he turned his senses back on and allowed the Pearl's signature scent, a blend of skillet grease, watered beer, and latrine bleach, to guide him in from twenty miles out.

"Pit stop, kid," mumbled Vern, hugging Squib close to his belly so he could benefit from some dragon dynamo heat. Dipping his flaps, he added, "Time to refuel."

The Pearl Bar and Grill sat back from the Slidell road on the southern border of Petit Bateau. The parking lot was lit up like a baseball diamond on account of the swamp hillbillies who insisted on using any dark corner to go slapping the tar out of each other. There were a couple of dozen flatbeds out front and the buzzy sound of amplified power chords pulsing through the screen door.

In his woozy state, Vern found himself missing company. For a fleeting moment he thought maybe he'd drop in for a rack of pool, seeing as he was already no doubt plastered all over the Internet. Could be that the Swamp Rangers were already on their way over here to throw some kind of weighted-net doodad over him.

Then he came to his senses and straight-A resisted the temptation to join the drunken ranks of humanity, instead swooping in round back, skimming a jagged mass of briar and cypress, and scaring the crap out of a sleeping crane.

"Fucking crane," said Vern, and as he decelerated, the blood which had, unbeknownst to him, been blowing over his back suddenly reversed direction and flowed down over his face, and he realized that he was bleeding again. A lot.

Hooke, he thought. *The gift that keeps on giving.*

There was more than battle disorientation going on here. *I am actually seriously wounded*, thought the dragon, and as soon as he thought it, he felt it.

He twisted in midair, misjudged the height of the fence, and clipped it with his tail, which would have been no big deal except that the proprietor had recently had it electrified and the resultant boost of his heart rate sent the blood gushing in Tarantino-esque gouts from his brow and skewed his coordination entirely. His claws spasmed, releasing Squib, who tumbled into the Pearl's yard, landing awkwardly but fortuitously on a pile of oat sacks, while the dragon himself crashed headfirst into a pyramid of oil barrels, scattering them like pins.

Bull's-eye, he thought. *All in all, a successful mission, Lord Highfire.*

And then he joined Squib in the land of shadows.

SQUIB EMERGED FROM the shadows first, mainly because of the lick of lightning bolt in a can that jolted his system before Vern jettisoned his cargo. The de facto defibrillator set his heart pumping and evaporated the mist from his mind. Fortunately, it did not burn off the anesthetic effect, so the boy lay on his belly for a spell, smelling the oats and thinking breakfast must be on a skillet nearby, while the world and all its travails gradually leaked in from the edges of his eyeballs.

Squib remembered the constable and his gut hook. He remembered those shining blue eyes that weren't a mirror to anything, because Regence Hooke didn't have no soul. He remembered the Marcello walk-in freezer, and how he'd imagined himself strung up with all those sides of beef. This was a troubling thought, and it might have upset the young buck even more had not his dragon friend rescued him.

Did he have a dragon friend in the actual real world, or was Vern simply a boy's fancy?

Squib took a few breaths to ponder this and arrived at the conclusion that he had a dragon boss with friendship potential. And Vern had delivered him from further harm in the Quarter, where further harm had most definitely been on the agenda.

This memory of harm reminded Squib again of his little piggies, as Momma used to call them on bath days in the blue plastic tub, some twelve years gone by now.

Three of my little piggies have done gone to market, and they ain't ever coming back, thought the boy. And he raised himself up from his inverted position on the sacks, for nothing moves a boy like the notion of taking a peek at his own scars.

I must be a sight, he thought. *Downright mutilated.*

Their arrival had activated a spotlight in the yard, and Squib knew at once where he was, for he'd been busting his hump in here for years.

So he was aware right off where he'd landed, but even so, he took a moment to study his left foot in the light of the halogen lamp. "Holy shit," he breathed. "Like goddamn taffy."

It was true. Vern's surgery hadn't exactly been cosmetic, and Squib's foot looked like a monkey had operated on it with a blowtorch.

"Cool," said Squib. "I can't feel a thing."

"Well now, son. That's about to change."

Squib looked up from his scrutinizing to see Bodi Irwin pointing a pump-action in his direction. The boss of the Pearl Bar and Grill was scowling through a prodigious gray beard and sporting a 2004 tour T-shirt emblazoned with the legend "American Idiot."

Which just about covered how Squib felt.

"Down you get from that pile, Squib," said Bodi, jerking the barrel of his shotgun, which Squib dearly wished he wouldn't. Waxman used to say that where "jerking" was concerned, weapons were like a fella's pecker and would respond in the same fashion. Squib had laughed along with that joke for years without getting it.

He got it now, though.

Yeah, I see, he thought. *That barrel is likely to shoot off with Bodi manhandling it how he is.*

"This ain't what it seems, Mister Irwin," he said, pointing

to his foot. "You know me. I wouldn't thieve from you. Look, I been injured."

Bodi glanced at the brutalized foot, but his expression softened not one whit. "Yep. You got a habit of misplacing digits, ain't you, Squib?"

"Come on, Bodi," said Squib. "This ain't a normal situation. Look at me, way up here."

"Seems normal to me," noted Bodi. "Some kid interfering with my electrified fence. Looks like you're planning to step up to major larceny."

"That ain't it," objected Squib. "We crashed, is what it is, I think."

Bodi frowned, which crinkled the beard covering most of his face. "'We' crashed? Who the hell is 'we'?"

It was Squib's turn to frown. "We" was difficult to explain without someone getting shot or fried, but he could see Vern's tail sticking out of a mess of oil drums, and the tail wasn't moving.

"Okay, Mister Irwin. I'm gonna tell you the truth, but you gotta stop waving that shotgun around. If it goes off and you hit Vern, he ain't gonna 'ppreciate it."

Bodi seemed to sense that something out of the ordinary was going on, and so he lowered his weapon maybe thirty degrees.

"You got ten seconds, Squib, more or less. Ten seconds to tell me who the hell Vern is, and to convince me why I shouldn't call the constable."

Squib took six of those seconds to plot out his various options and their possible outcomes. Most of them ended up with Bodi being dead. One of them ended up with Bodi accidentally shooting him with his final finger spasm, so before the ten-second deadline he piped up, "If you do call Hooke, I can guarantee that constable ain't gonna answer that call."

The idea that Regence Hooke might be incapacitated in some way cheered Bodi Irwin immensely. "I'm listening," he said.

VERN SLOWLY WOKE and his first thought was, *Oh, shit, something is Balls Out.*

He was right. Something *was* Balls Out—and in this instance, there was nothing metaphorical about the phrase.

He opened his eyes to find himself lying on what he initially thought might be a cloud, so soft and comfy was it. And in that state of utter relaxation that came with being electrified into unconsciousness, he had naturally enough relaxed his scrotal clench and allowed his junk out for an airing. Which would be fine at home on the bayou with nobody watching except maybe a gutsy squirrel, but whatever he was lying on now did not belong in his shack.

"Balls out," muttered Vern. "Balls way out."

He opened both sets of eyelids, let his pupils settle down, and saw the familiar roof beams of his own shack, which was a relief. But he also noted that he was being hovered over by two humans, neither of them Squib, which was the opposite of a relief.

Play it casual, Highfire, he told himself. "What the hell am I lying on?" he asked. "Because this shit sure is comfortable."

One of the humans squealed: a bearded man wearing a Green Day T-shirt.

But the woman held it together and said, "That's memory foam, Mister Vern. And perhaps we might drape a towel over you, for modesty's sake."

Vern glanced downwards. "No need, Miss. I can take care of that double quick." And he did the thing, withdrawing his tackle into its protective pouch.

The man, who, Vern had noticed, had a shotgun tucked under his arm, recovered enough to whistle. "Sorry about the hollering. Squib said you could talk, but I guess I weren't expecting a local accent."

"I'm a sponge that way," said Vern. "I tend to talk like where I hang my hat."

"Uh-huh," said the man, then, "That there is a neat trick with the crown jewels, son. Be handy in a bar fight."

"You said it," said Vern. "Ain't none of us relishes a Bud Light bottle in the nuts, am I right, fella?"

The fella agreed with a nod and another "Uh-huh." If there was one thing the species could come together on, it was balls ache, and the desire to avoid same.

"Memory foam," said Vern, testing the bed's surface with a knuckle. "I'll be goddamned. I seen the infomercial, but I never imagined. It's like cotton candy."

"It is pretty sweet," said the Green Day man. "The babes dig it. I got one just like it that's seen more action than Richard Gere in his heyday, I kid thee not."

"'Babes'?" said the woman, and Vern saw now that she had a look of Squib in her eyes and they both had pretty much the same haircut: a homemade job, by the looks of it, but it suited her, as much as hair could suit anything. "You ain't had a babe since Clinton left 1600 Pennsylvania Avenue."

"*Zing*," said Vern. "You got burned, Green Day."

Which was all by way of avoiding the elephant in the shack, who was in fact a dragon or a couple of humans, depending on your perspective.

Squib's mom took the initiative. "Mister Vern, first off, can I say thank you on account of what you did for my Everett. Saving his life and so forth. And giving him a job, I might add."

It took Vern a beat to remember that Everett was Squib's real name.

"He's a good boy," he said, finding manners somewhere. "Worth saving."

"Maybe he told you already that I'm Elodie Moreau? I'm the one who patched your wound. In truth, you should really get yourself a transfusion, although I wouldn't know where to begin finding you a donor."

Vern touched his forehead and felt a bandage cushioning the wound. "Thank you, Miss Elodie. I'd say that makes us square. And don't be too hard on the boy for keeping me a secret. That was a condition of his employment."

"I understand that, Mister Vern. Of course I do, you being how you are, all dragon-ish and such. But Squib had no choice but to come to us, as he was of the opinion that you might be dying. Squib said that he would surely prefer you alive and angry than dead and serene, and you was angry most of the time anyways."

This was a fair comment. Vern could certainly allow that

he spent a large portion of his conscious life in a state of irritation. Most of his sleeping life, too.

"This here is Bodi Irwin," continued Elodie. "He runs the Pearl Bar and Grill where you crash-landed. We come downriver on his boat. He donated the bed and supplies."

Vern shifted on the memory foam. "Much appreciated, Mister Irwin. Not a bad way to recuperate."

"Call me Bodi, please," said the Pearl's proprietor. "Young Squib also assured us that you would refrain from incinerating us."

Vern couldn't say that it hadn't occurred to him, but what kind of patient would he be, and so forth. "Rest easy, Bodi. You'll live to see *American Idiot* on Broadway."

Irwin laughed bitterly. "We got us plenty of idiots right here, Mister Vern."

It occurred to Vern that these people were being reasonably composed under the circumstances. Generally humans who set their peepers on him went plumb hysterical. Old Bodi had let out that single squeak, but that was about it. Elodie seemed positively relaxed.

"You people are mighty blasé," he said. "How long have I been out?"

"Three days," said Elodie. "We've been taking shifts watching over you. I had some leave coming from the hospital."

"Three days," said Vern. "I ain't *ever* been out for three days before."

"I hung your skin in my bedroom closet," said Bodi, which as non sequiturs go was a doozy.

Vern sat up slow. "You hung my *what* in the *where*?"

Elodie passed him a sippy cup of water. "You shed your skin back at the Pearl, Mister Vern, shucked it right off. We didn't know if you wanted it or not—for a ceremony or something? So we hung it in the closet. It's on one of them classy wooden hangers so's it wouldn't get marked. It's all in one piece, more or less."

Vern drank deeply. He wasn't due a shed for a couple of years, but trauma did sometimes bring it on. On the plus side, he'd slept right through the shedding, which was usually itchy as hell. In fact, this was the first time a skin had ever survived intact; usually he scratched it to ribbons.

"No, I ain't got no ceremony. But I'll need that skin back, 'Leave no trace' being my motto, for obvious reasons."

Bodi scratched his beard and whistled. "I dunno, Mister Vern. You left a helluva trace in New Orleans hunting after Regence. Not that anybody around here's sweet on Constable Hooke. He's been hitting me up for protection since he got here—he torched Jim Pooter's barbecue pit when he refused to stump up. There's rumors he disappeared people."

Vern couldn't refrain from boasting. "Well now, Bodi, I think you can rest easy on the Hooke front."

"Not yet I can't," said Bodi. "They ain't identified no body."

"I think it's safe to say he's gone," said Vern. "Things did not go easy in the Big Easy, not for our buddy Regence."

"We seen that on TV," said Bodi. "You kicked up quite a firestorm across the bridge. There's a special army unit from Washington dug in over there analyzing rocks with lasers, looking for your ass, but they ain't coming this way, not yet, at least."

Vern sucked the straw in the sippy cup, trying to get at the last of the water. He got plenty of air bubbles, but no H2O.

Elodie gently straightened the cup. "Don't tilt the sippy cup, Mister Vern. The straw goes all the way down."

Vern did as he was told, and this time he sucked the cup dry. "Memory foam and sippy cups," he murmured. "What a day."

"Quite a day for all of us," said Bodi Irwin.

"Take my word for it, Miz Moreau, you don't need to fret over Regence Hooke. He won't be making trouble for you no more."

"Lord forgive me for saying it, but you did the world a favor there, Mister Vern," said Elodie, hugging herself. "He's twisted, that one."

Vern grinned, anticipating his segue. "He's twisted all right. Into little pieces."

They all giggled at that, though maybe Elodie felt a touch guilty. Only a touch, though.

"Where's the boy?" asked Vern. "Where's Squib?"

"He went to the bar," said Elodie, "to fetch your skin and some barrels of oil. He said they might perk you up some."

Vern swung his legs from the bed. "That they surely would. I couldn't rescue no one in this state. Hell, I couldn't barbecue a chicken."

The dragon stood, and he felt as though the floor was pitching underneath his feet, although in reality, he was the one doing the pitching.

"I ain't all the way right," he said, resting a hand on Bodi's shoulder. "I might need some help. You up for that, Green Day?"

"Well," said Bodi, "I guess you ain't gonna murder me, huh?"

Vern said something along the lines of which he'd never said before. "Any friend of Squib's, I guess."

The dragon blinked, surprised at the words coming out of his own mouth, which were downright civil. *What the hell am I saying? Humans killed my entire race, more or less.*

Then he thought, *A long time ago. Long time.*

And then:

Not these humans.

CHAPTER 18

REGENCE HOOKE HAD NEVER BEEN A MAN TO WASTE TIME. WHILE it was true what his daddy always said re: idle hands doing the devil's work, Hooke reckoned that active hands must surely perform that work more effectively. So while other men might have hidden under the duvet waiting for Homeland Security or the Feds to follow a trail of blood from the Marcello debacle to Slidell's Deluxe Inn, Constable Hooke got busy on the phone and rethunk his strategy vis-à-vis Vern the Boar Island dragon, who was no doubt back on his patch pissing away his immortality.

First and foremost, Regence no longer believed that Vern's power could be harnessed, an idea he'd been tinkering with. This meant that Vern had to go, which could be challenging, but there was not room in this ward for them both. Plus Vern was injured now and, even more importantly, Hooke knew that he could be injured a lot more. No doubt the dragon and his pet boy were high-fiving each other over Regence Hooke's demise, so they would never even see him coming. It was true that Vern would be healing more with every hour that passed, which would diminish Hooke's own advantage, but even so, better to lay low for a couple of days, let the cinders settle, make a plan, and gather his troops.

Just leave, idiot! said his little voice. *You got a bag of cash and big prizes, so head on down south of the border and find yourself a Tijuana rose.*

But Hooke refused to listen to sense. *My name is Regence. I am a king and I will have my kingdom.*

He would never happen across another chance like this one. He had seen men seize their fortunes before, in Iraq. A man had to be ready for the vacuum, and when it came, he had to be willing to step into it. There was certainly a vacuum in the French Quarter now, and nature abhorred a vacuum. *Regence Hooke is just the man to plug that hole,* he thought, *but not just yet. First, I need to dispose of one scaly impediment to my ascension.*

And it cost him not a second thought that he fully intended to be the cause of an ancient species's extinction. In fact, he'd had a little practice in this area, having hunted and killed the last Caspian tiger seen in Iraq because it happened to wander into his sights during a desert stakeout.

He smiled at the memory. That tiger had had the self-same smug look that Vern favored.

You think you're top of the food chain, don't you, Vern, buddy? Well, you can discuss that with the tiger when you see him.

HOOKE HUNKERED DOWN for a few days and kept an eye on Fox 8 while he worked the prepaid phone he'd picked up in

RadioShack over on Gause. The Marcello "bombing" was the lead story for two days straight; then it dropped down to the second segment, but the various Vern videos boasted insane numbers on YouTube and Instagram and would go on to hang around home pages for years. Explanations ranged from "big dog" to "publicity stunt" to "total hoax," with only the usual conspiracy-peddlers actually employing the term "dragon." The people who believed it tended to believe that sort of thing, and the folks who didn't did not. So in many ways, it was business as usual, though the Marcello crater did become something of a shrine for the LOTRingers.

None of which Hooke could give a good goddamn about. All the constable listened for was his own name, and whether it would find its way into the narrative.

It did not. There was not a peep re: Constable Regence Hooke.

There was plenty of chatter about Ivory Conti and his place in the criminal underworld, but no mention of a mere constable out of Petit Bateau. Why would there be? So far as his own office was concerned: Regence Hooke was on vacation. Plus the one thing Hooke was grateful to Vern for was the lack of survivors. The dragon appeared to have carbonized everybody who might ever have had dealings with Constable Hooke in the Marcello.

It occurred to Hooke that he was free and clear, should he wish to remain that way, but this was a fleeting notion.

Free and clear so long as he kept his head way down. Who the hell wanted to live like that?

If there is a hell, then I'm going there anyway, so I might as well earn the ticket.

And if there wasn't a hell, then that would mean he had won at life.

On the third day, Hooke emerged from his motel room.

The third day, he thought, *like Jesus coming out of that cave, huh, Pops?*

The motel was not bad as these places go, but Hooke had finer things planned for his future. No more highway roadside stops for him.

I want to live somewhere that ain't within hollering distance of a Chick-fil-A—and no McDonald's neither, for that matter.

He didn't intend to go all Ivory-bling like every wannabe gangster he'd ever met. "But I won't be stepping out into a goddamn parking lot," he promised himself.

Dark wood. There would be a lot of dark wood, polished to a high shine. And one of those lounge chairs that came with a footstool. A coffee machine built right into something so it couldn't be moved.

Hooke laughed aloud at himself and his fancies.

You're a rube in that world, son. What you gotta do is cozy up to someone with class.

Someone like Elodie Moreau, he'd daydreamed until recently, but since her boy had joined the ranks of his abductees and survived, that was, he had to admit, a little unlikely now.

Still, Hooke thought, *there's more than one way to skin a cat.*

And by "cat" he meant Cajun lady.

And her son.

And a dragon.

So, three cats in all.

HOOKE ARRIVED AT the Seabrook Diner maybe forty minutes in advance of his noon rendezvous and ordered himself a twenty-ounce rib eye with the works. It came on an enamel tray with fries, mashed potatoes, biscuits and gravy, and kale chips, for some reason. He followed it with two beers and a slice of lemon pie submerged in whipped cream fresh from the nozzle. It was nice to be eating out in the open again, so to speak, and he enjoyed every mouthful.

The constable briefly considered actually paying for his meal, but decided that would send the wrong message, and so he contented himself with tipping the waitress and advising her good-naturedly that she might increase her percentages if she got those front teeth straightened out.

The diner had that vintage-Airstream kinda look that a lot of these places went for in thereabouts. Maybe the proprietors thought folks would be bamboozled into believing themselves in *Happy Days* or some shit by the red vinyl booths and menus secured under a sheet of acrylic bolted to the table.

While the girl cleared, keeping her lips buttoned, Hooke set out Ivory's notebook and his own map. Time for business.

He knew he was being surveilled through the diner window: Of course he was. He'd expect nothing less. No doubt there was a weapon trained on him right now, maybe two, but that was all right; they wouldn't go pulling the trigger unless they were real stupid. Or green. And these people were neither.

A thought occurred. *They could be crazy.*

He hadn't accounted for crazy.

But that was the thing about crazy: You *couldn't* account for it. Hooke had once ridden shotgun on an arms heist from an air base south of Basra where Colonel Faraiji, who had underwritten the operation, was forced to slit his own driver's throat during the robbery when the driver had lost his nerve and threatened to start shooting.

The colonel had commented later to Hooke, "My friend, when you work with disturbed people, it is like building your house on sand."

As usual, Hooke had wished the colonel didn't feel the need to talk in riddles, but now he appreciated the elegance of the image.

Have I built my house on sand? he wondered.

If he had, it was too late to do anything about it now. He wouldn't even hear the bullet that killed him.

He tugged at his left sleeve to reveal his watch, a fake Rolex he'd picked up in some souk or another. The thing still ran just fine, in spite of a dunking in the bayou. He raised his wrist and tapped the watch face for the benefit of anybody scoping him from the tree line across the highway.

Tick tock, ladies and gentlemen. We all got places to be.

Five minutes later, three striking individuals trooped in. Hooke studied them as they entered the diner and knew by their demeanor that he'd chosen well.

They'd all checked out their exits and sight lines. Pros, every one of 'em: a real kill-team.

Vern, that's all she wrote for you, buddy. If I can put one hole in your scaly hide, these guys will cook your goose for sure.

From Ivory's extensive list of bent cops, he'd chosen three pet pigs, all military trained. Two he'd heard of already. There was ex-marine sniper Jing Jiang, four feet eleven inches of laser accuracy who had once, according to barrack legend, put a 9mm slug into the eye of the Jack of Clubs through the window of a moving transport. That was Gunnery Sergeant Jing Jiang's specialty: moving targets. They said crazy things about Jing Jiang: Her old man was a ninja, her weapon's barrel was forged from the samurai sword of her ancestors, all sorts of stereotypical shit like that. One thing her current peer group in SWAT air support could agree on was that when they strapped Officer Jing Jiang into a chopper harness, she rarely missed who she was shooting down at.

Hooke was almost disappointed in her: Imagine going from decorated sharpshooter to working for Ivory. Ain't nobody's ancestors would be proud of that gear shift.

I shall be her redemption, Hooke thought, and that made him smile. Like a bloody limb makes a shark smile.

Second on the list was Army Corporal Jewell Hardy, originally from the south side of Detroit. Bare-knuckle bouts brought her to Hooke's attention; apparently she supplmented her army pay with illegal bouts off-base. She had to be quietly discharged when she stoved in one head too many during a tour south of Doha, as most folks were not aware the US even had a base in Qatar. Kid was barely twenty-five and already bigger than three average GI Joes strapped together, with fists like anvils and a forehead like the front end of a snow plow. Now she was a patrol officer, stomping the French Quarter beat with NOPD, and breaking bones for Ivory on the side. In looks, she was reminiscent of a grizzly bear in crew cut and moisture-wicking sports gear.

That girl will relish wrestling a dragon if she gets close enough, thought Hooke. *And she just might get close enough.*

And finally, the sailor: a lieutenant from the US Coast Guard, New Orleans sector, an Oregon native who grew up shooting the Celestial Falls long after they were closed down to kayakers. Some dumbass from NYC getting himself tangled up in his life vest and choking to death trying to live-stream his adventure put a stop to all that, so DuShane Adebayo sidestepped into the navy, a route which Hooke could appreciate, and put his nautical skills to good use manning a Riverine small boat buzzing the Fifth Fleet in the Persian Gulf. Word had it that DuShane did more than guard the fleet, spending his downtime during the oh-darks nipping ashore for shipments of opium and local girls to amuse the waterlogged salts. Lately, DuShane was turning a blind eye for Ivory in a different gulf, or rather, he had been. Now the lieutenant was at a loose end, with only his legit wages, and there weren't many people who could survive on what the USCG shelled out.

This guy is starving for extracurricular employment, thought Hooke, *and I have just the job interview.*

So the lineup was as follows:

Officer Jing Jiang, all J.Crewed up, looking twenty-two, although Hooke knew she was forty.

Patrol Officer Jewell Hardy, the baby of the group, in sports gear, like Ivan Drago's sister.

And Lieutenant Adebayo in camo vest and Beavers baseball cap, with a sour face that would curdle cream.

That's okay, thought Hooke. *I'll cheer this little bunch up quick enough.*

He was expecting the silent treatment from the bunch, in case this was a wire sting, although Hardy, he reckoned, might get a little verbal on account of her age, but it was Jing Jiang who let fly.

"What the fuck is going on here, Hooke?" said the countersniper, sliding in opposite him. "Cryptic messages? Summoning us here? Summoning? You think you're some kind of samurai warlord? I shoulda popped you from the parking lot. Fuck, I could've been back in New Orleans eating muffulettas by lunchtime."

A hothead sniper? thought Hooke. *That's unusual.* "I don't know about that," he said. "Traffic is pretty heavy on the bridge this time of day. You mighta got held up."

Jewell Hardy's chuckle sounded like a log going through a chipper. "Hooke is right, traffic on the bridge can be a sonuvabitch."

Youngsters, thought Hooke, warming to Hardy.

DuShane Adebayo sat, an intense-looking bony-faced man with gray twists in his goatee, sweat sheening his high forehead. He was a mouth-breather, sounded like, which could be a deal-breaker if Hooke was planning on sharing a sniper hide, but for water work it should be fine.

"This is some bullshit," said DuShane. "Are you shaking us down here, Constable?"

The "Constable" was thrown in so Hooke would know he was made.

"No, Lieutenant, I ain't shaking no one down," said Hooke equably. "What we got here is a trial by fire, followed by a business opportunity." He felt something nudging his groin under the table, flattening his ball hair. A silencer, he reckoned. Looked like Jing Jiang was not in the mood for no preamble.

Trying not to think about the bullet six inches from his nuts, Hooke got directly to the point. "Okay, people, here's the situation. Ivory is gone. We step in and move the black tar up from Mexico for starters. Then we sever ties with South America and switch to guns only. We cut out highways by using the Pearl River. Simple. Between the four of us, we marshal Ivory's pet pigs—that's what he called us— and we run this operation with a little military precision. I got nearly a hundred names in Ivory's notebook. Outta those I picked you three, 'cause you've all seen considerable action. All we gotta do is what we were already doing, only more so. There ain't none of us think that Ivory was officer material, am I right? All he had going for him was an inheritance. Little prick was pouring cash into that operation and barely breaking even. In six months we could all of us here be millionaires. In ten years we'll be billionaires."

Hooke was waiting for a reaction to his speech, but it did look like his chosen disciples were chewing things over and finding themselves pretty much in agreement with every point.

"Billionaire": that was the word that did it. A word like that carried weight. Hooke felt the silencer retreat a little, and his ball hair spring back into place.

Jewell Hardy spoke first. "Billionaires, huh? I bet you didn't run no numbers on that, Hooke. I bet that there's a sales pitch."

"Maybe," said Hooke, "but it's there or thereabouts. And I can hand over a hundred grand cash, right now, for today's work."

He laid three envelopes on the table, slowly and deliberately.

"One hundred thousand. Each," he said, tapping each packed envelope. "For twenty-four hours. After that you can walk away and I ain't gonna bother you again, but could be you like the sound of being a billionaire?"

Hardy chuckled. "They even got your constable stamp on the front of the envelope. Nice touch."

"So you don't forget where they came from."

"Might be you're full of shit, Hooke," said Adebayo, cracking a smile and looking like a different person. "But I do like the sound of a hundred grand." The pilot pocketed his haul. "Now tell me about this trial by fire."

SQUIB WAS BACK in the Pearl Bar and Grill lockup. *Same old, same old*, he thought.

Except this time he had himself a key—more than a key, in fact. A *fob*.

It might be fobs were commonplace out in the world where people had electric gates and hybrid automobiles, but

Squib was having himself a right old time clicking the hell out of that fob on account of it being the first one he'd ever held.

"Fob," he said, grinning like a loon. "Fob. Yep, got me a fob."

It was stupid, he knew, dicking around with electronics when his boss was languishing in the shack, but a big part of fifteen-year-old Squib was still only nine and the buttons on this plastic teardrop were super-satisfying to press, especially with the corresponding flashing light.

"That's right, Charles Jr.," he told his big-dicked friend, who was not even in the vicinity, "you keep fiddling with your equipment; I got me an infrared multifunctioned fob."

After this Squib indulged himself in a thirty-second laughing jag; then he knuckled down to business. After all, he had to get Bodi Irwin's cruiser loaded, unloaded at the shack, and back here before sunup.

Too many people up on Vern as it is, he thought. *I don't want no one quizzing me on why Bodi is fine with me ferrying supplies into the swamp.*

Squib surely did hope that Vern would not regain his senses while he was about his errands. The dragon might not be too thrilled to see strange humans in his shack.

At least he ain't in a position to fry my momma, thought Squib. *I'm certain of that.* He was as certain of Vern's condition as he'd ever been of anything; otherwise he would never have left his momma holding the reins upriver. *Boss man is in that in-between place he talked about, so I gotta get some juice into him before he crosses to the other side.*

Vern was so out of fat that his body had shut him down in

midflight; he wasn't going to be shooting off any bolts any-time soon, not until he'd glugged down a couple of drums.

So Squib was back in the lockup, but there was another difference, too, the second one being that on this occasion he was wearing a dragon skin with the head hooked over his own head like a scaly Batman mask, the arms tied about his waist and the rest trailing behind him like a bridal train.

This is probably offensive to dragons for some reason, he thought. *What say I never tell Vern it even happened?*

Even so, Squib snapped off a quick selfie, just in case he ever needed to stick it to Charles Jr.

The Pearl Bar and Grill had its own landing out back for locals who outfoxed the drunk-driving laws by cruising in for their beers. Even then, some guys got too wasted to even keep a boat between two banks of a river and so spent the night in their pirogues, tied up at the jetty, which explained all the alcoholic mosquitoes in the region. Bodi Irwin went even further to secure his custom by running a booze boat round the local inlets picking up strays.

"The three ins," Bodi always said. "Inlets, infirm, and inebriates: pick 'em up and deliver them to my door. Maybe it's time you did a shift on the booze boat."

Seemed like Squib would have himself another job if Vern ever gave him a slack minute—but first things first was to get his number one boss back to his regular disagree-able self.

Squib fobbed himself through the rear gate and onto the dock. There was only a single vessel moored at the wooden jetty, Bodi's own flat-bottomed aluminum cruiser, which bore the Pearl Bar and Grill logo along both sides in speech bubbles coming out of an artist's impression of a manga-looking Honey Island monster, which Squib knew would piss Vern off no end.

All clear then, thought Squib. *Lock and load—or in this case, load and lock.*

He laughed again, reckoning that he was funnier than Vern gave him credit for. Sometimes he thought of cracks so fast that Jimmy Kimmel would crap himself, but all Vern did was roll those slitted eyes all the way round and say something like, "Shit, boy, I ain't paying you to talk like you got hit in the head. Ain't you got some work to do?"

The lights went out, and Squib waved his arms a little to activate the halogen spots.

Less thinking, more moving, he thought.

It took him maybe thirty minutes to roll half a dozen drums onto a trolley, one at a time, wheel them down to the jetty, then unload at the other end. It didn't help none that he was down four digits in total, and three of his stumps were giving him trouble even though his momma had stuffed the toes of his Converse with cotton wool. It also didn't help that the trolley hadn't seen a squirt of oil since before he was born, and the jetty was probably Civil War era and was short a mess of its planks. Nevertheless, Squib persevered because he was the world's only executive assistant to a dragon, and that was a position he was eager to hold on to. He wrestled the six drums onto the *Pearl's* deck, and the booze boat settled a little lower into the river.

Still plenty of clearance, thought Squib. *She could take another couple easy and still pull up at Boar Island without no trouble.*

But time was ticking on and he could always make another run tomorrow. Best be on his way. He fobbed the electric fence, then cast off from the Pearl's jetty and went motoring upriver on low revs, keeping the churn down so even if someone did hear an engine at this god-awful hour, they wouldn't be able to tell which dock it'd slunk from.

Unless they're watching me with some kinda night-vision optics, thought Squib, and risked another ten percent on the throttle.

HOOKE AND HIS newly minted drug lords, minus Jing Jiang, were loading their gear into Willard Carnahan's RIB at the Petit Bateau dock maybe three hundred yards south of the Pearl Bar and Grill while Squib was giving his fob thumb a workout.

"This is a nice goddamn boat, brother," DuShane Adebayo commented, testing the inflatable tube running around the gunwale with the heel of his fist. "Stable as all hell. Nice-sized deck. Even these groundhogs couldn't turn this shit over. Where'd you get a rig like this, Hooke?"

Hooke thought of Carnahan keeling over into the swamp and that mutant-big turtle breaching right out of the murk. "A gift," he said.

"Yeah, sure," said DuShane, tossing his gear onto the deck. "I bet you get a lotta gifts, right, Regence?"

In truth, Hooke would have preferred his own cabin cruiser, which felt a lot more substantial than this glorified dinghy, but the lieutenant was all smiles and nods, and he knew his stuff on the water. Also, Hooke's cruiser was buried in swamp sludge twenty feet off the coast of Honey Island, so it wasn't like he had a choice in the matter.

"Do what you gotta do, Lieut," he said. "We're heading out as soon as Jiang shows up."

He had been sincerely hoping that Jing Jiang might be able to swing a chopper, but the markswoman had laughed at both this suggestion and his offer of the Barrett .50-cal, opting instead to retrieve her own sniper rifle from an off-duty stash.

"I gotta swing by a place for a thing, then I can put a hole in the New Orleans monster without getting within a thousand yards of it," she'd said.

Hooke was fully aware that the team didn't really credit his dragon story, not in their bones. They had all watched the footage and heard the chatter around the Quarter, but a thing like Vern had to be seen in person to be believed. If the shoe was on the other foot and he was the one being sold a line about dragons, then he, too, would take the wad of cash and watch how this thing played out, maybe see if it led to where the rest of Ivory's loot was at.

Tonight we are testing the waters in every way, Hooke thought. *And the best thing is, killing a dragon ain't even illegal.*

His gaze was drawn to the flash of Bodi Irwin's big halogens across the road in his yard. Hooke didn't really give much of a crap about someone snooping round back of the diner; this seemed like pretty routine law-and-order stuff. But he didn't need a monkey wrench in his own works at the moment. Technically, nothing unlawful was going down, but if these dockside shenanigans were stress-tested, then it was likely they would all be out of jobs, at the very least.

It's prob'ly some dumbass burglar getting barbecued by Bodi's fancy fence, he thought, but decided maybe it would be prudent to check it out, because who knew what the hell might be going on in this sleepy backwater town where dragons dressed like men and carried cell phones.

Might find myself a unicorn wearing suspenders, he thought. *Or a vampire chained down in the diner parking lot.*

So after patting his vest to check for his monocular, he trotted to the end of the jetty to see what the light show was about, and a couple of minutes later he was mighty glad he had, for it looked like Lady Luck was smiling down on him brighter than the lopsided grin of the Louisiana moon.

There's the kid, right there, wearing some kind of romper suit. "Well, if that don't beat all," said Hooke, delighted. "I guess good things do come to those who wait."

"Wait?" said Jewell Hardy, appearing beside him. "We only been here an hour or so."

"It's a saying, Hardy," he said, zipping the monocular into its pouch. Wasn't much need for it anyhow on a night like this. Sometimes when the stars were out in force, the swamp had a shine to it, like the whole river glowed with phosphorescence. Made the details stand out—even the shadows were sharper. "Ain't no call to dissect everything I say."

"Just making conversation, boss."

"Ain't no bosses," said Hooke. "We're all partners here."

Hardy punched him playfully on the shoulder. "Whatever you say, boss."

The constable found that he was warming to Jewell Hardy, which wasn't like him. "I like you, Jewell," he said. "I surely do hope you make it through the night."

Hardy considered this comment. "You're serious about this dragon fella Vern, right, Hooke?"

"*Right Hooke,*" he thought. *Nice.*

"Yeah, I'm serious," he said, keeping his eyes on Squib. *Kid's limping a little.* "Three hundred large worth of serious. What do you think, this is all some kind of elaborate setup?"

"Nah, I can't figure an angle for that level of convolution," said Hardy. "But maybe you're crazy. No offense."

"I gotta say, I'm a little offended. But you're young, so you get a one-time pass."

Hardy pocketed an imaginary pass. "Appreciated, chief."

"And to put your mind to rest, I ain't crazy, though it might be better for you if I was."

"'Cause if you ain't crazy, then I gotta take on a dragon, right?"

"That's right, Jewell."

Hardy stretched both arms in front of her, clenching her fists till they creaked. "If you guys can draw his fire, then I reckon me and old Vern will have ourselves a time."

Hooke didn't doubt it. He recognized a stone-cold killer when he saw one.

Takes one to know one.

Still, Vern had been at this business for centuries. "From what I hear, Vern favors his right hand. Also, those wings of his wrap around a motherfucker. You go in there, you ain't coming out."

Hardy nodded, taking it in.

"In-jab-out," said Hooke. "Keep dancing. You dance, girl? Sometimes the big ones don't dance."

"I dance fine," said Hardy. "I fought a tiger once in-country. You hear about that?"

He still had his eyes on the Pearl's yard. "Yep, I heard. Heard they pulled that cat's teeth and claws."

"That they did. Weren't no need. I could've done it anyway."

"I hope so, girl, 'cause with Vern, teeth and claws are present and correct. Still, could be it won't get that far."

"Could be it will," said Hardy. "I sure hope so."

Kids, thought Hooke. *Every one of them invincible. Jewell Hardy cannot wait to get up close with the creature who will most likely kill her.*

It occurred to him that he had never even heard Hardy come up to him. *Big and sneaky. Like those Trojans in the wooden horse.*

"Say, Hardy," he said, "you see that kid down there? It's gonna take him a couple of minutes to fetch another barrel."

Hardy grinned. "Way ahead of you, Hooke." And she took off down the dock.

DuShane Adebayo whistled from the boat, and Hooke turned to see Jing Jiang stepping down into the RIB cradling a rifle case like it was her firstborn.

"We heading out?" said DuShane.

Hooke checked on Squib again. The boy was done loading barrels of oil, looked like, and there was no sign of Hardy. He mused on this. *Barrels of oil. Barrels and barrels. Looks like the dragon needs him some fuel.*

Which would mean . . .

Vern is on empty, he realized. *There ain't never gonna be a better time.*

"Cast off, Skipper," he said, walking down the jetty. "Plans have changed a bit. I hope you're as sneaky as they say because I need to follow that kid upriver without him knowing. Is that a thing we can do?"

DuShane frowned in exasperation, like, *Why do I have to deal with these landlubber idiots all the goddamned time?*

"Just tell me, DuShane," said Hooke, thinking that maybe the Adebayo attitude might need some adjustment in the near future.

DuShane patted one of the RIB's twin outboards. "These babies are muffled, Constable, so all's we gotta do is hang back a little and that kid won't hear jack over his own engine. The only way he cottons on is if he decides to row that tug upriver."

"Well, all right then," said Hooke, deciding to keep it all congenial for the moment. "You good, Jiang?"

Jing Jiang was all decked out in camo, including a lightweight balaclava. "Good to go. I'm gonna set up on the prow, put one in the eye of this so-called dragon. Turns out to be a guy in a suit, then thanks for the easiest hundred grand I ever made."

"Listen to me, Jiang," said Hooke slowly. "First we ground the beast, then we assess. There's no kill shot till I give you the signal. This bastard has Rebel gold, and I want him to part with it before he dies."

Jiang's eyes narrowed in the balaclava's slit. "I'll try, Hooke, but sometimes the call has gotta be made by the finger on the trigger."

Hooke pinched the bridge of his nose, like, *I'm holding back my temper here.* "Jing, girl, we ain't on no official op. This here chain of command only got one link in it. I want you to do what I say to the letter. Ground him and let me work. Okay?"

But apparently Jing Jiang didn't get to be the world's preeminent female sniper by being easily intimidated. "I hear you, Hooke. And I understand you got all that testosterone swilling around your lusty balls. But if this Vern guy is a real live dragon, perhaps he won't let you work. Perhaps I'll have to make a split-second decision. You okay with that, Constable?"

Hooke nodded. He knew that a remote kill would be the best outcome all round, but a part of him didn't want it to go down like that, even if there hadn't been loot at stake.

What we got here is biblical, he thought. *Be a shame to finish it long-distance.*

A man only got so many epic nights in his life. Maybe he and the Hardy girl could beat Vern to death with their bare hands.

Beat a dragon to death. Now that would be something.

Also, "lusty balls."

Nice.

CHAPTER 19

Vern had Bodi Irwin help him to the landing, which barely qualified as a landing, overrun as it was with cypress knuckles, multicolored spores, and moss drapes. Vern had never fixed it up because he didn't want any swamp folk getting ideas and tying off there. One of the dragon's favorite tricks was to lie on his back in the shallow waters and punch dents in any hull that came too close, something he'd been doing for a hundred years. He called those punches "warning shots."

Here be treacherous waters, boys: You ain't getting onshore from here without perforations.

And so the tours knew to give Boar Island a wide berth on account of it wasn't safe to land there. Too many submerged rocks and roots. And if the water predators didn't get you, then the big cats and boars on the island would do the job. It was like the Bermuda Triangle for hillbillies: People went missing on Boar Island and the environs. And so the Honey Island monster legend grew.

Honey Island, which was fake news. Humans couldn't even get the island right.

But the point was, there was hardly a soul who knew the way through.

Waxman had known the path, and now that secret had been passed on to young Squib.

Vern sighed.

Waxman.

Damn, that old bastard had been a good friend to him. In less than a hundred years Vern had grown closer to that mogwai than he'd ever been to his own kin. The dragon's long experience of grieving told him that it would be decades before that pain dulled some, and it would never truly leave his system. Especially considering the way his buddy had checked out.

I been sadder for longer than any creature alive, thought Vern. *Ain't that a pain in the ass.*

Vern blinked his inner lids half a dozen times to clear off the film of gunk which had been bothering him thanks to the '70s chemical runoff from Exxon, which had permeated every molecule of water in the state and would take a million years to dissipate. His vision cleared, and he saw the *Pearl* motoring down the center of the river, Squib plowing up a wake like he didn't care who saw.

"I keep telling him," said Vern to Bodi, "low-profile. That's the whole goddamn point."

"Teenagers," said Bodi, feeling Vern's weight on his shoulder. "You give 'em access to an engine and all good sense goes out the window."

"'Cause sound travels like a motherfucker over swamp

water," continued Vern. "Skips right along like a flat stone. I swear I can hear the music from your joint most nights."

"You like it?" asked Bodi, hoping for an affirmative answer.

"A bit fiddle-heavy, if you ask me," said Vern. "Ain't you got any Linda Ronstadt on that jukebox?"

"I thought about it," said Bodi. "A little on the nose, maybe?"

"Or maybe not," said Vern.

"We'll have her on there Monday," promised Bodi. "'Blue Bayou' on repeat."

Squib must've spotted his boss onshore because he made a great show of throttling back on approach.

"Look who just noticed us standing here," said Vern, sniggering.

"James goddamn Bond himself," said Bodi.

"Guess how many people he's fooling with his *Look at me, ain't I careful* act?"

"Not a one."

"Goddamn right. I should dock his pay, I really should. But he is bringing in the goods. And trust me, Green Day, there'll be a reckoning for that oil."

Bodi wasn't sure he liked the sound of that. "'Reckoning' has different connotations, Vern. You ain't using the term in a negative sense, by any chance?"

Vern laughed and it felt good, but it also hurt his chest some. "Connotations? Well, fuck me, Bodi, ain't you the linguist? Nah, it ain't that kind of reckoning. I aim to fix up with you, is all."

"Fix up" didn't sound much better to Bodi, but he reckoned he'd let it go.

Vern watched Squib navigate the final stretch from the river proper into the barely visible tributary which ran into his little dock. The kid had skills, there was no doubt about that, tipping at the throttle with his left and adjusting the steering with the heel of his right, and right there Vern realized that something was missing—not from the world in general, but inside his own head, the psychological equivalent of rising hackles. Vern already knew that he liked the kid, but now he realized that he had faith in him.

This could work out, he thought. *Kid's young; we could do a half century.*

"You make enough noise, kid?" he called when the boat nudged against the half-submerged planking. "Shit, you wakin' up my ancestors."

Squib grinned. "Hey, boss. I sure am glad to see you back on your feet. I thought you were toast—and I need this job."

"He's a cheeky little cuss, ain't he?" Vern said to Bodi. "I'll show him toast."

And Vern wasted valuable energy spreading his wings. "Does this look like I'm toast, boy? I'll outlive all you puny humans."

And in that second, while he was all pumped up like that, Vern smelled something on the breeze: a scent he'd thought had been scorched from the earth.

Fucking Hooke, he thought. *Come the nuclear holocaust, it'll be just him and the cockroaches.*

Then he heard a sound like an old lady coughing across the river and he had two holes in his wings the size of dinner plates. Or maybe the holes came first.

Bodi was saying something about something, but Vern couldn't understand.

The old lady coughed some more, and Irwin was gone from under his arm, snatched away like he'd come to the end of his bungee.

Humans, thought Vern. *The angry mob is here.*

He looked to Squib, who was scrambling over the prow of the cruiser, desperate to help his master; then he, too, was snatched away, not by a bullet but by a hand on his ankle which yanked the boy backwards and sent him cartwheeling into the Pearl River. It might have been a lark, it looked so funny, but whatever was transpiring here, it wasn't no comedy. In Squib's place came the biggest human Vern had seen up close, swarming onto the landing like an angry bear. Vern had fought bears before and they weren't no pushover, even when he was at the top of his game.

It's fight-or-flight time, thought Vern, *and I am plumb out of flight.*

Which left *fight*.

On a good day it would have been an audacious creature indeed who would come at Wyvern, Lord Highfire, with nothing more than lead-shot-weighted sap gloves as weapons. But this was not a good day. Wyvern, Lord Highfire, was perforated, concussed, and out of juice, so no flame, no altitude, and very little balance. Whatever oomph he had, he sent to his armor plating so that he could at least roll with the punches.

And the punches were not long in coming. This human woman moved so fast that Vern wasn't sure he could have tagged her a good one even if he had been tip-top. He made the effort, though, swinging open-clawed so if he did make contact he might clip an artery and that would be the end of the story as far as this assailant went. But the woman went low, and Vern only managed to rake one claw along her buzz-cut skull, opening a shallow gash that bled a little but was nowhere near fatal. And of course then Vern had missed his window and the human was inside his guard.

She went to work like a surgeon, battering Vern's mid-section with a flurry of hooks and jabs, searching for weak spots. She found one or two, and Vern felt his armor plating groan under the pressure.

Come on, Highfire, he told himself. *You ain't no man-hands, right?*

Maybe "man-hands" was the wrong derogative in this particular situation. This lady's hands were breaking him down like an old chair. He felt his kidney plate collapse and his solar plexus wobble.

Too soon, he thought. *Get it together, Vern.*

The woman worked on the kidney area, and Vern felt a searing pain shoot from balls to throat.

"Mother—" he swore, and that's when Vern got a momentary breather.

Maybe the woman hadn't realized that it was Vern who had spoken earlier as she hid in the stern, or maybe Hooke hadn't mentioned the dragon's power of speech. Either way, Vern's expletive froze the woman just for a second and she came into focus.

Vern completed the popular insult. "—fucker!" he said, driving his fist down on the woman's head. It wasn't much of a blow, but it bought him a few seconds to back up and draw his breath.

The woman went down on one knee and shook the stars from her eyes. "That's it, Mister Vern? That's all you got in the tank? Shit, I'm gonna mount your head on my wall."

Vern clicked his jaws, trying to spark up, but there was nothing, not a single drop of fat. If only he could reach the oil barrels.

"What's up with your face, Vern?" said the woman, balling her fists. "You having some kind of fit? In case you want to know, the name of the gal whupping your ass is Jewell Hardy. Don't forget that name, will you, boy?"

"I ain't whupped yet, Jewell Hardy," said Vern, "so let's you and me get to it."

There was a blink of light from out on the river and then Vern got himself sledgehammered by a slug which pancaked on his chest. It was bad luck for the shooter, as the chest plate was close to impenetrable. Lack of penetration notwithstanding, Vern's lungs still emptied in a *whoof!* and he was sent ass-over-tail into the brush.

"Go, Jiang," said Jewell Hardy, whatever the hell that meant, and was all over Vern like a cheap cologne, which was as far as that analogy went because cheap cologne isn't normally in the habit of beating the bejesus out of its wearers. Hardy gave him a couple in the side of the head first to rattle his marbles, then probed his torso with her fingers, looking for a way in.

Vern's eyes rolled and he thought, *I cannot believe this week.*

The swamp mud squelched beneath him, and he felt the slick paste of Boar Island seep into his cargo pants.

New fucking pants, too. Well, newish.

"Ok-aay," said Jewell Hardy, which was ominous.

The fist-fighter had found a gap in Vern's ribs and jammed her fingers in, which tickled. But then she drew a knife from behind her back and tried to work it in the space.

This ain't gonna tickle, thought Vern.

The tip went in—but the secondary effect of this penetration was not foreseen by either combatant. The first effect was a stab of white-hot pain, which was to be expected, but the second was an involuntary revving up of Vern's neuromuscular system, which initiated a stretch of his muscles and woke up nerve receptors in his tendons, which kicked off an impulse transmission up his spinal cord, where it triggered a reaction to contract the muscle that was just stretched. Of course, Vern didn't know the science of this; all he knew was his knee jackknifed with a force he would not have thought currently in him, which slammed Jewell Hardy in the back, sending her tumbling into the undergrowth with every last breath of air driven from her lungs.

"Shit," gasped Vern. "Fucking beast of a human."

He'd been lucky, but a woman like that wasn't gonna lie down long because of a knee in the back; she wasn't out of the fight yet—you could bet your last dollar on that. And unless she stabbed him in the same spot, he had nothing in the tank.

"Vern," said a husky voice, and for a moment Vern thought his ancestors were talking to him from heaven where dragons were supposedly transformed into the seraphim.

"Is that the angels?"

"No, it ain't no fucking angels, leastways, not yet."

Vern looked sideways, and there was Bodi Irwin not

three feet away, the blood on his shoulder glistening tar like some kid had dumped a bucket on him.

"Bodi," said Vern.

Bodi tapped his chest weakly.

"I feel the same, buddy," said Vern, reckoning it cost nothing to be gracious since the human was probably checking out.

"No, fuckwit. Shotgun."

Ah, thought Vern. *Yeah, that makes more sense.*

Bodi had his shotgun strapped to his back.

Vern reached across, snicked the strap with one talon, then wiggled the weapon out from under Bodi.

"Goddamn," swore Irwin. "Take it easy."

"Sorry," said Vern. "I saw on Lifetime how a bullet wound ranks about the same pain-wise as childbirth, so suck it up, Green Day."

As Vern delivered this missal, he pumped a shell into the chamber, so that when two seconds later Jewell Hardy made a grab for the gun, he was able to blow one of her ears clean off the side of her head.

No more Beats by Dre for you, lady, thought Vern.

And he would have finished her off had Bodi's cruiser not exploded.

SQUIB FELT LIKE he'd come out the sphincter end of a water slide all wrong. He hit the river so hard he was certain he would split like an overripe banana, but somehow his skin held on to its integrity, even when he crashed into the river-bed barely three feet below.

No: *not* the riverbed.

The swamp bed didn't creak and buckle.

With remarkable presence of mind, Squib managed to assemble two rational thoughts:

One: *I think my ass is broken.*

And two: *Goddamn, if I ain't after landing on Hooke's sunken boat.*

It was good to know where the cruiser was, for future reference. If there was to be a future for him, which wasn't looking very likely.

Squib found that he could stand on the cruiser's keel, and once his lungs had been satisfied, he could take a peek at the situation, or situations, to be more accurate.

Seemed like there were two action zones.

Vern onshore wrestling with a WWE diva, looked like.

And a boat in the river, with someone taking potshots.

And wasn't much he could do about either.

I brung them here, he thought. *Those bastards, they done followed me.*

Squib's first instinct was to stay where he was, just bobbing here in the Pearl River, let this crisis wash over him. Vern could handle it—he'd surely handled worse. But that instinct faded fast, and he was ashamed of it.

Momma is on that island and all because of me.

So he made his choice based on desperation and a dollop of teenage stupidity.

I'm gonna swim ashore and give the boss some backup, at the very least come between that warrior woman and Momma.

So he made to push himself off the keel—then his foot snagged in something.

Goddamn gator's got me, he thought. *Spared by a dragon, only to be killed by a gator. That's some cosmic bullshit there.*

But it wasn't a gator; it was a cord or strap or something, caught tight around his ankle.

Squib took a breath and ducked under. He kept his eyes closed because there wasn't any point trying to see in a swamp at night, even on a clear night like this. He scrabbled at the strap looped around his ankle and wiggled his thumb in between the buckle and his skin, which was as much as he could do on the first breath. On the second, he widened the loop and slipped his foot out, then thought he might as well see if what'd snagged him could be of any use.

Turned out it could.

HOOKE FOUND HIMSELF watching a dragon getting beat up.

These are truly the best of times, Regence, he thought. *Things ain't never gonna be this good again.*

And it was true: If snipers shooting at dragons in a swamp at the dead of night was your thing, then right now Boar Island was the sweet spot of the universe.

Hooke's daddy had once told him, "You ain't nothing special, boy. All these sinful antics that in your opinion make you different from the rest of the world? You ain't different. There are a million other jerk-offs doing exactly the same thing you are."

Hooke smiled again. *Wrong again, Daddy.*

He was watching the onshore shenanigans through his monocular. Jewell Hardy was going fine till Vern caught her with the shotgun blast.

"Holy shit," he said to DuShane. "Now she's gonna be pissed. Take us in a little."

DuShane sat on the inflated gunwale. "Any closer and we're gonna be scraping the bottom," he said. His tone was weird, kinda hollow, like the pilot was in shock a little. Which could be the case.

Hooke didn't care, so long as he didn't lose control of the boat. "Fuck it if we scrape the bottom," he said. "Ain't my boat, son."

"That's what I thought," said DuShane; then he said, "Heads up."

Now ain't that a strange thing to say? thought Hooke, wondering whose head Adebayo was referring to and why it should be up, but these questions were answered when DuShane plucked something from the sky and held it to his chest.

"I caught her," he said, and proudly showed Hooke a grenade like it was a golden egg.

"Goddamn," said Hooke.

Adebayo's face collapsed like he'd been punched by an invisible fist as he realized what he was holding, and Hooke knew what was coming next. He'd seen it a hundred times. It wasn't like in the movies when some square-jawed, in-it-for-the-"right"-reasons soldier caught a pineapple neat as a third baseman and pitched it toward the enemy, destroying a tank and saving the village. In the real world, if some fool is unlucky enough to find a grenade in his immediate vicinity, he immediately regresses to his pass-the-parcel days and targets the nearest comrade.

Not tonight, thought Hooke. He reached down to grab Adebayo's ankle and with one heave he flipped the sailor out of the boat. He reckoned that he himself had maybe a thirty percent chance of survival.

As it turned out, Adebayo's body shielded Hooke from most of the blast. The pilot managed a semi-revolution before the grenade exploded, making spaghetti of his Kevlar vest and churning his organs to mush. He was mashed against the keel before sliding down slowly into the murk like a sports sock down a wall.

He was dead before he hit the water. Hot lunch for the alligators.

Hooke took a slash on the forearm and would have tinnitus for the rest of his days, but otherwise he was hale and hearty. Jing Jiang was not accustomed to being within one thousand yards of the action. Her reaction to an explosion inside that comfort zone was a convoluted string of swear words, followed by a swift decision.

"I'm making that call, Hooke," she called over her shoulder, and she swapped her .50-caliber for the rocket launcher, on which Hooke had written in Sharpie: "Last Rezort"—"Rezort" with a z, because soldiers surely loved that kind of rebellious misspelling.

The Russian MANPAD was a little clunkier around the midsection than the old drainpipe models, and the business end looked more like a paparazzi telephoto lens than a barrel, which made it difficult to aim precisely, and there was no time for digital sights, but Jiang probably figured it would obliterate most of her event horizon, so job done.

"Die, Gojira," she said.

Hooke was pretty sure that "Gojira" was a Japanese reference and Jiang was Chinese, but they could discuss that cross-cultural reference later, and either way, the latest re-boot was undeniably a hell of a movie.

And Jewell Hardy, thought Hooke, *she will die, too*. But his arm stung, and he had a ringing in his ears, so if Hardy had to go, so be it. It wasn't as if she had two ears anymore, anyway.

"Do it," he said.

"Like I need you to tell me," said Jiang. The sniper boosted herself to her knees and with only the most cursory of aim-taking, pulled the trigger at precisely the same moment a cluster of gators thudded into the keel while fighting over the remains of DuShane Adebayo.

It wasn't much of a thud—no one was falling out of the boat—but the prow dipped just enough to send Jing Jiang's rocket squirreling off course underwater.

"Shit!" said the sniper, watching the blurred taillight fade into the murk. "I don't even know if that's gonna—"

AT WHICH POINT the *Pearl* cruiser leaped into the air like a volcano had just erupted underneath it, and the consequences were multifold:

A tiny species of hydrophytic buttercup, indigenous to the swamp, was blasted into extinction. No one ever saw it, and no one would ever miss it—apart from the bullfrogs that ate it for its hallucinogenic properties. Cue thousands of cold-turkey bullfrogs croaking their sacs off for what was left of the summer.

Two million gallons of swamp water were violently redis-tributed by the rocket's release of energy, causing a six-foot wave to rise up from the depths like Poseidon's fist and dozens of stunned alligators to float to the surface, where they bobbed like healthy turds.

Bodi Irwin's cruiser flipped neater than a high school gymnast, landing square on top of Vern like he was in a Buster Keaton movie.

Squib tried to hold on to the keel of Hooke's sunken boat, but the mini tsunami ripped both him and a section of the boat free, and the boy literally surfed thirty feet onto the deck of Hooke's RIB.

Old Goatbeard, a legendary three-hundred-pound catfish who had been teasing fishermen for years, took a fin from the rocket in the brain.

NOISE.

Lotta coincidence and happenstance—but Wyvern the mythological dragon had brought that kind of thing with him from the early times.

VERN WAS SUDDENLY in the dark, but leastways that crazy warrior woman was off his back for the moment.

The keel shuddered above him, roaring directly into his face like a giant shell channeling the ocean. Also, he was covered in gunk.

What is this shit? Vern wondered, but then his scales instinctively opened to absorb it and he knew.

Oil.

Finally, Lord Highfire gets a break. Now all I need is a minute to convert.

That much-needed minute was not forthcoming, however, as no sooner had the sonic vibration ceased than someone had hooked their fingers beneath the inverted gunwale and begun to heave.

Someone, thought Vern. *Three guesses.*

No normal human would be capable of lifting the boat, but Vern got the feeling that this woman would find the strength somewhere—like it was a tree trunk and he was her baby pinned underneath.

And the momma was hell-bent on killing the baby.

So not exactly your normal tree trunk–baby scenario.

Vern could feel the gunk sinking into his pipes.

Couple more seconds is all I need to be battle-ready.

Granted, it would be a very short battle—no aerial antics or anything showy, just a quick burst. But it appeared that even a few more seconds were not in the cards, because the boat lifted with the groaning reluctance of a mouth opening for the dentist. Swamp glow crept into the gap, and Vern could see the oil on his scales trickling through the grooves.

Come on, gunk. Do your job.

With a final heave and a childbearing shriek, Jewell Hardy pushed the cruiser past the point of no return, revealing a prostrate Vern slathered with the oil from Bodi's busted barrels.

"Just a second," said Vern. "I'll be right with you."

"Death don't wait in line," said Jewell Hardy, which had a nice ring to it.

And to be fair to the girl, with half her face hanging off and blood drenching her torso, she did seem like some class of a harbinger, and Vern was inclined to believe that this moment really was his last when Hardy was struck from behind with an oar and the blow caused her to momentarily hunch over.

"What now?" she said. "Just *what the fuck now?*"

And there was Elodie Moreau come from the shack, trying to help out, putting her own self in harm's way for her son's boss.

"You just leave that old dragon be," she said. "Ain't you got no respect for endangered species?"

Which handed Jewell Hardy her comeback on a plate. "Lady," she said, shrugging off the blow, "you are something of an endangered species yourself."

Elodie went for another blow with the oar, but Hardy caught it and knocked the blade against Elodie's forehead. Squib's momma crumpled to the grass beside Bodi, where they lay like spent lovers.

"Nighty night, sweethearts," said Jewell. "Back in a sec."

She turned to the dragon and said, "Sorry to keep you waiting, Mister Vern."

"Ain't no problem," said Vern, and sparked up.

Jewell Hardy must have seen the spark because she endeavored to remove herself from the literal line of fire. Most of her made it, too, but not quite enough to save her life. Vern's blast of howling flame charred her to cinders below the waist, and her heart had given up the ghost before she hit the mud.

I got enough juice for one more blast, thought Vern. *And I know just the recipient.*

SQUIB DROPPED THE grenade launcher and thought about his favorite book as he surfed on a keel plate that moonlit summer swamp night. The book was *The Princess Bride*, and the part was where one guy says to the other guy following a series of barely credible events how "inconceivable" might not mean what he thought it meant.

Yup, thought Squib, though mostly he was screaming.

The rocket-induced wave propelled him bodily toward the boat he'd just tried to sink and dumped him gasping like a fish on the deck. The boat took the shock, and the excess water sluiced out through bilge ports, but in spite of his name, Squib was too hefty to squeeze through one of them bilge ports and instead lay blinking the scum from his eyes.

"Pennies from heaven," said a voice. "Inconceivable."

Hooke is alive, and he can read my mind, thought Squib, and he wasn't one whit surprised.

HOOKE LIKED TO believe himself godless, but when nature dumped the kid on his deck, he couldn't help thinking that some dark force was working in his favor and therefore an opposite force must surely exist.

"Pennies from heaven," he said. "Inconceivable."

The kid was a sorry sight, all mud-slicked and bashed up by recent events, but that didn't inspire any feelings of sympathy in Hooke. What he thought was, *Enough of this screwing around. No more strategy. I'm just gonna kill my way to the end of this situation.*

And so he grabbed at Squib. "C'mere, kid."

The kid backpedaled along the deck, but there wasn't really anywhere he could go besides into the water, and Hooke aimed to close down that option.

I'll shoot him, he thought, but then, *No, best not, not in an inflatable boat.*

"Let's go, boy," he said. "I got things to do." And he bent low with grabby hands and dug his strong fingers into Squib's lapels.

No, not lapels. Some kind of crackly hide.

"Is this—?" said Hooke. "Are you wearing a dragon suit?"

The nine-fingered boy showed some dexterity and stuck a thumb in the middle of the granny knot securing the suit around his waist. With one jerk the knot unraveled, which surprised Hooke almost as much as the existence of the suit itself.

"Well, if that don't beat all. David fucking Copperfield on a stick."

Squib slid between his legs and was gone over the side so fast that all Hooke could do was chuckle.

"Gators will get him," he said, but he didn't give much weight to his own words. The darned kid had as many lives as fingers. Like a fucking roach.

Then again, I killed roaches before.

Jing Jiang climbed down off the prow. There were tears welling in her eyes. "I lost Timberlake," she said weepily, and it took Hooke a second to catch on.

"Your weapon?"

"'Weapon'?" said Jiang. "'*Weapon*'? Timberlake was a friend of mine. Timberlake was a friend of the whole damn country."

Over her shoulder, Hooke saw fire on the island and thought, *Uh-oh. We awakened the beast.*

And he draped the dragon skin over his shoulders.

"I lost Timberlake," screamed Jing Jiang, "and you're playing dress-up?"

Hooke pulled his Vern hood over his eyes, thinking, *I must look like a big goddamn devil.*

"Hail Satan," he said. "I'm gonna kill Vern the old-fashioned way."

And then he followed Squib overboard.

Hooke didn't mean it—not about going overboard; that was on purpose.

And not about killing Vern; he absolutely meant that. That was an *if it's the last thing I ever do* kinda statement.

About Satan. He didn't mean it about "Hail Satan."

Regence Hooke worshipped no one but his own self.

VERN MANAGED A three-second blast.

His aim was a little erratic, shearing the Irish moss right off a row of cypress over on Honey Island, but at least one final second of dragon flame landed on Hooke's boat, melting it and anybody on it to a memory. One second might not sound like much, but it's a long time to be on fire, as Jing Jiang might have testified to if she hadn't been so incinerated. In fact, in the name of honesty, truer to say that Jiang wasn't incinerated as such, because Vern's final second was a bit breathy, as the last second often is, so the temperature dipped considerably, meaning that Jing Jiang was actually asphyxiated by melted plastic rather than burned outright, which was not really any comfort to the sniper.

Dragon flame was clean. Being cocooned in liquefied plastic? Not so much.

Vern kept on pumping till his molars sparked like an empty Zippo; then he keeled over into the mud and thrashed a little like he was making a swamp angel.

Bodi Irwin, trying to attend to Elodie, had something to say about the thrashings. "Vern, come on, dude. I been shot here, and Elodie's out cold. Quit spasming. You're tail-lashing me."

"Show some gratitude, Green Day," said Vern, though he did calm down with the tail. "I saved your hippie ass. And you ain't dying, in case you was wondering. If you was dying, you would be gone already. Plus you're talking up a storm."

"It ain't hardly a storm, stringing a few sentences together," argued Bodi. "And you ain't exactly keeping mum your own self."

Vern snorted. "You was afraid of me a minute ago. I miss those days."

"Yeah, well, a ruptured torso puts things in perspective."

Vern patted his stomach, which was now concave. "Perspective, Green Day? From which perspective ain't a dragon scary?"

"I'm still scared, Vern, but I'm more anxious."

Vern sniggered. "About Elodie?"

Bodi elbowed the dragon. "Screw you."

"She's a hell of a woman, if you like that species."

Bodi picked the hair from Elodie's forehead, taking a peek underneath. "This ain't the time, Vern. I been shot. You're close to a skeleton, and Elodie's knocked senseless."

"Check on her then," said Vern. "Lemme take a second here, then I'll retrieve our boy."

Bodi had a barman's experience with checking on

casualties, so was soon satisfied that at least one of them wasn't going to die anytime soon, though Squib's momma would have a bruise the size of a lily pad and could probably do with a couple of staples to the bridge of her nose.

"You see what happened to Squib?" he asked the dragon.

Vern hiked himself up on his elbows, thinking there was probably more oil underneath the *Pearl* cruiser or in the swamp pools hereabouts, and if he could just swallow a few quarts . . .

"He went in the water. After that I was busy getting beat on."

"Maybe you should take a look-see now?"

"Yeah. I surely would, if you could stop detaining me with conversation."

Bodi did not rejoin, preferring to lie back beside Elodie and put pressure on his own wound. The Lord knew he had thought about them lying parallel like this, but without the bullet hole and lily pad bruise.

"Guess I'll take a look-see then," said Vern, rolling onto his stomach. "Might have to drag this old carcass."

But he never had to drag the old carcass because Squib came lurching out of the water by the splintered remains of the landing.

"Momma?" he called. "Momma? Vern?"

"Heh," said Vern. "You ain't even in the circle of trust, Green Day."

Then he raised an arm weakly. "Yeah. Everyone's alive, Squib. I done saved 'em all. You shoulda seen me."

"The alligators look like sleeping turds," said Squib, sniffling.

It was plain that the boy was close to all-out bawling.

"I wanna hug my momma in just a second," he said.

"Just a second"? wondered Vern. *Why the delay?*

Squib squatted down, elbows on knees with the loose joints of childhood, which was pretty graceful, and then ruined the effect by throwing up a quart of swamp water onto the keel of Bodi's inverted cruiser. It was one of those effortless pukes, no painful retches: just open mouth and unleash the torrent.

"Shit, boy," said Vern. "You musta gone in with both ends wide-open."

"I been thrown in twice," said Squib. "My insides ain't nothing but swamp."

Vern had to laugh. Nothing funnier than watching a youngster throw up. It was a shame Squib hadn't been drinking, as then the dragon could've delivered a lecture, too. But puking would have to do.

"Get it out, son."

Squib wiped his mouth. "Nah, I'm done."

"You sure? Sometimes there's a round two."

But Squib did not oblige, and instead, Vern was forced to deal with the uncomfortable truth that he was lying exposed out in the open in the aftermath of an epic shit storm with the Feds one county south keeping their eyes peeled for exactly this class of a blip on the thermals.

Highfire, son, he thought to himself, *you don't wanna stop being mythical and start being real.*

This was surely true, as being real was only one step away from being extinct. Lying prostrate in the mud with holes in his wings and a head wound bubbling on his forehead, Vern had to admit that the one step between him and extinction was feeling like a baby step this fine morning as the sun threatened to push through over the gulf.

"Momma," said Squib. "Momma—your face . . ."

"That looks bad," said Vern, "but it's cosmetic—"

And then things got balls-nasty one more time because it looked like the Swamp Thing was coming out of the river. But it wasn't the Swamp Thing; it was Regence Hooke wearing Vern's skin like a cloak, limbs all blackened where they poked out.

Vern's response to this apparition was to unleash his junk and take an arcing piss.

The Swamp Thing sloughed off the algae and weed fronds to become, of course, Regence Hooke, blackened and blistered, but infuriatingly, undeniably alive.

HOOKE HAD FELT the heat of Vern's dragon fire moments earlier as he leaped from the RIB, but not as severely as he might have without Vern's own skin to protect him. Even so, his pants were frizzled away, and his hands scorched black.

Coulda been a whole lot worse, Regence, he told himself. *A dragon suit? Fuck me.*

Hooke wasn't the greatest of swimmers, but he plugged away, dragging himself through the murk-of-dawn swamp, trying to ignore the logjam of dazed alligators off his port side.

That's one for the Discovery Channel, he thought. *Shit, maybe I should board one of those brutes and paddle ashore.*

But he didn't want to risk waking the big lizards. It would be a shame to be eaten by a gator on the way to beat up a dragon.

Anyways, it wasn't more'n two pulls before his boots touched down and all Hooke had to do then was negotiate the submerged tree knuckles and dips of the swamp bed on his way to shore. He kept himself low, just peeking out enough to breathe. His sopping attire killed any buoyancy he might have had, so it was easy to keep himself mostly hidden. He saw Squib, that little pain in his ass, crawl ashore and throw his guts up. He saw the first rays of slanting morning sun catch Vern on the snout. That boy was tuckered the hell out and couldn't even manage a hug for his little familiar. And there was Bodi Irwin, all shot to hell. He might make it or he might not, but either way he wasn't up for fisticuffs right at the moment.

This is your chance, Regence, he told himself. *This right here is the golden opportunity people are always talking about.*

Sure, his Delta Force plan had gone completely ass-ways, but here was a shot at redemption.

Hooke counted to five, then waded ashore.

Squib never heard Hooke coming up behind him, being too busy boo-hooing over his precious momma. But Hooke knew the little seven-toed bastard would be like a gnat if he wasn't swatted, so he improvised a move, one of those maneuvers that he just knew was gonna work out before he even set himself in motion.

He could *visualize* it.

This is gonna be cool, he thought, and reached one of his massive hands beneath the gunwale of Bodi's boat. Making sure to lift with his knees, he hauled the craft maybe three feet up on one side, then whistled. "Hey, kid."

Squib left off his bawling for long enough to check out the whistle, at which point Hooke palmed him under the boat and dropped it on him like a coffin lid: the second time in as many minutes the cruiser had been used as a prison.

"Oh-ho," he crowed, "sa-*weet*. Whaddya say, Vern?"

The dragon's response to this was to take an epic piss.

"What the hell you doing, Vern?" asked Hooke. This wasn't no way for his nemesis to go out, pissing on his friends.

"You make me nervous, Constable Hooke," replied the dragon, "and when I'm nervous, I pee."

"Uh-uh," said Hooke, not really buying it, suspecting something. "You pee."

He peered around, looking for the blindside move, but everything seemed clear. The boy was banging on the hull, yelling about his momma and doing damage to his own eardrums. Bodi Irwin was bleeding out, and pretty Elodie Moreau sure wasn't pretty no more. As for the mighty Vern, he was on his ass, pissing on Bodi and Elodie.

"You squirt away, lizard. Either you let it out now, or I'm surely gonna beat it outta you."

Bodi, finding a smidge of gumption somewhere, started pawing at the shotgun by his side.

"No, sir," said Hooke, snatching the weapon away and checking the load. Empty. "I am done with inconveniences. You just lie still, and I promise to kill you quick."

"Ain't you got no soul, Regence?" Bodi rasped, his face cherry-red with indignation. "This here is the last of his kind. You wanna be the man who robbed the world of magic?"

Hooke spat in the mud. "*Magic*? Magic, old man? Your 'magic' is ass-deep in swamp mud pissing on your flank. I think the world can survive just fine without that kind of enchantment."

This was a good point, and as much as Bodi blustered and rasped, he came up short regarding an answer.

"That's what I thought," said Hooke. He cast around, looking for something in the blossoming light of a summer morning, the sun bleeding into the sky from out on the gulf and mosquitoes calling it a night.

"Aha," he said, like a movie psycho who's just come upon the biggest knife in the kitchen. But it wasn't a knife he'd discovered but the top half of Jewell Hardy, which was bled pale in the scrub.

"Shit, Vern," he said, peeling off her weighted gloves. "You done a number on this girl. I liked her, too, so that's coming out of your ass."

"Sure, Hooke," said Vern, whose tank was apparently empty. "You're gonna be the one. After all these years, it's gonna be Regence Hooke. Dream on, Constable."

Hooke tugged the gloves on as far as they would go on his massive hands. "A little O. J., right? I know. But still, it should be enough to do you in, Vern. You ain't got nothing left. No fire, no flight. Shit, you don't even got no piss anymore."

Vern grinned weakly, and blood bubbled behind his teeth. "I got one thing, shitface."

Hooke set himself up, planting his feet on Vern's wings, squatting low and snapping off a right hook to Vern's jaw.

"What's that, lizard? What's the one thing? You ain't

gonna say 'friends,' are you?" Hooke laughed. "Because I'd say your friends are just about as fucked as you. Five seconds after I beat your head off, I'm gonna take care of them, and what's more, it's gonna look like you was responsible. I'll be a goddamn hero, sheriff of whatever goddamn ward I choose. Shit, I might even run for mayor."

Hooke set about Vern's head with a flurry of jabs, snapping the dragon's head from side to side, drawing blood with each blow. Soon the dragon's face was a lattice of blood lines.

Vern's eyes rolled back, and it sounded like he was trying to speak, but all he could manage was a reptilian throat rattle.

Hooke was delighted. "Your buddy is reverting, Bodi. I beat him all the way back to the Jurassic age."

Bodi couldn't talk much; all his energy was going into anger, which was just pumping the blood out of him faster. "You . . ." he said. "You . . ."

"Yep," said Hooke, happier than he had ever been in his life. "Me . . . *Me.*"

Vern rattled some more, and coughed at the end of it.

"What you saying there, Vern?" asked Hooke, stomping on the dragon's jaw. "You calling for your dragon momma?"

Vern spat blood and one of his tusks, which Hooke picked up and wiped on his pants.

"Naw," gasped Vern, "I'm calling for the one thing I got."

Hooke had too much adrenaline rushing through his veins to catch the tone. "I'll tell you what you got. You got a hope in hell, that's what you got, Wyvern."

Vern rattled his throat one more time, then said, "No, Regence. What I got is subjects."

"'Subjects'?" said Hooke, then laughed. "Goddamn subjects. You're a one, Vern. Damned if you ain't, Your Majesty."

This relentless ragging must've got Vern's goat a little because he withdrew his junk with a defiant clanking. "And you're a dick, Regence. But not for long."

Hooke was bored now. Incredible, that a person could tire of beating up a dragon, but now the race was run, more or less, and he wanted to keep on keeping on. This situation needed tidying up before the Federales arrived with their tents and stuff to cross. He had all the *t's, dot the i's,* and drown the witnesses.

"Anyways, Vern," he said, "I reckon there's one thing that will surely slice through to a dragon's heart, if you're finished pissing on your friends, that is." He wrapped his fingers around Vern's own tusk, testing its underhand grip.

It was possible that Vern was slightly more pale than usual.

Everything looked red in this light, but he continued talking back to his last breath. "Ain't you never watched nature shows, Hooke? Ain't you never had a goddamned dog? I wasn't *pissing* on my friends. I was *marking* them."

Vern gave one more rattle, which gave Hooke a moment to consider the "marking them" comment.

"Bullshit" was his verdict on that. "Bullshit, Vern. Piss ain't no more effective than Rosary beads. Piss can't protect nobody from me."

Vern barely opened his mouth to answer. "Not from you, moron. You ain't nothing."

Okeydokey, thought Hooke. *Cab for one delirious dragon.* He made a few experimental thrusts with the tusk.

Nice heft, he thought. *I'm gonna have this tooled up. Put a handle on her. Kill everything with a dragon's tooth from this day forth.*

Constable Regence Hooke took a moment to appreciate his surroundings. *Live in the moment,* wasn't that what they said? All them gurus and so forth.

"There ain't never going to be another moment like this one, Regence," he told himself. All the elements were present for a unique-style memory:

1. The dragon dying on his ass.
2. The woman with her face all beat up.
3. The son trapped under an inverted boat.

It was almost demeaning to that bunch of details to include a bleeding-out hippie, but Bodi was part of it, so Hooke acknowledged him with a wink.

Ain't you never had a dog? What the hell was that about? Deathbed bullshit.

But the fact was that Regence Hooke never did have a dog as a boy, his daddy being dead set against them. But he had read up on them, back in the day, and he did know that dogs pissed on things to mark their territory. To warn off other dogs.

But there ain't no other dogs, that is to say, dragons.

Then Regence felt a clamping on his ankle, and now he understood.

Fuck.

Vern did have subjects after all.

Hooke looked down to see a big-ass alligator with what looked like a scorched head chomping on his boot. The creature's teeth hadn't penetrated the padded leather yet, but it was only a matter of time, so he nailed it right between the eyes with Vern's tusk, and it sank in like a spike through crusty bread, that is to say, a little initial resistance, then through to the sponge beneath. Trouble was, it didn't come out so easy, and there were a ton more gators slithering across the slick swamp grass.

"You prick, Vern," said Hooke. "You goddamn prick."

The first gator didn't relax its grip, even in death. In fact, its jaws ratcheted tighter and Hooke felt a bone snap in his ankle.

No talking now. No threats.

Hooke knew that he would need every joule of energy to extricate himself from this gator crisis, for they were coming in a sinewy wave over the verge, hides glistening red, some still half stunned by the explosion, turret eyes rolling, jaws wide like Satan's hedge clippers.

Hooke gave the tusk a couple more tugs, then abandoned it.

Better maybe, Regence, to abandon this entire conflict for now.

But first he needed to retrieve his foot. He stomped on the gator that had latched onto his ankle, stomping with his heavy boot until the animal's snout was only so much crazy paving, and twisted his foot out of the tooth trap. The broken bone hurt like hellfire, but he tucked that pain in his back pocket for now. He could take it out on someone or other later, when everything on this godforsaken island was dead excepting him.

He tried to run, but after three hobbling steps he knew

that two more would see him collapse into the mud, so he turned to fight.

Weapons?

He had lost pretty much everything in the swamp, but he still had his faithful gut hook, and so he armed himself sharpish as the sinewy sea of alligators swept toward him with a synchronicity about them that he had never seen in gators before, and he reckoned that was going to be all she wrote for his ass.

Still, a fella has to go down swinging, so the constable gamely sliced into the first alligator, hoping that the herd would be scattered by the death of their leader. It was only when the gators ignored the body of their comrade, clambering over it to get to him, that Hooke realized, *I'm going for the wrong creature. Vern is their leader.*

But he had no time to deal with that before the glistening mass of nubs and teeth was upon him, tearing him apart with all the eagerness of demons welcoming newcomers to Hades. Hooke watched as one arm was torn from his body and the blood spurted like oil from a nozzle; then he saw a gator take a chunk out of his stomach the size of a basketball and his own insides plop onto his lap.

Ripped right through my vest, he thought, *like it wasn't even there.*

Then he was lying on his ass and trying to punch his attackers with a hand he didn't have anymore, and he had to laugh at that, which was a mistake because a gator aimed its lower jaw directly into Hooke's open mouth hole and speared him right through the brain, which was an unusual move for that species, but it was effective as all hell because when the gator closed its mouth, Hooke's head cracked like a watermelon under the hammer.

VERN HAD EXPECTED to feel some kind of grim satisfaction. You watch your sworn enemy getting torn apart, and it's meant to feel good, right?

Hell yeah! That's supposed to be your reaction.

But Vern was surprised to find he didn't feel anything even close to exhilaration. It was too brutal a death, even for a cosmic-level asshole like Constable Regence Hooke.

Still.

Hooke was definitely dead this time, so there was that.

Vern watched as Hooke was completely submerged in a sea of alligators, then gave a rattle from his throat, followed by two brief whistles.

The gators retreated like they were on bungee cords, leaving Hooke's mangled corpse in an unnatural heap on the trampled reeds, looking like a butcher just poured him out of a sack. Buttons's corpse was lying maybe six feet away. Vern knew his buddies would come back for him when the ripples had settled.

Maybe just as well Buttons got plugged, thought Vern. *He mighta taken another shot at the king, and this time the crown woulda been his.*

But Vern didn't buy his own rationalization. He'd gotten Buttons killed, was the long and short of it.

He took a shaky breath, and even that hurt. He realized that it was quite possible Hooke would still manage to be the death of him unless Squib got his ass in gear and did his job.

"Bodi," he said. "You there, man?"

The response was slow coming. "More or less, Vern. Not for long, I'm thinking."

"How about Elodie?"

"I can hear her snoring. Nose must be broke."

"She's still beautiful inside, so don't you be forgetting that."

"Screw you, lizard," said Bodi, probably figuring he was dying anyway.

"Oh-ho," said Vern. "Green Day grew some balls."

And he closed his eyes.

SQUIB KNEW WHAT was going on outside his prison boat. He'd heard an alligator swarm in Vern's shack; he doubted that he would ever forget that noise. If he had to do a comparison, like for a school essay or something, he would say alligators swarming sounded a little like a billion punctured tires all leaking air at the same time—not normal tires, mind, but big tires, like the ones on them monster trucks.

Boss man's called in the cavalry, he realized. *Those gators will tear Hooke to bloody strips.*

His mom, too, most likely. And Mister Irwin.

It was the thought of them gators crawling all over his mother that gave Squib strength. Even though he was tuckered out beyond belief, what with all the swamp shenanigans, he threw himself at the cruiser's gunwale and heaved with every ounce of his newfound supernatural reserves. He managed to move it maybe half an inch.

Think, Everett Moreau, he told himself. *Think.*

He wiped his hands on his legs, which didn't dry them any, and ripped open the Velcro seal on his vest's phone pocket. His phone wouldn't be any use as a communication device, not out here in the dead zone, but at least he would have some light, presuming recent traumas hadn't done a number on his electronics. His luck was in, and soon the boat cave was awash in a spooky glow.

Outside, the alligator charge was continuing. Squib could hear the bastards scrambling over the boat to get at someone.

"Momma!" he called, his voice ragged with fear. "I'm coming!" For all the good the mighty Squib's intervention would do. But he had to try.

He wasn't shifting the boat, that much was clear, but there had to be a way out. He ran his torch around the gunwale again, but the craft was sealed pretty tight, sunk right down into the mud in some places. He could probably dig himself out if he had an hour to spare and a handy shovel, but neither of those things were presenting themselves. There was a patch of morning light shafting in through the engine port, but there was barely enough room for a baby rat to squeak through.

Unless I can get the engine off, he thought suddenly. The fifty-horsepower outboard was secured by two large butterfly clamps, and Squib attacked the first with gusto. Luckily, Bodi was a man who took care of his equipment and the nut barely put up a fight, spinning off in his fingers. Squib's luck held some more when the second clamp couldn't bear the weight of the skewed engine and was dragged off without him having to so much as say *Boo* to it. Now he had an escape hatch about the size of a cereal box. For once, being the runt of his generation was about to pay off.

"Pay off," he thought. *Well, if getting chewed up and swallowed by swamp gators was the kind of payment a boy was after.*

Nevertheless, and to his credit, Squib did not hesitate but dived into that hatch like there was a fantasy land on the other side where the folks were just waiting to dub him a prince. It was a tight fit. The mud insinuated itself into his every crevice, and Squib felt like he would never be clean again, but that didn't matter much, seeing as how he'd most likely be dead in a couple of seconds anyway.

They can bury me in mud, and no one will know the difference.

His hands scrabbled for the outside world. When he felt the air playing across them, he worried that some sharp-eyed gator would mistake his fingers for worms and chomp them right off his hands, but no such amputations occurred, and soon Squib Moreau was on his feet and blinking in the morning haze.

He was looking for his momma, his boss, and his other boss, and he found them laid out side by side by side. It was quite a peaceful tableau, if Squib ignored the wounds and bruises and blood, which he couldn't. He dropped to his knees in the squelch of swamp and waved his hands over his momma's head like an expert in one of those nontouching healing massage methods.

"Momma?" he said. "Are you dead?"

Elodie declined to answer, having been recently paddled by a bear-woman, but at least she continued to breathe, which was something, though her swollen nose made a whistling labor of the process.

"Nose, Momma," said Squib, pointing at the nose. "Your nose."

"Boy's some kind of genius," said Vern.

"Goddamn prodigy," agreed Bodi, who reckoned he was so deep in shock that he might as well converse like none of this was happening.

Squib wiped a tear from his nose. "What do I do, boss? Everyone's dying or plumb dead already. This situation is DEFCON 1 fucked."

Vern was okay for smart-assholery, but actual decisions were beyond his oil-starved brain. "Uh," he said. "Erm. Lemme sleep on that."

And he did, collapsing into catatonia.

"Balls," said Squib, crawling across to Bodi, who seemed to be chuckling at an invisible joke while blood bubbled on his chest. "Come on, Mister Irwin, I can't plan stuff. I done proved that over and over."

"Sorry, boy," said Bodi, "I can barely manage to stay alive. If you tell me something, I might remember it."

Squib suddenly felt as though the mud coating him was alive with critters and they were chewing ruminatively on his flesh. There were lives on the line and corpses to be explained. Everyone was dying and he had to fix it somehow—and all without a phone signal.

"Everyone is dying, Mister Irwin," he said desperately.

And then Bodi found a spark in his brain to say something intelligent. "Ain't nobody dying, Squib, 'cept maybe me. And by the sound of it, help is on the way."

Squib thought on this. *Nobody was dying.* Only Bodi Irwin was in need of urgent help, and the sound of sirens on the water confirmed that the cavalry was surging upriver. After the hoo-ha in New Orleans, there was probably a whole flotilla of lawmakers strapping on their Kevlar right now.

"Okay," he said. "Okay, I think I got something. It's crazy, but not as crazy as the truth."

And he told Bodi his plan.

"Yup," said Bodi. "That's just about the biggest heap of . . ."

Then Bodi joined the other two in unconsciousness, and Squib could only hope he had been about to say, *That's just about the biggest heap of genius I ever heard.*

Which was a well-known phrase, wasn't it?

Even if it wasn't, Squib had no choice, no help, and no better ideas, so it was either get busy trying or get busy waiting for the cops to arrive.

What would Vern do? he asked himself.

That was easy. Vern would cuss a little, scratch his behind, then get busy.

Well, all right then.

"Fuck a duck," said Squib, scratching the sopping ass of his jeans, then took his momma under the arms and dragged her toward the pirogue.

CHAPTER 20

VERN WOKE FEELING LIKE HE'D BEEN PASSED THROUGH THE KIND of malevolent mangler that Stephen King might have dreamed up. He felt so bad that it was quite possible he was actually dead and in dragon hell. Memories and personality meant nothing while confined to that fugue; there was just the punishing drudge of pain. No, that wasn't true—it wasn't all agony; there were parts of him that felt tender or nauseated, his brain for example. Vern would have said the word for the way his brain felt was "peeled." Which was never a good thing as far as brains were concerned. His ass also felt peeled, which didn't generally bode well for asses either.

Vern had no choice but to endure, which he did for about half a day till his cells had regenerated enough that he was upgraded from "at death's door" to merely "gravely injured." And perhaps half a day after that he regained control of his faculties, not all of them, but enough to marshal the energy to exclaim, "By the throbbing shaft of Azazel."

Which had been a popular expletive, back in the day.

He opened his various eyelids, all of which felt like they were coated in grit, to find Elodie Moreau staring down at him with a worried expression.

"*Groundhog Day*," said Vern. "I'm stuck in this dream where you're watching me recuperate."

"It ain't no dream, Mister Vern," said Elodie. "We're both here, sure enough."

"One of us smells like the inside of a deep fryer," noted Vern. "I'm guessing that'd be me."

Elodie raised his head and stuck a sippy cup straw in his mouth, and while Vern sucked she said, "Yeah, I guess. We've been getting oil into you any way we could. You've been guzzling in your sleep, and Squib borrowed my basting brush. You're like a Christmas goose with all the fat he painted onto you. No offense."

"None taken, Miss Elodie. It does seem to be doing the trick."

"We soaked bandages for your wings," continued Elodie. "I figured maybe something more refined for that tissue, delicate and all as it looks. So Bodi purchased some grade-A coconut oil for that."

"Well I never," said Vern. "I got me a regular spa going on here." He looked around the small room. "Where is 'here,' by the way? No memory foam today?"

Elodie smiled, a touch embarrassed. "Thing is, Mister Vern, you're in our tub. Seemed like the best place, with you being more or less submerged and all. I padded it nice with towels and one of those travel cushions for your neck."

Vern shifted a little and heard the slow slosh of oil around his flanks. "Fine idea. Yours?"

"No. Everett's been doing the thinking for all of us. Lord knows where he found the strength but he took me and you both down here in his canoe, evading the various members of law enforcement coming to storm your island. You should see that place now: like Disneyland it is, with all the lights and folks in space suits."

Vern sighed. "That's another safe house up in smoke, so to speak. How's Bodi?"

"Mister Irwin is all kinds of fine," said Elodie. "A hero, is what he is. He always suspected Constable Hooke was running drugs up the Pearl, and in the course of his snooping—a little white lie we concocted—he was caught in a crossfire of crooked cops, all part of Ivory Conti's operation that used to be, according to a notebook recovered from Regence Hooke's person.

"So Mister Bodi Irwin has been sworn in as caretaker constable by unanimous vote of the town council."

Vern whistled. "Good for you, Green Day. And Squib?"

"The entire plan was all my boy's. He's being run ragged, doing shifts at the bar and trucking oil over here. I am mighty pleased to see that young man has finally learned some responsibility."

Vern slumped down in his oil bath till only his wings and snout punctured the surface tension. He was feeling better by the second; his stomach was growing before his eyes.

"Your face looks okay," he said to Elodie.

Squib's momma glanced at herself in the bathroom mirror. "Oh Lord, that woman sure did put a hurt on me. I swear my entire head is still ringing. My face looks like I been in a cage fight."

Vern chuckled. "I'll bet Green Day don't mind. I swear that man is smitten."

"I'm a mite smitten myself, Mister Vern," admitted Elodie. "We go way back. And now that Hooke ain't marking his territory . . ."

This particular caused Vern to flash on that time he'd pissed all over Miss Elodie.

"Yeah, marking his territory," said Vern, sinking a little lower. "About that . . ."

Elodie waved away the looming apology. "God, no, Mister Vern. You were *saving* us. I get that now—and anyways, I was unconscious. My jeans did get a little bleached, though. Nice pattern, actually, all these interlocking loops. My dragon jeans, I call 'em now."

She's funny, thought Vern. *I see where Squib gets it from.* He sank entirely below the gloopy surface. *Looks like all's well, apart from old Highfire. He's up the creek, and it ain't the creek he lives in.*

Vern blinked up through the golden film and saw the Moreau bathroom grow convex above him.

I might stay down here a spell, he thought, *absorb some more of this fat.*

And for the thousandth time, he resolved to find out something about his own workings.

A dragon can't just go around ignorant his whole life.

There had been physicians back on Highfire, but Vern had neglected his sciences in favor of more outdoorsy activities, so intent had he been on proving his baby brother Jubelus wrong vis-à-vis him being a waste of space on the battlefield. And so now he had no one to ask.

So far as I know.

Maybe it was time he had a look for another dragon, took a more active role in his own future besides just lazing around in it. But there were loose ends to be tied up here first.

I need to do some deep thinking on these matters, thought Vern, and closed his eyes.

VERN DIDN'T COME fully out of it for another week, and by then the swamp sideshow was packed up, by and large, according to his sources. The dragon woke one evening to find the tub bone-dry, and his wings busted out of their bandages, so he elected to give his old bones a turn around the Moreau shack, the first time he'd so much as ventured outside the tub, never mind the bathroom. Following an undignified tumble onto the tiles, he found the quaint bathroom did not accurately preview the rest of Chez Moreau, as the rest of the small hut was bare wood and worn Formica, basic but clean, except where Squib left his teenage mark. The boy's main mess items were various chargers snaking across every surface, and water bottles stuffed behind just about anywhere a bottle could be stuffed—and a few places they could not, unless they'd been crumpled to fit.

"Goddamn, kid," muttered Vern. "There's a trash bin right there."

The shack was empty, but Vern could smell Squib close by.

"Still using that packet soap," he muttered, snagging a raincoat from a hook and draping it over his shoulders. His wings retracted with barely a twinge, and Vern thanked his stars for the restorative power of fat.

I don't know why the magic works, Highlander, he thought. *I'm just glad that it does.*

Vern peeked through the screen door, checking for stranger danger, but there was only one human in view: Squib, passed out in a lawn chair on the porch with a newspaper draped across his legs.

Newspaper, thought Vern. *They're still making those?*

He ducked outside and sat opposite Squib, reading the headline upside down:

HONEY ISLAND MONSTER REVEALED TO BE CROOKED COP IN COSTUME

"Heh," said Vern. "Nice."

"That was part of my plan," said Squib, who was apparently awake. "Wrap it up nice and neat for Five-O. All those monster clips? Nothing but a drug-running cop in a dragon suit scaring people away from his pipeline. They found a ton of evidence in the river, and I sent a photo of Hooke wearing the skin into the *Times-Picayune,* just to make sure we got a little traction."

"Clever," said Vern. "And the Feds bought that?"

Squib rubbed his eyes. "Nah. Too many holes. Like, what was Hooke doing playing dress-up in New Orleans? That sort of thing."

"But it keeps the public happy?"

"Yeah. It's much easier not to believe in you, I guess."

Vern propped his feet on the little lawn table. "Yup. That's the way I like it." Then he thought of something. "A photo? When did you take a photo of Hooke in my skin?"

Squib hummed and hawed a spell and then came out with it. "It weren't Hooke, boss."

"It was you," said Vern. "Couldn't resist it, right?"

"You know us young folk," said Squib. "We can't let a photo op pass us by."

"I hope you ain't signed your own arrest warrant with that photograph."

Squib waved that away. "Nah. I printed out a hard copy. Dunked it in a barrel of oil. Put it through the dryer then copied it in a printer. Don't look like nobody now but it all adds up to the public, I guess."

Vern squinted at him. "So you been gallivanting around in my skin?"

Squib stretched, then changed the subject. "Okay, so while you been healing in the tub, I've been thinking. Obviously the island is blown. The Feds have a dozen webcams running 24/7, and there are still a couple of agents boarding at the Pearl—real Mulder and Scully types, lady even has red hair. You believe that?"

Vern whistled the *X-Files* theme and realized that his missing tusk was growing back. A little stubby, but getting there.

"Exactly, boss," said Squib.

"I loved that show when it was monster-of-the-week," said Vern. "Then they started with the world-building shit and I lost interest."

"Too political," said Squib, not because he'd ever seen *The X-Files* but because they'd been down this conversational road before.

"Yeah, too political," said Vern. "Just shoot a chupacabra, for Christ's sake, and spare me that cigarette guy."

"*Die, chupacabra,*" said Squib, shooting finger guns.

"Anyway, kid, I cut across you there. You've been thinking?"

"I've been thinking: The island is too hot for now, but how long are those agents gonna hang out on the government dollar? Couple of months, tops, then we're back in business. *Highfire and Moreau, Part 2: The Burn is Back.*"

"Nice title. I can see the poster," said Vern.

Squib was encouraged. "So, Momma says you are welcome to stay here until the smoke clears or dies down or whatever. You can have my bed. And then by Christmas you're swimming with the gators. What do you think, boss? Makes sense, right?"

"Almost," said Vern, "if you squint at it. If you don't examine it too close."

Squib chewed this over for a minute. "The skin," he said at last.

"Yup," said Vern, "the skin. Lady Fed Scully is gonna analyze that and figure out it's not gator, kid. So at the very least those cameras ain't going nowhere any time soon."

Squib wasn't ready to cry uncle just yet. "I can fix the cameras—maybe point the lenses up a boar's asshole, or just bust 'em every coupla weeks."

"Nah," said Vern, "that's just drawing attention, and before you know it, there's a satellite taking shots from space."

"Okay then, we relocate to Honey Island. Island-hopping, right, like how all the celebrities do."

"That's a negative, son. I need distance—somewhere south of the border."

Squib knew where this was going; he'd been dreading it.

Vern had, too, truth be told.

"So we gotta leave?" asked the boy.

Vern almost went for that. Almost. But exile only worked solo. "'We'? That would be nice, kid. Real nice. But I gotta fly outta here stealth-mode-style. Ain't no passengers, not long-distance."

Squib covered his face with his hands, and Vern wondered what was going on behind there.

"When you going?" asked the boy, his words muffled.

"Soon," said Vern. "The authorities are gonna extend the scope of their inquiries, and we're the first stop on the river right here."

"Where you going?"

Vern flapped his lips. "Not certain exactly. South America, I think. Get outta the jurisdiction, you know. Sounds sensible. Also, I want to make sure I really am the last, and South America might be a good place to start. I always figured the Internet rumors were the usual bullshit, like that cat who plays a keyboard, but after my own reveal I've changed my outlook a little. Time to investigate."

Squib opened his fingers a little, revealing his eyes. "What about my job?"

"You'll be okay," said Vern. "I know Waxman wanted you in his boat house. That place is a palace. Everything hidden in there is yours and your mamma's."

Squib nodded. He had been hoping Elodie would move to Waxman's with him, but now with this new romance on the stove it didn't seem likely. Still, he had his own place on the water, which opened up a world of possibilities.

"What about you, boss? You gonna be okay? You lost your buddy. Old Wax was a character."

Vern shrugged. "I ain't been okay for a long time, kid. But I'm a helluva lot better with you on the payroll."

"So stay," said Squib. "You can tell me stories about Waxman. Work that shit out. I can be like a therapist."

Vern laughed. "I can't afford no therapist."

Squib didn't like that comment. "It ain't about money, boss."

"I know, kid," said Vern. "I was kidding. You've been invaluable to me. I never had a familiar like you. I would go so far as to say you're my partner. Junior partner, of course."

Squib dropped his hands, and he was smiling just a little. "Junior partner? I like that."

"In fact," said Vern, "as junior partner, it's your moral responsibility to look after my business affairs while I'm out of the country."

"You got business affairs, boss?"

"Sure I got business affairs. Real estate, for one."

Squib laughed. "I know you ain't talking about the shack?"

"Yes, the shack, but I got capital, too, and I can't be taking it with me."

"Capital, like *cash*?"

Vern grinned. "Like cash, but shiny. Confederate shiny."

The penny dropped on something Vern had said.

"Wait a minute, boss," said Squib. "You said 'while I'm

out of the country.' I am inferring from that that you're coming back."

"You're inferring? Well, fuck-a-ducka-doodah all the day," said Vern, straight-faced. "Miss Ingram is responsible for that term, I'm guessing. Maybe if you're inferring, I'm implying, huh? Not as stupid as I look."

"So you are coming back."

"Ain't that what I said?"

"I ain't certain, boss."

"Me neither. But I do plan to come back. Or bring you down to me when your schooling is done."

Squib blinked. "Schooling? *Schooling*? You ain't gone all Catholic on me, Vern?"

Vern leaned in, as if to impart great wisdom. "Most schooling ain't worth shit, that's no secret. Schooling in general is a broken system perpetuated by educators: 'You need what we got, so let us sell it to you.'"

"Exactly," said Squib. "I been saying that exact same thing for years."

"But," said Vern, raising one finger, "Miss Ingram seems like the real deal. So I want you to get your diploma."

"My diploma!" exclaimed Squib. "So what, I can wipe my ass with it?"

Vern wasn't finished. "And . . ."

"And? There's *more*?"

Vern sat back and folded his arms, waiting out the bluster, which took a full minute until finally Squib calmed himself.

"That was quite a display," said Vern, disapproval written all over his snout. "Not exactly junior-partner behavior."

Squib was sulking so hard his neck had disappeared. "Yeah, well, you's talking education. I ain't got time for that. I got shit to do."

"Damn right you got shit to do: You gotta manage my business, and you gotta find out everything you can about my dragon-ness."

"'Dragon-ness' ain't even a word."

"Maybe it is, maybe it ain't," said Vern, "and that there's exactly the kind of thing you need to verify. Far as I can see, there's a lot of knowledge neither of us is privy to that one of us needs to find out. Besides, in today's business market, I'd be a fool to employ a junior partner without no college degree."

Squib was like to fall off his chair. "*College degree?* I got to go to college now?"

"Damn straight," said Vern. "I need to know what makes the markets tick and what makes *me* tick, so you gotta do some kind of combination degree: business and dragon studies."

"Business *and* dragon studies? You can do that?"

Vern nodded with exaggerated confidence. "Sure you can—they got *everything* these days. You can do a *Star Wars* degree, Obi-Wan fucking Moreau."

"Cool," said Squib.

"So, you get some tutoring from this Ingram lady, then off with your skinny ass to UNO for a couple years, all the time monitoring my portfolio."

"You mean putting your stash in a hole in the ground?"

"Yeah, minus what you take out for your scholarship and salary. Keep records, mind. Of every cent."

This was a lot of long-term information to absorb for a young man who rarely thought past his next payday. "Can I think about it?"

Vern's expression said *no*, as did his voice. "Negative on that, kiddo. This here is what they call a once-in-a-lifetime opportunity, boy. I'll be fancying me some travel in years to come, and I'm gonna need a college-educated feller by my side. So there's the terms."

"I ain't never stuck at schooling, boss," whined Squib.

"Who the fuck are you? Huck Finn? Just take the goddamn deal." Vern stuck out his hand. "This hand goes away in five seconds. One-time offer only."

Squib took a good look at the massive scaly hand and the claws on each fingertip, which not that long ago had been on the point of slitting his throat. That seemed like a different time and a different Vern, and he realized that offering that hand was a giant step for Vern and taking it would be life-changing for him. He also knew that if he didn't shake Vern's hand, that would be it for him and the dragon, which was unthinkable.

Squib waited three seconds, then shook the hand. "Shit, boss. College. I thought we was like action heroes, all intrigue and rescues. Now I got to study?"

Vern was feeling all mentor-like. He said, "Students are the real heroes."

Which cracked them both up for near to a minute.

VERN WHISTLED THROUGH his shrinking tusk hole when Bodi Irwin explained step one of the plan.

"That is audacious shit," he said, "riding with the narcos. How you know all this shit, Green Day?"

Bodi was proud and offended at the same time, which translated to approximately the expression brought on by trapped wind. "Less of the 'Green Day.' It's *Constable* Irwin now. I ain't even wearing no Green Day T-shirt, see? I got a hat and shit. And I know this shit because I wasn't the law before yesterday and a fella has to get his weed somewhere."

They were assembled in the Moreau lounge, which was also the kitchen and Elodie's bedroom. Vern was squished into the single armchair, with a Moreau perched on each arm. Bodi had hunkered down hunter-style for a few minutes until his knees popped and he was forced to shift back onto the coffee table. Elodie gave him a smile as he scooched. Effort's gotta be rewarded.

"If you two are done mooning," said Vern, "then maybe we could get on. Word is the Feebs are knocking on doors as we speak."

"Hush your mouth, Vern," said Elodie, who had obviously grown accustomed to having a dragon in her parlor/lounge/kitchen. "Bodi is still healing."

Bodi appreciated the support. "Yeah, Vern, we can't all take a bath in a deep fryer."

"Zing," said Squib. "Burned, boss."

Vern worked hard to keep a straight face. "Zip it, Phi Beta Kappa. We ain't outta the swamp yet. How about jokes and shit when I'm safe in Mexico?"

"Actually, it ain't Mexico," said Bodi. "Colombia was the plan. Mexico ain't worth a flying goose shit to you at the moment, pardon my French, Miss Elodie."

And damned if Elodie didn't blush. "I can pardon you most anything at the moment, Bode, seeing as we're in the first flush."

"'Bode'?" said Squib. "You two have got endearments now?"

Vern slapped his knee. "My advice to you, kid? Buy some noise-canceling headphones or else be scarred for life."

Squib squirmed on his perch. He wasn't a kid in most ways now, but everyone's a kid when it comes to hearing about their momma's carryings-on.

"Colombia, boss," he said, steering the conversation into safer waters. "Because I found this video. I searched for a couple of days under 'dragon sightings,' and it was all bullshit, but then I tried 'gargoyle.'"

"Goddamn!" said Vern. "Gargoyles ain't even real creatures—they're statues. All you gotta do to sight a gargoyle is go down to New Orleans and look up."

"Anyways, they got more and more tourists trekking into the jungle to see the Lost City since the guerrillas chilled out a little."

"*La Ciudad Perdida*," said Elodie, laying on the accent for Bodi's benefit.

"Momma, please, cut it out," said Squib. "I'm working here."

"Sorry, son," said Elodie.

"More tourists means more videos," continued Squib, "and last year this pops up on the Internet."

Squib tapped his phone a mess of times, then swiped once, bringing up a YouTube video. The short film was shaky and dappled with shadow, but it showed something big and reptilian darting into the trees. Something big, with an anvil-shaped head.

Vern sat up straight. "Maybe," he said.

Squib played it again.

"Could be."

"Could be bullshit, too," said Bodi.

"Indeedy," agreed Vern. "But what choice do I have?" *I gotta leave anyway,* he thought, *so why the hell not go* toward *something?*

Vern was more than a tad anxious. He hadn't gone looking for his own kind for a long time, and he knew he was more than likely headed over the cliff of disappointment. Still . . .

"Yup," he said. "Yup, all right. So when do I go?"

"Next week," said Bodi, "if you're up for flying."

"Shit, Green Day," said Vern. "I was born to fly."

CHAPTER 21

SQUIB RECKONED THAT HE WOULD HAVE A WEEK TO FIND THE right words, but then a couple of days later the situation got critical, with Bodi getting back-channel news that the dragon skin had tested fireproof, and the FBI were sending down an additional twenty agents to blanket-bomb the area with investigators. So the newly minted constable had decided to accelerate the schedule, resulting in departure being moved up to that very night, which in turn resulted in Squib and Vern sitting in a Zodiac five hundred yards off the Pass-a-Loutre Wildlife Management Area in Garden Island Bay. Vern was swaddled in a triple-XL Pelicans hoodie so that any late-night crab-fishermen closer to shore wouldn't pay him no mind.

"You remember that stump out front of the shack, looked a little like Danny DeVito?"

Squib laughed. "I do. Darnedest thing. Danny goddamn DeVito. I love that guy."

"'Course you do. Who wouldn't? Pound for pound the funniest motherfucker in the world."

Squib felt there was more going on than a fond DeVito observation. "So what about that stump?"

"You should take a look at it."

"Shit, boss. You still giving me jobs? I thought I had to go to school."

"You do. Then college. What's under the stump will sort things out. Maybe you might fancy up your house a little—not enough to draw attention. But a little cable wouldn't hurt. Maybe even broadband. And a sofa, for Christ's sake."

"New PlayStation?" asked Squib.

"MacBook," said Vern. "Get yourself educated in between games. I don't want those gold ingots wasted. The Confederates didn't give them up easy. Dole them out to Bodi one at a time. He'll get a good rate."

"Under the DeVito stump, huh?"

"Yep. At the end of a chain."

They sat under a deep blue sky set with a spectacular sprinkling of stars, shooting general shit but not really coming close to communicating. The Zodiac bobbed a little on its anchor, which reminded Vern of a recent inflatable.

"Remember Hooke's boat, kid?"

Squib was glad to have a topic to latch onto. "Remember it, boss? Shit, I barely got my ass overboard before you blew her up."

"You ain't gonna be traumatized by all those goings-on?"

"I ain't so far," said Squib. "Maybe later on, you know. If I get depressed and such."

"*Boom*," said Vern, and chuckled. "I lit that sucker right up."

Squib felt kinda awkward about the whole "so-long" situation and didn't really know how to jump in.

Vern obviously felt the same because eventually he said, "We don't need to suffer through the usual farewell rigmarole because we know what's what, right, kid?"

"Right," said Squib.

"Me and you, kid, we done saved each other's hides. So there's always that."

"Sure is, boss," said Squib.

Vern seemed like he was chewing on his words. "And the whole kid-boss thing? Maybe that was it initially, but it ain't it now. Now's different. Unique. There ain't never been nothing like now before."

This was cryptic, but Squib got the gist.

"So what I'm saying is, kid: Keep on the path and stay straight. Got it?"

"Got it," said Squib. "Straight A's all the way. I'll spend your gold wisely and account for every nugget when you get back. And if you need me . . ."

"I'll holler," said Vern. "Count on it."

Squib scanned the sky. "I don't see nothing yet. Should be here by now."

"Delayed, is all," said Vern. "You ever been on a plane that left on time? Even a narco plane?"

"I ain't never been on a plane," said Squib. "Only time I ever flew was with you, and I slept through that."

"I ain't never been on a plane neither," said Vern. "Seems downright unnatural, flying *inside* something."

"You sure you can make it? Ten hours in the air?"

"Should be fine," Vern assured him. "I'll take a break in Havana when they stop over."

"Then turn right at the airport."

Vern patted the pocket of his cargo shorts. "Bodi gave me a GPS, so I can't miss. Don't worry about me, kid. Flying is my business."

"What if they see you?"

Vern shrugged. "Narcos fly quiet. They don't scan for nothing. And if they do see me, then someone's cash ain't making it to Colombia."

"I hope you find a lady dragon."

"Me, too," said Vern, with feeling. "I surely do hope that."

"Make sure you eat your fat," said Squib.

"Yep. And you make sure you don't."

Then Vern heard an engine maybe seven thousand feet up, and he scanned the sky with his night vision till he located a shape darker than the rest of the sky, and that was all she wrote vis-à-vis *au revoirs*.

"That's my ride, kid," he said, stripping off the hoodie. He stood gingerly, and Squib held onto the oarlocks.

"Send me your address if you can," said the boy. "I'll mail you a few *Flashdance* T-shirts."

"Maybe I won't need inspiration no more," said Vern.

The dragon squatted low, then leaped explosively, spreading his wings at the apex of the jump just before gravity took hold. He flapped like crazy for a few seconds, which must have been a strain, but he kept his features under control, which was cool; then his membranes billowed, and he caught the air, and with one sweeping beat he was gone like a rocket, with only the catspaws from his downdraft and the rocking of the Zodiac to prove he was ever there.

"Shit," said Squib in awe. "There goes my boss."

He scanned the sky, but he couldn't see nothing but stars.

But somewhere up there, he knew, there was a cartel light aircraft with a dragon riding shotgun underneath. If there was one group of people who knew how to evade detection, it was the narcos, and for once the dragon was chasing them instead of the other way around.

"Heh," said Squib. "The dragon's chasing them. I am funny, boss."

Then he put his back into pull-starting the little five-horsepower outboard. Bodi was waiting onshore in the truck, keeping one eye out for wardens, ready to flash a badge if someone noticed the boat was missing, but so far, nada. Bodi was saving his other eye for Elodie, who was keeping him company in the cab. God only knew what they'd been getting up to.

I don't want to know, thought Squib, pointing the Zodiac toward shore. *I swear those two are like teenagers.*

And then he thought: *Junior partner, huh?*

Wyvern, Lord Highfire, had no need to worry. Everett "Squib" Moreau would see to it that his business interests were well looked after.

A crane swooped past his starboard bow and Squib thought, *Don't fly too high, buddy. Vern might fancy him some spicy wings.*

A COUPLE OF weeks later, Squib found a postcard waiting on the dresser when he got home from his shift at the Pearl Bar and Grill.

A line drawing of a dragon.

Balls out.

ACKNOWLEDGMENTS

WITH THANKS TO EVERYONE WHO HAD A HAND, FOOT, EYE, OR tooth in dragging this book from my brain and into the real world. The only reason my Irish self-esteem will allow me to be so proud of *Highfire* is that you fine people were involved.

ABOUT THE AUTHOR

EOIN COLFER IS THE *NEW YORK TIMES* BESTSELLING AUTHOR OF the Artemis Fowl series as well as two adult crime novels, *Plugged*, which was short-listed for the Los Angeles Times Book Prize, and *Screwed*. He lives in Ireland with his wife and two children.